THE LOVECRAFT SQUAD
WAITING

Also available

The Lovecraft Squad: All Hallows Horror

THE LOVECRAFT SQUAD
WAITING

created by STEPHEN JONES

with

PETER ATKINS STEPHEN BAXTER
RICHARD GAVIN BRIAN HODGE
THANA NIVEAU REGGIE OLIVER
JAY RUSSELL ANGELA SLATTER
MICHAEL MARSHALL SMITH STEVE RASNIC TEM

and KIM NEWMAN

PEGASUS BOOKS
NEW YORK LONDON

THE LOVECRAFT SQUAD: WAITING

Pegasus Books Ltd
148 West 37th Street, 13th Floor
New York, NY 10018

First Pegasus Books hardcover edition October 2017

Interior design by Sabrina Plomitallo-González, Pegasus Books

ISBN: 978-1-68177-525-8

10 9 8 7 6 5 4 3 2 1

Printed in the United States of America
Distributed by W. W. Norton & Company, Inc.

They worshipped, so they said, the Great Old Ones who lived ages before there were any men, and who came to the young world out of the sky. Those Old Ones were gone now, inside the earth and under the sea; but their dead bodies had told their secrets in dreams to the first men, who formed a cult which had never died. This was that cult, and the prisoners said it had always existed and always would exist, hidden in distant wastes and dark places all over the world until the time when the great priest Cthulhu, from his dark house in the mighty city of R'lyeh under the waters, should rise and bring the earth again beneath his sway. Some day he would call, when the stars were ready, and the secret cult would always be waiting to liberate him.

—H. P. Lovecraft
"The Call of Cthulhu" (1926)

PROLOGUE

Howard's Way

HOWARD IS ALMOST NINE years old on his first day, and he's made to stand at the front of the class while the teacher introduces him. Aunt Lillian—having at last won the long-running the-boy-must-go-to-school argument—dragged his mother, Sarah, away as soon as Howard's foot was half over the threshold of the room. This marks the start of what he will ever regard as a loss of innocence.

His aunt insisted it was time for him to learn more, that he'd surpassed what even his grandfather can teach, and that Howard should become familiar with things other than merely those that interest him and Whipple Van Buren Phillips.

Howard knows, however, that she just wants him out from underfoot. She and Annie want to loosen the apron strings, free Sarah to visit friends and neighbors with them instead of leaning over his sick bed, worrying about his latest malady.

They want her to stop telling him how ill he is, as if that might act as some kind of cure for him. He watches his mother's departing back with yearning.

Miss Whatley, the teacher, is young and pretty and kindly, and she smiles at Howard, but she isn't Sarah; she does little to calm his nerves. The other children in the class—there are thirty, he knows, he counted them, but still they seem legion—stare at him as if they've never seen the like before. He wonders if there's dirt on his forehead, his cheeks, but resists the urge to raise a hand and swipe away whatever might be there.

He thinks of his face, how he's seen himself reflected in windows and mirrors, the waters of the fountain when the pumps are turned off just before evening falls. He stares at the children (Grandfather whispered *Show no fear!* before he left the house this morning), trying to find an echo of his own features there, just one who looks like him: thin nose, protuberant eyes a little too close together behind thick glasses, wide forehead, tightly pursed lips which—did he but know it—give him the same disapproving air as Aunt Annie.

The children, as if somehow sensing that he's found them wanting, determine unconsciously to pay him back.

Howard focuses on a small blonde girl in the front row; her plaits are secured with pink-and-white-checkered gingham ribbons. She stares at him, and somehow he feels like the others are waiting, waiting for her judgment. She begins, at last, to snigger.

When he is older, Howard will recognize in the gesture the action of a pack leader, and the following of her acolytes as only natural. As a child with no experience of those his own age, however, he merely smiles uncertainly, unaware for long moments that the joke is on him.

The giggling and guffawing rises until Howard's ears hurt and his temples begin to pound; he will have a headache by the end of the day, he knows it. Miss Whatley frowns and shushes the class, which gradually quietens, then she directs Howard to the only empty desk, beside the blonde girl.

The girl's eyes sparkle in a way Howard doesn't like—they appear cheap and mean, like glass cut to resemble gems. (Grandfather has shown him the difference, lapidary being one of the subjects they studied when Whipple undertook Howard's schooling.) She tracks his journey like a predator watching prey, still so as not to startle the creature.

Howard is almost terrified to take his seat; he stumbles, doesn't quite get his backside where it should go, must purposefully haul himself onto the chair. Vaguely he wonders if this might trigger some new reaction, but it does not. There's just a gleam and a flicker in the blue eyes, then a look of sudden satisfaction on the girl's face as if something has been decided. Then she hisses one word: "*Tadpole*."

They chase Howard home. He's unaccustomed to running—the air burns his lungs, esophagus, mouth; the lactic acid is quick to build in his muscles—but he's so very aware, though he cannot say why, that if he's caught, something terrible will happen.

The noise of the pack spurs him on, but they don't sound like dogs or wolves: They croak and call, *ribbit* and creak. They shout *frog* and *tadpole* and *freak*. Someone screams and he remembers the night-gaunts in Grandfather's stories, and he stretches his stride farther just when he thought he'd reached his limit.

At last, he trips over the raised step at the garden gate. His heart feels as if it drops like a frozen thing—he's not reached the bastion of his front door yet—but when he rolls over, expecting to be set upon, he finds that he is safe.

As he scrambles to get up, it becomes clear that none of the children will follow him. They stalk behind the blonde girl (*Deirdre* someone called her), but they will not come in, will not push in through the gate that still swings back and forth with the force of Howard's precipitous entry.

In the end Deirdre pauses, points at him, and hisses, "*Don't come back!*"

That night Howard does not eat his dinner. Sarah fusses, declares he has a fever. Aunt Lillian insists he have his vegetables. Howard forces them down. All are surprised when the greenery comes up again, all over the table.

Whipple carries him to bed. Sarah sleeps in a chair by his side.

In his dreams, Howard wanders.

There is a castle, dark and decaying, and he knows its every corner, every crevice; he has lived here an eternity, and suffered. The loneliness of his dream-self feels like a coat of cold slime, something that grips him and will not let go. He is hungry and thirsty and has been thus forever, or so it seems to his sleeping mind. (If, indeed, he *is* sleeping.) When he thinks of others (others, so long ago!) he imagines them in terms of sustenance. Imagines the warmth of gore, gouts of ichor pulsing in a dying rhythm down his throat, tearing meat from bones while shrieks fill the air, resound in his ears (odd things he feels as nothing more than holes either side of his unnaturally round head).

And there are books, so many of them lining the walls, and where they do not fit in shelves, they are stacked on chairs and tables, on beds in which no one sleeps, piled high on moldy covers and damp sheets. They are spread across floors of cracked marble, across rugs so threadbare that only the merest hint of a pattern remains. Some lie in purposeful fans, others are simply scattered like scree or animal scat, discarded. He cannot recall the last time he picked one up, opened it, read it, although there is a distant echo of having done so, once upon a time.

They line the stairs, even, all those myriad stairs that climb up and up and up. Outside the windows are rows of high, lightless trees and he wonders sometimes, when his mind settles and focuses, if they too might be made of books. Towers, trees, constructed of paper and leather and thread.

One night—in his dream it is always night—he is seized by the urge to ascend, to take those stairs and see where they might lead, perhaps to a place where his loneliness or hunger might be assuaged; to company or food or both. He climbs forever, it seems, past windows, past paintings of folk he cannot remember ever seeing, past tapestries, past doors open and closed, past rooms filled with naught but dust, and past the ever-present books, books, books. Because his night never shifts or changes he cannot tell how long the journey takes, but at last, miraculously, there is a door above, a trapdoor he supposes, a thing of wood and iron. It opens only with objecting creaks and groans, its weight making his shoulders and back ache as he heaves and pushes, at last wins.

Here is a church. Here is a steeple. Where are all the people? It is night, still; as below so above, but there is a moon here, though he's not sure how he recognizes it. A large silver-white object suspended in a sky that is nowhere near as dark as his own. He surveys the churchyard, the small houses that cluster around the low stone wall; not a single gleam shows. Ah, but on the hill, on the hill! So many lights, pouring from windows and doors, a halo of gold that pulses around the great edifice. *There*. That is where he will go.

The journey is strangely more arduous than the one from his own ruined castle. He's distracted, tormented by the scent on the wind of warm sleeping bodies, of unguarded flesh. Sometimes he stops in the middle of the stone-cobbled road that leads to his goal and sniffs like a dog tormented. But the locks he tries are held fast and no windows have been carelessly left unlatched, so he must continue his weary way up and up and up, toward the glowing bastion.

He needs use no cunning to enter the castle, the doors have been thrown wide, they are unattended by servants and he wonders if they've sneaked off to indulge like the old cook, Keziah, sometimes does, sitting quietly in the pantry to drink her special tea that smells like Grandfather's whiskey. He wanders though a grand foyer, looks into chambers untroubled by dust (there are, he notes, no books here and the lack disturbs him). He walks and waivers, roams until he comes to the entrance to a grand ballroom. Two men in matching livery watch as he approaches, their expressions becoming more and more concerned the closer he gets, until at last they shout and flee. The noise of their distress is lost in the crescendo of music; a waltz is being played and danced, all eyes, all ears, all feet and hands are concentrating on getting their steps correct, so he is free to enter.

Slowly, then more quickly as they notice him, the dancing crowd parts. They bolt, and their fear gives them such speed that they escape his sweeping grasps, his clawed hands, though the talons catch the edges of pretty trailing lace and long skirts; though they tear he cannot get a grip on such fripperies. Thus it goes until he comes to the center of the ballroom, to the place where clever artisans have embedded gems and mother-of-pearl in the floor in the shape of a radiant sun.

This is where he finds her.

She has not heard him, for whatever reason—perhaps she is transported by the dance—alas, her partner, less chivalrous than he'd like anyone to know, has long since fled. The girl turns and turns and turns, eyes closed, lost to the music; unaware she's easy prey. He takes a moment to observe her, finds her familiar, then realizes the features are known to him—or to his true self, to Howard who dreams and sweats, ridden by a nightmare from which he cannot wake—realizes that it is *Deirdre*, the pack leader, the mean girl, only grown, just a little, her face older, her hair longer, her dress from a different era. And with this realization, Howard in the dream and Howard in the bedroom in 194 Angell Street, both let loose a howl that's inhuman; both strike out, one with a hand that has talons, the other with neatly-clipped nails. The dream-hand catches the girl's throat and rips her red; the boy's swats at his mother, waking her from a restless sleep.

Sarah sits up, grabs at Howard, steadies her son, holds him immobile while he struggles, holds him until he awakens weeping and sobbing, drawing in great gasps of air.

Howard does not tell her his dreams. He does not tell her what he did or who he was in either that darkened castle, or that castle burning with light. He does not tell her that he did not, could not wake until he'd seen himself reflected in the mirrors of the ballroom ceiling, watched himself devour his tormenter in a punishment that seemed all out of proportion with the nature of her sin.

Howard is ill for days.

Howard does not go back to school.

The house at 194 Angell Street is where Howard was born and, even before his father was taken away, spent many happy hours. After Winfield's "removal," moving in there seemed barely much of a change at all. Indeed, his grandfather greeted him with the words "Welcome home, son."

The structure is handsome—one of the most handsome in all of Providence, it is generally agreed—with its wide windows, and verandas, the ivy growing over the porch providing extra shade in summer, and the broad gardens and park with winding paths, a neat picket fence and a magnificent fountain.

The building is huge, and Howard has always indulged in explorations of corridors and rooms, chimney corners and cellars, but he is certain he never finds *all* the spaces; remains certain that nooks and crannies stay hidden. In the attic in particular, partitioned off into areas to store servants from a time when the house had more, there are strange angles and curvatures that seem not quite right, seem not meant to go together, and in between their junctures lie voids filled with dim and murky air that he feels might well hide something *other* were he to look closely enough, long enough. Sometimes he plays a game of chicken with the twilight abysses, staring for minutes on end . . . but he is always the one to look away.

And then there is a *thrum*, which sometimes pulses through the floors and the walls; it seems constant but perhaps is not, yet Howard is so used to it he barely notices its presence—only its absence. It is most strong, he has noted, on those nights when the moon is full and his mother and her sisters let their hair hang loose. Those are the nights when he is sent to bed early.

Howard's aunts are not kind. They behave a little better when his mother is around, but not much. Lillian was given to pinching the soft flesh of his inner forearm, until Sarah found the marks. After that all he had to deal with were the snide remarks, the things forgotten: a blanket missing from his bed in winter, no fire lit in his room on icy nights, food he was allergic to appearing on his plate.

But Grandfather gave no sign of noticing his other daughters' inimical dislike of the boy. And he certainly never partook of it; indeed, loved the boy to distraction, and never made any comment about his father when Howard had, for a brief period, asked questions about Winfield Scott Lovecraft.

"Your father's not a well man," was all Whipple had said.

"Nervous exhaustion," Sarah avowed with the same fervor others reserve for prayer.

"Acute psychosis," announced Aunt Annie firmly, with a kind of satisfaction and that little tilt of her head, a lift of the lips.

"Neurosyphilis," Aunt Lillian had muttered darkly when Sarah was out of earshot; Howard didn't know what that was, but it didn't sound nice.

Howard has only vague memories of the day his father was taken away. Wispy visions like old flickering film of Winfield's thin, bearded face with its veneer of sweat despite the winter's chill; the tall man pacing with a limp in his step that had manifested as his mental state had deteriorated. That, and the twitching hand, the right one, he held to his chest and beat out a rhythm, the same one every time, eight quick beats, three slow, always in an identical pattern as if he described the main points of interest on a map. That, and the shouting, the shrieking, as two men from the Arkham Asylum came and took him; the whimpering after they'd locked him in the back of the ambulance; the spots of blood on the verandah steps where a cut on Win's forehead bled copiously.

After a time, Howard stopped asking and largely put the matter of his father out of his mind, taking up little more than the shape of a silhouette. Winfield's departure, Howard decided, was intentional, an active desertion.

The boy has a child's sense of betrayal that undermines his mother's assurances—regular reminders, as if she puts them in her diary on a weekly basis—that his father loves him.

But Howard only really recalls Winfield's existence on those rare days when he sees a letter arriving from the asylum, when he recognizes the color of the stationery and the coat-of-arms the place probably isn't entitled to.

Today was one of those days and, for reasons he cannot quite explain—although it might have been the rare absence of the humming in the walls, the floor—he has been unable to sleep, at least not for long.

He'd dreamt that a trophy in his grandfather's library—one of those things Whip had collected in the days when he traveled to exotic places, or so he said—had come to life. A green jade amulet, some bizarre breeding of imagination and chimerical fancy, carved in the shape of a winged dog, had fallen from its shelf. Yet before it hit the carpet to either bounce or break, it hovered in the air, the hindquarters stretching downward to the floor, its head remaining in place where its only change was an increase in size. When it took on its final form it had opened its many-toothed mouth, unleashed a bark that smelled of long-dead meat, then leapt across the space between it and Howard. Its fangs closed on his throat just as he awakened with a shriek.

"What did you think would happen, Sari?"

Howard is standing outside his mother's bedroom door, hoping perhaps to be allowed to sleep in Sarah's bed, although he knows his aunts disapprove of this too. His fingers, stretching toward the handle, are arrested at the sound of Aunt Annie's voice. He pulls the hand back, knuckles the sleep from the corners of his eyes.

Annie's tone is exasperated, but her use of a childhood nickname makes Howard recall that dislike of him does not extend to his mother. There's an unintelligible answer from Sarah, and Annie repeats, "Well? What did you think would happen?"

"I don't know," sobs Sarah, louder now. "I thought we'd be happy. I thought he'd love me enough."

"Enough for what? To obey the rules you imposed? To respect that even after years of marriage? To not ever wonder what his wife did once a month on the full moon when she locked herself in the spare room?" Aunt Annie makes that disapproving clicking with her tongue. "If he didn't love you enough to respect that simple request, Sarah, then he didn't love you at all." His aunt's logic is always narrow. "If he couldn't keep his own mind intact when he found out—"

"Don't say it, Annie." Sarah's voice breaks. "Was it so much to ask?"

Howard doesn't open the door. He doesn't think to offer comfort, knows somehow that he should not be hearing any of this, wonders if this relates to the letter that arrived today. Wonders if, if he's found out, he will suffer the same fate, the same *crisis* as his father?

Howard imagines his aunt leaning into her sister's much prettier face as she says, "Yes, Sari, it was too much to ask. And before you wail and howl yet again, how can you expect the truth of what we are to be bearable for anyone? Lillian and I made the choice never to marry—"

"I don't recall anyone ever asking," his mother says bitterly.

"—*chose* not to marry. Mother and Father shared secrets, shared lineage, they were *between creatures* as are we. But you . . . you had to marry *out*." Then his aunt's tone turns mournful. "We are so few! Neither one thing nor the other, our blood so thin!"

"Then why are you so cruel to Howard?"

"Because his blood's thinner yet than ours! He's further from us than we are from *them*, and it renders him even stranger! The ill health, the dreams, the things he says, the things he hears! Don't think I don't know! He listens, I see him sometimes, just standing there, head a'tilt—"

"Annie."

"You could have chosen any of our own. You might even have chosen one of *theirs*, strengthened the bond, brought us closer. But you chose *Winfield*, a man whose mind broke at the first sign of weirdness. Imagine what Howard might have *been*!"

"He wouldn't have been himself," says Sarah firmly, and Howard is heartened to hear her come to his defense. "He is who he is, Annie, and *he is mine*."

Neither one says anything more for some time, until his aunt mutters reluctantly, "What did Doctor Walcott say in the letter?"

"Only that there's no change for the better. Although *he's* stopped talking about *them*, it's not because he's stopped believing that he saw what he saw." Sarah sighs. "But . . ."

"What?" Annie's tone is sharp, demanding.

"He's tried to escape three times."

"But they've caught him?"

"So far. Whatever other failings Winfield has, a lack of determination is not one of them."

"Then let us not worry about it for now, Sari."

Howard hears the noise of silken skirts moving and he imagines his aunt crossing the room to stand beside his mother . . . but there's not just silken skirts rustling. Does he hear something else? Or imagine it? There is a low sound, a crooning that reminds him of the hum he hears in the walls, under the floorboards, a sound like a lullaby, a comfort.

Inside the room, his mother begins to weep softly.

What could his father have thought he'd seen? How can his mother be anything but his mother? He bends his knees a little, puts a hand against the doorframe to steady himself, and leans in to press one eye to the keyhole.

A hand clamps over his shoulder; the touch is gentle but inexorable. Howard twists his head, sees first the flash of gold, the signet ring, engraved with the image of some mythological creature, set with rubies for eyes, then Grandfather standing there, a sorrowing serious gaze directed at him. Whip lifts a finger to his lips, and draws the boy away.

Outside Howard's own room, Whipple crouches with a cracking and creaking of knees, and stares at his grandson for a few moments, lips pursed in thought.

"Sometimes," he says. "Sometimes, we simply must not look. Even if we can, we must not. Remember Lot's wife. Sleep well, Howard, you've been dreaming, my boy, sleepwalking as you do. Forget these fancies."

And the old man kisses the boy's forehead, opens the door and tenderly pushes him inside.

Howard stumbles toward his bed, head filled with something he may or may not have seen, a long green-gray limb trailing behind his mother as she sat on her bed, a similar appendage at Aunt Annie's hems as she sat beside her sister.

Perhaps he has been dreaming after all.

Several days later, when Aunt Lillian returns to her *idée fixe* on Howard's education over breakfast, Whip decides to take the boy from the house.

Howard wonders if his grandfather wishes to discuss the keyhole incident, but no. It's worse.

Whipple takes him to Watchaug Pond—a lake really—and rents a small rowboat from a man who sits in a tiny hut at the landward end of a thin jetty. Howard waits while his grandfather counts out the hire fee. He watches the boats bobbing at the end of the pier, tethered like anxious hounds; the thought of anything even vaguely canine reminds him of his nightmare, of the jade dog-sphinx, and he shudders.

After Whipple hands him onto the seat, Howard decides he does not like boats anymore than he likes dogs. He doesn't like the way it rocks beneath him, as if trying to tip him out. The boat, he decides, is treacherous. The boat, he thinks, is plotting his demise. It's not a stable thing, not like the solid and reliable ground he's used to.

They have not gone out too far onto the water, but the boy feels ill, his fear increasing with each yard they traverse. Howard is about to tell Grandfather that he wants to go home, even though he knows this will not please Whip. Foolishly, he abruptly stands, forgetting he was told not to, and turns, tilts, and tips, all to the sound of Whipple's bellowed warning.

The boat does not capsize, although Howard does. One moment there is sky above, the next everything is sideways—and he sees, he sees, by the edge of the water, a bearded face, a man ducking behind trees—and then there is a splash, a journey through wet glass, and Howard sinks, sinks, sinks.

After the initial shock of the cold wears off, he begins to panic, to thrash, to try to propel himself upward, to where there is light, a filmy filtered sky.

He kicks out, but feels on his ankles, his calves, his knees, the thin grasp of fingers, the thick grasp of flattened palms. If he were able to pay attention to more than the burning in his lungs, he might notice there seems to be webbing between those fingers, that those palms are wider than they should be, their architecture of flesh infinitely stranger than it might otherwise be.

He is pulled down. Deeper, deeper, to where the light is a weak echo of itself, so pale he feels that even if he could break free, he wouldn't know which way is up.

Howard is swallowing water now; it's both warm and cold, tastes of salt and sediment. He knows he'll never get the sourness out of his mouth, the smell from his hair, his clothing—if he ever surfaces again.

He looks down—at least he thinks it's down—to where his feet are, where those grasping hands are and sees, though he knows he should not be able to, not in the darkness of the churned waters, a face. Two faces, three. Wide eyes, ichthyoid and protuberant; lips pouting, flat noses; hair so black it's barely distinguishable in the dark liquid. Queens of their kind, whatever kind that might be: weirdly beautiful, pitiless, terrifying.

They seem to be smiling. Not nicely, however. No, triumphantly. One opens her mouth, rows of tiny glowing teeth like sharpened pearls ring the aperture. The others follow suit, lips move and Howard hears even though he should not, perhaps in his head and not in his ears, one word:

Ours.

And abruptly there's pressure around the crown of his head, a desperate searching touch, then fingers twine in his hair, and Howard is drawn swiftly upward. There's a brief resistance from the hands of the queens that makes him feel he'll be pulled apart, but quickly their fingers slide away.

There's only the strong hand, its digits thickened with arthritis that Howard can feel, clutching his own hands around the rescuing limb; and there it is, the thing he recognizes by touch alone: the ring, thick gold engraved with the strange carving, set with rubies.

Soon he's lifted into the bottom of the small, traitorous boat, soaked, coughing, prone, and suddenly so very, very cold. He blinks the fluid from his eyes and watches his grandfather. The old man is rowing, rowing, rowing, powerful shoulders heaving beneath his jacket, and Howard finds himself thinking of an ox at a plough.

But Whipple's face is pale, paler than his snowy beard, his eyes are wild. Howard is almost distracted enough by the sight of his grandfather's panic to not notice that his own shoes and socks are missing, that his toes appear elongated and webbed as if the brief dunking has changed him—but this illusion only lasts for a few moments.

When the sun comes out from behind the clouds, everything is normal again; Howard glances at his hands, thinks that he's too late to see what they might have been, but he can feel the strange itch of transformation, as if his skin has recently shrunk to accommodate a restructured skeleton and musculature.

But it makes him wonder if he imagined the state of his feet; if the lack of air, the taint of the brackish water, his own fear and the incipient headache that he knows will grow and leave him abed for days, all took their toll and made him imagine things.

He knows his perceptions are off, for otherwise how could Grandfather have reached him? Perhaps he was not as far down as he thought?

Why else would he have imagined a face he recognized, just before he went in the water, a face he's not seen since he was three when his father was institutionalized?

He stares up at the sky and shivers. There's no warmth in the sun.

Whip is still rowing, rowing, rowing, muttering to himself, lips pinched, eyes all pupils, as black as night. When at last the lake becomes too shallow and they hit the shore, Whip keeps rowing as if he'll row them home, across the park, along the streets, right into the front yard. His stroke is so powerful it digs into the muddy earth, pulls them from the water, and two or three feet up the bank.

"Grandfather?" says Howard, then louder, "Grandfather!"

Whipple Van Buren Phillips stops abruptly, midstroke. He stares at Howard for seconds that seem to drag on forever. His gaze focuses on his grandson, actually sees him; Whip's face, stiff, stern, stony, finally relents and relaxes. He clears his throat, forces his lips to smile though they appear reluctant to perform this service.

He says, "Well, boy, what an adventure." He tries to make his tone jovial, but it's too much for him and the pitch is flat, affectless. "You gave this old man a fright. And what did I tell you about rocking the boat?" He forces out a laugh. "You'll know better next time."

But Howard senses—with an immense relief that makes him a little ashamed—that there won't be a next time. Somehow he knows this, understands this. But what he doesn't understand is why his grandfather kept repeating as he rowed them across the lake the words "Not yours, not yours, not yours . . . !"

Howard might have been pulled safely from the lake—*pond*, Aunt Annie keeps saying as if to make it mean less—but he feels it has not let him go. Indeed, as if the immersion, the swallowing, have conspired to make an eternal connection between himself and the water. It's *inside* him, now and forever; he wonders if he will ever sleep again without the sensation of sliding under the surface being the first thing he encounters when slumber takes over.

In his dream the queens are there, too, waiting and watching in the liquid shadows, eyes bright points in the darkness. They don't drag at him this time, do not insist, but move their arms and hands in elegant gestures to direct his attention to the scene below: a gleaming city, shining spires, precarious towers, great dead houses where great dead things lay dormant though not expired, not properly. As he stares down, Howard wonders at the drowned city, at its luminescence as if the moon holds sway beneath the waves.

When the queens' pantomime becomes impatient—*You must come, you must go, you must see!*—Howard remembers to be afraid. He kicks his way up, cuts through the dream-sea, desperate to be away, to escape the queens and their wrath, their thwarted wants. He breaks the surface, dragging deep gasps of air into his lungs (even though he'd felt no sense of need until now) and splashes about in a circle to see where he might be.

Here, too, there is moonlight that seems to burn, that illuminates the surface of the water like fire, and shows his salt-stung eyes a place of safety: a reef, a rock formation, lapped at by the waves, but not overcome by them, and much closer than the nameless seaside town the lights of which can barely be seen in the foggy distance. In his nightmare he strikes out with an assured stroke toward the ridge made of coral and stone.

It is only when he is almost ashore that he realizes there is movement on the rock, low to the ground, a kind of wormlike progression, almost peristaltic. Soon he realizes it is more than one figure, more than one body proceeding in this manner; some, he sees, sit upright as if bathing themselves by the moon. Like the mermaids in the fairy and folk tales Whip reads to him; but not really like mermaids, not at all. Not pretty or alluring, with none of the weird grace of the queens, either. Green-gray, round heads, with fins on spines and shoulders, hips and flanks, webbing betwixt fingers and toes, wide mouths emitting a frog-like croak.

Howard begins to push himself back out into the dream-sea where only the most desperate hope of escape waits—but then comes the all-too-familiar feel of hands around his ankles, calves, knees . . .

When Howard wakes, tearing himself from sleep, he fears he has wet himself, but soon it becomes clear that the entire bed is awash. When he rolls over, there is so much water that the mattress and linens *slosh*. He can smell, for no good reason, salt and seaweed. Just as he is frantically trying to come up with an explanation that will placate the Aunts—or is it possible he can simply hide the mattress? Leave it somewhere to dry? Burn it?—the waters inexplicably retreat like a wave withdrawing from a beach. He cannot say where they go, but somehow they disappear into the darkness, into the slivers and cracks of the spaces between breath and sleep.

A few days later, when Howard has ostensibly recovered from the dunking and the inevitable illness it brought on, when the dreams have for the most part receded (he's told no one about the queens, not even Whipple, whom he suspects knows already), Aunt Lillian calls him into Grandfather's study, although Grandfather is not in evidence.

Lillian sits beside Aunt Annie, and both are smiling; this would make him nervous, but for the fact they're not smiling at him. Someone is sitting across from them, his back to Howard, a man with thin shoulders and dark thick hair slicked to his skull. The suit he wears is brown and Howard, coached by Whipple to recognize quality and believe that one must not compromise, gives an approving nod; little does he realize he's been given a set of values it will be hard to live up to later in life, after the family fortunes are lost and he finds himself utterly unfit for earning a living.

"Howard, we have wonderful news," says Lillian, her tone sweet, and Howard doubts this most sincerely.

"Yes, Howard, come and meet this lovely gentleman who's the answer to all our prayers." Aunt Annie is doing something strange with her face, her lashes batting up and down like a butterfly's wings, her lips quirked and a little rouged if he's not mistaken. This is the way she looks at the butcher's boy when he makes deliveries.

Howard wonders where Mother and Grandfather are, but he obeys the Aunts. He rounds the chair where the man is sitting and stands on the afghan rug, feet squarely set on two flowers as if he's grown from them. He looks at the visitor.

Thin nose, protuberant eyes a little too close together behind his thick glasses, wide forehead, and even though he is smiling nervously there is still something that hints at a habitual tight pursing. The white of his shirt looks not bright enough against the intense pallor of his face, and the hands that hold his hat tremble just a little.

Howard sympathizes: the presence of the Aunts often sends shivers down his spine, though he is surprised to note an adult feeling the same effects. The man, intuits Howard, doesn't want the Aunts to know, however, and is doing his best to not show fear. Howard wonders at it for a moment, then decides there's no reason for anyone to be different to him.

"Howard," says Aunt Lillian, "this is Mr. Kindred, and he has kindly agreed to be your tutor."

"My tutor?" asks Howard.

"Well, we tried you at school and we all know how well that went."

Aunt Lillian's tone is as bitter as old almonds. She laughs to take the edge off the comment, but it leaves a cut thin as something inflicted by paper. Howard notices the tutor suppressing a shudder.

"Perhaps Howard would feel more comfortable if he and I were to talk together?" says Kindred and the Aunts, though they appear a little taken aback, nod.

Perhaps this will help keep their plans on track; perhaps Howard will be less inclined to sabotage their schedules with his illness, his attention-seeking, his apparent determination to get his own way. He can almost hear their thoughts, almost feel the thudding rhythm of their resentment.

They nod, and rise, and leave the room, closing the door quietly behind them.

Howard and Kindred stare at each other for a few moments, then the tutor smiles, a strange nostalgic thing, almost fatherly. "Please sit down, Howard."

Howard does so, but continues to stare at the young man, waiting.

"I understand you are sometimes vexed by your aunts."

That surprising pronouncement—a truth, though it is—shakes Howard somewhat. He nods.

"They don't like me," he confesses, wonders if the Aunts had managed to hide this from the young man. Wonders if Mr. Kindred will report back to Annie and Lillian, and Howard's life will be made that much more difficult.

"I suspect it feels that way, Howard. But sometimes when people are worried they express it badly. When they fear for someone they care about, it comes out as anger. They simply do not know how to express themselves properly. Do you think perhaps your aunts might be like that?" The young man's tone is so kind, so reasonable that for a moment Howard considers the proposition.

Then he shakes his head. "No."

Surprisingly, the tutor laughs and the sound puts Howard at ease. So much so that he asks, "Do you believe in monsters?"

Kindred examines him with that muddy green gaze that makes Howard think he's staring into a pond, then nods slowly. "Of course."

"Well, I think the Aunts are monsters," says Howard quietly, but he does not mention the night that might have been a dream or a truth, when he saw tails trailing from beneath his mother's and aunt's skirts. Kindred laughs again, a not unsympathetic laugh.

"We're all a little monstrous, Howard. They're not so bad, the Aunts, just different. Impatient. When the time comes, they will be there for you."

Howard gives the tutor a look of frank disbelief. Kindred smiles and says, "Or perhaps not. Shall we discuss a program of study?"

It has been two months since Kindred (his first name is Ward, Howard has discovered) joined the household at 194 Angell Street, and Howard wonders how they ever got by without the man's quiet presence. The Aunts, if not loving (that would be too much to expect), are at least unwilling to risk the tutor's ill opinion and so are solicitous to their nephew. Sarah and Grandfather, initially displeased at Lillian and Annie's highhandedness, were soon charmed by the young man's manner and intelligence.

He has been kind and considerate, uncomplaining and happy to undertake extra duties such as escorting the women of the family on shopping trips, carrying their parcels home again, and spending evenings in the study with Whipple discussing—while Howard listens with wide eyes and wide ears and a mouth tight-lipped lest they remember he's there—history, politics, astronomy, physics, and mathematics of a very strange sort indeed, the sort that opens doors between worlds and dimensions.

"A purely theoretical idea, of course," says Whip after a particularly intense discussion about gates and gods and doorways and demons. He laughs a laugh that Howard recognizes as the one he gave after their adventure on the lake.

"Yet some swear the great Abdul Alhazred's formulas can be made to work under the right conditions," says Kindred politely. The old man nods.

"The *Necronomicon*. You know," Whipple pauses. "You know, my great-grandfather claimed to have owned a copy. Never saw it myself."

"When I was younger—"

"Lad, you're barely out of short pants!" shouts Whip with a snort.

Kindred takes it in good spirit. "*Much* younger, then, I traveled to Egypt and was there shown a copy by one of my hosts, a man of terrifying and voracious scholarly habits."

"And did you read any of the spell-formulas?" asks Grandfather rather eagerly.

Ward Kindred shakes his head, smiling. "To what end? Had it worked my host might have been most put out as his own efforts had never borne fruit. Had it not worked, would I not have looked the fool?"

Whipple Van Buren Phillips chuckles and sits back in his chair. "True."

Later that evening when Kindred escorts Howard to bed (Ward himself has been given one of the small attic rooms), the boy asks a question that's been burning the inside of his mouth for hours:

"Are dreams doorways, sir?"

Kindred stops in his tracks, tilts his head and examines Howard as one might a babe in arms who has suddenly addressed one in a fluent and full sentence. "I'd not thought of them as such, Howard, but I suppose they might well be. How your mind works, young man, is a constant delight."

Howard, no more immune to Ward's complimentary pronouncements than the rest of his family, blushes.

"But I think they must be more personal thresholds, Howard, not necessarily something one can pull another through. A doorway for one's daydreams and dreads." Kindred smiles and touches the boy's thin shoulder. "Sleep well, Howard."

"Yes, sir," says Howard with certainty, for since Ward Kindred's arrival his dreams have been serene. Neither the queens, nor the dog-sphinx, nor the man-thing that climbed the stairs of the dark castle have made an appearance in Howard's nightly theatre of slumber. Nothing has troubled him, not even hints of Grandfather's fairy-tale night-gaunts.

When Howard is older he will realize this period as the calm before a storm. He will experience many such occasions in his life, sometimes knowing them for what they are and using them accordingly; other times he will be too rushed, too stressed, there will be too many voices in his head and he will forget to take a brief safe harbor. But now, at this moment, this evening, Howard does not think of such things. He has begun to take peace for granted.

And so it is only fitting that this night is a point on his timeline when there is a great turning of fate.

His sleep has been so deep that it takes a while for the rough hands to shake him awake in the dark watches. There is no light from the open curtains for the moon has hidden away—like Howard's mother, for this is one of the times she demands for herself—but there is a glow, a faint violet, tender and fragile emanating from somewhere in his room. A dark shape moves against it, blocks it for a moment, then Howard is shaken again and again, half-sits, is half-pulled into a sitting position.

"Howard? Howard! Get up, boy."

He does not recognize the voice, it's neither Grandfather nor Mr. Kindred, and certainly not Mother or the Aunts. It is a man, his tones low and rough, as if he's not spoken for a long while. The covers are thrown back and the boy is hauled to his feet. He's distracted, looking around for the light source but cannot find it; somewhere in the back if his mind the word *witchlight* is whispered, a memory seeded long ago by one of the servants or the Aunts or his mother when no one thought he was listening. Perhaps even Whipple in one of his stories. The illumination is omnipresent.

The man crouches in front of him; Howard can smell him now, stale sweat, foul breath, other things too that do not bear thinking about. The boy tries to breathe shallowly to lessen the effect. Matters do not improve when the man shoves his face close to Howard's and talks. "Hurry up, boy. We need to be away. Are you scared? Don't you recognize me? How can a boy not know his own father?"

And Howard realizes then that the pale face in front of him with its matted beard bedecked with flecks of food and old vomit is that of his departed paternal-type parent. It's the face he glimpsed that day by Watchaug Pond when he fell in. His father has been watching him. Did Sarah know Winfield had escaped? Did the asylum doctor write and let her know? Who has been hiding this secret?

As if divining the boy's thoughts, Win grins, showing that his remaining teeth are blackened. "In and out, boy. I can do that now, since I figured out the right order of things. No one knows I'm gone. C'mon, I'll show you."

And so saying, Winfield wraps a hand around Howard's mouth as if he senses the boy is about to cry for help, and with the other hand he draws—using a cut finger that still oozes ichor—a series of signs and sigils on the pristine wall beside Howard's bed. The marks almost look like equations, but there is something almost too elegant and artistic about their fluidity; Howard thinks of Grandfather's talk of eldritch mathematics, Mr. Kindred's comments about the formulae of Abdul Alhazred having worked under the right circumstances. As the thoughts coalesce in his sleep-heavy mind, he watches the wall: The bloody marks act as if they are blunt knives or brushes laden with acid. Where a sign has been drawn the wallpaper and the wood beneath it peel away. The spaces between disappear and, faced with a newly created door, Howard forgets the urge to scream, just for a moment.

His father tries to shove him forward, but Howard resists. Winfield cuffs his son hard, and the boy's ears ring. He stumbles, directed by the rough hands of Winfield Lovecraft, the father he's mostly forgotten.

The humming is terribly loud here, the humming he's heard for much of his whole life. The thrumming rhythm that's been the lullaby of his nights, the comforting white noise of his days. Now, unfiltered by walls or planes or dimensions, it is as powerful as blood rushing in the ears.

There is the sound of water, too, rushing, and Howard's feet are wet. He's afraid to look down at them lest they be transformed like that day in the lake. His father's hand is still hard on his shoulder and he feels the flesh bruising.

"Father—"

"Shut up, boy. Can't hear myself think." As Howard watches, Winfield shakes his head, more a nervous twitch than a voluntary movement, and he raises his right hand to tap out the rhythm on his chest, the sequence, which is the strongest memory Howard has of his father. It is also, he realizes, the sequence in which Win wrote on the wall of his room to open the door *through*.

"Have you been here before, Father?"

But Win doesn't answer. He keeps a tight hold on Howard and pulls him along in his wake as he wades through the cold groundwater. Mist hovers just above the surface of the liquid; there are no trees here, just a lot of rock and, Howard sees, an arched stone roof, a natural configuration. The farther they go into the cave—for a cave it most certainly is—the louder is the humming, as if pressed from many throats, and the light grows stronger (although not quite as violet).

They come to a place where the tunnel opens into a much larger cavern. A huge rock formation dominates the center and, covered as it is with creatures of green-gray with round heads and wide mouths, it puts Howard in mind of his dream of the rocky reef off that nameless seaside town. There is no sign, however, of the gleaming city beneath the waves, with its dreaming spires and rising towers.

And atop the rock, Howard recognizes the three queens. They lie, preening—it would be basking if there were any sun. Around them are creatures like them, but not alike. *A different bloodline*, Howard ponders, *a different strain, a different caste, just as bees are divided into drones and workers and queens*. Howard is terribly startled when his father shouts.

It is not any particular word, it is a formless kind of a cry, but it does what Win intended it to and it attracts attention. The queens, their courtiers, all heads turn, bodies slew, arms outstretch and webbed fingers point. The three queens slither down the rocks at an incredible speed, almost serpentine in their motions, then they come to stand not far from where Howard and Win wait. The boy cannot believe how quickly they move, that they slither then become upright on two feet as if they're closer to humans than *reptiles*, than *fish*.

Winfield drags Howard against him as if the boy might provide a shield. One hand goes into the pocket of his ragged coat and pulls out a knife with a long stained blade. He rests the dull edge against his son's neck, the cool of the metal a brisk contrast to the warmth of the skin where the blood flows so close to the surface. A tiny cut is made as Win's hand shakes, and Howard does not know who to fear more: his father or these strange queens.

"I've brought him!" shouts Winfield as if addressing a rioting crowd even though the creatures before him are silent and still; he gives a sort of broken bow and Howard is struck by how the gesture weakens Winfield. "Take him back. Take him, he's yours. Give me my mind once again. Return my wife as a normal woman, as she was before the child! Just take the boy away. Get out of my dreams, make me forget and all will be well again!" He sobs and says words Howard's heard from another mouth. "Is it so much to ask?"

Had he spent more time with his father, had he truly known him at all—or at least the man he *was*—Howard might have felt more betrayed than he does. The queens remain silent, swaying back and forth where they stand, like snakes hypnotizing small, stupid prey. A whimper escapes Win's lips and he lets go of Howard. The boy has the presence of mind to step away as his father sinks to his knees, sobbing; Howard then moves behind Win, all the better to put something between himself and the queens.

"I've brought him home," weeps Win. "Back to his spawning pool, back to the birthing ground. Isn't that what you want? Isn't that it? Tell me, tell me it's what you want! Take him! Take this little tadpole and give me back my life."

In later years Howard will wonder if it was simply a childish desire to pass on the hurt, but his deepest self knows that it was the anger to hear the little pack-leader's words, Deirdre's words, come from his own father's mouth. To feel that somehow there should have been more loyalty than *this*.

He pushes his father. He raises his hands and shoves Win squarely in his shoulder blades. The man, already unbalanced from his own rocking, is easy enough to tip, and he doesn't try to save himself. He falls, unmindful of the dagger in his hand; he falls until he is stopped by the soggy ground, by the blade that enters his stomach, and is pressed in farther and farther by his body weight. Again, Winfield does not try to save himself; he gives only a brief, sharp cry, then subsides to a kind of relieved weeping.

Howard, vaguely horrified, vaguely fascinated, backs away, whispering, *I'm sorry*, though he's not entirely sure he is.

The queens shriek and howl, and the noise is taken up by the creatures around them, the sound becomes deafening. Howard fears his ears will bleed. He backs away, unable to take his eyes from the scene of his father writhing in the few inches of water that's become pink, now cherry, now burgundy, now black as his lifeblood leaks into it; or the scene of the queens and their acolytes, screaming and shuddering. He backs away because he cannot shake the idea that once he turns to run they will be upon him with preternatural speed.

Yet still they do not approach.

Howard is taking more backward steps, unsure he will be able to find his way through the tunnels, find the door, find his home, when he bumps into something. No. There is the weird give and resistance of a human body: *someone*.

He twists his neck to see, but keeps his frame facing toward the pack as if that will somehow keep them at bay.

Ward Kindred stares down at him, his expression a mix of relief and concern. His glance takes in Win's now-still form, the now-silent queens and their court, the now-sluggish creep of blood from Howard's neck. The tutor places a hand on the boy's head, a reassurance, a benediction, and says, "Wait here, Howard."

Howard watches as Kindred walks with assured steps through the water, stopping just short of the queens. He does not bow, makes no obeisance. Howard hears Kindred begin to speak, but he does not recognize the words. They are not English nor any other language he can identify. The boy listens carefully, trying to map the syllables onto his memory so he will know them if he ever hears them again. They are the sound of the waters, of amphibian creatures, sounds made by mouths uniquely evolved to press them out.

The conversation is short; at its end the queens nod, and Kindred comes back to Howard with quick steps. But Howard is not really paying attention to his tutor, for the crowds of creatures have turned their rounded heads, their ichthyoid gazes, toward him, toward Howard.

All of them, all in their rubbery, amphibian monstrosity, all bow to him now, croaks diminished to a respectful thrum, a chorus of awe.

Kindred's hand on his shoulder startles him. "Howard, come away. Come home, Howard, it's not time for this yet."

Kindred escorts him to the doorway that stands as a silver tear in the air, and beyond its ragged edges is Howard's room and Whipple Van Buren Phillips, looking even older, as if his vitality has been sapped by the past—minutes? Hours? Days? The tutor helps him step through into Whip's waiting arms. Grandfather is shaking so tremendously that Howard fears for the old man's health.

"It's all right, Grandfather, Mr. Kindred saved me." He strokes the old man's cheek gently and smiles, then turns to Ward Kindred, expecting the young man to step through the doorway, too, to join them.

Kindred shakes his head. "Howard, I cannot go with you. We have spilled blood *here*, pure human blood, and for that atonement must be made."

"But you saved me!"

"It does not matter, Howard—this was my agreement with the monarchs and I shall honor it." Ward crouches down so he can look the boy directly in the face. "You're different, Howard. Listen to me, my young friend: you'll always be *between*. Between dark and light, earth and water.

Neither one thing nor the other. You'll hear voices, voices beyond those around you, and it will get worse as you get older. Don't always listen to them, or they'll drive you mad."

Howard has so many questions they all push at his mouth, get caught like a log jam of curiosity so none of them make it out. Before he can say anything, Ward Kindred straightens and peers past the boy, speaks to Whip, "And now it is time to begin Howard's *true* education. I know you have dreaded this, sir, put it off as long as you felt you could, but the boy must be trained. Forewarned is forearmed and things will only get worse for him as he ages, as the layers of his mind become more sensitive, more receptive. At least allow him the ability to defend himself."

Reluctantly (Howard thinks), Whip nods.

"Promise me," insists the tutor. "Swear it."

"I promise. I swear on the blood of my dearest, dead wife."

Kindred nods, a single sharp movement of satisfaction. "Goodbye, Howard."

And Howard still cannot say anything. It will be one of his greatest regrets, this last moment, this first great failure.

As the tutor walks away, his thin back growing thinner and more indistinct as the distance increases, the door between dimensions begins to close, a process that is simultaneously too slow and too quick. At last there is a sort of searing *pop* and the threshold is gone, no evidence left on the wall that it ever existed, not even the bloody marks Win made there. No trace.

No trace in the morning either of Ward Kindred when Howard wanders into the tutor's room, seeking some sign that he did but dream the night's adventures. The small chamber is so neat it seems there's no proof of him ever having been there, ever having existed. Howard feels strangely bereft.

In days to come, the newspapers will report Winfield Lovecraft's death at Arkham Asylum. The printed letters will gleefully dwell on the method of demise: Choking on his own tongue at the height of a psychotic episode. An empty coffin is buried in a quiet ceremony, and none of the paid pallbearers comment on the lightness of the box.

Howard has already told his mother and the Aunts and Grandfather what happened in that *other* place, of the facts of his father's true exit, and although Sarah weeps her last tears for her lost husband, she is pleased and proud of her son; she hugs him close. The Aunts, their demeanor altered, exchange a glance with each other and then, to Howard's great astonishment, face him and drop into flawless curtsies. While their relationship to the Nephew will never be without pressure fractures, bumps, and incidents, from this day forth it will be changed.

And finally, one day, when the bruises have faded from Howard's shoulder, the tiny cut on his throat has healed, on that day Whipple Van Buren Phillips appears at the door of the boy's room and announces, "Now, m'boy, it's time to begin your true education."

And Howard Phillips Lovecraft picks up his pen and begins to write . . .

ONE

Shadows Over Innsmouth

IT WAS A CHUMP'S assignment from the start, the sort of goose-chase the Bureau might send an agent on to keep him earning his kale before they showed him the exit.

Dobbs understood that. He'd grasped it the moment the special agent in charge of the Boston field office laid it out for them. Hewlitt, now, he didn't get it. He didn't yet know how these things worked. Hadn't learned enough about the shifting politics of the situation to recognize the warning signs. Ridley Hewlitt was a bright fella, quick on the uptake, but he was green. He hadn't been privy to the bloodbaths of the past three years, since J. Edgar Hoover took over as director of the Bureau of Investigation. The agents who'd been fired, maybe they hadn't been the best, but jumping Jesus, they'd been axed with all the care a sawbones might show a gangrenous limb.

Dobbs could only imagine the discussion in Washington, the chain of decisions to even take this report seriously and how to scratch it off somebody's checklist.

We need somebody from the Boston office to go up to Danvers and interview a patient who's been in the asylum there for the past six years. See what he has to say, if there's anything sensible to come out of him. And if there is, if any of it squares up with the report from this Robert Olmstead. He's the one who went sightseeing to a town in the northeast corner of Massachusetts and came out telling the wildest tales you've ever listened to. A place called Innsmouth.

Innsmouth? Never heard of it.

No reason you should have. Hardly anybody has. It's this wormy little run-down seaport that fell on hard times before the Civil War, and times there have only gotten harder since. It's hanging on up there like a barnacle.

What's our interest? Isn't this something a state agency should look into?

You know the director. He just wants to be thorough. Doesn't want anything slipping past him while his eye's on Capone. It's probably nothing. But, say somebody in that town thinks they have a good reason to put on crazy masks and run off outsiders. Better we know about it than we don't, right? But, if you ask me, it's a bunch of bushwa from a couple of hop-heads.

In that case, send Agent Dobbs, why don't you? Archie Dobbs. It'll keep him out of trouble before the hammer comes down.

It must have gone about that way, more or less. Dobbs was as glum about the prospect of the day as Hewlitt was sunny, the kid seeing this as a chance to get paid for spending a couple hours enjoying the scenery between Boston and Danvers. Trees were fiery with October glory, and after a miserable summer the air was nippy enough outside the Studebaker to make a fella glad to be alive, if he was lucky enough to have gotten out of bed that morning without worries.

But good luck trying to hang onto that in Danvers.

The state asylum loomed over everything, an architectural monstrosity on a hilltop. Its central building alone looked grim enough to throw a bruise-black cloud over anyone's day, a gentleman despot's idea of a castle, the last façade a person might see before his life went down a hole . . . but the place just kept going. He'd never seen anything like it. On either side of the central building, a series of wings receded back, one after the other, set corner to corner.

"They say, from the air, it looks like a bat," Hewlitt told him.

That figured. Even without knowing this, there was no missing that it looked like a place ready to suck the life out of anyone who got close. Had he ever seen anything as demoralizing? Not on these shores. Not in this decade. He'd have to go back ten years, to France, to the kind of ruins left after a day of artillery.

This place was intact, but it oozed the same hopelessness. As if your world were ending, and tomorrow was already gone, and your head was up too high while you listened for the whistle of that one last shell coming down to finish the job.

The loony's name was Mayhew. One of the doctors ushered them down a series of hallways to go meet him, and Dobbs spent every step tuning out the moaning and the babble. For as enormous as the place looked from outside, it felt too close within. He had the kind of hulking frame that filled doorways, shoulder to shoulder, and often had to duck through even when he wasn't wearing a hat.

Lionel Mayhew didn't like to leave his room any more than he liked to go five minutes without a ciggy. His fingertips were yellow with them, and his teeth brown. He had a smile fit to frighten the Devil himself, as if he'd forgotten what a smile was and when it was appropriate, so the best he could manage was a random, jerky skinning of his lips back from his teeth like his next trick would be to bite the head off a lizard.

They'd driven all morning for *this*.

Mayhew had been a life insurance man for Metropolitan. Before he ended up locked away, he'd been under the pressure of a company-wide squeeze to bring in new policies, fresh premiums. MetLife had taken it in the balls at the close of the last decade, paying out over $8 million in claims from the Great War, and nearly $28 million more in the wake of the Spanish Flu.

Which was how Mayhew had found himself in Innsmouth. Nobody for miles around had anything good to say about the place, but folks there should need life insurance the same as anywhere, right?

"No!" he said, a fierce rebuttal to his own question.

All of this was verified, and so far Mayhew seemed lucid enough, if twitchy, in recounting it.

"No, they do *not* need life insurance there. They do not need my services at all. What they need, what they demand, is everything else, my life my soul my skin my bones my organs my seed. The greediest ones are the greenest ones, the ones with the widest mouths and the sharpest choppers. That's how you know. As if the look of any one of them isn't enough to tell you you're in the wrong place when you stick your pushy little foot in the wrong door."

He flashed his ghastly brown smile, his teeth a row of slimy brown Chiclets.

"They're the ones who hop. Are you following me? A pair of fine fit specimens such as yourselves should have no trouble getting approved for a double indemnity clause. So you should be able to run faster than they can hop. And you'd have to. Life soul skin bones organs seed—you have them too."

Mayhew fumed like a smokehouse chimney and grew agitated as he spoke. And he paced. At some point during his years here, he'd used some tool to score a ragged line in the floor tiles, wall to wall, six feet from the barred windows. He seemed careful to not cross it.

"I was a godly man, sir," he said. "Me and mine in the fucking pews every Sunday, sir. Do you know how to tell us Christers from the rest?"

Dobbs wagged his head as though maybe he did and maybe he didn't. "I'd like to know how *you* do it, Lionel."

Mayhew appeared gratified to share his expertise. "We're the ones with the broken knees from all the groveling. That's our reward. A lifetime of broken knees. And cricks in our necks from looking up up up." He spat toward the window. "Wrong direction. In Innsmouth, their roots are the same as their gods. They run deep there. Deeeeep."

Mayhew found this privately amusing. As readily as he snickered, he scowled.

"How could he let it happen there? Anywhere?" Mayhew whispered now, the hushed disbelief of a man still trying to work through the worst betrayal of his life. "In this world he told us he made. How could he let things like this take root and grow?"

Mayhew flashed his pearly browns.

"Do you know how much of the world is water and how much is land? Neither do I, exactly, but there's far more room for *them* than there is for us. And every Sunday I took us to the pews and fell to my poor sore knees and I thanked that wretched God of mine for making it that way. Because I used to love a good swim! What do you think of that? What do you think cows and pigs would say about God if somebody told them he'd made them for *our* teeth?"

He skinned back his lips again, this time to grind his teeth back and forth, and side to side. They made a most unnerving click.

"Show me the face of my old God, is all I ask. Half a chance, that's all I want. Let me see him, and I'll chew the nose from his face and spit it into the abyss."

The best they could tell, separating the fragments of his recounting from his interjections, and piecing them together on the fly, Mayhew had spent a long, fruitless day in Innsmouth with nothing but red knuckles to show for it. He'd knocked on a lot of doors. Most remained shut, even when he could hear the bumps of something shifting on the other side. A few places opened up, usually just wide enough for a face to fill the gap, but there was more disappointment waiting when they did.

The residents, more often than not, looked peculiar and smelled worse, like fishermen who'd given up on washing when they came in from their boats. To a man, they were as churlish as convicts, even the women, dead-eyed and unfriendly, plagued with baldness and rashes on their wattled necks, and skin so sallow they seemed to have spent their entire lives under a scum of clouds.

Mayhew had expected a seaside town full of rubes, and rubes they were, but his advantage ended there. A man who knew how to close a sale could handle rubes, as long as he could talk long enough, but in Innsmouth he never got going with them. Not a one. They couldn't even be bothered to speak properly. They slurred and grunted and gurgled like they'd been blotto from bathtub hootch for so long they were no longer capable of holding a respectable conversation.

The normals weren't much better, urging him to go peddle his papers elsewhere.

After a thankless day of this, Mayhew confessed that he'd been ready to indulge in a little rudeness himself. If these clods were going to give him the bum's rush out of town, then he might as well earn it. He always wore the shoes for it, fit to wedge open a door until he'd had his say, given his spiel.

Mayhew ground out another shit-colored smile.

"I only wanted to see how they lived. On the inside. So I could inform my idiot sales manager why I'd wasted an entire day. That was when I saw the ones they must have been trying to hide. And there's so many more of them than the ones they let outside."

He jutted his lower jaw into a grotesque underbite and chomped at the air.

"They came for me then. A flood of them spilling out of one house, then another, and another. I'd had my fill of them and they'd had their fill of me. Or would have, if they'd gotten their scaly paws on me. Their webbed fingers. Tongues the size of shoe soles, some of them. Life soul skin bones organs seed . . . they would've had them all from me if I'd been any slower."

According to Mayhew, he stood rooted in shock from the spectacle, and they were almost upon him when he bashed one across the skull with his briefcase and ran. He feared there was no time to start his Model T, from '18, the year before the change to electric starters. These monstrous townsfolk would catch up to him as he labored over the engine crank.

So he left everything behind—briefcase, flivver, and all. Career, too, and at some point, everyone agreed, his mind. He abandoned everything and ran. For miles. He found the road he'd taken into town and followed it back up to Newburyport.

Next day, an Essex County sheriff's deputy had taken a run up, to check things out. There had been no sign of his car, no one to admit they'd seen him, no evidence he'd been there at all.

"*To* you, they look like something you'd drag up from the bottom of a pond and throw back. Only bigger. That's enough fishing for today," Mayhew said. "But *at* you . . . they look *at* you with the arrogance of men. You wouldn't know it from their eyes. But they're haughty, and how. Royalty, is what they think they are. They rise up before you like they're kings of the world, because the world is wet. I read people, is what I do. There's triumphant men and there's beaten men, and I know the difference in the way they stand. Two of them, I saw, they were even wearing shiny gold-like crowns on what passes for their heads. That's how I know. They've already crowned themselves the new kings of this world."

Look for details that square up—that was the assignment, and here was one of them. Queer headgear. Robert Olmstead, the latest fella to come raving out of the place, said the same. This wasn't some random fluff anyone might pick out of the air. It was specific. With Olmstead, there was even a trail he'd picked up on, just such a piece kept on display at the Newburyport Historical Society. It had been around long enough to be regarded as an odd bit of jewelry whose origins were unlikely to ever be known. Some mysteries didn't want to be solved.

"Let's hear about these shiny gold crowns, Lionel," Dobbs said.

Mayhew glanced about as if he'd never broken himself of the habit of looking for something to write on, draw with. He settled for his tobacco-tattooed hands. Pressing the tips of his thumbs and pinkies together, he made a circle—squashed a little, but rounder than not—then mimed setting it atop his own noggin, the rest of his fingers splayed up and out like rays.

"There. That's a proper crown, see. Any king would be proud to wear it and the fit would be perfect."

He lowered his hands again and studiously adjusted the shape. The distance between his thumbs and his pinkies lengthened; his palms pulled closer; the circle became a narrow oval. His other fingers bunched at the tips to suggest a rising peak or overarching loop. Mayhew shuddered with disgust, then made a show of how ill suited it was to fit his head.

"It's not for a human skull anymore. They have heads made like lima beans."

He dropped his hands as if he couldn't bear to hold them this way anymore and gave his fingers a fierce shaking out.

Mayhew wasn't good for much else, and it wasn't clear how much he'd been good for in the first place. What he'd done, though, was tell a remarkably similar story to that of Robert Olmstead, whose trip to Innsmouth had ended the same way: chased out of town by bogeymen, and desperate to convince anyone who would listen that something rotten was lurking beneath the surface of a busted-up, broken-down seaport that nobody had much reason to visit anymore.

After an hour with Lionel Mayhew, it was easy to see why people had written him off. If he hadn't gone to Innsmouth broken, he'd left that way. He wouldn't have been the first salesman to crack under the pressure of quotas he couldn't fill. He was fit for cutting out paper dolls with dull scissors, and that was about it. A man like that might beat his gums with all kinds of silly stories not worth the time spent listening to them. He was easy to ignore.

Olmstead, on the other hand, must have come across as clearheaded enough to impress someone to take him seriously.

Forget the bogeymen for a minute. Those crowns . . . diadems . . . tiaras . . . that was a singularly consistent detail. Whatever they were, they had to fit something, right?

Back down at the Studebaker, Dobbs spread his road map over the hood. Hewlitt watched him trace his finger from Boston to Danvers to Innsmouth itself.

"We're almost halfway there already," Dobbs said. "We'll have to give it a look-see sooner or later. Do you really want to turn around and have to come back this way all over again tomorrow?"

The farther northeast from Danvers they got, the worse the roads became. It had been a long time since they'd seen fresh gravel and tar. Eventually they dwindled to hard-packed dirt. Farms and pastures sat back from them, winding down for the season, a time for mending fences and culling the herds and turning over the fields one last time before the earth froze. It took a lot of cursing to keep the Studebaker on the move, as its tires caught the ruts and put up a constant fight through the steering wheel.

By their watches it wasn't much past midday, but the closer they got to the coast, the more like evening it seemed. The sky grew dark with an unbroken ceiling of clouds, thick and low and turbulent with snatches of rain that spattered the windshield then let up as if to tease them onward with a promise of something clearer just ahead.

Finally, Hewlitt uncorked what he'd appeared on the verge of bringing up half a dozen times already.

"What's eating you, pal?" he said. "You've been a sad sack all day, even before we got anywhere near the bughouse."

Dobbs worked his tongue in his cheek and scowled at the day outside awhile. "You've never asked for any, but if you want some advice, here it is for free, just the same."

Dobbs looked him over, his partner a regular Joe Brooks in that spiffy tailored suit, that herringbone Chesterfield overcoat, the fedora that probably had never once blown off his pretty head. He came from money and looked it, six years out of Yale Law and destined for great things. He hadn't spoken much about his college years, just enough to give the impression that he'd excelled at every sport he tried out for and studying came just as easy. He couldn't hide all that, although it was obvious he'd been making an effort to leave behind the fraternity boy inside him. It was easy to imagine Hewlitt and his buddies going ape on weekends, sneaking off to the best juice joints they could get a line on and making time with all the vamps and flappers they could slip their arms around. A regular Rumbleseat Ronnie.

"If you want to keep this job, do yourself a favor," Dobbs told him. "Look sharp. Always look sharp. You've got the kind of look Hoover likes. Hang onto that as long as you can. Shave twice a day if you have to, and say no to second helpings at the supper table. The last thing you want is to let yourself get to looking anything like me."

He could see Hewlitt's gears turning. Maybe Ridley didn't want to look like his partner—Dobbs with his slab of bohunk face, a gap between his front teeth for God's sakes, a face made for snarling—but he didn't necessarily see a problem with it either. Nothing wrong with looking like somebody the hoods and thugs should fear. Enough height, enough muscle, enough ugly . . . in their line of work, that wasn't a bad set of qualities to bring to the table.

"It's Hoover. All Hoover," Dobbs went on. "He's got this vision. The Bureau did fine without him, then he waltzes in three years ago and he's been making it over to suit his image ever since. He's got it in for guys like me. We don't fit in anymore. His words, not mine—if you look like the kind of lug who should be driving a truck or working a loading dock, he doesn't want you."

Hewlitt looked incredulous. Because he still could. "You get the job *done*, though. Doesn't make a lick of sense."

"It's as much image as results now. And I don't just look wrong, I've got the wrong pedigree too. You know how I got hired on with the Bureau?"

Hewlitt shook his head no. "It's never come up."

"My pop grew up with Senator O'Dwyer. He called in a favor or two, and that was it. I had the kind of war record that looked good to the right people, so I was in. The Volstead Act hadn't passed yet . . . they didn't farm us out helping Treasury chase down moonshiners . . . those were different days. It was a different job. But men who came on like that, Hoover wants them gone too. Him and his brown-nosers, they find their reasons."

Hewlitt looked embarrassed for him, staring out his window.

"Just you wait. Prohibition can't last. Everybody knows it was a mistake and nobody wants to be first to come out and say so. But it'll fall. Trust me. And by the time it does, you won't recognize the Bureau. It'll be all guys like you, with your law and accounting degrees. That's why Hoover keeps bringing you in."

Now Hewlitt looked as if something that never fit for him finally clicked into place. He laughed with the hesitation of someone who wasn't sure he should. "*That's* why you've been taking those night classes?"

"Was. I quit this week. I don't know what I was thinking. I thought if I showed them I knew how to read a ledger . . ."

Dobbs glowered out the window as they trundled along. Lillian was glad he had more time at home again, but if he lost this job, his wife would see there was such a thing as too much time.

"I don't have the brain for it. I'm in a class with a bunch of Caspar Milquetoasts ten years younger than me, every one of them I could break in half, and they all cipher rings around me. But that's how Hoover thinks he might take down Capone and Moran and Lansky and the rest. If he can't get them on their actual rackets, he's going to trip them up on their taxes. Sounds like a load of applesauce to me, but that's what he's got in his head. And he's still doing it half-assed. He wants accountants but he doesn't want Jews. Go figure that."

Hewlitt finally looked as if he got it. That nobody was safe. That anybody's days could be numbered. As long as he remembered this, he might be okay.

"I don't know what to say, Arch. I'm sorry? That doesn't cut the mustard."

Dobbs shook his head. "There's nothing *to* say. If that's my hand, I'll play it 'til they take away my cards. Call me dumb, call me ugly, fine. Just don't say I was ever half-assed about anything. Send me to the nuthouse, send me to Innsmouth, I don't care. If something's up here, I'll find it."

They clattered into Innsmouth from the south, along the road up from Ipswich, the final leg of the journey cutting across desolate stretches of sandy ground that grew nothing taller than hearty clumps of sedge grass and wind-gnarled shrubs.

When they crested the rise before the road made one final dip toward the town, Dobbs cut the throttle and coasted to an idling stop so they could take their time with the view. Even from this far, anyone could tell that Innsmouth must have been grand once, a jewel by the sea, fed by trade and fattened on the wealth of the world. A few streets held rows of legitimate mansions, and others weren't far behind, roofs bristling with multiple chimneys and widow's walks. But something had gone wrong here. The outside world had gone on without them, and what remained of their own was left to decay.

Its homes and shops marched toward the sea down hills and plateaus cut in half by the Manuxet River and a series of low waterfalls. A refinery, its chimneys smokeless, was perched on the north side of the final falls, where the river widened into the mouth that met the sea. The harbor's surface was calm, the surging of the ocean held back by a spit of land and breakwater that speared down from the north and turned the bay into a loop of wharves and docks and warehouses. Out to sea, a mile or two, ran a forbidding black line of stone called Devil Reef.

He saw more movement in the ocean than he saw in the streets below.

"How many people are supposed to live here, is it?" Dobbs asked.

"Three hundred or more, four hundred tops."

"That's a lot of real estate for no more people than that. Even if most of it *is* falling to pieces."

"What are you thinking? Rumrunners coming down from Canada?"

"It'd be a good place for it." Dobbs pointed past the reef, where the clouds met the sea. "Looks like a place that gets a lot of fog."

He trained a pair of binoculars on the lighthouse at the tip of the breakwater. The tower had shed a lot of bricks, most of the glass in the lantern room was smashed out, and the lamp lens looked no better. It wasn't going to be guiding anyone in safely.

"If a captain knew what he was doing, he could use the fog to slip the Coast Guard, and be in the harbor and unloaded before the cutters caught up with him."

At eighty or ninety simoleons per case of the good stuff, it was a risk a lot of captains would be willing to take. If a smuggler's boat was far enough offshore, the Coast Guard couldn't touch it—officially, at least—even if everyone knew it was bringing all the Canadian Club in the world. Had to nab them while offloading it onshore. Sometimes the boats from both sides of their war sat on the open ocean for weeks at a time, playing cat and mouse games. The Coast Guard waited for the smugglers to make their move, and the smugglers waited for the chance to do it.

Hewlitt took the binoculars for himself. "They could be bootlegging it themselves down there too. Like you said, that's a lot of real estate for four hundred people. A lot of room to hide a barrel house somewhere."

They weren't going to get a better read on the place up here. Dobbs drove on.

It wasn't that he didn't believe the stories Olmstead and Mayhew told about their encounters here; more that he couldn't believe the conclusions they'd drawn. Both of them had experienced *something*. The tales they'd told were too similar, and the fear was real. But if two years of bullets, bayonets, and artillery had taught Dobbs anything, it was that the memories of frightened men couldn't be trusted. They couldn't help it. Fear bent the truth out of shape in a hurry.

If the choice was between bootleggers and bogeymen, he figured he knew the real score around here.

At the southwest edge of town, the country road turned to a thoroughfare called Eliot Street, according to a rusty sign that listed toward the intersection. It cut through Innsmouth's grid on a diagonal until it brought them to the town square, a hub where several streets came together like spokes on a wheel. Things looked livelier here, a few residents shuffling along with their heads down, people with nowhere to go and all day to get there. The square was ringed with businesses—a drug store, a grocer, and off to the left was the five-story Gilman House, where Olmstead claimed the townsfolk had first come for him, trying to peel their way past his door while he slipped away through the connecting rooms and out onto the neighboring roof.

From behind every window, Dobbs got the prickly sense of being watched. This town had a lot more eyes in it than it liked to let on.

"The place definitely gives me the heebie-jeebies," said Hewlitt. "Do you think they know who we are?"

"Count on it. They'll be thinking revenuers. Close enough. We don't stop."

Hewlitt already had his Roscoe out, resting on his thigh with his thumb on the hammer. Smart lad. Dobbs preferred the solid, comforting heft of the Colt automatic under his arm. If it was good enough for the army, it was good enough for him.

They left the square by another street called Federal. It took them across the Manuxet, swollen with autumn rains, on a creaky bridge that had gone years too long between repairs. Another block later they came to an unkempt circular green, fronted by a pair of old New England churches that didn't look to be saving many souls these days.

Hewlitt pointed across the green to another building, better maintained despite the creepers and vines climbing its walls. It looked like a lesser temple from ancient Greece, more stone than wood, across the front a short row of columns holding up a triangular tympanum—not a church, but a lodge. Freemasons, he would've thought, until Hewlitt read the rough letters chiseled across the lintel.

"'Esoteric Order of Dagon' . . .?" he said. "What's that supposed to mean?"

"It means keep out and keep moving, you gullible suckers."

A block later they turned east, facing the harbor that every prickly instinct Dobbs had told him wasn't nearly as tranquil as it looked from up here. They cruised as far down as they could, hooking a right at Water Street so they could backtrack across the river and make their way south again.

Between them and the harbor's waters sat a long row of warehouses being pried apart by time and the slow predations of the sea air. Dobbs cranked down his window and had Hewlitt do the same, so the breezes might blow through and tell him what they could.

This was a vile place.

Dobbs had been in fishing villages and harbor towns before, on both sides of the Atlantic. Over here and over there, they all smelled more or less the same. Their air, their very essence, was saturated with the ancient scents of fish and briny water, and the boreal forest smell of wood so wet it might never be truly dry. All of that was here . . . but underneath was something else, something foul, a sour, living odor, like the musk of some predator that hid itself in the trees or tall grass until it was time to pounce.

So now they knew.

They wouldn't get far by day here.

They'd have to come back by night.

It took a month to secure the go-ahead.

Dobbs's recommendation: if they were to get to the bottom of what was going on in Innsmouth, they needed someone who knew how to come in quiet, poke around, and slip out with the goods before anyone knew he was there . . . and he was the right man for the job. For obvious reasons.

Simple enough, but the SAC of the Boston office refused to proceed without express approval from Director Hoover, and was slow to seek it. He disliked Dobbs's idea from the get-go. It could spiral wrong in too many ways. They were investigators, not infiltrators.

Sit tight and watch and wait—that was SAC Swindlehurst's idea of caution. He wasted weeks liaising with local law enforcement, trading favors to get prowl cars to lay low and keep eyes on the roads between Innsmouth and the nearest towns: Newburyport and Kingsport Head, Ipswich and Rowley and Arkham. If they noticed trucks, or those fast, roomy Lincolns that rumrunners liked, that would reveal a lot.

Surveillance turned up one big fat goose egg. The only vehicle observed that could've hauled any sort of load was the rattletrap daily bus to Newburyport, and that was typically light even on passengers. Nothing going in, nothing coming out. Add in what the Coast Guard had sighted, and all they had was a bigger, fatter egg.

Clearly, in Innsmouth, they were smarter than most of them looked.

"If you wait much longer," Dobbs warned Swindlehurst, "we'll have to hold off until spring, unless you're willing to belly crawl through miles of snow *with* me."

Which finally jarred things loose.

The challenge was how to get in silent and unseen, yet have the means for a speedy retreat if things went bad. Innsmouth was nothing if not isolated, inconvenient from anywhere. Forget driving, and even walking the roads was a bad idea, in case they stationed lookouts. Neither was Dobbs keen on hoofing it over miles of open ground, against the hostilities of a northeastern November. He'd be half-sapped by the time he got there, maybe no good when it counted most.

In the end, it was Hewlitt to the rescue, suggesting the abandoned railway between Innsmouth and Rowley. If Olmstead had used it to escape from town while staying clear of the roads, why couldn't they do the same, in the opposite direction?

It was a sound idea. The rails were still in place, rusty but not impassable. The terrain was mostly sandy grassland and scrub. No trees to fall across the tracks, no roots to buckle them from below. If they requisitioned a handcar from the Boston and Providence Railroad in Rowley, they could cover the distance down to Innsmouth at ten or twelve miles an hour—faster than walking, stealthier than driving.

Now, finally, they were hitting on all six.

But if planning was on their side, the weather was not. Wait too late to decide, and this was what you risked. Things never changed—it was never the man holding things up with his fat ass parked behind a desk who paid the price. No, that fell to the men in the field.

For days, their team was stuck operating out of a Rowley hotel room, nothing to do but smoke and wait out the rains that were too stubborn to clear. When the report came in that the season's first snow was on the way, it was move now or postpone everything until next year. Conditions wouldn't likely get any better for months, only worse. This was their shot.

An hour after a wet, gray dusk, on the night before Thanksgiving, Dobbs and Hewlitt set off from the Rowley train station on their rolling platform of wood and iron. In oilskin ponchos and fisherman's hoods, each pumped one end of the lever mounted in the middle of the railcar, a seesaw action that propelled them across the countryside, under a drizzle of rain that turned to a slap whenever a gust of wind blew through.

They got a rhythm going, and for the first miles allowed themselves the luxury of a carbide trainman's lantern at the front end, to warn of blockages. They were a quarter-hour out before the going felt smooth enough to start talking again.

"You were wondering where I went yesterday. I didn't just slip out because I was getting itchy in the hotel," Hewlitt said over the spatter of rain and grind of wheels on the rails. "The name on that lodge, the first day we were up here . . . the Esoteric Order of Dagon . . . that wouldn't let me go. So before we left Beantown, I went to a couple libraries to see if I could dig something up on it. They weren't much help, but one librarian, she said if I wanted to know bad enough that I didn't mind some driving, I should head up to Arkham and check with the library at Miskatonic U. If anybody could help me, that would be the place. So that's where I went yesterday."

Dobbs pumped the lever a couple times and kept his eyes on the lantern's cone of light. He was facing forward, Hewlitt was making the trip backward. Up to him to make sure they didn't collide with the unexpected.

"Somebody there knew something?"

"And how. They've got all kinds of creaky old books there. The order . . . it's a genuine cult. It goes back at least ninety years . . . maybe even longer. It's what the people turned to when the fishing went bad for them. This Dagon, he's some sort of fish-god. With a consort called Mother Hydra. But they're not worshipped for themselves. They're the go-betweens to other powers . . . more remote gods."

Dobbs had to snort. "Fish-gods, huh? Guess I should've brought a filleting knife, instead."

"I know how it sounds. That's not the point." Hewlitt peeked over his shoulder as if having second thoughts about where they were headed. "I know what's going on in Innsmouth is probably bootleggers who cooked up a new way to scare off outsiders. But jeepers creepers, Arch, if you chisel a name into a building, it's not just for show. I think we might want to consider that whatever else these rumrunners may be up to, this is something they actually believe in."

Impulse wanted to keep scoffing, but Hewlitt was right. Fanatics could turn to bootlegging the same as plain old greedy sons of bitches, and the zeal of true believers could be a lot more dangerous than pure self-interest.

"Good work," Dobbs said instead.

By the time they neared the coastline, the lights of Innsmouth a dim glow ahead, it was raining pitchforks. They backed off the lever and coasted to a stop, then reversed the railcar's direction and set the brake to hold it in place. Dobbs shucked his poncho and hood, his clothing soaking through as he stashed the foul-weather gear beneath the cart.

"If I come back yelling bloody murder," he told Hewlitt, "you have this heap moving before I even get to it."

With that, he was off. He was dressed for movement, not for keeping dry—a snug pullover sweater, pants just loose enough to maneuver, and lace-up boots fit for the trenches. Sheathed at his waist was the biggest pigsticker he'd been able to drum up since he'd known this night was coming. No gun. He didn't need the bulk, and firing it would only give away his position to more of them than he could shoot.

He jogged beside the tracks to the outskirts of town, then slipped along the north side, pressing toward the curl of land that enclosed the harbor while keeping the houses to his right. It was questionable whether anyone lived in them, or would want to. Even through the rain they appeared unkempt, perhaps last tended to before his lifetime.

He could be quick and nimble for such a big man, at first glance unlikely to have amassed the kind of kills he had a decade ago. He still couldn't say why he'd done it. He hadn't hated the Hun any worse than the other doughboys sent to France. Crazy from the shelling, maybe, but rather than dropping fetal and trembling to the bottom of a trench, he'd made a savage game of leaving its safety entirely.

How far could he creep past the craters and shattered trees of the no-man's-land between sides? How easily could he thwart the barbed wire fences? How deep into the German front line could he go? How quietly could he cut the throat of a drowsy sentry, then slip back unseen? Could he leave them gutted, strewn along the ground? Could he manage two? Three? Could he take souvenirs?

He'd never known if the Hun had a name for him, this phantom butcher who for six weeks came in the night and opened them steaming in the cold autumn air, then returned to his own lines with blood on his face.

Why in God's name do you keep doing this? His buddies grew nearly as frightened of him as the Germans must've been.

Can't sleep. It was the best answer he had. *Might as well keep busy.*

The scrape of his boots drowned out by the rain and the surf, Dobbs scrambled down a shallow embankment to the wharves and warehouses ringing the harbor. Stone quays and timber docks jutted into the water, the gunwales of a few moored boats thudding gently against them.

He crept along the wharf, hugging walls when he could, advancing piling to piling when he couldn't. Whenever he found a door, he eased it open and slipped inside—nobody kept anything locked here—then listened for movement. Once he was satisfied he was alone, he slipped his Nassau lighter from its oilskin pouch and used the flame to see what might've been stashed away.

In hovel after hovel it was the same story: a lot of nothing, only accumulations of seafaring debris left by grandfathers who'd lived through more prosperous times. They didn't even look disturbed, as if recent loads had been moved in and out. But there was a lot more to search, and the night would be long.

Too long, maybe. However relentless the rain, it wasn't enough to tamp down the pervasive smell of fish and worse. Innsmouth was saturated with it, stewed in it. Only stone seemed immune. Every wooden surface—railings and stairs, the planks of walls and walkways—felt slick to the point of loathsomeness, so spongy with the rain and sea that grinding a hand against it sloughed off a wad of soggy splinters.

As Dobbs lingered in a shed's doorway and rubbed warmth into his hands, he stared out across the harbor, past a row of empty pilings, and finally put a finger on one thing that had bothered him about the October afternoon they'd driven through. Birds should have been perched on places like those pilings. Birds should've lined the peaks of roofs. The lower sky should have wheeled with gulls and terns and shearwaters, yet he'd neither seen them nor heard their keening.

What kind of a port was this when even seabirds shunned it?

He worked his way around toward the town's centerline, to a cluster of wormy storage buildings just north of the Manuxet. Visibility was better here, light filtering down from the last working gas lamps along Water Street.

Here, for the first time, he picked up a sound he couldn't dismiss as wind or rain or waves. A sharp sound of cracking—that he could hear it at all, so near to where the river's mouth spilled into the sea, meant it was close, very close.

Stepping lightly along the stones of the wharf, Dobbs followed the sound to its source. Somebody was out there, squatting on the soft wood of a dock, next to a piling that looked bristly—like others he'd passed, crusted to the top with barnacles. A man? Sure, why not. Women had better sense than to be out in weather like this.

Seen from behind, the man was an indistinct shape, broad-backed and thick, hunkered down next to a bucket. Every so often he reached in to dredge something out and fumble it to his mouth. After a few crunches and a sound of guttural slurping, he'd sling something into the water, except for when his throw fell short and pieces clattered to the dock.

Shell fragments and legs.

This couldn't be what it looked like. No. Dobbs didn't care how dumb they grew them here in Innsmouth. A man couldn't be out there eating raw crabs by cracking them open with his teeth.

He heard a splash, then a series of wet grunts, and moments later another one heaved into view, up a ladder Dobbs hadn't noticed next to the piling. A second man? Sure, why not. But a man misshapen, plopping onto the dock with a squelch and a splat, banging down a mesh-bottomed bucket that rattled and streamed water.

The newcomer raised his slippery-looking head into the light, facing inland.

How, Dobbs wanted to know. How did rain and dim light distort a face so badly it looked like *that*? Masks, he'd thought since Danvers. They wore masks here, to scare away unwelcome visitors. But under no circumstances could he imagine rumrunners so committed they would maintain the charade while diving for shellfish on a rainy night.

That out there? He stood like a man . . . sort of . . . but wore no man's face. Bug-eyed and bullet-headed, his big hands didn't look right either, with sharp-tipped fingers and flanges at the wrist as if he wore blades.

And he was looking right this way. Dobbs didn't move, didn't breathe, did all he could to knit himself into the shadows. But whoever, whatever, was out there, had eyes that seemed made for the murkiness of water and low light, and found him. He pointed and bellowed with an airy, hissing screech.

The other, still hunkered next to his bucket, spun around to face inland, and this one looked even worse. His skull peaked with an absurdly narrow crown, then flared down and outward into a brutal, underslung jaw jutting with teeth like spikes. If he was ever a man at all, that part was all but gone. His face looked more like that of a wolf-eel than anything human. His eyes were as sharp as his companion's, and his reactions frightfully quick. He seized his bucket by the handle and flung it through the rain.

Before Dobbs could react, it crashed into his right shoulder and his arm went numb. When the bucket clattered to the dock, it scattered crabs that scuttled around him. Staggered already, he slipped on them in his retreat, trying to buy time to get some feeling back into his arm.

They were after him in a heartbeat, moving as unlike men as they looked. One hopped like an enormous toad, the other waddled with great, strenuous strides—exactly as Mayhew and Olmstead had claimed about the people here. To his advantage, they seemed better suited for water than for land, but were relentless and croaked for help in their ghastly voices.

Dobbs had always liked to believe he never ran from anyone or anything, but no more. Whenever he'd stood his ground before, he knew what he faced. There was no shame in running when you had no idea what to even call what was after you.

He raced north up the wharves, careful to keep his footing on the rain-slick stones. From behind, and to his left, came the sound of doors opening, of others joining the chase, with ungainly bodies and huge slapping feet and a wet slopping mimicry of human voices. He drew the pigsticker knife with his left hand, and when one of them lurched from behind a shack to bar his way, he slashed the heavy blade across its throat before he even registered that his assailant's neck rippled with what looked like the beginnings of gills.

As he was reeling from that, another came at him before he could draw back the knife to slash again. This was the most like a man of the lot, but with a mouth so freakishly wide he could've worked a carnival circuit. Dobbs seized him by one arm and went with his momentum, spinning across the stones and flinging him off the wharf into the harbor.

He got far enough north to lose himself in the deeper shadows, where maybe they could still see him and maybe they couldn't. He was betting if he could reach the embankment where he'd come in, he could climb better, faster, than they could.

Feeling was returning to his arm, and if it felt clumsy he could at least use it again. When another pair came at him, he swung his right as stiff as a tree limb, the meat of his fist bashing into the side of the nearest head. The impact was unexpectedly painful, the heel of his hand jabbed as if by the spines of a fish's fin. It came away bleeding as he staggered into the second of the pair, and slammed the knife into its belly and yanked up toward its ribcage. He smelled its entrails and its burst of breath, an odor of fish and water, of seaweed and slimy mud.

But by the time he reached the sheds along the harbor's northern rim, he knew it wouldn't be enough to escape with nothing more than the same story that had brought him here. *Where's the proof, Agent Dobbs?* They'd ship him to Danvers and lock him in a room next to Mayhew until he started drawing his own do-not-cross lines on the floor.

It was his incursions against the Hun all over again. He'd have to take souvenirs.

Dobbs pressed close to the waterlogged walls, slowing the thud of his heart and listening through the rain. In his head, he retraced his steps from where he'd first come in, the buildings he'd searched and the detritus that filled them. He broke cover and, at a scurry, by the flame of his Nassau, searched the most likely shacks until he found the pieces of the past he'd seen earlier, reminders of when the town had taken from the sea in the usual ways, and grabbed what he needed.

Then he found a barrel sturdy enough to support his weight so he could clamber up onto one of the roofs. He lay flattened out, peering south through the gloom, pelted by the rain and assailed by the smell of sodden wood. He'd never been this wet. He'd never been this cold. He'd never cared less about either.

Soon, they drifted along, the original hideous pair of townsfolk he'd seen. They'd been the first to give chase and hadn't given up on him yet. Keeping his head low, Dobbs groaned as if wounded, softly, scarcely loud enough to catch their attention and lure them in. Maybe it was because they looked like such poor climbers that neither of them thought to glance up at the roofs.

Close enough. He rose and whirled the old fisherman's net over his head, then cast it over theirs. The pair floundered beneath it, slashing their way through with their sharp-looking claws. Rotten as it was, the net wouldn't hold, but Dobbs needed them surprised only long enough for him to swing down from the roof and go to work on them with the oar he'd left propped against the side wall.

He swung it like a club, then like an axe, chopping at them with the blade of the oar until it broke, leaving him with a jagged length of shaft. The bullet-head dropped with a gargling moan, then lashed out to catch Dobbs by the boot and bring him down as well. As he fell, Dobbs bashed the wolf-eel in the knee.

They wallowed in the rain, man and monstrosities tangled in the shreds of net. He felt something rake his side, a sting of cold fire that ripped through sweater and skin alike. His blood was the first warmth he'd felt in hours. He swung the shard of oar blindly, until he felt it punch into one of them, then traced the same arc again and again, until the wolf-eel quit moving and he couldn't yank the wood free of its body anymore.

But he still had the knife, and now it went easier. The bullet-head was half dead already. He just finished the job.

For a few moments, Dobbs lay motionless, sprawled atop the bodies, sucking air until the cold got him moving again. And the smell. Everything shit when it died. He'd thought nothing was worse than men. He was wrong.

The others would still be looking for him. He rolled upright again and dragged the corpses into the nearest shack, then cleared away the tatters of net and pieces of oar. Let the rain take care of the blood.

By the flame of his Nassau, he studied their inhuman faces, then set the lighter aside. This wasn't the time or place. He could spend years trying to figure them out.

Where's your proof, Agent Dobbs?

Here. Right here, you pencil-pushing shit-for-brains.

He unsheathed the pigsticker one more time. Two heads, one clawed hand. That should be enough evidence for anybody. He hunted until he turned up a burlap sack, then dropped to his knees and began to saw.

Severed heads weren't something to take on the road, certainly not as far as D.C., so J. Edgar Hoover came to them. The director was a traveling man anyway. Scuttlebutt got around, how he and his entourage might show up at a field office unannounced, like a surprise inspection in the army, looking for, *hoping* for, reasons to send good men packing.

Like in Denver. *Would you like a drink?* the SAC had asked one of them. He was out in the street on the spot.

Dobbs had never seen a more officious-looking man. Hoover was trim and no-nonsense, and kept his oiled hair combed straight back into a tight black ridge over his brow. He'd showed up skeptical, as if he'd listened to everything SAC Swindlehurst had told him over the phone and concluded they couldn't possibly have this right.

They'd been stowing the heads and claw on meat trays in the icebox. As soon as the trays came out onto a tabletop, Hoover's skepticism vanished. Give him credit for one thing: he could roll with the punches and adapt. Whereas everyone else wanted to keep their distance, seemingly fearful the heads might still bite, Hoover got up close, hands on his knees and leaning in eye-to-dead-milky-eye.

He prodded at them with a pencil, used it to flip the claw over and back again, to push at the webbing between its fingers. He toppled the bullet-head onto its side and poked at the nub of vertebra jutting from the meat of the neck. He knew cut-marks when he saw them, too, distaste flashing across his face before he bolted upright again and dropped the pencil into the wastebasket.

"And this is your handiwork, Agent Dobbs?"

"Yes, sir." It was two days on, and he was all kinds of sore, bruised, bandaged where anyone could see it and stitched up where they couldn't. He itched, as he might after getting scratched by a cat, only worse.

"Well," Hoover said, "I don't suppose they would've posed for photographs."

If they'd been nightmarish on the wharves, here they seemed unreal. The heads were green-skinned, mottled, and hairless. As individuals they looked nothing alike, but were the same species. Obviously. What else could they be? There was little human about them, yet he'd seen them walk and give chase, labor together and communicate and fight. Most worrisome of all, they kept themselves hidden in a town of people who themselves were reviled for their peculiar ways and appearance, emerging only when they felt certain no one else would see them. A town that worshipped gods they thought lived deep in the sea, a notion he'd found easy to laugh at.

Nobody was laughing now.

"I believe we can conclude that we're confronted with something other than bootleggers here," Hoover said. "Given all we know about creation, or think we do, these things shouldn't exist. But I'm looking at them. Can anyone explain to me how such a thing is possible?"

It was Hewlitt's turn. He'd actually enjoyed digging into this.

"It's just legend and gossip, sir. People of the neighboring towns have plenty to say once you get them going. I think we might find the truth woven into it somewhere," he said. "For more than a century, Innsmouth has been under the control of one family, mainly. That would be the Marshes. The first patriarch of note was Obed Marsh, a ship's captain who spent much of his life at sea. He was an active trader and importer.

There's a loose consensus that things in Innsmouth started to change for the worse in the early 1800s, after a trip Captain Marsh made to the East Indies and elsewhere in the South Seas. Cutting through the hooey, it sounds as if he may have brought back some highly unusual people. If not as passengers of their own free will, then we have to consider he may have regarded them as slaves. The town was isolated enough, and they wouldn't have known any better."

At this, Hoover seethed. Slavery was something they still fought now, the worst kind of men running kidnapped women, and people too poor and ignorant to know what hit them after they came through Ellis Island. If a person was helpless enough, there was always someone eager to turn them for a profit.

"But I suspect Marsh may have brought back something else he didn't intend," Hewlitt went on. "Something that got into their bloodlines. A skin disease, maybe."

"A skin disease." Hoover's voice went flat. He picked up the smallest of the meat trays, the one holding the severed claw, and leveled it before Hewlitt's nose. Hoover grimaced as if its very existence annoyed him—the lengthened fingers, their razored tips, the webbing, the ridges that swept back like rudimentary fins. "Would a skin disease do this? Would a skin disease look so functional? So . . . symmetrical?"

"It's just a supposition, sir." Hewlitt looked cowed. "I came across a quote in the Ipswich newspaper that called Innsmouth 'an unsavory haven of inbreeding and circus folk.' I was reminded of rare conditions that leave people no choice but to make a living in the carnival circuits. Alligator-men and the like."

Hoover smacked the meat tray back to the tabletop. "Agent Dobbs, you're the one who's come into the most direct contact with them. Is it your opinion this is a skin disease?"

"It's not for me to say, sir." Damn right this was no disease. But he wasn't going to call Hewlitt mistaken, to Hoover least of all. "That could be part of it, but I think whatever's wrong with them there goes more than skin deep."

Hoover saw through it and didn't respect him for it one bit. "Very diplomatic of you, Dobbs." He furrowed his brow and jammed his fists against his hips, glaring down at the evidence he'd demanded and now gotten. He had a big hard-on for Al Capone—rooting him out of Chicago's Metropole Hotel, shutting him down in Cicero—and this was what he had to deal with.

Although it was, in its way, an echo of a decade ago. While Dobbs was in France, Hoover, barely out of law school, was serving stateside in the War Emergency Division, heading up its Alien Enemy Bureau. A discovery like this had to play to fears he hadn't had to worry about since Germany signed the armistice.

"If these are not people as we generally conceive of *people* as God makes them . . . if their roots aren't even American . . . if there's an established history of them being willing to kidnap and kill to keep their existence a secret," Hoover said, "then I think we have no choice but to take that town apart and see how deep this threat actually goes."

He waved for someone to return the heads and claw to the icebox, out of his sight, then stepped closer to Dobbs, more than a head shorter and straining to flex his reach in other ways.

"Make no mistake, Agent Dobbs," Hoover said. "My intention is that, in ten years' time, this Bureau will reach the point where we'll no longer need men like you. But that day has not yet arrived. You've proved useful here. I'm sure you won't mind being at the front of the column when we go back in."

Dobbs shook his head no. "I wouldn't mind that at all, sir."

Thinking if the brass couldn't get rid of him one way, they'd get rid of him another. Throw him in the grinder and hope for the best.

Had it been up to Dobbs, they would've back gone into Innsmouth right away, before its residents, denizens, muck-dwellers, whatever they were, had much chance to react to the havoc he'd caused.

But it didn't happen that way. Which probably explained why he'd never made higher than corporal in the army, and was now facing a future with the Bureau that got shorter all the time.

The domestic invasion of a town in New England, cradle of the country's founding . . . that took time to plan. The war on rumrunners provided a cover story, but everything else had to spin off that to hold together. Which limited the personnel they could use.

Just as well. Because nobody, not J. Edgar Hoover, not even President Coolidge, could call up a battalion of the army and turn them loose on U.S. soil. Washington would be full of screaming congressmen before the smoke cleared. It had to be an in-house job, and the smaller the house, the better. Those heads in the icebox . . . matters like that needed a tight lid.

Through December, over Christmas, and into January, the task force gelled, agents handpicked from within the Bureau and Treasury—heavy on the Prohibition boys, plus the Secret Service, who knew a thing or two about discretion.

When in mid-February it was time to rendezvous in Boston, they came up from New York, and in from Chicago and Kansas City, and from half a dozen other places. The fellas from Miami may have been a mistake, because they spent most of their time bitching about the cold.

Numbering upwards of 140, they set up a final staging ground on the field beside a dilapidated barracks north of Arkham, unused since the Civil War. It was a frosty February morning when they gathered, an army in every sense but official, in uniforms of trench coats and fedoras, stamping their feet and blowing into their hands for warmth.

Not a one of them knew why they were really here. They still thought they'd been brought in because they were the best of the best, gathered for some high-level bootlegging raid nobody else could be trusted with.

The briefing set them straight. There were words from Bureau and Treasury brass, off the back of a truck, then they turned it over to Dobbs himself, because nobody else could speak with the same authority of experience. That was how they'd sold him on it, anyway. More like he was so goddamn big and mean-looking that he compelled the kind of attention it took to put the gravity across.

"Once we get inside this town, you're going to see things you never knew could be alive," Dobbs boomed out to them. "You'll wish they weren't. You're going to have to get used to that idea really quick. Some of you are starting to laugh already, I know, because I would too. But that's what's waiting for us. I've seen them up close. I've tangled with them and I've got the scars to prove it."

They passed out photos next, shots taken in late November of the meat trays and what they held, and things got sober fast. Dobbs heard the murmurs: *That can't be real.*

Better yet if they'd still had the heads to show, but Hoover had taken charge of those in early December, passing them along for study and analysis. The man was on a mission to quietly set up a new department in some laboratory somewhere, answerable only to him, and preparing for whatever came out of this raid: prisoners, corpses, things they couldn't yet anticipate.

"Innsmouth isn't supposed to have more than four hundred people in it, but there may be hundreds more like these in hiding," Dobbs went on. "I don't know what they are or what they're up to. That's what we're here to find out, instead of one day wishing we had. All I know is you don't want to underestimate them. A couple months ago, while you were tucking into Thanksgiving dinner with your families, I was out here instead of with my wife, getting stitched up from what two of these things did to me. Just two."

The faces out there, hard-looking men one and all . . . they were shaken. He'd never seen expressions like this during his years with the Bureau. For this kind of dread, he had to go back to the war. Waiting for the shelling to begin again, or the clouds of mustard gas. Waiting for the Hun to charge. Waiting to go over the top and leave the trenches behind.

"What happens today stays between us," Dobbs told them, going beyond what he'd prepared to say. He didn't know where it was coming from. "Whatever you see, whatever you do, you lock that down in a place inside you and don't speak about it to anyone who wasn't here with you, and you carry it to your grave. Live with it. Live with it the way some of us do with what we saw and did in the war.

"You're here because you're good at your job and somebody thinks you can be trusted to keep secrets. So keep them. Remember that, if you get an itch to beat your gums about it. Ask yourself if the things in these pictures are something you want people out there knowing about. Your neighbors, your friends. Your mothers. Ask yourself if it's something you want to explain to your wives. If you want to sit with your kids after they wake up dreaming about what's out here, and try telling them with a straight face that the monsters aren't real."

They loaded up and set off on the final miles, a convoy of two dozen trucks and automobiles bouncing along the ruts of the winter-bogged roads to the coast. They came into Innsmouth from the south, one direction only, not bothering to split up and converge from the roads from Ipswich and Rowley and Newburyport.

Whatever was hiding under the surface of Innsmouth, it wasn't going to flee inland.

As they rolled through in a roar of motors, under a sunless gray sky, Innsmouth coiled still and silent around them. Arkham Road turned to Federal Street, taking them to the town square that Dobbs and Hewlitt had traversed on their first visit here. They paused long enough to drop off a dozen agents to remain in the heart of town and question the residents who still showed themselves by day.

When they continued, half the vehicles took the south side of the river down to the harbor, the other half crossing the bridge to the north bank. At the bottom of the slope, they fanned out along Water Street, the bulk of the task force bailing out of their vehicles to hit the ground running. Most bristled with shotguns and BARs and drum-fed Thompson submachine guns, while a handful of sharpshooters clambered up to the tops of the trucks, ready to train their rifles on anything that moved.

They broke into units of ten and began the search. Four teams took the homes and businesses on the west side of Water Street. The rest split above and below the river, to clear the warehouses along the wharves, their plumes of breath following them in from outside. The cold kept down the worst of the smell permeating the waterfront, but every building felt like an icebox, their rotting timbers rimed with salt and frost. As chilled and quiet as stone tombs, their lonely inner silence was made more manifest by the constant surging wash of the sea.

On the wharf, Dobbs took point with the first team and had Hewlitt stick close behind him. From structure to structure, they advanced north, toward the worst of the decay, the stretch of sheds where in November he'd skirmished tooth-and-claw. Same as the rest of the teams, Dobbs and his agents poked and prodded through the leavings of the years—crates and barrels cracked open by age, upended rowboats abandoned untold seasons ago, and pieces of bigger vessels left in states of disrepair. Ignoring it all, looking for more recent signs of life.

They'd been at it for more than two hours when the attack came.

The spot seemed safe, as deserted as everywhere else they'd been, a corridor leading out of one of the more cavernous warehouses, whose floor space was divided into a warren of passages and rooms left open to the rafters.

Dobbs heard a thud and a scream from behind, and whirled in time to see one of the Treasury agents rush headlong into the wall as if he had no will of his own. Jutting from the man's spine were the last inches of the barbed head of some sort of iron spike—there one moment, then withdrawn back through him with a cracking of bone as the man crumpled to the rotted boards. An instant later, another spear punched through the planks of the wall into empty space, then a third from the other side, this one slashing a gash across another agent's thigh.

Harpoons.

They were attacking with harpoons that hadn't seen a whale in generations.

Dobbs swung up his Browning Automatic Rifle, the same as he'd used in the war, and fired a burst of rounds through the wall on one side, then swiveled to target its opposite. Behind him, agents backtracked through the corridor's entryway, or dropped to the floor, below the level of the harpoons, and fumbled to engage their weapons. The planking disintegrated under fire, rotten slabs of wall falling away to uncover hidden corridors that ran parallel to them.

They stood revealed, creatures made wholly for neither the land nor the sea, that skulked beneath the surface of the town. Twenty or more, they ran a gamut from those who looked almost like men, to cousins of the wolf-eel whose head he'd taken. Some were dead, some were dying, some continued their assault. In the chaos, an agent was skewered where he lay, while another was felled by a rusty cargo hook swung into the base of his neck, then wrenched down to rip him open from throat to breastbone.

Beside him, Hewlitt was screaming, firing his shotgun repeatedly into the same malformed and bulbous creature, dead already but not dead enough to suit him.

It left Hewlitt distracted enough that he didn't see the next one, vaulting over the bodies of its comrades with neither hook nor harpoon. But it had jaws. It grappled onto his shoulders and bore him down before he could react, lunging and snapping as they fell. Hewlitt dodged by instinct, but his attacker's lantern jaws, brimming with needle teeth, clamped shut over his collarbone.

Dobbs took his finger off the trigger; couldn't fire downward without shooting through the thing's body into Hewlitt as well. He flipped the BAR's muzzle toward the ceiling and spiked the butt into the back of the creature's skull. It relaxed its bite long enough for Dobbs to snatch it by the straps of its filthy overalls and hoist it up and off Hewlitt, heave it away, and gun it down while it staggered.

Did these things even care about their own lives? Undoubtedly they did . . . but they cared about Innsmouth more, perhaps, or the others of their kind that were left. If Dobbs had thought them inhuman before, he found it a worse shock to think they were at least human enough to sacrifice themselves for the rest. To strike a blow they knew they might not survive, that their targets would never forget.

He pulled Hewlitt onto his feet again, wild-eyed and shrieking. The wound was a bleeder, as ragged as whatever remained of his nerves.

Dobbs slapped a handkerchief over it, got Hewlitt to hold the compress in place, then was back in the fight again.

From outside came the sounds of distant gunfire, south along the wharf, as other teams either came under assault, or rushed forward, drawn by the noise of this one.

Their surviving attackers, wounded and untouched alike, fell away in retreat, ducking deeper into the warehouse, losing themselves amid the maze of crates and makeshift walls. Dobbs chose not to follow, and instead charged the rest of the way through the corridor, into daylight and under open skies, the freezing wet wind a revivifying jolt.

The wharf was swarming with them now. Some plunged into the icy waters of the harbor. Others straggled along in their peculiar gaits and made for the buildings ahead.

Dobbs was wearing a bandolier stuffed with box magazines for the BAR, twenty rounds apiece. He ejected the spent one onto the stones and reloaded, then leveled the rifle from his hip and held it steady by the wooden handle mounted on the barrel. It all came back as though he'd never left it, firing the way he'd been trained a decade ago, to clear the way for his squad: advance and fire, short bursts, advance and fire, target wisely, advance and fire, eject and reload, advance and fire. The crack of it rolled like thunder along the wharf and over the tranquil waters of the harbor.

He zeroed in on one of the sheds where he'd seen them converge, chewing away at its walls and supports, churning up a blizzard of splinters and shards until the structure collapsed into a pile of rotten wood. He took down another, leaving a trail of empty magazines behind him, and let up only when he realized he hadn't seen any of them moving for at least a minute. The last of his volley of fire echoed off the sea-cliffs to the north and died away beneath the surf.

Strange—he was certain he'd seen more of these monstrosities scurry into these sheds than they looked capable of holding.

Stranger yet—when the survivors of his team rejoined him and dragged aside the wreckage of roof and walls, they didn't find a single body.

Once they dismantled the site a little further it became clear enough, a vital detail he hadn't seen, or even considered, when he'd poked around that rainy November night.

Tunnels. Some of these shacks were merely fronts for tunnels, concealed beneath the crates.

As the sea-wind whipped them and the cold bit for their bones, Dobbs and the others stood around the opening, staring into it, ancient brick and shaped stone, with a ladder affixed to one side, rungs worn smooth by generations of inhuman hands.

Like a throat, it yawned and waited, daring them to enter and sighing with the dank breath of the sea.

They returned in two days, this time packing in dynamite.

Every hour, another tunnel or two was discovered. They linked structures to one another, or structures to the sea, beginning in town and terminating in tight caves that perforated the rockier stretches of coastline. They made such a labyrinth that exploring them seemed a job better suited for miners. Some looked wholly natural; others bore chisel marks and utilized support beams. Interrogated residents spoke of them being used since pre-Revolutionary days, when colonial smugglers sought to evade the trade regulations of British rule.

And now? Now the tunnels appeared to have been utilized much as the trenches of the Great War had—for shelter and safety, as the foundation of an entire unlikely culture whose population wanted most of all to keep their heads low and intact. They were littered with the bones of fish, the shells of crabs and lobsters, oysters and clams, with scraps of clothing and makeshift beds and the crudest of weapons left behind in the haste to evacuate them for good.

In this much, at least, Dobbs found he could understand them, even grant them a grudging admiration, his disgust at what they were tempered by measures of pity.

Nobody chose to live that way if they could help it.

Throughout the second day, into the third, the waterfront boomed with the blasts of demolition. Buildings came down, tunnels collapsed or filled with debris, and little by little the Innsmouth skyline of rooftops and steeples, cupolas and widow's walks, was reshaped.

Beginning that second day, they had eyes on them from the seaward side, as well—Hoover's doing. A pair of Coast Guard cutters idled in the choppy sea past the breakwater, while an O-class submarine, up from Division 8 of the Boston Navy Yard, prowled the deeper waters beyond the grim black line of Devil Reef.

The refugees had fled there, if the sharpshooters and other high-vantage spotters in town were to be believed. They claimed to have seen numerous swimmers heading toward the reef throughout the first day, surging in and out of the water like seals. If true, it accounted for why no one had encountered any of Innsmouth's more bestial residents since their initial attack.

In town, up and down the hills on both sides of the river, the sweeps continued, from the humblest cottages to the once-grand mansions of Washington and Lafayette Streets. Some of the residents they let go, others they took into custody.

It was easy to weed them out now that it was apparent what to look for, and why. In the neighboring towns here in the northeast corner of Massachusetts, folks had spoken of it for decades, in a hush and often with abhorrence: the "Innsmouth look," they called it. Townspeople born generations apart, to different families, with no known blood connection, came to look remarkably alike, more so than typical siblings and their parents in decent places.

In Innsmouth they aged quickly, it was said, and badly, then they were never seen in public again, yet their kindred spoke of them as though they were still alive and well.

Dobbs didn't know what Darwin would've made of such a thing. But with their balding heads and bulging eyes, their flaking skin and widened mouths, their clomping feet and oversized hands, they looked to be the landlocked forerunners of the ones who'd made their escape to the sea.

Frightened or sullen, few had anything to say to their interrogators, although one of them turned chatty. A skinny fella in his late teens, with a shock of floppy dark hair, Giles Shapleigh didn't yet bear the look, and was so full of the cockiness of youth it would have felt good to swat him down a few pegs. Better, though, to let him talk as long as he wanted.

However hard it was to listen to.

Giles Shapleigh spoke of heritage, of how he knew where he came from, boasting that his bloodline was older than that of Pilgrims or Indians or the first Christian man in pagan Europe to drop mewling to his knees and beg favors from a nailed-up god dead long before that man was ever born.

He had come from water, Shapleigh said, and would return to it, no matter how long it took to get there. Years meant nothing. This skin he wore now? It was just a shell, and would molt away the same as any transitory form did when it had outlived its use.

Deep Ones, was what they were, Shapleigh said. They were in the process of becoming Deep Ones, and in a thousand years he would swim over his captors' bones after their graves sank beneath the world's oceans.

He sounded like a madman.

But so had the fellas who'd warned them of exactly what they would find here.

When they swept through for the third time, to Dobbs's eye most of his fellow agents appeared to have aged ten years in just a few days. Haggard and worn, with the distant stares of combat veterans, they had more interrogations to run. More arrests to make. More prisoners to transport. They did their jobs with the plodding determination of men who wanted to see it done so they could go home, drink themselves to sleep, and hope the place didn't follow them into their dreams.

At midday, he was helping clear one of the last manses left on Lafayette when a commotion rippled through the town. The last to know? Maybe he was.

Dobbs was lingering in the chilly parlor of this grand old house built by the fortune of another age, lived in and loved well, then left to go to ruin. Even now, he probably couldn't afford it. He stood at the baby grand piano, its lacquered maple dulled by years of sifting dust. Lillian played. She would've been thrilled to have an instrument like this. Would've been thrilled to have the room for it. With clumsier fingers than his wife's, he pressed a few yellowed keys and winced at the discordant clang of neglect.

He hadn't seen the fellow Bureau agent hustle in off the porch. Losing his edge? Maybe he was.

"There's something big going on out by that reef," the agent said.

Dobbs sprinted for high ground, taking the broad steps of the main staircase two at a time, three stories' worth. At the roof, he burst out onto the widow's walk where, in the Golden Age of Sail, a woman must have maintained a vigil to watch the eastern horizon for the ship that would bring back someone she loved.

The day was cold but clear, visibility good and the wind like a knife at his skin as he peered past the breakwater, out where the spine of rock called Devil Reef cut a ragged slash across the untamed waters of the open sea. As they'd fled the town, heedless of the cold and pounding waves, the Deep Ones had made for it, and no one could fathom why. They hadn't gathered on it, as if waiting for a ship. They'd simply gone no farther, then disappeared.

It was a fool's wish to conclude they'd drowned; unthinkable to speculate they might've had a whole other home out there waiting, once they were ready.

He'd think about that later. Right now, the Atlantic Ocean had a hole in it.

How wide? Wider than the reef, and certainly wide enough to swallow the Coast Guard cutter that appeared to be frantically trying to chug away from its pull, a circular depression into which water was pouring from all around, as if the drain plug had been yanked from a tub. It churned deep, deeper, revealing more of the reef like a cliff-wall as the motion began to swirl with purpose and direction, into a vast whirlpool.

In the greater distance, the submarine's conning tower marked its course as it swung around in a wide arc, until it pointed in the direction of the reef. It submerged, the tower and its thicket of masts and scopes slicing beneath the waves as smoothly as a diving shark.

Ever since the raids began, one of the hardest things to manage was sorting fact from rumor. Nobody knew what was true and what wasn't unless they'd seen it with their own eyes, and even then it could be hard to know.

What he'd heard? That the waters ran *deep* out there. That the shelf of land fell gradually away from shore, then in one broad spot abruptly plunged into an anomalous abyss. The depth soundings and other sonar readings the submarine had taken couldn't tell what or why, only that it was a rift of immense dimensions. The sub wasn't built to operate much past three hundred feet down, and it hadn't come anywhere near the bottom.

For no reason Dobbs could see across the surface—he had only a sense that it presaged something worse—the whirlpool slowed, stopped. The depression in the sea collapsed inward, the ocean colliding with itself as water rushed back in to fill the void and rebound with a foamy geyser as tall as the house beneath him. He saw it first, and seconds later heard it, a roar like an awakening leviathan.

It had barely settled again before the water was roiled a second time—smaller disturbances now. Dobbs gripped the walk's railing until the cold iron seared his hands. A series of four, he counted, then a brief wait and another four.

Torpedoes. The submarine must have fired its torpedoes.

And then . . . calm.

But calm was deceptive. Calm could never be trusted. Calm was a sunny, blue-sky day pierced by the whistle of an incoming shell, not knowing where it would land until the arms and legs went flying. That was calm for you.

As the afternoon wore on, the sky blackened and turned against them one last time, spitting down a freezing rain that stung Dobbs's face until his cheeks and chin went numb. He hated the place and it hated him back, and he couldn't say he blamed it.

They'd done what they'd done and, after tonight, wouldn't be returning.

Had it been worth it? He supposed that depended on what would've unfolded here if they'd never known enough to smash the place apart.

Maybe it was a question better put to the widows and children who would be denied the truth of why their husbands and fathers had come home in boxes. Or put to Ridley Hewlitt, if he could give a coherent answer, because if the kid wasn't bound for his own stay at Danvers . . . well, if not, maybe then Archie Dobbs could start believing in God again, instead of sitting in the pew each week beside his wife like a morally upstanding agent should, feeling like a fraud.

After the disturbances near the reef, rumors were quick to float up from the harbor, carried by agents and brass alike. The Coast Guard, they said, had made a few slow, back-and-forth runs over the site. The cutters' hulls plowed through a spreading field of some thick jellied substance that bobbed to the surface from below. For half an hour, it rose in noxious dark clots and globs, some the size of a side of beef, but formless and translucent. Every now and again, one popped or bubbled with the suggestion of an eye.

The crews tried to dredge a few samples on board, a frustrating and futile endeavor. As with so many things, the harder they tightened their grasp, the quicker it slipped free, until the whole ungodly mess dissolved into an iridescent slick that drifted away on the tides and left them with nothing.

Just rumors. He hadn't seen it with his own two eyes.

But it *sounded* true.

He couldn't leave soon enough.

It didn't matter where in town he stood, looking out over Innsmouth's moldering roofs and forsaken steeples, its once-proud docks eaten down a sliver at a time, its harbor and breakwater and reef. All of that was just the mask. What he was really looking out over was an entire way of life that had come and gone, risen and fallen and become something else, something malevolent beyond understanding, while hardly anyone had noticed.

The sea was a vast and hostile thing, less a place than a force, and hid its secrets well. It devoured at will and never gave back.

And one day, he feared, one way or another, it would rise to devour the world.

TWO

Ec'h-pi-el

I

April 11, 1937

WHENEVER NATHAN BRADY WAS summoned to the office of Mr. J. Edgar Hoover, he felt nervous. An atmosphere of power and menace, assiduously cultivated by Hoover himself, surrounded the director of the FBI like a force field, and it threatened even Brady who had never suffered its ill effects.

It so happened that Brady was one of "the young men," as Hoover liked to call them, who had found favor in his eyes. Tall, well-dressed, handsome, Harvard-educated, daring in his actions, observant and yet discreet in his reports, Brady met with Hoover's approval in almost every respect, except perhaps for his literary and artistic leanings. Mr. Hoover regarded an over-pronounced taste for literature and the arts to be, as he termed it, "being too clever by half." What precisely he meant by this is uncertain. After all, *could* you be too clever by any sort of fraction, however vulgar, if you worked for the FBI?

Despite his apprehensiveness, Brady knew better than to knock hesitantly at the director's door. A sharp double-rap was met almost instantly by a characteristically staccato "Come!" from within. Brady entered.

The agent sometimes wondered, without naturally ever voicing his wonder, whether Hoover had taken a leaf out of Signor Mussolini's book. Like "Il Duce," Hoover had had his office built on the grand scale, calculated to intimidate the visitor, with a huge desk at one end of the room opposite the door. It stood on a dais so that anyone, whether seated or standing before the director, would have to look up. Mr. Hoover was somewhat self-conscious about his lack of inches, and wore built-up shoes.

The floor was of polished black marble relieved by a fine Turkish rug or two. To Brady's left as he looked down the room were bookcases filled from floor to ceiling with gilt-tooled, leather-bound volumes that the director would never open. To his right, three tall windows looked out onto Washington, D.C., and the Capitol Building, gleaming like a wedding cake in the spring sunshine. On the wall behind Hoover's desk was a full-length portrait of himself, left hand tucked Napoleonically into his double-breasted jacket, looking even more menacing, and rather more soigné than its subject currently did, crouching in shirtsleeves behind a battery of telephones, intercoms, and neat stacks of paper. He was a squat, squarish man, with oiled hair combed straight back into a tight black ridge over his brow and round, slightly protuberant eyes that seemed to penetrate the soul of whatever came within their range. *The face of a power-worshipper, if ever I saw one*, thought Brady, who did not himself pay homage at that particular shrine.

"Come in, Brady," rasped Hoover in a tone that implied *approach the presence, if you dare*. "Take a seat, young man." He waved him to an uncomfortable-looking Chippendale dining chair that had been placed some five feet in front of Hoover's desk. "I've read your report. How in hell did you get to know about this in the first place?"

Brady held up a rather undistinguished-looking octavo volume. It was hardbacked with a white dust jacket on which was printed in gray lettering the words *Shadow Over Innsmouth* and, below it, the author's name: H. P. Lovecraft.

"I take an interest in this kind of literature, sir," said Brady. "I have read some of this man's work before. In *Weird Tales*."

"*Weird Tales*! You, a Harvard man, read garbage like *Weird Tales*!"

"We all have our faults, sir," said Brady, instantly regretting his levity; but the director did not seem to notice. Perhaps it was just as well that J. Edgar Hoover, like most power addicts, was a stranger to irony and humor. He determinedly pressed on: "Lovecraft's stories in 'The Unique

Magazine,' as it calls itself, have included such titles as 'The Horror at Red Hook,' 'The Call of Cthulhu,' and 'The Dunwich Horror.' I have been looking back through the Bureau's files, and I've discovered—"

"Do you play golf?" Hoover interrupted.

"No, sir."

"Then, take it up, Brady. That's my advice to a young man like you. It's a decent open-air kind of pastime. Takes you out of yourself. *I* play golf, Brady."

"I'll bear that in mind, sir."

"Take up golf, young man. Don't mope around reading trashy books and pulp magazines all day. Still, in this instance, I'm very glad you did. You realize this darned book is potentially a thousand tons of high explosive just waiting to blow our asses off?"

"That's why I have brought it to your attention, sir."

"Well, Brady, you did a good thing there. Consider yourself commended." It was not a particularly gracious phrase, but it was the highest accolade that Hoover ever offered his subordinates, and that sparingly. "You say in your report that only two hundred copies of this thing were issued last year by some vanity publisher out in Pennsylvania?"

"That is correct, sir."

"Well, you must make darned sure there are no more published. And I want every available copy destroyed, if possible. Without attracting undue attention, naturally."

"I have already taken steps to ensure that, sir."

"Good man, good man. Shows initiative. I like a young man with initiative, Brady. But you can take a thing like initiative too far. It's like the game of golf. You can try to hit your ball all the way to the green in one, and land yourself in a bunker—"

"Yes, Mr. Hoover."

"—Or a goddamn lake . . . So who is this sonofabitch Lovecraft anyhow?"

"He is a writer, impoverished, something of a recluse. Comes from an old New England family. Not very well known, though highly thought of by a small circle of admirers. Divorced, lives with an aunt, somewhat eccentric."

"Is he a commie? A Bolshevik sympathizer?"

"Very much not, sir, I understand."

"Well, that's something anyhow. Is he a fag?"

"I don't believe so, sir."

"Not a commie fag. That's encouraging. So how in hell does this guy know about Innsmouth? I thought we had well and truly buried that shit nine years ago with that hothead Dobbs, and now this cockamamy sonofabitch comes up with his book that spills all the beans."

"It *is* supposed to be fiction, Mr. Hoover."

"I know that, Brady. Do you take me for some kind of a dumb-ass?"

"No, Mr. Hoover!"

"Fiction is only a fact disguised as a lie. You know who said that?"

"You, Mr. Hoover?"

"Correct! Note it down, Brady."

"I will, Mr. Hoover."

"In this case very thinly disguised. What's this guy's game, Brady?"

"I don't know, sir."

"Then find out, godammit!" Hoover banged the desk with his fist in the manner approved by all men of power. "And find out what else he knows. You never know, he might be useful to us."

"Have I your permission to go and interview Mr. Lovecraft, sir?"

"Yes godammit, but be discreet about it. You know we are literally sitting on a goddamn volcano at the moment. If it blows, our asses are toast. Literally toast!"

Brady, being a Harvard man, deplored the misuse of the word *literally*, but he understood what the director meant. He nodded agreement.

"So get to it, young man," said Hoover.

The meeting was at an end. Brady rose and went to the door. Before he reached it there was one further instruction from the man behind the desk.

"And get yourself some golf clubs, young Brady!"

April 19th, 1937 (from the diary of H. P. Lovecraft)

A young man called Nathan Brady has written to me. He claims to be an admirer of my work and wishes to discuss it with me. A Harvard man, I note with approval. Well, I will see him. I feel thoroughly out of sorts and I am, as usual, plagued by ailments mostly of the gastric variety, and perhaps he may bring cheer to my benighted existence. Yet another bad night, full of the phantasmagorical visions which have plagued me since my youth. Aunt Annie tells me she heard me cry out in my sleep, though what I said she could not make out. "It was some awful foreign or Negro tongue," she informed me. I wonder if I have the courage this time, or the energy, to translate my dream into story. My nightmares are a plague, an alien infection; something is trying to speak to me through my slumber, I am convinced of it.

I found myself in of all places a theatre. Sometimes my dreams are confused. It was a new theatre and they were still excavating its nether regions while on stage a rehearsal was in progress. A whole line of "hoofers," as I believe they are termed, in their rehearsal clothes were thundering away in their tap shoes to the accompaniment of an upright piano. I couldn't make out the words, but I know they were inane. As for the music, it was some vile jazz-infected Negroid muck that banged its way into my brain and now won't come out. Those odious jungle rhythms! They stayed with me as I seemed to descend below the stage and into the depths of the theatre where workmen were excavating so as to put in machinery for a revolving platform for the dancers. (How I knew this was so, I cannot say.) I saw them stop as they dug and listen for a while. Below the chattering of the stage piano and the clattering of metal-shod feet that battered out the rhythm of their tawdry dance came another sound, darker, deeper, still more primitive than the music above and yet almost, though not quite, in step with it. The sounds were like a boom, an echo from beneath, as if the very earth were responding to the shallow travesties of dark rites from above. I saw the workmen stop, hesitate, wipe their grimy faces, look for a moment with astonished terror at each other, then resume their labour.

And then it was as if I had descended farther into the earth than they and had entered into a vast space, like a long gallery, barrel-vaulted and illumined by the pale eldritch light emanating from some fungoid growth on the walls. These walls were cunningly built of vast cyclopean blocks of masonry that might have seemed rudely antique, but for the subtle precision with which they were locked together. Moreover, upon them had been carved many runic signs and bas-relief sculptures of figures, monstrous, shambling, and piscine: hideous to behold. Yet I was enthralled by the cunning with which the carver had limned them as if from the life.

Then I heard the sound as of a thousand marching feet, yet not like the boots of soldiers, nor yet the rhythmic fusillade of those "hoofers" from above. The sound they made was a kind of thousandfold slap as if a myriad great splayed or webbed feet were stamping onto smooth rock through a thin integument of standing water. They seemed to come nearer, and their hastening was a doom-laden terror to me, and as they came they let out cries, piercing and hideous, yet clearly discernible above the monstrous rhythmical din of their approach. One cry in particular was borne in on me.

"*Rghyyeloi fo Xhon! Rghyyeloi fo Xhon!*" And it seemed as if I knew by some dreadful instinct what these horrid intonations signified. It was "*The Armies of the Night! The Armies of the Night!*"

Nearer they came and nearer, by which time I was half-conscious that I was dreaming and must need shake off the surly bonds of sleep to rid myself of this mounting terror. I felt like a diver who realises belatedly that he has gone too deep and must struggle upwards, almost despairing that he may reach the surface, gulping for air where none exists. I shook the thunder from my brain and gasped. Almost it seemed I was sinking back into that unspeakable subterranean cavern, then with a final lung-tearing, heart-pounding effort I broke the surface of wakefulness and found myself panting and sweating in my narrow bed at 66 College Street, Providence. More than ever does it seem a blessed haven and a refuge.

Yet for a long while those terrible cries still echoed through my brain: "*The Armies of the Night! The Armies of the Night!*"

I had barely dressed and made my toilet when Mr. Brady was knocking at the door of Number 66. My visions had completely shaken the thought of him from my mind; so that my usual punctiliousness was confounded. I showed him what courtesy I could in my distracted state and he reciprocated. He seems a most gentlemanly fellow with the clean-cut Aryan features of which I approve. His clothes were enviable, evidently the work of the best tailors in Washington whence, he tells me, he hails. I asked him his occupation and he replied, somewhat nebulously, that he worked for the government, though in what capacity he would not specify. However, all misgivings that I might have had evaporated when he offered to take me to luncheon.

I told him that there was an excellent hostelry nearby where for $2 a very decent noontide repast was to be had. Moreover, I added, I was not a drinker and never had indulged in the kind of libations with which many of my fellow scribes seek to stimulate their genius. My muse is solitude and the dreadful blessing of dreams.

My new friend Mr. Brady seemed somewhat dismayed at the prospect of taking luncheon at the Providence Temperance Hotel and Coffee Rooms which is the establishment I favour, but thither we repaired, and, having reconciled himself to my modest requirements, Mr. Nathan Brady proved to be a most delightful companion. I must say he is gratifyingly well acquainted with my oeuvre, as I may term it, but he asked a number of questions whose import I could not entirely fathom . . .

Extract from FBI report from Agent Nathan Brady, April 20, 1937

. . . Mr. Lovecraft has been most communicative. He is a good and fluent talker and, as far as I could make out, an honest one. In the light of what he told me, however, this may be questionable. He was certainly well informed about the Innsmouth incident; accounts of events at Dunwich and Red Hook conform with and may even exceed the very confidential information that we possess. Using what tact and discretion I could, I tried to find out precisely how Mr. Lovecraft had gained access to this knowledge. Though he made reference to certain printed or manuscript sources, including the *Necronomicon,* of which we were led to believe there is but one copy, and that in the library of the Miskatonic University under lock and key, Mr. Lovecraft claims that his understanding of certain events derives from dreams or "visions," as he sometimes calls them. This may or may not be the case, but it would seem that Mr. Lovecraft is in possession of valuable insights. I recommend that an agent remain in regular contact with him. I suggest myself for this task if only because I have already established cordial relations with this source and a new and inexperienced contact might arouse suspicion.

I attach an invoice for expenses. The bill for the meal at the Providence Temperance Hotel and Coffee Rooms amounts to $4.75, including a 25¢ tip. The meal itself, foul beyond description by the way, came to exactly $4 but Mr. Lovecraft demanded several extra cups of coffee, under which influence he talked, as he would say, "volubly" . . .

April 28, 1937

"Well, Brady," said the director. "I have read your report. I like it. You're a smart kid. I gather you've been seeing this Lovecraft character on a regular basis. The guy who lives with his aunt?"

"Yes, Mr. Hoover."

"There's no funny business going on between this guy and his aunt is there?"

"No, Mr. Hoover. I have seen the aunt and the possibility seems vanishingly remote. In any case, I believe Mr. Lovecraft is largely asexual."

"A sexual? What sort of a sexual? A homosexual?"

"No, Mr. Hoover. Just no sex at all."

"Then why not say so? You want my advice? Don't mess with sex. If you don't mess with sex, sex won't mess with you. Note that down, Brady. And you think this stuff Lovecraft is giving you is on the level?"

"It certainly tallies with the reports we've been getting through from other quarters. And in some cases he anticipates them."

"Anticipates? How?"

"He claims that he dreams them."

"Dreams? Brady, is he leveling with us? Or is he giving us the *phonus balonus*?"

"He has been accurate so far, but we have a way of testing his veracity, Mr. Hoover."

"Never mind that. I just want to make sure somehow he is on the level."

"Well, Mr. Hoover. He has been talking to me recently about some disturbances beneath a theater, which seems to be a Broadway theater in New York. It would appear that, according to him, that this is the site of the next intrusion of these—phenomena . . ."

"Yes, yes. I get it."

"Now we have yet to have any report of this from other sources, so I suggest we investigate this to see if—"

"I got it! We investigate this, and if it turns out to be true we know our guy is on the level and not the *phonus balonus*. And we get to burn these dam bums before they get really dangerous. What do you think of my plan, Mr. Brady?"

"I think it is excellent, sir."

"It *is* excellent, Mr. Brady. And I am appointing you to investigate. You leave for New York tomorrow. Young man, allow me to let you into a big secret, which on pain of having your ass diced and then fried on the hot plate you will keep under your Stetson. After nearly a decade of trying to get those so-called politicians on Capitol Hill to agree with my plans, I'm finally going ahead myself and forming a secret body of men to combat this new threat to our great country. I'm going to call this covert organization the Human Protection League, or HPL for short."

"How very appropriate, Mr. Hoover—"

"Appropriate, my ass! It's the right thing to do, for America, Brady. And when America's ass is on the line, J. Edgar Hoover is there to defend that ass at all times. I am appointing you, Nathan Brady, as Agent Number One of the HPL, and you will be directly answerable to me alone together with my assistant director, Mr. Clyde Tolson. Is that clear, Brady?"

"Yes, sir!"

"Good man! You want to know something, Brady? The commies are at the bottom of all this somehow. I've got a feeling in my water. You mark my words. This is a plot masterminded in Moscow to undermine our American way of life."

"I'll bear that in mind, Mr. Hoover."

Most agents knew that the director could under no circumstances be contradicted. If he said anything with which they could possibly agree, they replied with a smart: "Yes, Mr. Hoover, sir!" If the director, as he was prone to do from time to time, made a remark so wild and fantastical that a self-respecting agent needed to distance himself from it, the response would be: "I'll bear that in mind, Mr. Hoover." But the director, for all his faults, was a shrewd man, and one could never be certain that one's evasion had not been noted and filed in that voluminous and vindictive brain of his. Like the Bourbons, Mr. J. Edgar Hoover very seldom learned anything, but he forgot nothing.

"Oh, yes. It's the commies all right. Brady—I'm going to call you Nathan—"

"Thank you, sir."

"And you can go right on calling me, Mr. Hoover. Nathan, I want you to nail these commie bums for me. Nail them! See my secretary Miss Gandy in the outer office. She will furnish you with all the requisite travel passes, weapons certificates, and expenses forms. Nail those goddamn bums, Nathan!" Hoover's fist banged emphatically on the tooled leather surface of his Bureau, and with that the meeting was at an end.

In the outer office Miss Gandy was at her desk, a large, pleasant middle-aged blonde woman, puffy and powdery and wreathed in smiles. She appeared to know exactly what Brady required before he even asked for it.

But the room had another occupant. A tall man stood silhouetted at the window, gazing out toward the Capitol. At first he seemed to take no notice of Brady, then he turned and advanced toward him. Brady noticed that, as he did so, Miss Gandy's manner became at once more flustered and more formal. He immediately recognized it to be Hoover's assistant director, Clyde Tolson. They had never met before but Brady knew him by sight and reputation. He was a good-looking, impeccably dressed middle-aged man with a fishy eye and a glacial smile.

"Ah, Mr. Brady, isn't it?" Brady thought Tolson was going to put out one of his hands to shake; instead he clasped them behind his back. It was as if he was out to disconcert his subordinate.

"Yes, Mr. Tolson."

"I hear you are a coming man in this Bureau, Brady."

"Thank you, sir."

"Oh, don't thank me, Brady. For that you must thank our lord and master, J. Edgar, eh?" He winked conspiratorially. Brady sensed that this was a trap, and that if he responded with too much familiarity he would be rebuffed, so he merely bowed his head. Tolson seemed both gratified and frustrated by Brady's ritual submission. As he came closer, Brady caught the distinct smell of peppermint on his breath. Was it to disguise the alcohol perhaps?

"Yes," said Tolson almost in a whisper, "A coming man, but—a word of warning, young Brady: don't try to come too far."

At that moment the door of Hoover's office opened a fraction and the familiar rasping voice was heard.

"Is that you, Clyde? Get your ass in here. I want you!"

Tolson looked furious for a second, then disguised his rage with a sickly smile and went in to his "lord and master."

Brady and Miss Gandy heaved a sigh of relief at almost exactly the same moment and smiled at each other in mutual sympathy.

II

April 29th, 1937 (from the diary of H. P. Lovecraft)

I am become a martyr to dyspepsia. Aunt Annie wishes me to see a doctor, but I have no wish to commit myself to the costly and generally futile ministrations of the medical profession. However, the other day I found a bottle of Dr. Ogmore Van Bogusteen's Patent Gastric Preparation in the secret drawer of my escritoire. It may be rather old, but my esteemed grandfather Whipple Van Buren Phillips always swore by it. Well, I took a tablespoon full of the greyish glutinous liquid for my stomach ache yesterday afternoon. At least, I think it was yesterday and the afternoon—I cannot be positive on that—but whenever it was, it did wonders for the pain, despite tasting like the pus from a diseased reptile. Shortly after taking it, however, I fell into a deep sleep, then, waking of a sudden at some remote hour of the night or the morning, I lay on my bed incapable of motion but without any discomfort save a certain mental agitation at my incapacity. Having lain like this for I do not know how long I began to dream. "Yet 'twas not a dream neither," or if it was, it was such a dream as I have never had to this intense degree, and I am a man prone to such things. It was more like a waking vision. I seemed to be fully conscious throughout my reverie and was able to reflect on my being an unwilling witness to the events I must describe. It was as if I were a prisoner in my own body, trapped, unable to move so much as a finger and yet able to see and hear with a distinctness that rivals or even supersedes my current awakened senses.

I am back in the basement of that infernal theatre again. The workmen I had seen before are having an altercation with some men. These men are all wearing dark double-breasted suits with a wide chalk stripe and those vulgar two-toned shoes. One of them has a knife. They are swarthy of complexion and I have no doubt they are of Italian extraction and "hoodlums": dago vermin from the lowest stews of Naples or Palermo. One of them has a missing finger, the other a pencil moustache so thin it looks like the gash from a knife. I can hear their voices but cannot tell what they are saying, even though I suspect it is English, of a kind, and not some greasy foreign tongue.

In these visions, I am endowed with a supernatural understanding, yet the language I understand is not my own, but a deep remote tongue that comes from the stars, a language of aliens.

It seems to me that the workmen and the hoodlums are in some dispute over working conditions and pay and that the hoodlums are threatening them. All but one of the workmen maintains some defiance in the face of threat and eventually put down their tools and leave the basement where they have been working. The one who remains behind is a young man, tall, but not very well set up, and he seems fearful. Perhaps, I divine, he has a wife and young children to support and cannot afford to leave, much as he might like to. When the others are gone the hoodlums give this man a cursory nod, as if they approve of his conduct, but also secretly despise him for it.

The young man continues to work. He is wielding a pickax to the floor of the basement when there comes a rending and cracking sound, and then the sound of large pieces of masonry falling down a deep chasm. The man surveys his handiwork and sees that a large black hole has appeared in the floor at which he had been hacking. He stares in wonder at it, then, seizing a lantern, he lies on the ground next to the hole and shines the lantern into the black depths. I cannot see what he sees but something makes him drop the lantern accidentally down the hole.

Then I see the man in a quandary. He hesitates. Finally he takes another lantern and gingerly descends a flight of rough stone-hewed steps into the darkness beneath the floor. It seems that in my vision I follow him. The sense of dread is now magnified and palpable, but I cannot escape. My body is trapped, held in a vice by my own paralysis.

He descends from the floor above until he reaches an uneven pile of rubble and debris at the bottom of which lies the lamp, now extinguished. I see him stop several times during his cautious descent to listen. His features are taut and white. The man reaches the bottom and is in the long barrel-vaulted chamber or passage that I have seen before. Its walls are slicked with a damp wetness from the green lichen that spreads over it like a disease. On it are incised signs whose meaning I cannot fathom and carvings in bas relief of monstrous ichthyoid forms whose heads sprout long and fibrous tentacles and whose vast saucer eyes look out at me even from the stone in which they are graven.

He stoops down to pick up the lamp, though as he crouches he looks round in wonder at his surroundings. He starts at a single sound, like that of a large splayed foot stamping in a puddle, innocent in other circumstances perhaps, but hideously disconcerting here and now. He calls out hesitantly and such is the strangulation that his nerves are causing him that his voice is a shrill pipe in the throat. The voice is answered by a deep boom, and then terror absolute and unadorned seizes the wretch.

He turns and, abandoning both lanterns, begins to scramble up the rubble incline towards the steps above. In his terror and desperation he begins to slide and stumble amongst the fallen masonry. He cannot get a firm grip; his hands are slick with sweat. I watch paralysed, unable to move or even cry out. I am present in his agony and at the same time I know that I am miles away.

It is pitiful indeed to watch a man so abject with terror, but this is nothing to what happens next. As he struggles helplessly among the sliding scree, trying to gain some purchase and reach the floor above, dark shapes are seen moving in that subterranean chamber. I do not see one of them whole—mercifully I am spared that!—just a limb here, the misshapen outline of a head, a tangle of lank, coarse hair. Their shapes are anthropoid, but neither are they wholly human, their skin being hard and squamous, like that of a reptile. I sense that the creatures are of both sexes with perhaps the females predominating, for they are the ones who now surround the workman, pawing and caressing him with their powerful scaly arms. Their fingers are long and prehensile but are webbed together by a translucent skein of skin. It is hard, thankfully hard, to see clearly in the subdued light, but it seems to me that the hue of their flesh is vilely iridescent, like a slick of oil on stagnant water.

Then all at once they pounce and engulf him. He gives a despairing cry and for a moment it is as if I am one with him, suffocating under a sea of slimy, scaly possessing flesh. I am struggling now to escape not from my body but from his. All goes dark and I hear again the voices pounding against me.

"Rghyyeloi fo Xhon! Rghyyeloi fo Xhon!"

"The Armies of the Night! The Armies of the Night!"

Then I am lying on my bed, every item of clothing on me soaked in sweat. I know I am once more in Providence, but what day or what hour it is, I cannot say. There is daylight, of a sort, to be seen through my curtains.

I had barely recovered from this hideous adventure when there was a knock at the door. It was my new acquaintance, Mr. Brady, come to pay a call. Fortunately by this time I had found myself a fresh shirt and a reasonably clean collar, so that I was "clothed and in my right mind" when I answered the door, but he could see that all was not well.

Mr. Brady was most solicitous. He took me out to dinner—Yes! It was the hour of the evening meal!—but not, alas to the Temperance Coffee Rooms, but to the Arkham-Biltmore Hotel where he had a couple of highballs—not, it goes without saying, available at the Temperance Coffee Rooms!—before we both partook of a sumptuous repast which was a little too much for my delicate digestion. He asked me to describe my dream (or vision?) in the greatest detail and I was happy to oblige. He seemed highly gratified by my account though I cannot quite fathom why. Is he perhaps an aspiring writer looking to plunder the resources of my perfervid subconscious? This seems to be the only probable explanation.

At all events, his pleasure in my society seems to know no bounds and he asked me if there was anything he could do for me. I immediately said to him that I would be much obliged if he could secure me some more bottles of Dr. Ogmore Van Bogusteen's Patent Gastric Preparation as my local pharmacy seemed unable or unwilling to sell me same.

At this Mr. Brady looked somewhat shocked. Did I not know that Dr Van Bogusteen's Preparation had long ago been proscribed, as it contained various highly narcotic substances? I said I did not care, as it was the only thing that relieved my stomach problems of which I gave him a comprehensive, indeed exhaustive, summary. He took my "organ recital" very well, considering, and asked me if I had seen a doctor. I replied that I had not. He seemed perturbed and said I should do so at once, and that his "Bureau" would defray any expenses; then, immediately correcting himself, he said he would do so personally. I really cannot fathom this young man; but then, as my literary friends keep reminding me, an understanding of human nature has never been one of my strengths as an artist or as a man.

A further oddity occurred, for when I happened to mention that the vividness of my visions of late may have been due to my ingestion of Bogusteen's Preparation, he immediately said that he would "see what he could do," but he also insisted I should visit a doctor. We took our leave most cordially. I cannot help liking Mr. Brady. He is obviously a gentleman, even though he appears to work for a living. What precisely is the nature of that work, I have yet to discern.

April 30, 1937

The first thing Brady did after checking into his hotel on West 54th Street was to call up his friend Charlie Chin. He and Charlie had been star pupils together at the Harvard Law School and an immediate friendship had been formed that, despite the fact that Charlie was a New Yorker and Brady was based in Washington, D.C., had endured. After Harvard, Charlie went back to New York to help run his father's very successful string of chop suey joints in the Broadway area. Brady, whose family had lost everything in the Wall Street crash and subsequent depression, needed to earn money fast and so joined the FBI straight from graduation.

Charlie, whose energies were prodigious, had, in addition to running the chop suey establishments, set up a law firm on Broadway, specializing in show-business clients: theater contracts, copyrights, and the like. He had immediately written to his friend Brady offering him a partnership. Brady, who had begun to find his work at the Bureau engrossing, had reluctantly declined, but not without the warmest expressions of gratitude to his old friend Charlie.

They met, that evening, at Sardi's on West 44th Street, in the Theater District. Both men were delighted to see each other again, Brady noting that his old friend looked the very image of prosperous contentment. But it was not long before Brady came to the point. He wanted to know if Charlie—whose store of show-business gossip had always been prodigious—had heard about any trouble going on at a theater that was under construction or renovation in the area.

Charlie Chin leaned back on the banquette and studied Brady with an anxious, puzzled look on his face. It was unusual for Charlie to look anything other than completely at his ease.

"You wouldn't like to tell me exactly what all this is about, Nathan?" he asked.

"It's an FBI matter. We've heard some rumors. I'm afraid I can't be too specific."

"All right, Nathan, but you're going to go carefully aren't you?"

"Okay, so what have you got, Charlie?"

"Ever heard of Micky 'the Angel' Buonarrotti?"

"I am familiar with his reputation. The Bureau has him on file."

"Well, then you know he is not a man to be messed with. He is sometimes just known as 'Micky Angel'—so-called because he was once an altar boy in the church of St. Ignatius in the Lower East Side and looked angelic. Once. Then came puberty and he joined his uncle—Joe 'Claw Hammer' Buonarotti, so-called because, well, you get the picture. Joe specialized in liquor importation and extortion, and young Micky Angel learned his trade quickly and developed it to include prostitution, numbers rackets, you name it. He is now one of the most notorious and powerful hoodlums in all New York. My advice, Nate, is on no account to seek acquaintance with this guy. He has a way with a sawed-off that is in no way gentlemanly, and his close associates are no longer choirboys either."

"So? Where does the theater came in?"

"Micky Angel is an empire-builder. He is always acquiring businesses and property—legit or illegit, it makes no difference to him. Well, one of the properties he acquires is a run-down old theater on Broadway called the Roxy Palace and he is in the process of restoring it and putting on a swanky show there mainly for the benefit of his current doll, a Miss Billie Bernard, a Broadway hoofer with ambitions to be a star."

"So?"

"So, they have completely renovated the stage area, including putting in a revolve and a hydraulic system under the platform, but there is a problem. The builders and workmen he has hired are refusing to work down there. Micky throws threats and money at them in equal measure and still they refuse, and many, including Micky, natch, are beginning to suspect that Leo 'the Artichoke' is at the bottom of it all."

"The name is not familiar to me, Charlie."

"That has been til now your good fortune, Nate. His full name is Leo 'the Artichoke' Vinci. He is a big hoodlum and maybe the only one who can make Micky Angel still look like an altar boy."

"Why 'the artichoke'?"

"Believe me, Nate, you do not want to know."

"So?"

"So, in the first place Leo runs a fashionable nightery called the Garden of Allah, which is just a block away from the Roxy, and does not take too kindly to Micky Angel setting up an even classier establishment on what he considers to be his territory. And second of all, Miss Billie Bernard used to be his doll and used to sing and dance at the Garden of Allah. Well then, these guys start turning down well-paid work in Micky's theater and won't give no clear reason. Then a couple of nights ago, something else happens."

"Tell me, Charlie."

"This is only rumor, mind you, and I had it at third hand, so you didn't hear it from me, and anyway the details are so hazy . . ."

"Yes, yes! Well?"

"Some guy who's still working at the Roxy disappears. Just vanishes. And while he's working in the building. Honestly, that's all I know."

Brady shivered. It may be that Lovecraft's vision had been accurate. It was a thrilling and decisive moment, but something in him wished he had been wrong.

After a pause, Brady said, "So how do I find out more, Charlie?"

"I suppose you will not take my excellent advice and have nothing to do with this?"

"Charlie, I took an oath to the flag and to J. Edgar."

"You always were such a Boy Scout, Nate. All right then. My advice is to hang around Mindy's, the restaurant. It's where all the showpeople go, it's cheap and if you don't prefer chop suey as you should, the food's not half-bad. And you know how showpeople gossip. There's bound to be someone in from rehearsals at the Roxy. Make yourself out to be some kind of an agent—a theatrical agent, I mean, not a G-Man, for Christ's sake! Or a newspaperman. Most showpeople have an inordinate and misplaced faith in agents and newspapermen, until they become old and cynical, so pick on the young ones. You never know, you might find it amusing. You look like you need some recreation."

"And you won't tell me why this Leo guy is called 'the Artichoke'?"

"My lips are sealed. Have a Cognac."

March 1st, 1937 (from the diary of H. P. Lovecraft)

My dyspeptic condition is no better and I am running out of Dr. Van Bogusteen's Preparation. Ever since my vision, the phrase "The Armies of the Night" has been echoing through my head like some execrable tune by Messrs Gershwin or Berlin. Well, having nothing better to do by way of editing or writing, I decided if I might try to see what it signified. Among the volumes bequeathed to me by Grandfather Whipple was an ancient and battered copy of Dr. Dee's translation of the *Necronomicon* (1598). It is, alas, incomplete and in some respects inaccurate, but I have been denied access (as has everyone) to the only copy of the more comprehensive and accurate Latin version by Wormius (from which, in any case, Dee derived *his* version) at Miskatonic. Well, enough of this pedantry! Following a minute perusal, I did come across the following:

It is written that the Great Old Ones shall lye a-dream till certaine awakenings shall happen. Then they shall mingle with mortalls—perforce, or by the debased and willing subjection of some—and bring forth a race accursed, a half-broode. And these shall be called the exercitus noctis *or armies of the night, or, in their owne blasphemious tonge: Rugelloi fo Ixion* [as usual, Dee, never having heard the language spoken, has transcribed it inaccurately]. *And they shall rise up from beneath the earthe and smite all in their pathe, and though many perish, they cannot be subdued till one shall perform the three Voorishe Invocationes under the protectioun of the Hand of Glorye.*

The *Hand of Glory*, I understood. It is an ancient magical instrument made from the severed hand of a condemned man, but the "Voorish Invocations" I could not fathom. I knew that the Wormius *Necronomicon* contained a section at the end (which Dee had not translated) on ancient Voorish magic, so perhaps the invocations were there. But the Miskatonic *Necronomicon* was no longer available to scholars such as myself. Long years ago I was briefly granted access to their copy, but, alas, I only took a cursory glance at that last section because it was in some form of code. No doubt that was why Dee made no attempt to translate it, though he was a friend of Trithemius and something of an expert in cryptograms.

My friend Mr. Brady called on me. He expressed great interest in my researches and asked me some detailed questions about the possibility of gaining access to the Miskatonic Library in order to examine the Wormius *Necronomicon.* He seems to have some ulterior motive in wanting all this information from me, which I cannot fathom. Still, he is a gentleman and treats me like a gentleman, and that is a rare thing.

He gave me the name of a physician whom I should see for my gastric problems, telling me that I had no need to trouble over the expense as he and others who admired my work had arranged for all bills to be paid. He also gave me a bottle containing a liquid which, he told me, would have much the same effect as Bogusteen's Preparation. I have tried it and it does, but it is not nearly so foul to the taste as the Preparation. For some reason, this is rather a disappointment; my Puritan blood runs deep.

March 2, 1937

When Brady got to Mindy's he sat himself at a table near the wall so he could watch all comers and goers. He ordered a coffee and a plate of ham hock and sauerkraut, which, he was told, was Mindy's specialty. It was six o'clock, which was about the time that most Broadway players come in from rehearsals, or to grab something to eat before doing a show. Brady watched the clientele with the fascination of a born observer as they came in and out, insisting on their favorite tables, or, eyes wandering, looking for a friendly face: the almost-famous who made a grand entrance to attract attention, and the already-famous who tried desperately to avoid it.

Brady was on his fifth cup of coffee and Mindy, the proprietor, was beginning to eye him unfavorably, when a group of chorus girls came in and sat themselves in the booth next to Brady's. They exuded life, vitality, and laughter, and it seemed to Brady that they were taller than the average hoofer. Brady was struck in particular by one of them, darker than the rest with jet-black shingled hair, golden skin, high, aristocratic cheekbones, and wide, smiling eyes. A slight Southern drawl permeated her Brooklyn accent. They began to gossip about the show they were rehearsing and much of it, suffused with giggles, was incomprehensible. But then he began to hear odd fragments of conversation which interested him.

"So what's with this revolving stage?"

"They've stopped working on it."

"For Micky Angel? That's bad news for them. What's the beef?"

"Someone said the smell. Like a million-year-old dead fish. Haven't you caught it even in the dressing rooms? And it's worse down there. Much worse."

"So there's a smell down there. So can't they wear masks or something?"

"And then this guy who's working down there just vanishes. Young guy and all. With a wife and kids. And Micky goes ape."

"Why, it's not the poor guy's fault. Maybe he just—I don't know . . ."

"No. But Billie says Micky thinks it's the Artichoke at the bottom of it!"

"Jeez! Keep your voice down, Ellie. You don't know who might be listening."

Suddenly a blonde, bubble-curled head appeared above Brady's stall.

"Excuse me, sir. But might you be earwigging on a private conversation? If so, please desist forthwith or you might get a sock in the kisser."

Brady remained calm. "That would be regrettable, Miss—?"

The blonde who, in spite of herself, seemed favorably impressed by what she saw, introduced herself as Lisa Bolt. The others were also introduced by name, including the dark girl who was called Miss Ellie Jackson. Brady bowed formally and told the girls that he was Nick Carraway of the *New York Sun*.

"But I assure you, ladies," he said, "that I will regard anything you say as off the record."

"Oh, yeah!" said Lisa. "I've heard that one before."

"Aw, give the guy a break," said Ellie. Brady caught a smile that was echoed in her eyes.

"*You* give the guy a break, sister. I'm off home to give my kitty his tuna au naturel. Are you coming girls?" The others, apart from Miss Ellie, followed Lisa Bolt, who was evidently a leader of women. The one left behind was neither leader nor led—and Brady registered the possibility of a kindred spirit.

"May I join you?" he asked.

"It's a free country."

"I hope so, Miss Ellie," said Brady, seating himself opposite those smiling brown eyes. "My view, for what it's worth, is that the jury's still out on that."

"My! A newspaperman *and* a philosopher. I've never met one of those before. Or are you a newspaperman, Mr.—what was it?—Nick Carraway? A swell literary name that. Now where could I have read it before?"

Brady had reached a moment of decision: to trust or not to trust. He plunged.

"You are working at the Roxy Palace?"

She nodded. "And you?"

"Nathan Brady, FBI. I'm very pleased to meet you, Miss Ellie Jackson."

Ellie had little more to add to the information Brady already had about the situation at the Roxy Palace, but she promised him that she would observe. She admitted that she had been troubled by what had happened and that the place "had a bad feel about it." To lighten things, Brady ordered two dishes of Mindy's famous apple pie and asked her about the show.

Ellie explained: "It's a musical called *Zip Ahoy!* It's about this guy called Johnny Saint who's an inventor, like poor but honest, that stuff. And he's soft on this doll, right, and she's like a big star called Dorita Sunshine, or Sonnschein, only she's not Jewish or nothing. And she's a great doll because she loves Johnny, even though he's poor and stuff. And this guy Johnny invents this zip fastener, see. Only it's a great zip, like a million times better than the ordinary zip and he's going to make a whole lot of potatoes from it. Only there's this Ritzy gangster, called Rocco 'the Slasher' Golstein—but he's not Jewish, neither, he's kind of Jewish-Italian—so he blackmails Johnny and steals the formula and he says he's not going to give it back or nothing unless he can have Dorita, and Johnny says nuts to that, but Dorita she wants to save his invention 'cause she really has the hots for him and wants to be his ever-loving wife and all that, so she says she don't love him no more and they all get on this ship where Dorita is singing in the cabaret and there's this big mix-up over some missing pearls which end up in Johnny's cabin so he is arrested and put in the sneezer on board. But there is this doll on board called Ruby Emerald and she's a jewel thief and Dorita recognizes her and threatens to tell the cops and put *her* in the sneezer unless she steals back the zip and anyway it all ends happily. And I'm a hoofer in the chorus and understudy for Ruby Emerald, who is played by Miss Billie Bernard, Micky Angel's doll."

"I see."

"Sounds a bit of terrific, huh?"

"I hope Billie Bernard is prevented from playing Ruby Emerald so I can see you in the role."

"Don't you wish that on me, Mr. FBI. Micky Angel will not be pleased if Miss Billie Bernard is stopped from being a big star, which is what this show is all about. Anyway, Billie is an okay broad and I would never wish harm on her."

"Can I pick you up after rehearsals tomorrow?"

"You may, Mr. Brady."

"Thank you, Miss Ellie. I'll be outside the stage door."

III

March 4, 1937

"You seem to have done well, young man," said Hoover. "And this informant of yours. Miss Ellie Jackson. Is she to be relied on?"

"I am sure of it, Mr. Hoover."

"Hmm. She is, however, a woman, Brady. And a woman, Brady, is always a woman. Note that down."

"I'll bear it in mind, Mr. Hoover."

"The next thing is to gain access to the theater."

"I am working on that, Mr. Hoover."

"Good man. Now this stuff about the three invocations and the Hand of Old Glory."

"Hand of Glory, sir."

"Hand of Old Glory. What are we doing about getting hold of them?"

Brady explained the difficulty of acquiring the invocations without access to the Miskatonic Library; and getting hold of the severed hand of a condemned criminal also presented problems.

Brady added: "But all this is just superstition, Mr. Hoover. In an old book."

"Don't knock old books, young man. They may be old, but they can sometimes give you the low-down, such as the saying: 'There are more things in heaven on earth.' Do you know who said that?"

"I think it was Hamlet in—"

"A great American called Buffalo Bill said it. Not a lot of people know that."

"No, sir."

"We need to get hold of one of these Hands of Old Glory. It may be, as you say, the *phonus balonus*, but we need to make sure. So we got to find the severed hand of an executed criminal. Am I right?"

"Yes, Mr. Hoover."

"And it's got to be fresh, I reckon. Let me just check out who's coming up for the hot squat." He pressed a button on his intercom and spoke into it. "Miss Gandy, will you bring in a list of the folks who are going to the electric chair in the coming fortnight?"

Brady heard a faint "Right away, Mr. Hoover!" and surprisingly soon Miss Gandy was in the office with a neatly-typed list which she laid on Hoover's desk before leaving the room, casting a quick friendly smile in Brady's direction as she did so. Hoover studied the document.

"Huh, so there's 'Machine Gun' Willie Biggs down in Idaho, but he's got a mother who'll kick up hell if we take the body. These mothers of condemned criminals are the pits. Officially we need consent from the penitentiary and the prisoner and the relations to get hold of the body. Then, there's Velma van Horn, but just maybe she didn't hack her husband to pieces and feed him to her pet 'gator, and her uncle's a Congressman. Could be a reprieve for the broad . . . Steve 'Slugger' Smith . . . No. He's got God, so he won't buy it—Wait a minute! Here's Obadiah Willums in Sing Sing. An old guy: cut off his wife's head with a pruning hook because she yacked too much. He's got no one who cares about him, least of all the relatives who get the farm. He might just say yes. We tell him the FBI laboratories want his body for studies in the brain of the superior criminal or some such *balonus*. That might hook him. Now when is he due to meet Old Sparky? Sing Sing on the thirteenth! New York State. We're in the money, young man. Ever been to Sing Sing, Brady? I'll get Miss Gandy to arrange a visit as soon as possible."

March 4th, 1937 (from the diary of H. P. Lovecraft)

When Mr. Brady called yesterday I was able to tell him I had seen the Doc he recommended. Apparently he was already acquainted with the results of my examination, and had made provisional arrangements for me to go into hospital to undergo further tests and possibly an operation.

I protested in the strongest possible terms at this intrusion into my personal affairs. Mr. Brady listened patiently to my outburst, then remarked quietly that my continued health and well-being was his greatest concern. He told me that all expenses for my treatment and operation would be taken care of, but before that could happen, he would ask one favour of me. I told him to name it.

"I would like you to help me to break into the Miskatonic Library and steal the *Necronomicon*," he said.

My utter astonishment can without difficulty, I presume, be imagined. I asked him in crudely vernacular terms what his "game" was, and he, as the vernacular also has it, "came clean."

After he had explained, it took several minutes for me to regain my customary coolth and composure. So the visions were real! My dismay that I had been something of a dupe these last few weeks was mitigated by Mr. Brady's sincere admiration for my work. And, after all, I am a patriot and my respect for that great American Mr. J. Edgar Hoover knows no bounds. It would seem that I am to become an ex officio G-Man! Mr. Brady enjoined on me the utter secrecy of this mission, which not even Aunt Annie must know about. I agreed.

Last night my visions took me back to that accursed theatre. Brady was there and in mortal danger. I tried in my dream to cry out to him to be wary, but no sound came. I await news from him with trepidation. For all his underhandedness he is, like me, a gentleman, and I can't help liking the fellow.

March 5, 1937

As Hoover had correctly surmised, Brady had never been to Sing Sing. He had interviewed prisoners in other penitentiaries, but never one of the condemned on Death Row. The prison governor seemed most anxious to assist and asked Brady to convey his best regards to "Mr. Hoover." Brady found this degree of courtesy, often to the point of obsequiousness, among officials where J. Edgar Hoover was concerned, and wondered if the director "had something on" the governor. It was usually the case.

As he led Brady through a succession of metallic passages and locked doors, he said, "You'll find Obadiah Willums a queer sort of guy. I reckon he's positively looking forward to the chair. Why does the Bureau want the body, by the way? If you don't mind my asking."

"Our forensic laboratories are conducting a number of highly advanced scientific experiments on brains that will enable us to identify the criminal mind almost from birth in the future." Brady was astonished and ashamed at his ability to come up with this sort of nonsense.

"Really? Really? Modern science is a wondrous thing, sir. That's most interesting. Mr. Hoover is a truly great man."

"He is indeed, sir."

"But I wouldn't say Willums is exactly a criminal; more crazy. He told me that this kind of weird creature came out of the well in his yard and told him to snuff his old lady. I reckon he ought to be in a booby hatch rather than Sing Sing, but he won't have it. He says he's sane and he wants to go to the chair, but if he really wants to sit in Old Sparky he *must* be bughouse."

"Mr. Hoover is particularly interested in the criminally insane."

"Well, okay then. Mr. Hoover is one hell of a great guy. And you be sure to tell him I said so."

"I certainly will, sir."

"And if he—or you—ever want to come down to see an execution with Old Sparky at work, you only have to ask. You will be most welcome."

"Thank you, governor. That is very generous. I am sure Mr. Hoover will appreciate the offer."

"I sure hope he does. Well, here we are: Death Row. You'll notice I have just had everything repainted. Cerise-pink. My wife, Florine, chose the color. It's part of our humane policy to make things feel kind of homey here. I'll hand you over now to the Reverend Mortice, our Death Row chaplain. He does a great job here with the prisoners, saving their souls and such."

The Reverend Mortice was a small, round, smiling individual with the manner of a practiced receiver of confessions, like a solicitor with extra unction. As he led Brady to the interview room, he smiled at the guards in the corridor and spoke to each by their Christian names and waved to all the men in their condemned cells.

"I have a great love in my heart for Obadiah," he told Brady, "but, sadly, I cannot get him to repent. If only they repent then they can go straight from that chair of death into the life eternal of paradise. It's the free gift from the Lord to all us sinners. But if they will not repent, then they must go to Hell. It gives me great distress to think of any of these poor souls in a place of eternal torment. Perhaps *you* can persuade him to repent."

"I think that's your job, reverend. I am here to—on another mission." Then, witnessing the crushed look on the Reverend Mortice's face, he added: "I'll do my best."

Mortice beamed. He opened the door of the interview room, which was painted the same hideous shade of "cerise-pink" as the corridor. It reminded Brady of flayed flesh. "Someone to see you, Obadiah."

A little wizened, bald old man in dungarees sat rigid and upright at a table. He glanced with scorn at Mortice, but showed mild interest in his new visitor. He did not speak until the chaplain had left the room and then he fixed Brady with a disconcertingly mild gaze.

"You can see me, son," said Obadiah Willums, "but I ain't going to say no more. Tomorrow I'm going to meet Old Sparky and we'll get along just fine."

In quiet, respectful tones, Brady stated the purpose of his visit, which was for Willums to sign a paper giving consent for his body after execution to be handed over to the FBI for "research."

"Search?" said Willums. "Search for what? You won't find nothing save bones and a bit of old gristle. What's the use of searching for that?"

"Well, in that case, that is what we will find out, Mr. Willums."

"You folk are the darndest fools. Still, ain't no concern of mine. But I done nothin' wrong, son."

Brady looked at Willums enquiringly. A miscarriage of justice would complicate matters beyond measure.

"Oh, I killed the old beaver all right. Cut her head clean off." Brady heaved an involuntary sigh of relief. "Nice and neat too. But I had to, son, and I don't regret it, no, sir. The Old One tells me to."

"The Old One?"

"Yes. The Old 'Un. Ain't you heared of the Old 'Uns? You college-educated boys don't know nothing, do you? Up Dunwich way where I lives, you get the Old Ones. They comes up from under and speak to you, not in words like other folk, but like light through the brain. And they smell like thunder, and sometimes you see them and sometimes you don't, but you sure know when and where they've been. For they come with all Hell in their wings, which they stretch up to the stars from where they come a long way back. My grandaddy spoke with them and taught me to speak with them too. And we had an Old 'Un specially ours and he lived in that there old well in our backyard. And every midsummer eve we'd lay flowers on the well and throw a cow down there or maybe a couple of hogs, but mostly a cow, hogs being too valuable. And the Old 'Un'd come up and maybe show himself or maybe not, but my wife, Martha, she never see'd him because she didn't hold with the Old 'Un, being in with the Holy Joes up the Baptist Chapel. And she called the Old 'Un all kinds of names, like Old Moloch and Beelzebub and Satan's Brood and such, and the Old 'Un took it til one day he says to me, 'Oby'—that's what he calls me, see—'Oby, that old lady of yours don't like me, nor you, nor your hogs, and she ain't no use anymore. You give me her head; I'll see you right.' So that's how it come about. And so one night close to the end of summer, when the whippoorwills were a'screaming in the dusky air, I picks up my pruning hook and I snips her head and I throws it down the well to the Old 'Un. And the Old 'Un goes *Boom!* And up comes a smell like thunder, and all the whippoorwills stop their screeching, and a great peace comes down on the earth. And later comes the po-lice and all, and they find Martha sitting upright on a kitchen chair with the gurt old Bible open at the fifth chapter of Matthew in front of her on the table, but no head to read it. So here I be. And you can do with my old body what you like because Old Sparky, he's going to take my soul right back down to the Old 'Un, where I belong."

There was a silence in the room when Willums had finished speaking. For a full minute Brady hardly dared move. Then, slowly, he took out a pen and passed it across the table with the paper for Willums to sign, while the old man hummed gently to himself.

"What do you think I've ordered for my last meal, son?" said Willums suddenly.

Brady shook his head.

"Pork!" And he chuckled with delight. "I've always kept hogs, see, since I were a young shaver. I was known for my hogs, so I'm going to have pork. Best darned meat in the whole world, pork. That's one reason why I had to kill my old lady. The Old 'Un told me she didn't respect my hogs no more. I couldn't have that, so I got out my old pruning hook—not a gun. I don't hold with no guns, ever since my Daddy shot off his foot chasin' a bear—and I sliced off her mean old head neat as you like. So I'm going to have some nice fat pork with a bully piece o'cracklin' before I sits me down in Old Sparky. Do you think you can fix me that, son, for sure? Nice piece o'cracklin'?"

"I sure can, Mr. Willums."

"Then I'll sign your paper. Anything more I can do for you, son?"

Brady, who felt unaccountably sorry for Mortice, gently hinted that Obadiah Willums would make the chaplain very happy if he repented of his crime.

"But I don't repent it, son," said Willums. "I'm darn glad I sliced off her mean old head. She was all dried-up like a stick, with not an ounce of juice left in her. That Old 'Un had the right of it."

"But you could *say* you repent, couldn't you Mr. Willums? Just to keep Reverend Mortice happy. You don't have to *mean* it."

Willums was silent for a while, considering this, then he slapped his thigh and let out a yell of laughter.

"My! If that isn't the durndest thing I ever heared of! I'll give him repentance, the old coyote! I'll lead that smirking, psalm-singing preacher man in a square dance he won't forget, no sir! And inside, me and the Old 'Un will be laughing fit to bust. Here's your paper, son. Signed and sealed. Darn me! That's the biggest laugh I've had since old Great Aunt Thirza fell into the grain silo and drownded herself in corn!"

As he left the interview room, Brady could still hear Obadiah Willums chortling to himself. In the corridor he met Reverend Mortice, who heard the noise and looked at him enquiringly.

"He is sobbing over his sins," said Brady. "Give him a few moments. I think you'll find him ready to repent."

"Bless you, Mr. Brady," said Reverend Mortice, a wide smile splitting his round face. "And Praise the Lord! Today you and Mr. Hoover have saved a soul for paradise!"

It would have been inhuman of Brady not to feel a little ashamed; still, the body of Obadiah Willums, condemned murderer, now belonged to the FBI.

THREE

The Armies of the Night

I

March 6, 1937

NATHAN BRADY'S SEAT AT the Roxy Palace Theater was some way toward the back of the circle, but he had a good view. It had been kind of Miss Ellie Jackson to secure him the complimentary seat. He looked down into the audience. Most of the men were wearing black tie and dinner jackets, like him, though a few people in the boxes were in white tie and tails. Among them, Brady was astonished to see his own director, J. Edgar Hoover, with his faithful assistant, Clyde Tolson. Brady noted, with something of the innate snobbery of the well-favored, that a white tie did not in any way diminish Hoover's air of squat brutishness.

But his boss's farouche appearance was nothing to the man in whose box they were evidently guests. A huge man, mightily built though not grossly fat, stood behind them smiling proprietorially on the proceedings. He was florid in his complexion, and his black curly hair, sleekly oiled, was abundant. His features, apart from a calamitously broken nose, were still classically regular, and Brady could just imagine that he might once have been a handsome, even a pretty youth, though more Murillo urchin than Botticelli angel. For this, as Brady knew from consulting the photograph in his remarkably slender FBI file, was Micky "the Angel" Buonarotti. But what were the director of the FBI and his assistant doing in his box?

Brady decided to dismiss this puzzle from his mind as the conductor, to a ripple of applause, took his place and the overture began.

He was no connoisseur of musical comedy, but Brady judged that *Zip Ahoy!* might well be a hit. It was certainly cheered and applauded enough to give that appearance, though Brady knew that it was the Broadway critics who would have the last word. The numbers were perhaps a little too big and brassy for his rather over-refined taste but, whenever the chorus came on, his attention was instantly drawn to Miss Ellie Jackson. Her golden skin and lustrous eyes marked her out. Was it just his own personal preference? She certainly danced superbly, with a lithe and natural grace, and Brady thought he could pick out her voice among the others: lower, smoother, silkier.

She had one line to say, and it got a laugh. Was he falling under her spell? Given Mr. Hoover's less than advanced views on race, it was a dangerous thing for Brady to do. He dismissed the thought from his mind—theirs was a purely professional, albeit friendly, relationship, he told himself.

He made a note, too, of Miss Billie Bernard, who played the part of Ruby Emerald, the jewel thief. It was a showy part with one or two good numbers, and Billie Bernard had made a fair fist of it, he supposed. She danced well, but her voice was a little thin and her personality didn't run to much.

While the audience was filing out, Brady made his way toward the pass door to the stage at the right-hand end of the circle. Ellie had told him that she would leave it unlocked. Once through, Brady found himself on a metal walkway above the stage where, behind the fallen curtain, he could look down on the heads of the cast still milling and hugging.

Brady waited until they dispersed and only stagehands were present, moving scenery into place for the start of the show the following night. Unobserved, he moved across the walkway and through a second pass door into the upper dressing room corridor, where the chorus lived.

On one of the doors Brady knocked and asked for Miss Ellie, opening it a fraction to do so. Presently she slipped through the aperture and came out into the corridor.

She had her hair up and wore a long white silk dressing gown, tightly belted to show off her exquisite figure. Though she was out of makeup and *en déshabillé*, Brady thought he had never seen anyone look more glorious. She gave him that warm generous smile that could melt an iceberg a league away.

"Thank you for those lovely flowers, Nathan. All the girls in there think you must be my beau."

"I hope I am your very, very good friend, Miss Ellie."

"You see that door at the end of the corridor? That's the wardrobe, and nobody will be in there till six tomorrow morning at the earliest. I had a key copied. Here. Now you go in there and lock yourself in. I'll make sure I'm one of the last to leave, and I'll knock on the door three times to let you know it's clear. But you watch yourself. Micky Angel don't like anyone creeping round his theater, 'specially not the FBI, I guess. Are you packing a rod?"

Brady opened his jacket to reveal a Colt .38 special neatly tucked into a leather holster strapped close to the left side of his ribcage.

"My!" she said. "It doesn't show with your tux buttoned at all!"

"I told my tailor to make allowances," said Brady, a little self-consciously. "What are you giggling at, Miss Ellie?"

"Oh, nothing! Just that for a G-Man, you really are quite sweet." And she kissed him on both cheeks. Brady blushed. "Remember. When you're done with the snooping, I'll be at the show party at Sardi's all night."

"I'll try to get there."

Ellie blew him a kiss and tripped back into the dressing room. Brady heard whoops from the other chorus girls as she did so, and he rapidly made his way to the wardrobe room at the end of the corridor.

Brady did not have long to wait before he heard three sharp raps on the wardrobe room door, but he did not immediately come out, and it was as well he didn't. Soon after, he heard footsteps coming down the corridor and the door being tried. Fortunately, he had locked it as Miss Ellie had suggested.

Twenty minutes later he emerged to find the theater apparently deserted and in darkness. He nevertheless moved silently, having taken care to put crêpe on the soles of his patent-leather pumps. He came down two flights of stairs, hearing and seeing nothing, but when he came to the stage level, he heard a noise coming from one of the star dressing rooms. He crept closer and found an alcove from which he could hear unobserved what was going on.

"No, Micky, no!" said a high, slightly nasal voice, which Brady recognized as belonging to Miss Billie Bernard. "I will not come to your ball. I know when I'm not wanted. I was lousy tonight and I know it."

"But, honey, you were great! I did all this for you."

"I know, Micky, I know. And I'm grateful believe me. But I just can't take it. Aw, Micky just leave me."

"You are coming to Sardi's, doll. I said so."

"Let me go, you big ape!"

Brady heard sounds of a struggle, then a grunt from Micky and a scream of pain from Billie. He peered out of his recess, darting back just in time to avoid being seen by Micky, who emerged from Billie's dressing room nursing what looked like a scratch on his right hand. Brady saw him turn a corner and then, beyond Brady's line of sight, begin to speak in muffled tones to some person or persons.

Brady heard the words: ". . . and see she shows up" from Micky, followed by a "Yeah, boss," which was echoed by another. Then Micky left, slamming the stage door behind him. Meanwhile, a sound of sobbing was coming from Miss Billie Bernard's dressing room.

Brady was just about to emerge from his hiding place when two large men came round the corner and walked purposefully toward Billie's dressing room. Their faces were shapeless and pockmarked—one of them had the little finger missing from his left hand, the other a pencil-moustache so thin it looked like the gash from a knife. Incongruously, they were immaculately costumed in midnight-blue dinner suits with wing collars and black bow ties.

They paused before Billie's dressing-room door and knocked.

"We've come to take you to the party, Miss Billie," they said.

"Scram, you great lunks!" screamed Billie from within. "I'm not going for you or anyone!"

"Boss's orders, Miss Billie," said Pencil Moustache.

The one with the missing finger who seemed, if possible, even more brutish than his companion mumbled: "Boss's orders." Then they both entered Billie's dressing room.

Presently Brady heard scuffles and screams and the smashing of glass, followed by the heady odor of cheap scent. A bottle of perfume had been thrown. Brady wondered if he should intervene, but this was not what he was here for. Besides, it sounded as if Miss Billie Bernard could look after herself. Then there was a further crash, and Billie came bolting out of her dressing room. She wasted precious seconds trying to lock the two mobsters in her dressing room, but they forced the door open, pursuing her down the corridor past where Brady was concealed.

Billie tried to dodge through the door to the stage, but they blocked her way. There was now only one possible route of escape—the staircase down to the understage, and this she took with Pencil Moustache and Missing Finger in close pursuit. Brady decided to follow at a discreet distance. Billie was screaming, the two hoodlums bellowing—it was a primitive scene.

Brady followed them down to beneath the stage, where he was just in time to see Billie take an unwary step and half-slide, half-tumble down a ragged hole in the floor of the basement. Pencil Moustache and Missing Finger followed her down the steps more carefully, using their cigarette lighters to see where they were going.

Brady came to the edge of the hole to watch the descent of the thugs at a safe distance. He had a flashlight, but would not use it unless absolutely necessary. He could hear the hollow echoes of Billie's cries and the splashy echo of her footsteps as she wandered blindly in the spaces below.

As soon as Pencil Moustache and Missing Finger had reached the bottom of the steps and negotiated the uneven pile of rubble at their foot, setting off in rather hesitant pursuit of their quarry once more, Brady started his own descent into the depths.

The first thing he became aware of on reaching the bottom was the smell. It was ancient and putrid and fishy. The atmosphere down there was not, as he had expected, close. There was air coming from somewhere, almost like a breeze, but the odor it carried was all decay and death. The walls Brady touched were mostly smooth and clammy, though in parts it felt as if they were covered with coarse wet hairs: some sort of moss or weed, he presumed. The growth was faintly bioluminescent, and of a greenish-gray color, like a vast hirsute glowworm.

Brady risked a quick flash of his torch, and what he saw astonished him. It was just as H. P. Lovecraft had described: He was in a vast barrel-vaulted corridor with smooth walls, some of them masked with the coarse subterranean growth he had felt and seen. Other parts of the wall were damp and naked but intricately carved, either with lettering which Brady identified as Runic in character, or with grotesque bas-relief sculptures. He had no time to examine them because, ahead of him, Pencil Moustache turned around, uttering the words, "What the—!" Brady immediately snapped off his flashlight.

Ahead of him, the two thugs had other things to occupy their minds. Brady saw them halt and hold up the flickering lighters to stare around them. The vaulted gallery had debouched into a wide, almost circular chamber from which numerous passages wound off like tentacles from the head of a monstrous beast. They evidently could not tell which way Billie had taken, and were dazed by the awesomeness of the structure that they encountered.

The roof of the space was conical, like the beehive tombs of pre-classical Greece, and every inch of the smooth cyclopean masonry with which it was built was covered in carvings of strange and hideous creatures, coupled with what looked like astronomical charts featuring constellations and planets.

Brady came up close to the two men unobserved, and watched as they stared in horror and wonder at the chamber they had entered. For a moment there was complete silence, then a scream was heard coming from one of the tunnels that led out of the space they were in. It was Billie.

Pencil Moustache and Missing Finger had some discussion as to which tunnel Billie's voice had come from. Eventually, Pencil Moustache overruled Missing Finger and plunged down one of them, the latter following, disgruntled. Brady thought he rather favored Missing Finger's decision, but decided to follow them at a discreet distance.

As soon as Brady entered the tunnel he was aware of a thicker, more oppressive atmosphere, the fish-corpse odor now so powerful that he could hear the two hoodlums ahead of him choke and retch. Brady conserved his strength and took shallow breaths. The two men began to call out: "Miss Billie! Miss Billie!" trying vainly to sound conciliatory. but nothing except the hollow echo of their cries was to be heard.

Then came another sound. At first it was no more than a pulse in the earth that could have been mistaken for the thump of Brady's own beating heart. Rapidly it grew louder and began to boom like the vibrating skin of a vast drum. Pencil Moustache and Missing Finger were still moving forward ahead of him, but slowly, tentatively. Now the booming sound was accompanied by the splashy patter of splayed feet advancing over puddles. There was a curious hissing noise before Brady heard Pencil Moustache say, "Son of a—!" Then things began to happen rapidly.

There was a swishing sound, and Pencil Moustache was swept off his feet by something like a giant arm. Missing Finger pulled his gun and started firing indiscriminately until the clip of his magazine was exhausted. Brady switched on his flashlight to witness a scene of such horror that for a few seconds he could do nothing but stare.

Pencil Moustache was being held aloft by a giant arm or tentacle, and he was either dead or unconscious, but his eyes were wide-open and staring. Most of his right leg had been torn off and was being devoured by a host of creatures, half-human, half-piscine, and of unimaginable hideousness. Meanwhile, Missing Finger was bellowing and struggling among a roiling mass of creatures.

Above it all, a half-human voice cried out triumphantly, "*Rghyyeloi fo Xhon! Rghyyeloi fo Xhon!*" And it was taken up by many more: "*Rghyyeloi fo Xhon! Rghyyeloi fo Xhon! The Armies of the Night! The Armies of the Night!*"

Brady considered intervening, but it looked as if Pencil Moustache and Missing Finger were doomed, and perhaps not to be much missed. He would be better employed trying to rescue Miss Billie Bernard. He switched off his flashlight and ran back down the tunnel toward the central hall. As he did so, the dreadful bellowing of Missing Finger stopped in midscream.

When he reached the hall, almost without thinking he darted down the tunnel from which he and the late, lamented, Missing Finger had thought

Billie's screams were emanating. Losing all caution, he switched on his flashlight and ran, calling out, "Miss Billie!" as he went. The passage became narrower, and Brady noticed that it was now constructed from homely brick. He heard what he thought sounded like a muffled human cry. Brady turned a corner without any precaution, his light flashing over the rough brickwork as he ran. He did not even draw his pistol. Then, before he saw him, he heard a man say: "Stand right where you are!"

Brady halted, cursing his own recklessness. He shone his flashlight directly ahead and saw a big man standing in a blade of light made by a half-open doorway. In his right hand he held a revolver, which was pointed directly at Brady. His left arm encircled the frail form of Miss Billie Bernard, who struggled feebly in his grasp, and the massive left hand was clamped tightly over her mouth.

"You better come with us, punk," said the man, a vast Chinaman, almost as wide as he was tall, "unless you're looking for a gut full of lead." Brady was not, so he followed instructions and preceded Billie and the Chinaman through the door and up a narrow flight of stairs. From somewhere he could hear the sound of laughter and a very capable dance orchestra in full swing. Brady felt the almost irresistible urge to ask the Chinaman if he knew his good friend Charlie Chin, but felt this was neither the time nor the place. But he did ask where they were. They were not in the Roxy Palace, that was for sure.

"You dumb or something?" said the Chinaman. "This is the Garden of Allah, and I am taking you to see the boss, Mr. Leo Vinci."

"Oh, you mean Leo the—" Brady just restrained himself from uttering the dreadful word *artichoke*. "Mr. Vinci. Yes, of course."

"And," added the huge Chinaman, rather superfluously, Brady thought, "Mr. Vinci will not be very happy to see either you, Mr. Smart-Ass, or Miss Billie Bernard!"

II

March 7, 1937 (early hours)

The office of Leo "the Artichoke" Vinci was situated at the top of the building which contained his highly fashionable nightclub, the Garden of Allah. It would not, however, be true to say that the aforementioned establishment owed any of its success to Mr. Vinci. It had been bought, for a very reasonable sum, from the club's original proprietor and creator who had got into difficulties with Vinci and been made, as they say, "an offer he couldn't refuse."

Mr. Vinci, however, was not a man to deny himself credit, even if it was undeserved, and he made sure that everyone knew that he was the Garden of Allah's sole director, and that the excellence of its orchestra, the refinement of its food and liquor, and the slenderness of its chorus girls' legs were all thanks to him. His office was the epitome of what was considered in his world to be sophisticated modernity.

Whatever was not chrome-plated was gold-plated, and the elegance of his moderne furniture was only matched by its discomfort. Behind his desk, a portrait of Vinci by the artist of the moment, Tamara de Lempicka, was a miracle of popular cubism and shameless flattery.

He himself was not a thing of beauty, even though the Polish-born artist had done her best to imply it. She had certainly caught the angularity of the man. He had an abominably long, thin face, which had been likened by no less a person than Miss Dorothy Parker to "two profiles stuck together." His nose was a beak; his lips were exiguous. That narrowness of aspect reminded Brady, when he first came into his presence, of his new friend Lovecraft; but this was a demonic version of the lantern-jawed sage of Providence, Rhode Island.

The Chinaman had been right. Vinci was not pleased to see them, though Brady doubted whether the man sitting opposite him and playing with a dangerous-looking steel letter-opener was ever pleased to see anything except his bank balance.

"I found these guys in the basement," said the Chinaman.

Vinci was enraged. "Haven't I told you, Hang, never to let anyone go down in that goddamn basement!"

"But, boss, they didn't come from the Garden, they came in some other way."

"What! Is this true?"

"It's true," said Brady.

"And who the hell are you?"

"Nathan Brady, FBI," he began to reach for his badge, but as he expected, was stopped.

"Keep your hands away from your pockets, punk!"

"Very well, then, Mr. Vinci. If you or your assistant reach into the right-hand outside pocket of my jacket, you will find my authority."

"Do it!" said Vinci to the Chinaman, who extracted the badge and threw it onto the desk in front of Vinci.

"So, Mr. FBI," said Vinci, lacing every syllable with sarcasm, "you expect me to be impressed."

"Not impressed, but perhaps better informed."

Vinci's eyes narrowed. "Would you like to tell me how in hell you got here?"

"It's very simple. I was following this young lady here. Miss Billie Bernard."

"Yes, I know her name, thank you, Mr. FBI. We know each other well, do we not, Miss Bernard? Have you come back to me, then, Billie, begging for forgiveness? Have things gone sour between you and that hulking great sonofabitch, Micky Angel? Is that your game?"

Billie, released at last from Hang's debilitating grip, began to show spirit. "Listen, Leo," she said. "I know I was your doll once, and I know you are pretty mad at me for throwing you over for a sap like Micky Angel, but that is not here nor is it there. And how I got here, I do not truly know, and who the hell this G-Man is and what he is doing shnozzling around after me, I know not neither. Now, will you kindly release me from your extremely classy joint? I have a party at Sardi's to attend, following the premiere performance of a show named *Zip Ahoy!* at the Roxy Palace, with which you may not be entirely ignorant." And, with that, she began to march confidently toward the door of Vinci's office.

"Not so fast, sister!" said Vinci. "At this moment my betsy is pointed at your ass, which is a very fine ass as asses go and would not benefit from being rearranged by the insertion of lead."

Billie halted. She knew Vinci well enough to sense that he meant business. She turned around to see that Vinci's revolver (pearl-handled and gold-plated) was indeed pointed directly at her nether regions.

"Aw, Leo," she said, "it is truly touching that you still have my best interests at heart."

Vinci, a stranger to irony, did not smile. "Park your ass, doll, and lay off the gabbing till I tell you to gab." Billie sat down in the chair that Hang indicated with a flick of his pistol. "Now I want to know how in hell you got here and where you came from, or I shall loose Mr. Hang on you with some methods of persuasion that you will not like."

Brady explained that there was a route from the basement of the Roxy Palace to the basement of the Garden of Allah, which had been discovered, and that he had followed Miss Billie Bernard there. He did not think it appropriate to mention the part played by Pencil Moustache and Missing Finger, or their unhappy fate.

"And why were you following Miss Billie?"

It was a question that Brady had been expecting and dreading. "That is a confidential FBI matter and no business of yours, Mr. Vinci."

"Oh, no? And suppose Mr. Hang here makes it relevant, punk?"

"Mr. Hoover would not be happy with you, Mr. Vinci. And when Mr. Hoover is not happy, consequences follow."

"Oh, yeah? And if you end up in the East River wearing the concrete overcoat, who's to know?"

"Mr. Hoover would know. He knows enough already, and he always gets to know everything in the end. I will give you plenty of five to seven on that. I can only guarantee your safety if you let me go unharmed." This was, of course, as Mr. Hoover might say, the *phonus balonus*, but it seemed to impress Vinci. Like most people of a criminal persuasion, Leo Vinci was superstitious, and had bought into the myth of the FBI's omniscience.

The proprietor of the Garden of Allah considered a moment, then spoke. "Okay, Mr. Wise Guy. I'm going to let you go, but you do exactly as I tell you. You go to Micky Angel and you tell him that I have got Miss Billie Bernard, and that she does not go on tonight or in any show ever, unless he comes and does business with me. We will meet in a friendly way, and our people will be carrying the minimum of weapons. And I expect his answer by tonight. I am done with Mr. Buonarotti muscling in on my territory.

"First he steals my broad, then he builds his theater a few blocks away, then he comes at me from under my building. This is not the action of a guy who used to be a buddy. Micky and I grew up together. Hell, we used to run a whorehouse together! Best goddamn whorehouse in Brooklyn too! Together we buried 'Feet' Macorquodale alive for singing to the cops about the Hoboken bank heist.

"Now he's in cahoots with your director. What's his hold on the guy? Why does he not share it with me? Where is the comradeship? Where is loyalty and honor? Where is the old pals act? It is all gone. I tell you, Mr. FBI, this country is taking the A train to Hell. Now get your ass out of here."

"Do I have your assurance that Miss Billie Bernard suffers no harm?"

"You do, but she stays in my keeping until Micky Angel gets his ass over here and starts talking business. And no FBI in on the act. Capeesh?"

Brady, who was a linguist, indicated his understanding with a nod and was released.

March 7, 1937 (later that morning)

It was fortunate, Brady reflected, that Mr. Hoover had been at the first night of *Zip Ahoy!*, because it might mean that he was still in New York. This proved to be the case. A phone call gave him the information that he was at the New York FBI building in downtown Manhattan, and by ten o'clock Brady was standing opposite him in the director's office. With Hoover was his assistant, Clyde Tolson, watchful, enigmatic, and cold.

Brady gave them an edited, but, he hoped, credible account of the events of the night before, leaving out some of the more outré aspects of his adventures in the subterranean tunnels beneath the Theater District. He was listened to in silence.

"Well, young man," said Hoover, "we have ourselves a situation. Mr. Buonarotti is as far as I know a man of good standing in this city—"

"I understand that you and Mr. Tolson enjoyed his hospitality last night."

Hoover stiffened; Tolson glared. Brady had taken a risk, but he had wanted to gauge their reactions. Vinci's remark about Buonarotti's "hold" on Hoover had impressed him.

"Mr. Brady," said Hoover, "I did not ask you to interrupt while I was speaking." The coldness was evident, but he was clearly on the defensive. "A lot of nonsense in this city is talked about so-called mafias and organized crime. There is no such thing. There are just criminals. There is no organized crime. There is no 'mob.' Do you understand, Brady?"

"I'll bear that in mind, Mr. Hoover."

"Mr. Buonarotti is a businessman in good standing; he owns a theater which is under threat from these communist rats. There is your organized crime, if you like. Now, I know nothing of this dispute he has with Mr. Vinci. That is not FBI business, but this dispute should be resolved. After all, Mr. Vinci is also a businessman, though I am not personally acquainted with him. Your task, Mr. Brady, is to give Mr. Buonarotti every assistance in ridding himself of these commie bums. I do not want to know how you do it, but you will do it. It will be a test for you. Do I make myself clear?"

"Absolutely, Mr. Hoover. I have your permission to act on my own initiative then?"

"You do, Brady. You may hit your approach shot any way you like, so long as you get your ball in the hole. Do you have a plan?"

"I believe I do, Mr. Hoover."

"Well, don't tell me about it, just get going and kick some ass. And, Brady—?"

“Sir?”

“By the time you get back to your hotel room, a parcel should have arrived for you. Special delivery from Sing Sing. Via our laboratories. Understood?”

“Understood, Mr. Hoover,” said Brady. Out of the corner of his eye, he noticed Tolson look enquiringly at the director. Evidently *he* had not understood; there were some things that Hoover kept even from his closest associate.

The rest of that morning and afternoon Brady spent mainly with Mr. Buonarotti who, after an initial explosiveness, proved most accommodating. Brady also made other arrangements. The last task on his list, and not the least important in his eyes, was to see Miss Ellie Jackson, who took the news he had to give her with a kind of sober level-headedness, neither fearful nor exultant, which only enhanced his admiration for her. Then she, too, had her preparations to make.

They met again only shortly before curtain-up on the second night of *Zip Ahoy!*, in which Miss Ellie was to take over the leading role of Ruby Emerald owing to the indisposition and absence of Miss Billie Bernard. As the overture was playing, they stood together in the wings.

“Miss Ellie,” said Brady looking into those wonderful eyes, “I want you to go out there and come back a star.”

“You honestly think I can do it, Nathan?”

“I *know* you can, doll.”

“Oh, Nathan! You called me doll! How thrillingly ungentlemanly of you!”

“I am now going to *do* something ungentlemanly,” he said and kissed her full on her soft lips. “Now go out there, Miss Ellie, and knock ’em dead!”

And she did. Watching from the back of the stalls, Brady felt immense pride, but also something else: something deeper, more primitive, and, somehow, purer. Hoover would not have approved; but to hell with Hoover. Miss Ellie Jackson came back a star.

Later that night, having congratulated Miss Ellie on her superb performance, Brady went down to the basement beneath the stage, where he was presently joined by Micky "the Angel" Buonarotti and what seemed at first like a dozen musicians, for they were all carrying instrument cases. However, their pin-striped suits and two-toned shoes were not particularly musicianly, and their features would not have suggested to a casual observer the subtlety and sensitivity of the musical mind. Brady was hardly surprised, when the men began to open their cases, that none of them contained a violin, or even so much as a trombone.

"Okay, you guys, listen up," said Micky Angel. "This dude here is Mr. Nathan Brady. He is a G-Man—" There were murmurs of faint disapproval as Brady stepped forward, revealing himself to the assembled hoods. "But don't you give him no lip, see. I can vouch for him. He is a regular guy, and he is on a special mission from my very good friend, Mr. J. Edgar Hoover, to help us get that sonofabitch Leo the Artichoke who has nabbed my doll and done other goddamn lousy things that no decent guy like you gentlemen here would speak of, let alone do." At this, the assembled men looked at each other with a surprised complacency, and some began to burnish the barrels of their Thompson submachine guns and sawed-offs with handkerchiefs.

"Now we are going to conduct a raid on this lousy sonofabitch and teach him a lesson in honor, because this roach is also trying to muscle in on my territory by building a tunnel under the Roxy and hiring a lot of bums to scare the pants off my employees. Mr. Brady here tells me that Leo the Artichoke has got these lousy bums up in some goddamn scary costumes, like fish or some such, so don't you go running off saying you seen a ghost or any of that *crapola*. Hell, you are Americans, and proud of it, so just go right ahead, do your duty as citizens of the Land of the Free, and fill their lousy guts with a bucketful of lead. Gentlemen, let's go down there and kick some ass!"

This rousing speech received a muted cheer. Then Brady said: "This way, gentlemen, but tread carefully!"—and led the way down into the subterranean chambers.

Micky Angel and his army of mercenaries followed, and if he was a little surprised that Brady did not advise his men to keep silent and stop flashing their flashlights around, he did not voice his misgivings. During their long and complex interview, Brady had managed to inspire confidence: it was one of his gifts.

The men could not help looking around and wondering at the monumental architecture that surrounded them. Brady explained that the galleries in which they were walking had probably been built as water conduits by some of New York's very earliest inhabitants.

"You mean, like redskins?" asked one of the men incredulously.

"Very likely," said Brady shortly. He was becoming increasingly nervous. The plan he had devised was beginning to look more and more foolhardy. He held up his hand for silence.

Faintly at first, but becoming louder by the second, they heard a rhythmical booming sound that echoed through the underground chamber like the throb of a heartbeat. This began to be accompanied by strange half-human cries that even Brady, who had heard them before, found troubling. He could just make out the words—if they can be called words.

"*Rghyyeloi fo Xhon! Rghyyeloi fo Xhon!*"

"Forward, but steady as we go, gentlemen," said Brady who surprised himself by not sounding fearful or hesitant. They had come almost to the vaulted circular chamber with its numerous passageways leading off it and, as they did so, the tension increased. No one spoke, and all the men were checking their ammunition. Brady's flashlight began to make out vague shapes waving and shaking in the distance. He told the men to dip their flashlights until they got to the opening. Confident as he sounded, he realized that from now on he must rely on improvisation. A faint gray-green light came from the lichen, which bearded the slabs of masonry that lined the gallery walls. Brady drew his automatic from its holster and felt for the other weapons at his disposal.

The booming became louder, as did the slap and rustle of great wet feet. Now they were in the vaulted space. Brady flashed his flashlight around it and the others followed suit.

Nothing could have prepared them for what they saw. A great roiling mass of organic life stood before them. The shapes were a grotesque parody of the human, the skin glaucous and scaly, the eyes saucerlike, while the gaping mouths crammed with needle teeth embedded in gray flesh with mucous strings of slime hanging from them were beyond hideous. The beasts stared at their human adversaries. There was a moment of motionless stunned silence as each side contemplated the other. Brady saw the men recoil, not least at the appallingly corrupt stench the creatures gave off, but they steadied themselves and began to aim their weapons. Micky Angel was the one to break the silence.

"Hell! Those are some crazy costumes, all right! I always knew the Artichoke was one mean sonofabitch, but this is booby-hatch time!" There was another short pause during which everyone considered this profound reflection, then Micky said: "Okay! Let 'em have it, guys! Right in their ugly kissers!"

The sound of gunfire in that vaulted, confined space, was all but deafening. The whole cavern was ablaze with the flare of tommy guns and the angry flash of the double-barreled sawed-offs, no sooner discharged than reloaded and blasted again. Brady shot off a clip from his automatic, and then withdrew from the front line to observe better and decide on tactics.

The ichthyoid creatures were falling under the storm of bullets, it was true, and they seemed to have no weapons with which to retaliate, but there were so many of them, and they seemed curiously, flabbily resilient. Even when they had fallen, a part of them seemed to stir and grope forward toward their killers. But the men did not falter once they had begun. The scaly monstrosities seemed to react slowly, but they were staggering toward the line of firing men, stumbling over their fallen comrades, dull but undeterred. Micky's line of defense did not break, but it began to fall back.

Meanwhile, Brady was reloading and considering his next step, when he felt a touch on his arm. He started violently and spun around to find himself staring into the lovely shadowed face of Miss Ellie Jackson.

"Good God what are you doing here, Ellie? Go back at once! This is no place for you!"

"Hell, no! And what gives you the right to tell me what to do, Mr. Brady? I came here to help rescue Miss Billie and that is what I will do, and the hell with you!"

"Okay, Miss Ellie, but, as you may have noticed, things are getting kind of hairy around here. Are you armed in any way? Have you packed a rod?"

"Have I packed a rod? Is the Chief Rabbi Jewish? You bet your sweet ass I've packed a rod, and I can shoot straight. I come from Harlem, remember?" The automatic she removed from her stocking top was an elegant piece, and so was her stocking top, but there was no time for that.

"Very well, Miss Ellie. Keep close to me and watch your back."

"What the hell are those?"

"The Armies of the Night. I'll explain later."

Micky Angel's men were still firing and still bringing down the creatures, but there were so many of them and they kept coming, scrambling over the bodies of their kind whose limbs still twitched and struggled. Two of Micky's men had exhausted the supply of ammunition for their sawed-off shotguns and were using knives.

"You see that passageway opposite you, Miss Ellie? That's what we need to aim at to rescue Billie."

"My God! You mean we have to climb over those bodies?"

"*You* don't have to. You can leave now."

"I don't quit."

"Then keep up with me, and make every bullet count."

"Nathan! Behind you!"

Brady turned and saw a group of the mutant creatures shambling toward them from the long gallery. If there were more of them, Micky and his men would be surrounded and that would be the end, however many they killed. There was only one thing for it.

"Okay, Ellie," said Brady. "You hold them off with your rod while I do this." From the inside of his pocket he drew a thin object wrapped in brown paper, about the size and shape of the baguettes they sold at the French *boulangerie* on Spring Street.

"If this doesn't work, we're sunk. Aim for their eyes," Brady told Ellie.

Ellie began firing and made every shot count. As the creatures fell, they made a strange hissing sound as if air was escaping from their bodies, but still they twitched. Brady tore the brown paper off to reveal the object.

"Christ! What is that?" said Ellie, as she plugged another assailant.

"The hand and forearm of Obadiah Willums, wife-murderer," said Brady. It was indeed, a withered hideous thing, rigid and stiff as if desiccated, but it was an authentic Hand of Glory as stipulated by the *Necronomicon*. "It is a traditional magical instrument which makes any person or persons who hold it invisible."

"Baloney!"

"Quite possibly, but it's our only hope just now. I need a steady hand, so I am going to hold this up and give you my lighter. Now all you have to do is light each of the fingers. They have been prepared with a mixture of tallow and human fat, so they should light easily."

"What the hell is this?"

"Please! Just do as I say! This is our last chance!"

Without further discussion, Ellie took the lighter and applied the flame to the top of each finger in turn, as if to a candelabrum. From each finger shot a pure flame of bright emerald green. Brady made Ellie grasp the withered arm with him and held it aloft.

"Behold!" he shouted. "The Hand of Glory!"

The effect was almost instant. The creatures that had been advancing on Ellie and Brady stopped in their tracks with something that looked like bafflement on their subhuman faces. Brady and Ellie had the sense of being surrounded by a slight mist through which they could see, but which formed a barrier between them and the outer world. One of the creatures, more enterprising than the others, began to grope its way through the mist. He had almost touched the hem of Ellie's skirt when, with her free hand, she raised her automatic up to the beast's head and fired. The head exploded into a starburst of glaucous slime. The other creatures immediately turned tail and ran off howling.

Meanwhile, Micky's men were slowly being overwhelmed. Two men were down and one was struggling to hold off a mass of sharp claws. The sawed-off shotguns had been abandoned as firing pieces due to lack of ammunition and were being used as clubs. The men with tommy guns were eking out their last rounds sparingly. Micky's depleted mercenaries were on the retreat.

Then, suddenly, came a burst of gunfire. Out of one of the tunnels brandishing Thompson submachine guns came six men who immediately began firing on the mutant multitude. They were followed by Leo Vinci, languidly holding his pearl-handled revolver in his right hand, while with the left he occasionally fed his mouth with a Havana cigar.

This sudden incursion with new ammunition was too much, even for the subterranean hordes. With strange grunts and exhalations they began to retreat down various tunnels. Brady heaved a sigh of relief. His plan had succeeded, and his message to Leo the Artichoke that Micky Angel was planning to invade his territory with a whole lot of his actors dressed up as fishlike creatures to scare him had got through.

The last of the wholly alive members of the Armies of the Night were gone and the firing ceased. Across the vaulted hall, in which lay a sprawling, hideous mass of quivering subhumanity, two groups of men faced each other. Micky, with his ten still-able men, though seriously short of ammunition, against Leo Vinci with his six, slightly more adequately equipped.

"So," said Vinci, "Mr. Buonarotti. We meet again." In his mouth, Vinci's cigar glowed and faded, glowed and faded, like a wicked winking eye.

Micky said: "Where's Billie, you punk? You've got my doll, and I want her back."

"Not so fast, lunkhead. What are you doing dressing bums up in stupid fish costumes and coming on my territory?"

"*Your* territory! Baloney! And don't pretend that those fish-men are my bums, because they're your bums. I don't need no fish costumes to protect myself."

"Are you calling me a liar, you sonofabitch?"

"You bet your ass I'm calling you a goddamn liar, Artichoke!" There was an audible gasp from Vinci's associates, and a similar reaction from Micky's. This was followed by an impressive silence before Vinci spoke.

"You just called me Artichoke."

"Sure I did . . . Artichoke!" Another gasp.

"Nobody calls me Artichoke and lives. The last guy who did that is asleep in the East River with a very big rope around his guzzle."

"Well, Mr. Ar-ti-choke," said Micky very deliberately. "I am about to prove the exception."

"Don't be too sure of that, Micky Angel, you big fat sonofabitch!"

Then it all happened in what seemed to Brady and Ellie like a split-second. Vinci had begun to raise his pearl-handled revolver rather languidly, but Micky, who was holding his automatic in his jacket pocket, fired from the hip four times into Vinci's torso. Vinci collapsed, then Micky took the gun out of his pocket (now pretty much destroyed by the blast) and emptied the last two rounds into Vinci's convulsing body.

Vinci's men looked at him in astonishment, then one of them started firing, missing Micky, who had dodged behind his men to reload, but hitting one of the foot soldiers. Then a battle began between Micky's ten men and Vinci's six. Vinci's had the advantage at first because they had more ammunition and firepower, but soon this position was reversed when Micky's men charged their opponents and the struggle became hand-to-hand. Fists flew; knives flashed.

"Come on, Ellie, now's our chance to get Billie. If we can reach that tunnel over there, that should take us to her."

"But we can't get past all these guys beating the hell out of each other."

"We can if we use the Hand of Glory. They won't see us. It's worked so far. Do you want to save Billie or not? This way!" And with both of them still grasping the burning withered limb, they began to skirt the battlefield.

Whether it was the magic or the intensity of the struggle between the two gangs, nobody took any notice of Brady and Miss Ellie Jackson as they edged round the strangely carved walls of cyclopean masonry toward the tunnel. Having reached it, they ran through it. As they did so, the Hand of Glory began to sputter and, with some relief, they both, with one mind, let go of the thing. Then they were hurrying through the door and mounting the staircase that led to Vinci's office.

At the top of the stairs, before they burst in, Brady took out his automatic. Ellie followed directly behind him. In the office they found Billie trussed and gagged in one of Vinci's most elegant and uncomfortable chairs. Behind her stood Mr. Hang, holding a revolver, which he pointed directly at Brady.

"Drop the rod and put up your dukes," said Hang. Brady did as he was told, letting go of the automatic and raising his hands into the air. No sooner had he done so than he heard a bang by his right ear which temporarily deafened him. Then he saw a blood-red flower unfold in the center of Hang's forehead as he dropped heavily to the floor like a sacrificial ox. Miss Ellie had fired her automatic from behind him over Brady's shoulder.

"Good shooting, kid!" said Brady, his right ear still singing.

The next moments were spent untying and ungagging Miss Billie Bernard. The first thing she said when the gag was off was: "Hell! What kept you?" Then she gave vent to a torrent of colorful language aimed at no one in particular. It was strange to see it come from someone who, despite her long ordeal, was still coifed and pearled and gowned for a very classy first-night party in Sardi's that was long over.

At length she calmed down and began to study the huge bulk of Mr. Hang, lying face down on Mr. Vinci's fine Bokhara rug.

"Is the Chink a stiff?" Billie asked.

Ellie prodded Hang's bulk with an elegant foot. "The Chink's a stiff," she said.

"Where's the Artichoke?"

"He's a stiff too," said Brady. "Micky Angel plugged him."

"Well, Hallelujah for that!" said Billie. "Listen, kids, I owe you for this. Anything I can do for you, say the word."

"Well, to begin with," said Brady, "You could tell me why they call Leo Vinci 'the Artichoke.'"

"Don't you know? Jeez, I thought everyone knew. So Leo Vinci is much enamoured of a doll called Nancy Spider who is a hoofer at the Garden of Allah. This is some time before I became Leo's doll, so this is ancient history, right? And Vinci, as you know, is not a guy who takes kindly to any other guy taking a peek at a doll he regards as his, but Miss Nancy Spider in no way sees herself as any guy's exclusive goods. So along comes this dude called Artie 'the Ant' Millstein. And do not ask me why he is called 'the Ant' because you do not want to know. And he is a handsome dude and has plenty of potatoes, whereas Leo, though he too has plenty of potatoes, is no oil painting, except that oil painting by Miss Smart-Ass Lempicka. Well, Artie and Miss Nancy start taking peeks at each other and the next thing you know, they are holding hands at a table in the Garden of Allah between floor shows. So Vinci, he gets mad at this, but rather than blasting Artie with a sawed-off like a normal guy, he gets all subtle. Perhaps he wants to keep the right side of Miss Nancy. Well, he invites this Artie to supper at Luigi's to discuss, as he says, a matter of business, and Artie goes, all unsuspecting. Well, at Luigi's, as you may know, the specialty is a codfish cooked in the South Italian style with a tomato sauce. So they order the fish, then Vinci and two of his loyal colleagues who happen to show up, force the *spécialité de la maison* down Artie's throat, bones and all, with the result desired."

"He makes *Artie choke* to death?"

"You got it. And one and all, excepting everyone who knows of course, thinks it is by natural causes that Artie the Ant puts on the wooden overcoat."

"Well, thank you, Miss Billie."

"It is a pleasure, Mr. Brady, to enlighten such a well-educated and high-toned dude such as yourself. Needless to say, when Mr. Vinci's new sobriquet gets around he is not best pleased, for Leo 'the Artichoke' Vinci is not by nature a guy with a big sense of humor. And now he is no more—God rest his soul—plugged by my ever-loving Micky Angel. Listen kids, I am busting to split from this lousy joint. If I don't get out of this goddamn wet ballgown and into some very dry Martinis eftsoons, I will go apeshit."

III

March 13th, 1937 (from the diary of H. P. Lovecraft)

I write this from my comfortable bed in the Jane Brown Memorial Hospital in Providence, where I am currently undergoing tests and sundry examinations for my ailments. Aunt Annie seems content that I should be here, for of late I had been, as she put it in her demotic way, "looking rather peeky." This is hardly surprising given the severe physical and spiritual ordeal I have lately undergone.

Three days ago Mr. Brady called on me and asked me if I had considered the matter of purloining the *Necronomicon* from the Miskatonic Library. I told him I had, but that it was a venture both morally dubious and fraught with risk, whereupon he replied that no venture was morally dubious nor too risky when the very safety of the United States of America was at stake. As a patriot I saw the force of his argument; as a gentleman, I sighed but assented. After some prolonged discussion we settled upon that very night as the time for our adventure. I protested that I was not in a fit condition for an escapade of this nature but he insisted I accompany him, for only I could identify the volume in question and knew precisely where it was to be located in Miskatonic's labyrinthine *bibliotheke*.

A gibbous moon was riding high in a firmament laced with silver cloud as we drove in Mr. Brady's Packard through Arkham County towards the Miskatonic University. When we reached Dunwich, Brady stopped the car and offered me a slug of bourbon from his flask. I declined, for I never touch intoxicating liquor, but asked if he had any of Dr. Bogusteen's Preparation on him. He said he had not and that, besides, we needed to keep all our wits about us for the coming venture. As we went over once again our strategy

I heard the whip-poor-wills making their eldritch cries in a nearby brake. Having concluded our deliberations we proceeded on our way, arriving at the outer limits of the Miskatonic campus at a quarter after midnight.

The gates of the campus had been locked for nigh on two hours and there was a high wall surrounding the whole, but Mr. Brady had come well-accoutred with grappling hooks and a rope ladder, in addition to carrying on his back a haversack containing other tools to facilitate breaking and entering. Despite these useful adventitious aids, I found the climb over the high flint wall arduous, and needed encouragement, sometimes amounting to threat, to complete the task. We descended into a belt of trees on the other side of the wall whence we could see but not be seen. I myself had selected the spot where we might scale the walls undetected and Mr. Brady commended me on my excellent choice of location.

Before us, glaucous under the pale moonlight, lay a great expanse of grass, sometimes used, I believe, by the alumni for football and other recreations. Beyond it reared the gaunt and Gothick edifice of the famed Miskatonic Library, looking ancient, monastic, and somewhat eerie in the lunar effulgence.

I had warned Mr. Brady about the guard dogs which roamed the campus at night, ready to apprehend the intruder or the errant sophomore. He said he had anticipated their possible intervention, but, fortunately there seemed to be no evidence for their being in the vicinity. Nevertheless we proceeded with caution, crossing the football field on swift but silent feet. Arriving at the foot of the library, I directed him first to the alarm bell on the wall of the building. With an agility that astonished me, he climbed the rusticated masonry on the lower courses of the edifice, and, by clinging to the wall with one hand, with the other he succeeded in cutting the wires which attached the bell to the system within. Back on the ground he took from his haversack what he told me was a "jemmy" with which he forced open one of the library's casement windows.

We found ourselves, by an irony which did not escape me, in the "law" section of the library. There we crouched under one of the tables and, with the aid of a flashlight, consulted the rough sketch map I had made of the place. We thought it best to proceed, as far as possible, unlit by artificial light, and, though the moon was not full, its illumination via the great Gothick windows was enough to help us on our way. But the library is vast and the way to the Camera Librorum Prohibitorum where the *Necronomicon* was kept, long and involved. Many were the times we had to stop in the protecting shadow of a wall of books to consult the map. A library by day or well-lit is to me the most welcoming of places, but in the dark of night it assumes an aspect of menace. Several times I fancied I heard the tread of furtive feet behind me, but I dismissed this as idle imagining and pressed on, though I noticed Mr. Brady once or twice cast a hasty glance behind him.

At length by devious ways and by descending several flights of steps into the vaulted cellarage of the library we arrived before a low Gothick doorway of heavy oak bound with iron on which the following was inscribed:

C L P [for *camera librorum prohibitorum* or
"chamber of forbidden books"]
STRICTLY NO ENTRY EXCEPT BY EXPRESS PERMISSION
OF THE PRINCIPAL AND GUARDIANS

The arch which formed the doorway had as its keystone a grinning head of such menacing and malignant appearance that we were both taken aback and around it was carved the following inscription:

CAVE, QUAESITOR, CUSTODEM ENIM
SUPER HANC PORTAM POSUI

The inscription, translated means: *Seeker, beware! For I have set a guardian over this doorway.* Of what nature the guardian was or whether this was a mere idle threat we did not pause to consider, but neither the inscription nor the carved keystone had been present on my last visit to the library.

From his haversack Mr. Brady took a curious metal instrument which, he told me, had been developed in the FBI laboratories, but which looked to me like a version of the old skeleton key. This he applied to the lock, which after several tentative turns yielded and the door swung open.

The small vaulted chamber that revealed itself to our torchlight looked at first like a kind of mausoleum. It was windowless and painted black. On all walls were shelves housing a number of ancient leather-bound volumes as well as several iron-bound muniment boxes, no doubt containing loose manuscripts. What gave me something of a shock, I must own, was that in the centre of the room was a small wooden table covered in a red velvet cloth fringed with tarnished silver thread, and on the cloth reposed a heavy volume bound in black and heavily corrugated leather. I recognised it at once as being the Miskatonic's copy of the *Necronomicon*. It was as if the book itself had been expecting us.

Latent feelings of terror and misgiving, which had been present with me as soon as we entered the building, suddenly became urgent. I turned round to see the door of the chamber beginning to swing shut. I hurled myself upon it, anxious beyond reason that it should not close upon us and managed just in time to interpose myself between the door and its frame. My slender body felt that it was being crushed; yet the air was close and still, and I could feel no trace of a breath of wind which could account for the door's movement. Brady picked up the volume, thrust it in his haversack, and then with me forced the door open. Once we were through it closed with a deafening clang and we were horrified to see two heavy steel bolts descend vertically from either side of the keystone and settle themselves over the door. Had I let it shut Brady and I would have been immured.

It was then that something like a panic seized us both and we began to run. Brady, being now burdened by the considerable weight of the book on his back, could go no faster than I. Several times we had to stop reluctantly to catch our breath and in those dreadful moments the silence was punctured not only by the gasping of our exhausted lungs but also a strange pattering, rustling sound as if someone or something were in pursuit. Sooner than we would have wished we felt compelled to run on. Several times we lost our way among the dark and brooding stacks, which compounded our terror.

At last we reached the law library and the open casement. Through the great Gothick windows we could see wind-driven clouds racing across the moon, sometimes obscuring it entirely and plunging the law library's great hall into Stygian darkness. The pattering sound came closer, and was in the hall as we scrambled our way to the open window.

We had reached the window when Brady, in a moment of absurd folly, turned round and shone the torch back into the obscurity of the library. It caught a whitish object. I saw it for barely a second but the memory of it will remain with me til the day of my death and—who knows?—beyond. It was roughly human in shape and monstrously tall. The head, like the body, was featureless and entirely composed of what looked like scraps of paper or parchment on which signs and sigils had been inscribed. The thing was forever shifting and turning as if a whirl of wind were keeping it in shape. On it came rustling dreadfully and intent on some nameless harm. Brady turned me about and bodily pushed me through the casement.

I collapsed in a heap outside. Meanwhile I saw him pick up a sheet of paper from one of the desks, squeeze it into a ball, light it with his lighter and then hurl it at the oncoming spectre. It burst into flames and only then did Brady follow me through the window.

We began to race across the playing field towards the belt of trees and the wall, but our peril was not over yet. I heard the barking of dogs and then I saw, galloping over the grass towards us, the shapes of several massive hounds, bullmastiffs by the look of them. They gained on us rapidly but we managed to reach the belt of trees. Brady shouted to me that I should climb the wall first while he held off the hounds, but I said I was too weak to climb by myself and needed to be hauled up from the top of the wall. The dogs were almost on us and I also saw several human figures hurrying towards us in the distance.

One of the animals, outrunning the others, leapt upon us but Brady struck it on the nose with a densely folded copy of *The Arkham Observer*, upon which it slunk away whining. The rolled-up newspaper, he later informed me, was a sovereign remedy against aggressive canines, a stratagem he had learned during his boyhood in Maine.

Brady climbed up the wall and tossed his rucksack containing the book over the other side. Then he told me to take hold of the rope that was hanging down and he would drag me up. I caught the rope but just then I felt a sharp pain in my ankle. It had been seized in the jaws of one of the mastiffs. I shook it off, losing my shoe in the process. Brady by this time was pulling me steadily up the wall, but then another of the hounds leapt up and seized hold of the seat of my pants. I was, perhaps fortuitously, wearing a pair of particularly old pants—and nearly all my garments are somewhat threadbare—so that the cloth ripped easily and the mastiff fell to earth with nothing but a piece of old tweed and a few minor abrasions on my posterior for his pains.

At last I was pulled to safety and sat for a moment atop the wall while the dogs yelped and barked beneath it. I looked across to the library and saw to my horror that the interior was illumined by a sheet of yellow flame. Then Brady was enjoining me to hurry. I climbed over the other side of the wall and dropped onto the soft turf beneath. Then, bruised and panting, my lower garments in a state of hideous disarray, I staggered over to the Packard whose engine Brady had already begun to stir into roaring life. The next moment we were speeding away from the Miskatonic along the midnight roads of Arkham County.

March 13, 1937

That morning, Miss Billie Bernard had invited Brady and Miss Ellie Jackson over to her apartment (lavishly paid for and equipped by Micky "the Angel" Buonarotti) for cocktails. Neither Brady nor Miss Ellie were in the habit of drinking dry Martinis at such an early hour, but they thought it churlish to make their reservations known. After her ordeal, Billie had been off sick from the production of *Zip Ahoy!* but she had summoned them to announce that her absence from the show would become permanent and that Miss Ellie Jackson, formerly the understudy, was now confirmed in the part of Ruby Emerald. As the show was now a popular and critical success with Miss Ellie in the role, not even Micky Angel had raised objections.

"Micky has asked me to be his ever-loving wife," said Billie, "and I have agreed. He may be a big sap, but he's my big sap. As for the show business, you can keep it, and I hope it keeps fine for you, Miss Ellie. Me, I am going to have six kids, and make cupcakes and become a member of the Manhattan ladies sewing circle. Hell, I might even start going to church, for Micky Angel is very big on the Pope, whom he regards as a regular guy. Though how the Pope sees Micky Angel might be not quite so dandy. Mr. Brady, I wanted to thank you properly for your rescue of me from the clutches of the Artichoke, and as a token of my thanks I am giving you this, which may help you in your further career. I obtained it from my ever-loving Micky Angel, who does not know that I have it, and if you ever breathe a word to him or anyone that I have it, I will personally use you for target practice, and though no Annie Oakley like Miss Ellie here, I am also no beginner with a betsy."

She handed him a thin brown Manila envelope, which Brady immediately put in his inside jacket pocket. When he had done so, Miss Ellie took hold of his hand and squeezed it. He squeezed back.

"You have my word I will not split on you ever, Miss Billie." said Brady.

Billie smiled on them both. "You may now kiss the bride," she said.

March 14, 1937

The train had just left Pennsylvania Station, New York, bound for Washington, D.C., when Brady, alone in a compartment, opened the envelope:

It contained two glossy full-plate photographs. One of them, a flash-photograph, showed Mr. Hoover wearing a sparkling sequined ball gown (oddly similar to the one Miss Billie had been wearing on the night of her abduction), an elaborately curled blonde wig perched on his toad-like head. As female impersonations go, it was unconvincing in the extreme; Mr. Hoover's customary swarthy scowl was the antithesis of feminine charm. The second seemed to have been taken clandestinely through a window, but it was quite clear enough for Brady to make out Hoover, still in his ball gown, engaged in a very intimate act with his assistant director, Clyde Tolson, who was *not* wearing a ball gown, or anything else, for that matter. Brady shuddered at the thought of ever having to make use of these striking pieces of evidence, as no doubt Micky Angel had, but he decided to keep them safe. Along with the purloined *Necronomicon*, they would be put in a very secure place indeed.

The photographs did have one almost immediate effect on Brady. When, later that day, he knocked on the door of Hoover's office in Washington, Brady did so without even a trace of nervousness or apprehension. Having heard the word "Come!" he entered directly and found Hoover standing by the window staring out at the Capitol Building. Brady could not help, just for a second, re-clothing him in his mind's eye in that sequined ball gown and grotesque wig. When Hoover turned toward him, he must have noticed some change in Brady's manner because he took a step back, then mounted the dais where his desk stood.

"Ah, Brady. Good man." His tone was slightly hesitant; it might even have contained a touch of obsequiousness. "So," he went on, "we nailed those commie bums, but you know and I know that it doesn't stop there. You are Agent Number One of the Human Protection League and I want you to help me to recruit a whole bunch more. We've got one hell of a fight on our hands, have we not, Mr. Brady?"

"We have, sir!"

"Good man! You've got spunk, Brady, and I like a man with spunk. Have you any further suggestions for recruits, then?"

"Just one at present, Mr. Hoover."

"I'm listening, Brady."

"Mr. Lovecraft, sir."

"Lovecraft! That cockamamy sonofabitch! You want *him*?"

"He has been very useful to us so far. Tomorrow he is undergoing an operation at the Jane Brown Memorial Hospital in Providence. It is for cancer of the small intestine, but we are hopeful of a successful outcome. If that occurs, I suggest that we relocate him to a safe place where he can continue his invaluable researches. He has yet to decipher the three Voorish Invocations, but given time, he will do so, and that may prove invaluable in our fight."

"And this Lovecraft guy agrees to this?"

"He suggested it himself. It appeals to his reclusive nature. His Aunt Anne will be suborned and we will, of course, supply him with all the comforts and resources he requires, but he is not a man of extravagant tastes."

"You seem to have got this all worked out."

"I apologize, Mr. Hoover, if I have over-anticipated your intentions."

"Well I was going to put forward something on those lines myself, so consider yourself pardoned, Brady. Mr. Lovecraft can become officially HPL Agent Number Two."

"An excellent idea, Mr. Hoover."

"It *is* an excellent idea, Brady. These excellent ideas come to me all the time. That's why I am the director. Bear that in mind, young man. Now about the Roxy Palace, you're sure those commie bums—Armies of the Night, or whatever they call themselves—have been eliminated?"

"For the time being."

"Consider yourself commended, Brady. You hit a hole in one there. You and your lady-friend who seems to have helped out. What was her name? Ellie?"

"As a matter of fact, sir, Miss Ellie Jackson and I were thinking of getting married."

"Well, I can't stop you, Brady. And at least it shows you're not a goddamn fag. But if I were you I'd take up golf instead. You can't do both golf *and* marriage in my experience, and golf's one hell of a lot easier to get right."

"Thank you for the advice, Mr. Hoover, sir. I'll bear it in mind."

"The Eyrie," Weird Tales *Vol. 29, No. 6, June 1937*

> Sad indeed is the news that tells us of H. P. Lovecraft's death on March 15, in the Jane Brown Memorial Hospital in Providence, Rhode Island. He was a titan of weird and fantastic literature, whose literary achievements and impeccable craftsmanship were acclaimed throughout the English-speaking world. He was only forty-six years of age, yet had built up a following such as few authors ever had. As a child he was a prodigy. He learned the alphabet at two years of age, and early developed a liking for old-fashioned and fantastic books. Always a weak and nervous child, he managed to stick out four years in high school at the cost of a breakdown which kept him from college and put him virtually out of the world for a number of years. About 1920 his health began of itself to effect that mending which specialists for thirty years had sought in vain to bring about; and shortly afterward he began traveling, visiting new places and meeting old friends whom he had contacted through his wide correspondence. He had a masterful command of several languages; and, as E. Hoffman Price once remarked, "There is scarcely an artistic or cultural subject on which H. P. Lovecraft cannot learnedly hold forth, and with an unfailing hold on the attention of the listener." As for his hobbies, let us quote Price again: "His hobbies? This is not a catalogue; let me short-circuit that by saying that the range must be from architecture to zoology." Between 1917 and 1936 Lovecraft wrote forty-six stories, each of which is a tour

de force in itself. He invented the Lovecraft mythology (the Necronomicon, Abdul Alhazred, etc.), which has been adopted by many other writers of weird fiction. With all his studies, his capabilities, his wide knowledge, and his vast intelligence, H. P. Lovecraft was a kindly, generous human being, modest as to his own work, and ever ready to lend a helping hand to others. He carried on a voluminous correspondence with over seventy-five weird-fiction enthusiasts, and endeared himself to all of them with his kind patience and generosity. His death is a serious loss to weird and fantastical fiction; but to the editors of Weird Tales the personal loss takes precedence. We admired him for his great literary achievements, but we loved him for himself; he was a courtly and noble gentleman, and a dear friend. Peace be to his shade!

FOUR

The Olde Fellowes

CARL WAS PUTTING HIS jacket on when his wife came into the apartment's small, frigid bathroom. She tutted, stood in front of him, and deftly made his tie look the way it should. With a pretty-recently ironed blue shirt and an only slightly-creased black suit Carl looked as smart as he was ever going to, though he'd been told more than once that he'd come out of the womb rumpled and there wasn't anything he could do about it. Usually by his wife.

"It has to be now?"

"It does."

"Even though you know what's cooking?"

Michelle would be the first to admit that in general her cooking was workmanlike at best, but her famous meatloaf—learned at her mother's knee, doubtless with plenty of contradictory advice from her grandmother, the crankiest woman on God's earth—was the best Carl ever expected to taste. There was sage in it, or something. His stomach had been growling the whole time he was getting ready. "Even though. You'll leave me some, right?"

"Stranger things have happened."

"Not many, with the way the kid eats now."

"I'm certainly not promising anything."

Carl Jr. was at the table in the cramped living room, puzzling over homework by the light of a small lamp. Michelle refused to use the overhead lights on the grounds the harsh glare made the rooms look tired and sad and low-rent. She was right. This way, the room was almost cozy. With little choices like that she made a big difference in their lives.

Carl Jr. looked even more puzzled when he saw his father was headed out. "Where are you going?"

"Work."

"But it's nighttime."

"It's only six o'clock."

"It's dark, and that makes it nighttime."

Carl conceded this. His son had recently developed a pedantic streak. Apparently that was common at around nine years old, especially in boys. They suddenly understood the importance and precision of the way words structured the world, and cottoned onto the idea that they might control it too. "You have two tasks while I'm out, okay?"

"Depends what they are."

"Finish your homework, and leave me some food." Carl Jr. made a noncommittal sound. "Seriously. On both. But mainly the meatloaf. Okay?"

His son smiled, suddenly, the kind of smile you only ever see from your own child, and when they're still young. Not a judged or chosen expression, a smile of a particular kind, not a genre of smile or a smile that's supposed to reassure or convince or mislead or do any kind of job at all. Just a kid's face, reflecting what's fleetingly inside, to the person who's half of their universe. "No," he said.

Carl laughed and gave him a hug. "Love you, kiddo."

"You too," his son said, turning back to his homework. "But I'm still not leaving any meatloaf."

As he left, Carl turned back and saw his wife setting a plate on the counter, and knew she'd put some food aside for him. "Not much longer," he said.

"Good."

"And I won't be late," he said.

"Also good."

But he was, and he never saw either of them again.

When he stepped outside the building it was dark and cold. The McCray was a looming Victorian on top of Beach Hill, looking down toward the ocean half a mile away. Built as a private house fifty years back and for a while the town's social hub, then a high-end hotel, its glory days were long behind it—and you got the sense the building knew this. The outside needed repainting, badly. The gardens were overgrown. The rooms were all by-the-week rentals now, and Carl was looking forward to not renting one of them any more. Michelle was too. People tended to assume that because she was pretty and quiet she was also dumb. They were wrong. In addition to being whip-smart she was good at listening, at making people feel comfortable enough to talk in the first place—and with the intuition to know who'd be worth talking to. It was Michelle who'd heard about what happened four years before, in 1933, when a female resident shot her ex-employer on the grounds for reasons that were never established, and how thirty years before, one of the mansions on the next street had seen a retired army major killing both his daughter and himself on the anniversary of his wife's death. Not to mention that the old woman who lived in the corner room on the first floor of the McCray had even told Michelle that back in 1908 plumbers doing work under the street outside had uncovered the remains of an actual Indian burial ground.

Carl didn't know whether that last was true or not, but Beach Hill had a weird vibe either way. The whole damned town did. Sure, it was attractive, with unspoiled beaches, seventy miles of emptiness north until San Francisco, and forty miles of the same south until Monterey. There was a fishing industry, mainly in the hands of Italian families, and overall the town was weathering the Depression better than some, helped by the "Suntan Special"—a Southern Pacific train that rounded up families from Palo Alto and San Jose and brought them over the mountains to spend their money every weekend at the popular boardwalk. After six months in town, Carl still didn't like or trust Santa Cruz, however, and he hoped that—if tonight's business was successful—they could soon be on their way. He didn't know where. Somewhere. Anywhere. The League would tell him when the time came.

He got in his car and drove along the steep road down the inland side of the hill, and up through the center of town along Pacific. A few miles along the highway and then a turn into the lower slopes of the hills which ringed the town. That was one of the strange things about Santa Cruz—the way how, surrounded as it was by either mountains, wilderness or sea, it could seem like an island, cut off from the rest of California and even the United States in general. The area seemed to attract an unusual number of crackpots too—like William Riker, who'd bought a hundred and forty acres on the other side of the summit and established a community called Holy City, based around a set of half-baked ideals he called the Perfect Christian Divine Way. On a practical level this primarily seemed to involve selling groceries and cheap gas to people headed one way or the other over the mountains, although the tiny town also had a zoo and an observatory and a bunch of other weird shit. Though Riker preached abstinence in most things, he had a tendency to drive his car off the road while drunk, and—if you were in the know—also plied a discrete trade in other methods of intoxication, examples of which were lodged in the inside pocket of Carl's jacket.

It was Carl's job to know people, and know things, and get things done. And tonight, more than anything, it was his job to change someone's mind. But first he had to find her—and Marion Hollins could be hard to track down.

He arrived at Pasatiempo ten minutes later. Pulled up at the gate and winked at the guy in the booth.

"How's it hanging, Jimmy?"

"Cold," Jimmy said. "Cold, is how."

"You got that right. Know where she is?"

Jimmy shrugged, looking even vaguer than usual. Jimmy was in his midtwenties and had the demeanor of a guy who'd be performing low-level tasks in a booth for the rest of his life, and be happy with the arrangement so long as not much in the way of thought was asked of him. It wasn't his job to know where the boss was at any given moment. To know, or care. "Around. I guess. Here, or there. Hell, you know what she's like."

"I do." Carl reached in his jacket, glanced back along the road, and tossed something to Jimmy.

He caught it—barely—and made the small package disappear into his pocket. "You're a gent."

"Use it wisely."

Jimmy raised the bar and Carl drove under it and up the long, curving road toward the clubhouse. He'd try there first, though the thing about Marion Hollins was that she was a body in constant motion. You wouldn't expect that if you saw her from a distance. She was forty-five, stocky, plain to the point of homely. Though by all accounts one of the best female golfers in the country—and thus the world—she didn't look designed for movement or attention. When you got closer you saw the truth was very different. She had an aura. Carl didn't know how you'd put it any other way. She made you feel the night was always young and that there were forever good times to be had. She was smart. She took risks. She was fun.

She made things happen too. Back in 1927 she'd been horseback riding in the hills of what was then the Rancho Carbonero—owned by William Bickle, a character who'd allegedly buried treasure on the property from he and his brother's privateering activities (needless to say, never found, though that didn't stop people from looking)—and decided it would make the ideal spot for a country club. Funded by a lucky score in oil a couple of years later, she made it happen: hiring a guy she'd previously used down in Carmel for Sam Morse's celebrated golf course at Pebble Beach, but keeping so close an eye on the process that not a single tree was allowed to be felled without her permission. Having spent a fair bit of time with Marion over the last months, Carl absolutely believed the story.

He parked up and walked into the club. Soon as he was inside he was hit by the noise. People talking loud and hard. A jazz combo in the corner, belting out "Sing, Sing, Sing." Raucous laughter. Red faces. A good time being had by all. Carl spotted a familiar face on the other side of the room and made his way through the throng to a table in the corner where a woman sat at a small table by herself.

"Good evening, Miss Pickford," he said.

Mary looked up. Her eyes were hazy and her voice a little slurred. "Mr. Unger. A pleasure, as always."

"Alone this evening?"

"My husband is . . ." She looked around the room. As usual—Pasatiempo hosted everyone from movie stars like Pickford and Charles "Buddy" Rogers to the Vanderbilts and other notables—nobody in the room stared at her. Marion had a knack of getting people to rub along happily, even mixing the Hollywood crowd with East Coast socialites, a combination that didn't usually come off. At Pasatiempo everyone knew to play it cool in the presence of fame, and that what happened in the club stayed there—whether it be someone seen leaving a cabin in the dead of night (and one that didn't hold their own spouse) or a rich young scion lying drunk in the bushes to the side of the 16th fairway. "Actually, I have no idea where he is. Nor, at the moment, if I'm abso*lutely* honest, do I much care."

Normally, as part of his loosely defined role at the club, Carl would have spent a while talking with Mary. Since her divorce from Douglas Fairbanks the year before, she'd not been quite the cheerful presence people remembered in the past—despite her marriage in June to Rogers, yet another Tinseltown actor (nobody expected it to last). Right now, however, he didn't have the time.

"Have you seen Marion?"

"Of course," Mary said. "You know dear Marion. Sit in one place for long enough and she's bound to stride past."

"Recently?"

Pickford frowned, looking a lot like one of the curly-haired moppets she'd made her career portraying. Like that, and even more drunk. "No," she said. "Now I come to think of it, not for hours. Why don't you sit with me, and we'll have a glass of Champagne and wait for her together."

"Can't, I'm afraid."

"Aha. Some secret mission to perform. Forever working in mysterious ways."

"I help things run smoothly, that's all."

"You're a dark one, Carl. Well, when you find her majesty please tell her that I'm rather bored and require her to come and get disreputably drunk with me."

"I'll do that."

On his way past the bar, Carl told them to send more Champagne to Miss Pickford's table. As he left the clubhouse he glanced back and watched the scene for a moment. All over the country people were on their uppers, struggling to get by, pecking out a living in the dust bowl. Starving, in some cases. You wouldn't know it from the atmosphere in here. At Pasatiempo the party was always in full swing, and you could believe that it always would be.

If you didn't know what Carl knew, of course.

He walked quickly along dimly lamp-lit walkways through the trees toward Marion's house. She'd called it "Sleepy Hollow," and Carl knew she was well-read enough for this not to be an accident.

As he turned up the path toward it he heard something, and stopped. Stood absolutely still for a moment. The noise of leaves rustling in a light, cold breeze. The quiet sound of his own breath, until he held it. But something else.

He turned, looked out into the darkness. In the distance there was a twinkle of light outside someone else's door. Between there and here, an inky emptiness. And a silence that was not quite silence.

"I know you're not there," Carl said.

The silence became more silent. The darkness a little blacker. The lamps along the path seemed to contract, to become smaller and brittle and wan. Carl felt suddenly tired and old and a little afraid. Not because something was there. There wasn't. *That* was the problem. This was an absence, a pulling-out of everything that should be present. He'd learned over the years to sense this lack. Others would feel it merely as a dip in energy, a deep feeling that things were not okay and might never be again. They would turn and look behind, convinced something was there, too, relieved when nothing was visible to notice that the shadows weren't in the right places. Carl had felt this in other locations in the world, but nowhere as strongly as this part of California, and specifically here in Pasatiempo. The place was not right. He believed that Marion knew this, too, at some level. He hoped so.

He did not show his fear.

He turned and walked up the path to the house. The sound of music came from somewhere inside, but he had to stand with his finger on the push-bell for three minutes before he saw a shape approaching. Even through the frosted glass he could tell it wasn't Marion. It was far too slim, and moving too slowly.

The door opened. "About time," Kitty said. "For goodness sake."

"About time for what?"

The girl blinked. Attractive, but pale, and too thin. An expensive dress, on backward. "I called you hours ago."

"No, Kitty. You called me two days ago. I came. You didn't call me tonight."

She blinked. Looked confused. "Oh. Then why are you here?"

"I'm looking for Marion."

"She's not home. At least I don't think so. I hope she's not, for sure."

Carl gently pushed past her and into the house. As usual it looked well overdue for a visit by the maid. Marion didn't care too much about such things. She also received regular houseguests. Other golfers, ne'er-do-well relatives come to sponge off her success, the society set of San Jose and San Francisco. She was welcoming, and always tried to help people out. Kitty was the current case in point, the wayward daughter of a friend back East. She'd been here five weeks and had spent most of that time either drunk or stoned. Marion hauled her out of bed every morning, made her go play golf or try to learn polo—Marion's other passion, at which she was also apparently one of the most accomplished women in the world. Kitty actually looked a good deal better than when she'd arrived, though still a long way from the straight and narrow.

Carl walked downstairs to the main living area. A few people were spread around the space, dancing vaguely to the gramophone in the corner—also playing Goodman's "Sing, Sing, Sing," as though this house were part of the same scene up at the clubhouse—or drinking cocktails out on the terrace. He recognized a few of them, without enthusiasm. Party people. No sign of Marion, naturally. Stoned though Kitty was, she'd have been likely to notice Hollins if she'd been in the same room.

Carl quickly searched the rest of the house. No sign. When he started back the other way he realized Kitty had floated along behind him. "She's not here," he said.

"That's as well," Kitty said. "She doesn't like Max, much. Or Jillian. Thinks they're a bad influence on me."

"They're a bad influence on everyone," Carl said.

"Do you . . . do you have anything for me? I mean, I know I didn't call. But do you?"

Carl raised an eyebrow. "Already?"

She shrugged girlishly, for a moment looking about the same age as Carl's son. "Some of the fellows upstairs . . . Marion's always generous. I like being generous too."

Many people do, when it's other people's money. Carl pulled out the second of the small packets he'd brought with him. The contents had been cut—Carl had meticulously performed this task himself, at home on the kitchen table—making it a little weaker than his previous delivery. He'd been doing the same, gradually lessening the dose, for three weeks. Marion knew about this. Kitty didn't.

"You're a doll, Carl."

"Keep it to yourself this time. I'm not doing this for the freeloaders upstairs."

"You got it."

Back in the living room Carl helped himself to a scotch. He took it out onto the terrace and stood right behind a couple there until the woman took the hint and wandered away. The man took his own good time in turning to look at Carl. Max Fleming's tie was loose and he had a cocktail in one hand and a cigarette in the other.

"Ah, Carl. I'd say it's a pleasure, but then we both know that I'd be guilty of a mistruth."

"That's an old one, Max."

"So let's dispense with the niceties. They're hardly your forte, after all. What do you want?"

"Stay away from Kitty."

"Pardon me?"

"You heard. Stay away. Don't sleep with her. Don't take what's hers. Don't encourage her to behave any more badly than she's already bound to."

"Are you serious?"

"Do I look serious?"

"And what would happen, should I choose to ignore these wholly inappropriate requests?"

"I'd break your fucking face," Carl said, evenly.

Max was momentarily shocked into something like sobriety. Nonetheless he took a leisurely sip of his drink and looked away toward the woods before responding. "I think you may have forgotten who you're talking to."

"No," Carl said, keeping his voice pleasant and low. "And that's why I'd do it. I wouldn't have to. One word from me and you'd never be allowed in Pasatiempo again. I may do that anyway. But I'd break your face purely because someone's going to do it sooner or later and it may as well be me. Not least because I'd really enjoy it."

Max looked Carl up and down and realized the man meant what he said. He rolled his eyes. "Whatever you say. One must stay on the right side of the help, after all."

"That's better. Any idea where Marion is?"

"I suspect she's left the reservation."

"What do you mean?"

"An hour ago. Actually, probably two. I was here on the terrace. Saw her striding by in the twilight, *thump thump thump*, as she does. Such an ungainly woman."

"Where was she headed?"

Max leaned back against the railing, and pointed. "Toward the gate."

Carl nodded. "Remember what I said. I mean it."

As he turned to go, something happened. A noise, so low that it was more like a sensation, a folding over in the gut. A juddering, brief rumble.

From inside the house, the sound of the chandelier tinkling, and then a couple of small smashing sounds as glasses fell off tables, or perhaps from someone's hand. When the tremor was over, there was a moment of leaden quiet. Then conversation started up quickly again.

"Goodness," Max said. "That's the second in three days. Mother Earth is rather out of sorts, evidently."

Carl walked quickly away. On the way out he passed a room where Kitty lay sprawled on a bed. She turned her head slowly when she heard him. Her eyes were far away.

"Goodbye, angel," she said.

He drove up to the kiosk. Jimmy saw who it was and pulled the lever to raise the bar. Carl didn't drive on, however. He sat looking straight ahead. After a few minutes Jimmy came out of the kiosk and over to his window.

"Everything okay?"

"Not sure," Carl said.

"What's the problem?"

"I don't know that either."

"Not really getting you, Carl."

"Just talked to a guy. Now, the guy's a world-class jerk, so I don't know. But he said he saw Marion headed this way a couple hours ago. She was on foot, but I know she often leaves her Duesenberg just over there because I've heard you bitch about it a hundred times. The car's not there now and it wasn't when I got here either, come to think of it. So I'm wondering whether she left before I arrived."

"Right," Jimmy said, quickly. "She did. A while back. I was going to tell you."

"When."

"Now."

"Why didn't you tell me earlier?"

"To be honest with you, Carl—I forgot. Until you'd gone in. Then I thought maybe she'd come back through the other gate, so you'd find her anyway and it probably didn't matter. Sorry, man."

Carl looked up at him. "You been smoking on duty, Jimmy? Did you maybe slip away into the trees this afternoon, and take a toke or two?"

Jimmy looked sheepish. "That may have happened."

Carl kept looking at him. He knew that though Jimmy was not smart, he understood very well that the packages of reefer that came his way were not free, and that Unger expected something in return. Intel. Information on who came through the gate, and who went out, and with whom. Any other bits of skinny that might come in handy.

"I'm sorry, Carl. Seriously. Sorry."

"You aren't, Jimmy," Carl said. "Not sorry enough, anyway. But you will be if it happens again."

He wound up his window and drove away.

It took him twenty minutes to get back to Santa Cruz, another ten to get across town to the west side. There he turned up High Street, the road leading to the upper part of town, an area sparsely occupied, a few small farmhouses. Then ever farther uphill along Spring Street, so called because it ran past one of the natural watercourses that had fed the gardens of the original Spanish Mission, without which there wouldn't have been a town.

At the top stood Windy Hill Farm, quite a different enterprise to the smallholdings he'd passed. A few fancy cars were parked along the street. None of them Marion's, but Carl got out and walked up the drive anyway. Fifty yards along was a cluster of buildings, an interior courtyard behind an ornate copper gate. Well-kept and grand, Arts and Crafts–style. Stables on the side for horses and dogs. The man of the house was a renowned breeder of both. But it wasn't him that Carl wanted to talk to.

When he got to the door he heard the sounds of restrained revelry within, and wondered if he was going to spend the entire evening dipping into other people's good times. Perhaps his entire life. It felt that way tonight. It was coming up for eight o'clock. There would be—if his son hadn't gotten to it—a plate of meatloaf and mashed potatoes waiting for him back at the apartment. He could go home, eat, spend time reading on the couch. Go to bed like a normal person. Get up the next day. Go do a regular job.

These thoughts floated across his mind like a story about someone else. He pressed the doorbell.

Deming Wheeler opened it a few moments later. At nearly sixty he remained a trim, imposing figure. Fitter than most men half his age, an expert horseman, the man responsible for bringing polo to Santa Cruz.

"Carl," he said, warmly. "Didn't realize you were expected tonight."

"I'm not, sir," Carl said. "It's more of a business matter. I'm looking for Marion."

"Aha. They seek her here, they seek her there, eh? Hard to keep up with, Marion. Well, she's not here, I'm afraid. Or not yet, at least. But come in, come in."

Carl followed Deming into the house, grateful for the warmth. It wasn't the first time he'd been in Windy Hill, nor the first time he'd reflected how much he'd like to own somewhere like it himself one day, however unlikely the prospect. Wood paneling and subtle brickwork. Every single thing within vision—furniture, glassware, paintings, the rugs, vases of flowers—chosen by a person of taste. A long window on the other side yielding an extraordinary view over the lights in the distant downtown, and on a good night, straight across the bay to Monterey.

A few prosperous-looking folk were gathered around the large stone fireplace. Several sounded like they were speaking French. Members of the international polo set, most likely. A couple watched Deming lead Carl across to the drinks table, nodding and smiling in his direction. People with manners, and goodwill. A man like Max Fleming, Carl was confident, would never be allowed to cross the threshold of Windy Hill Farm.

He let his host pour him a large scotch and then asked Deming if he might have a word with his wife.

"By all means. She's in her study, chasing down some photograph or other—trying to win a bet against Pierre over there. Wouldn't do any harm to flush her out. It's been a while. You know where it is?"

"I do."

Carl walked down the corridor to the room at the end, where he found Dorothy Wheeler bent over a desk. All the drawers had been pulled out, revealing a chaos of memorabilia. She heard him coming and turned.

"Dratted thing," she said. "Can't find it anywhere."

"It'll be where you first looked for it."

"I'm sure you're right. But one has to go through the process, doesn't one. And what are *you* looking for tonight, Carl? You have that air."

He smiled, and took a sip of his drink. As it flowed into him, warming his stomach, he realized both that he probably shouldn't have another after this, and also that he wanted one.

Dorothy waited for him to answer. She was closer to medium-build than Marion, and blonde where the other woman was brown. There was a strong resemblance nonetheless. Both keen sportswomen, of course—the Wheelers, predominantly Dorothy, ran the polo club up on the Pogonip, open country that started at the top of the road and stretched up into the mountains almost as far as Pasatiempo. Dorothy was no mean golfer herself, and said to be the first white woman ever to complete the Iditarod, driving a team of dogs from Anchorage to Nome while on honeymoon with Deming at the tender age of twenty.

She and Marion had become firm friends since the latter came to town, and there were those who hinted the relationship was even closer than that. Personally he doubted it. Marion was what she was, of course, though extremely discrete. Though Dorothy was two decades younger than her husband, and his first cousin, and there had been no children, Carl declined to speculate on the details of her personal life. It wasn't his business, and he didn't care.

The most telling resemblance between the women was their extraordinary force of character, the fact that though both were constrained by society to behave as though men ruled the roost; the reality was very different. In this town, and much of the world. The real power has always lived in the shadows. It gathers strength there.

"Marion," he said.

"Ah. Not here, I'm afraid. Nor expected. She's motored down to Carmel for a lavish feast with her pal Morse. It's her birthday tomorrow, of course."

He hadn't known this. Dorothy caught the look on his face and frowned questioningly. "What?"

"There's a problem," he said.

"I know."

"You know?"

"I had luncheon with her yesterday. She . . . she perhaps drank rather more than usual, and was frank with me."

"About?"

"Financial matters."

Carl nodded. Though he had been given Dorothy Wheeler's name as a contact before he moved to Santa Cruz, all their conversations had been oblique. Nothing direct had ever been said between them, nor so much as acknowledged. As a result he was unsure how much the woman knew, or even if she was aware of his role and occupation. "Things are tight, certainly. Nobody else at the club is aware."

Dorothy sighed. "She's generous to a fault. Always making sure people have the best of everything—friends, relatives, even appalling little parasites like that Fleming fellow."

"You've met him?"

"He rolled up at the Pogonip club a few evenings ago. Quite drunk. With that young Kitty creature, who's very sweet of course but distressingly dim. I let them have a drink but then encouraged them to understand they might enjoy their evening far more back at Pasatiempo."

"Good for you. But yes, all that. And not selling sufficient house sites on the course fast enough to pay for the constant improvements she's making."

"You know she imported the clay for the tennis courts all the way from Europe?"

"That's exactly the kind of thing I had in mind."

"I'm sure things will level out."

Carl nodded again, though he was not sure of this at all. He looked out of the window as he took another long draw on his scotch, which was excellent, of course. Far below he could see fog starting to creep in from the bay, blotting out the tiny points of light downtown.

The bay was very, very deep.

When he looked back he saw Dorothy's eyes upon him, her expression serious now. "What is it, Carl?"

"I'm worried," he said.

"About? Be frank."

"Marion is considering an offer for a portion of her land. For far more than it's worth."

"From whom?"

He chose his words carefully. "People who cannot be allowed to own the earth so close to a fault line."

Dorothy Wheeler blinked. At that moment her husband appeared cheerfully in the doorway, holding the scotch bottle. He poured another large slug into Carl's glass.

"I shouldn't," he said.

"Nonsense, young man. It's a cold night."

"We're almost finished, dear," Dorothy said. Deming took the hint, winked, and strode affably back toward his other guests. Carl threw back his drink in one.

"Go find her, Carl," Dorothy said, when her husband was back out of earshot. "Sam Morse enjoys a long meal, so I'm sure she'll be in Carmel a while yet. If not, she always drives home by Watsonville road. Go now."

Carl felt his chest tightening. "And?"

"What you speak of cannot be allowed to come to pass. I'm empowered to instruct you to tell Marion whatever it takes to convince her not to proceed."

"Empowered by . . ."

She looked him in the eye and finally confirmed what had been unspoken between them for six months. "Nathan Brady."

He hadn't been anticipating anything like this long a drive tonight, and so stopped for gas at the top of Pacific Avenue. While the attendant filled the tank, Carl considered going via the apartment to warn Michelle. It was almost nine o'clock now, however, after the time Carl Jr. went to bed, and he knew he'd get no thanks for waking him. Michelle would know that Carl would be back when he could, and that if he was late, it was unavoidable. Not for the first time—he seemed prey tonight to revisiting well-worn trains of thought—he realized how lucky he was to have found her: a woman who could accept that she was not allowed to know the details of his profession, but would love and support him in it anyway. He remained in the Buick and, when the tank was full, drove quickly out of town.

The road was dark and empty and long. Carl sped through the wide flat arc of the Pajaro Valley toward Monterey, his car small and lonely under a vast sky.

This time at least he was saved having to go inside. When he pulled into the lot of the Pebble Beach golf club a little over an hour later, he saw Sam

Morse—the man people were starting to call "the Duke of del Monte"—standing bullishly with a cigar outside the entrance, gazing up at the stars. Carl parked and walked quickly over to him.

"Carl Unger, as I live and breath," Morse bellowed. "Hell are you doing here?"

"Looking for Marion," Carl said, for what felt like the hundredth time.

"Well you've come to the right place. She's saying goodbye to our friends. Then driving home. You've just caught her."

"Excellent," Carl said, with relief.

"Nothing wrong, I hope?"

Carl knew an outright untruth wouldn't work. He was a long way from home on a cold December night, and Morse was smart. Though built like a bull and bluffly hail-fellow-well-met, his developments across the peninsula were well-conceived and profitable, despite the unfashionable efforts he went to in protecting the environment. A further testament to his character was the fact that though Marion had formerly been his employee, leaving to found a golf course that now rivaled his in fame—and attracted a greater number of celebrity guests—he'd remained both unfailingly supportive of her, and her friend.

"Nothing dramatic," Carl said, therefore. "But urgent enough that it's best I speak with her right away."

"Of course, of course." Morse stubbed the remains of his cigar in the ashtray by the door. "I'll let her know you're here. Come—wait in the bar."

Morse led him there, and firmly instructed the nearest waiter that Carl was not allowed to pay for anything. The waiter appeared to take this as an instruction that *he* was not allowed to not let Carl have something to drink. A large scotch arrived quickly. Carl was most of the way through it when he saw Marion, thankfully alone, striding along the hallway. She saw him and bustled into the bar.

"Carl. It's lovely to see you, naturally. But what on earth is it that can't wait until tomorrow?"

"Could we speak outside?"

"Of course not, Carl. It's freezing."

Carl moved so that his body was between Marion and the rest of the bar, and pitched his voice low. "You can't sell the lower meadow."

"What? Why ever not? And how do you even know that I'm planning to?" Carl didn't answer. "I'm sorry—but this is really none of your business. I'm selling the land and that's the end of it."

"You can't. It isn't safe."

"Isn't *safe*? What on earth are you talking about?"

"The people who made the offer. What do they say they want it for?"

"Oh, a facility of some kind. A cemetery, was it? I didn't really listen. They're prepared to pay well over the odds and that's the only thing I care about right now."

"You cannot sell it to them."

Marion seemed caught between amusement and irritation. "Carl, it's going to happen. It has to. And soon. I need the money, and we're meeting over it tomorrow morning, bright and early."

"At least delay the meeting."

"I can't. Their person is coming from the other side of the country."

"From where?"

"Oh, I can't remember that, Carl! Why should I care? Ended in 'mouth,' I think. What matters is that he's the only person who can authorize the payment quickly."

Carl took a deep breath. "Marion, listen to me. These people. They call themselves the Olde Fellowes, yes?"

"How on earth do you know that?"

"I just do. Do you understand who they are?"

"Of course. Like the Rotary. They've had a presence in town for years. Good works, business networking, that manner of thing. Dull but worthy."

"Yes. But no. That's what they appear to be. In fact they . . . they're something else. Something very *different*. They're extremely old and go under many names. They have a hidden purpose. It is a very dark one. I work for a covert organization whose task it is to stand between them and the completion of their agenda."

"What are you *talking* about Carl?"

"Marion—when you stand outside at night in the dark at Pasatiempo, do you not sometimes feel something? A lack? A sense that the world is thinner than it should be?"

"Carl—how drunk are you?"

"The fabric of reality cannot be taken for granted, Marion. It can be worn away. It can be *torn*. That is what these people are seeking to do, and they want to buy your land because it is close by something that would enable them to cause extraordinary havoc—damaging the world in a way from which it might never recover. The portion they're after stands directly over a subdivision of the San Andreas Fault. It is *imperative* that they be kept away from it. Not just the world, but the entire universe may be in danger."

"*Universe*? Danger? From *what*?"

"The endless void. The Crawling Chaos."

Marion stared at him for a long moment. And then, suddenly, began to laugh. Her laugh was famous. Loud, unbridled, and infectious.

"Oh Carl," she said. "You are priceless. And kind. It's a long way to come to gift me with a good laugh the night before my birthday, but that's you all over. Thank you. But now I'm going home, and you should too."

She patted him on the cheek and strode out of the bar before he had time to realize what was happening.

He dropped his glass onto a table and hurried after her, but there was no sign. She seemed to have totally vanished.

He trotted up and down the lines of the lot, looking for her Duesenberg J. He was right down the far side when he heard the sound of one leaving at the other end.

Of course. She'd parked right near the exit, as always, regardless of whether it was allowed.

Carl swore and ran back to his own vehicle. By the time he'd turned out onto the road Marion's car was out of sight. He paused a moment.

The last scotch had been a mistake. His head didn't feel clear. He wondered—did he even have to do this tonight? He now knew for sure that the meeting was happening tomorrow. Marion rarely interacted with people before ten, however, and so "bright and early" didn't have to be taken literally. He could go home, eat, sleep. Get to Pasatiempo before eight. Talk to her then. Tell her more about the League, if necessary. Tell her whatever it took.

No.

It wouldn't work. He'd seen it in her eyes and in the offhand way she'd dismissed what he'd said and hurried off. She wasn't listening, and she wasn't going to. The club was her life. She'd put everything into it. Heart, soul, all her not-inconsiderable financial resources, now gone. And she was proud. She'd evade him in the morning just as she'd evaded her many creditors this year, using every tactic from charm to simply making herself scarce for a while. The meeting would take place and the land would be sold.

That couldn't happen.

It simply couldn't.

Carl sat, hands gripping the steering wheel, cursing himself for not being quicker when she'd walked out—and feeling the stirring of real panic in his guts.

Then he remembered something Dorothy had said.

She always takes Watsonville road.

He'd lost only five minutes, ten at the most. Though Marion was well-known to enjoy pushing her Model J to the limits, Carl was confident he'd be able to catch up. His car was smaller, lighter. He knew what he had to do. He'd never driven Watsonville road himself, but had a good idea where it went: veering somewhat inland, cutting off the angle toward the north side of Santa Cruz. The only question was how you accessed it out of Carmel.

He found it quickly, and pushed his foot down on the pedal. Pretty soon he had a suspicion why Marion favored this highway, over and above the minor time-saving opportunity (she was a woman who always wanted to get where she was going as fast as possible, if not a little faster). Once you left town and got out into the countryside, it became clear that the county had decided there were more important roads upon which to spend scarce tax dollars. It was uneven, and pitted, the camber wonky even to the naked eye. Driving fast along it was exactly the sort of adventure Marion Hollins would enjoy.

It was empty for the time being, too, so Carl steered for the centerline and hammered along up the middle of the road. The Buick bumped and clattered frantically, occasionally bouncing hard enough to raise him out of his seat. The effects of the last drink kept settling deeper—he knew that he should slow down, but also that he couldn't.

He flashed past some two-horse agricultural town, a battered hut by the side of the road shaped like an artichoke, a nest of old, tilting farm buildings. None made the scene look any more occupied. If anything, they accentuated how much of the landscape was empty. The flat valley. The low mountains either side. The wide sky above, eerie with moonlight. There were parts of this country that made you realize how late an addition to the picture humankind had been, and this was most definitely one of them. This was land biding its time and waiting until everything had passed. It could not be trusted. It was no friend to him, or to anyone.

He slowed a little to take the narrow bridge over the river, site of the incident from which the area had got its name. Hundreds of years ago a band of exhausted Spanish soldiers, forging their slow way north to establish missions up through what had then been a province of Spain, had come across an abandoned village. It had been burned to the ground. A huge black condor, ten feet across its wingspan, had been nailed to the side of one of the buildings. Some kind of warning, the soldiers realized—but they didn't know what of. Carl did. He'd even spoken to a few surviving members of the Ohlone tribe and heard what they knew about areas of nothingness up in the mountains, places where the gaps between trees in the forest were not what they seemed: areas where appalling dread seeped up from the rock, as giant things stirred far below. Things like—

There she was.

As he finally rounded a long bend, Carl saw Marion's convertible a quarter of a mile ahead.

He pressed harder on the gas pedal, streaking along the bumpy road, feeling his teeth vibrate. Marion knew his car. She'd see him in the rearview and pull over. He ran over what he'd say, what, if necessary, he could promise her. He might not be able to carry through on it without agreement from Washington, but if it were enough to stop her taking the meeting tomorrow, that would be all they needed for the time being. Now that the veil of silence between him and Dorothy Wheeler had been twitched aside, perhaps they could work together, meticulously plan what happened next, how to close down this particular incursion forever.

He was close now, close enough that Marion must be able to see his headlamps bearing down upon her.

She didn't slow, however. Perhaps her mind was on other things. Carl was sure she would have taken freely of Morse's doubtless well-stocked wine cellar too.

He sounded his horn.

She noticed that, certainly. He was close enough to see both the slight swerve it provoked, and then her eyes in the rearview mirror.

To see, also, the look of irritation and determination in them, as she accelerated away.

She knew who was following her well enough, but she didn't wish to enter into further conversation, and had no intention of stopping.

Carl maintained the distance and tried to work out what to do. They were traveling at his car's maximum speed now, or close to it. Far too quickly for this road, in the dark. His front left wheel caught a bump and for a moment the Buick was in danger of slewing badly, but he managed to bring it back under control.

Marion's car inched a little farther ahead.

This is dumb, Carl thought. *Dangerous and dumb.* Yes, it remained imperative that he talk to her tonight, but he knew where she was going, after all. He should slow down, follow her back to Pasatiempo. Do whatever it took to gain and hold her attention there. Chasing her across the country like a lunatic was the product of panic and half a pint of expensive whiskey that he hadn't paid for.

Slow down, Carl: slow down.

It took a physical effort to ease his foot back off the pedal. A gathering of will. Judgment too. He couldn't afford to fall too far behind. She and Mary Pickford were thick as thieves. Their joint ingenuity would be considerable, and if Marion told Mary they were playing a jape on Carl—her fondness for practical jokes was legendary—the actress would play along and Carl wouldn't stand a chance of being able to find Marion tonight.

So he gently pressed on the accelerator again. Marion had evidently been monitoring his actions, however, and did the same—her Duesenberg surging forward, leaving him for dead.

Carl swore. As they flashed past a sign warning of a junction ahead, he increased speed again, more subtly this time, hoping at least to be able to keep the car in sight. He didn't need to be right on her tail.

But Marion kept increasing her speed, faster and faster. Perhaps to try to leave him behind—perhaps only because she liked to play the game, to live life at maximum volume. Carl increased his speed also.

Suddenly there were lights ahead.

A terrible screeching noise.

Carl dropped his foot on the brake hurriedly—hard, but not too heavily. He still nearly lost control.

As he was wrestling the vehicle back onto a straight course, he heard a loud crunching sound ahead, and another, not as loud.

He pulled over onto the shoulder, kicking up a hail of gravel, and got out and sprinted up the road toward the crash. One car lay diagonally across the road.

Another had rear-ended it, the front half-concertinaed. Marion's convertible was off the road, lying on its side.

As Carl ran up to it her saw her face, staring up through the windshield into the black sky.

Half an hour later he stood next to the cop as Marion was loaded into the ambulance.

"Concussion. Pretty bad, the doctor said, but she should be fine in a couple of days."

Carl breathed out heavily. "Where are they taking her?"

"Monterey. It's nearest."

"And they'll keep her overnight?"

"Twenty-four hours minimum. That was a heck of a bump on her head. You're a friend, right?"

"Well, colleague. But a friend, too, I hope."

"Anybody I need to notify right away?"

"No," Carl said. It would be better if the people who turned up at the club tomorrow morning—assuming that's even where the meeting was taking place—were faced with incomprehension. If they were told the situation, he wouldn't put it past them to seek Marion out in her hospital bed and do the deal there. Far better to deliver the news tomorrow afternoon, when it was too late. "She has no family here. And she's going to be okay. But I'll let the relevant people know tomorrow."

The two other parties involved in the accident were standing together smoking cigarettes. The accident hadn't even been Carl's fault, or not completely. One driver—who'd spent not only the evening but the afternoon in a bar in Salinas—had entered the junction and swerved onto the highway at too high a speed and with nothing like due care and attention. A second driver had been forced to veer into the other lane to avoid running into the back of him.

Marion hadn't seen any of this coming until suddenly the second car's headlamps were bearing down upon her. She pulled hard to the right, and nearly made it. The front of her vehicle was clipped, however, hard enough to spin her into the ditch and crack her head into the windscreen.

The meeting with the Olde Fellowes wasn't going to happen.

"You okay?" the cop said. He sounded suspicious.

"Fine. Why?"

"Just that you smiled. As if there's something going on that I don't know about?"

"Just glad she's going to be okay, that's all."

By the time he turned up the road that would lead him to the top of Beach Hill and the McCray, Carl felt he had his ducks in a row. Tomorrow would disappear into holding the fort at the club, and driving down to check on Marion. She'd be angry as hell that the meeting hadn't happened, but he'd reassure her that Pasatiempo's looming financial problems could be sorted out in some other way. Perhaps they even could. The League's field operations were still chronically underfunded, but this represented a clear and present danger. Perhaps he'd be able to get it passed up the ladder, maybe even with Dorothy Wheeler's help.

Either way, the danger had passed for now. He'd done his job, even though very few people would ever know it. And his wife never would.

As he got out of the Buick outside the hotel, he glanced up at the windows of the apartment, looking forward very much to being inside.

The lights were on in there. On brightly.

All of them.

"No," Carl said. "No no *no*."

He lunged back into the car to grab the Colt he kept hidden under papers in the glove compartment. This prevented him from seeing the two men converging rapidly upon him until it was too late.

Jimmy knocked him to the ground with one blow to the temple from a billy club.

As Carl collapsed into the gutter onto his back, staring uncomprehendingly upward, Max Fleming's crooked smile appeared above him.

"The Olde Fellowes send their regards," he said. Then he shot Carl in the face.

The two men dragged the body a few yards along the street and stowed it in the trunk of Jimmy's car.

"A good job well done," Max said, after he'd closed it again. "And our reward beckons. Make sure the boy watches, eh? Our masters are very fond of that kind of suffering."

"If you say so."

"I do. Play your part, and I'll try not to break the little wife too badly before you've had the chance to enjoy some fun and games with her too."

In the trunk, in the dark, the last part of Carl heard the sound of their words but thankfully could not understand them. As the final lights went out in his mind, like stars obscured behind a black cloud that would never go away, he sensed the approach of the shadow-things that live in the void beyond, their dread fingers and howls, as they came to claim him at last.

But sometimes the universe is kind, and he died just in time.

Standing across the street, well back in shadow, Michelle Unger watched the two men stroll up the path toward the entrance to the McCray. Tears rolled slowly down both cheeks, and her jaw was clenched.

Part of her wished that some intuition, a quiet voice inside, hadn't suddenly told her that Carl was late, very late, *too late*, and she hadn't bundled up the child half an hour before, and left the apartment. This part of her wished she was standing behind the door inside the apartment, holding the big knife she'd used to slice the meatloaf, a chunk of which—cold now, cold *forever*—still sat on a plate on the counter.

But she knew Carl would not have wanted it that way.

"What are we doing, Mommy? Why are we out here?" Carl Jr. had not been able to see what had happened on the other side of his father's car. A small mercy.

Michelle wiped her face. "We have to go now."

"Why? Where's Dad?"

"He . . . he had to go somewhere."

"Where?"

"Somewhere a long way away."

"Is that where we're going?"

"No. Not that far. But we need to leave right now."

"Who were those men?"

"Bad men. Working for very bad people. And one day, when you're older, do you know what you're going to do?"

"What?"

"You're going to find those people and you're going to kill them."

"But killing's wrong."

"Not always."

She put her arm around her son's shoulders and hurried him away into the darkness.

FIVE

Randolph Carter, Secret Agent

SHE WAS EXPLORING AN underwater cavern. Despite the depth, she wore no equipment other than goggles. Somehow her lungs had mutated—she believed she might stay down for hours. But there were things in the cavern beyond what she could see, things that buzzed and flapped and let her know she had no business there. And yet she continued to swim in their direction, into warmer water, into fire. And then the fire alarm went off, and both rock and sea began to fracture.

Lieutenant Dorothy Williams, Army Nurse Corps, bolted awake. She groped around for her alarm clock, which she always kept on the other pillow, then realized it was the phone ringing. She reached up to the vanity and grabbed it off the receiver. "What is it?"

There was a loud buzzing and her anxiety climbed. Then the operator came on. "Miss, you have a phone call from Butler Hospital for the Insane. Doctor Andrews."

"Put him through." Her eyes found the clock, still sound asleep on its pillow. Three o'clock, middle of the night. The same time in Providence. She recalled small bits of the dream, flowing shadows with uncommon shapes on undersea walls. Randolph had always offered to teach her how to remember more of her dreams. Once again she was grateful she'd declined.

The line crackled at the same time lightning struck outside her window, followed by a burning spread of light through the clouds. "Dorothy? What the hell is going on down there? Our special patients are climbing the walls! Where's Carter?"

"I . . . he should be asleep." She could hear screaming in the background. And Daniel, she'd known him since college, and she'd never heard him raise his voice this way before. There was a sudden loud slapping noise, a series of dull thuds. She remembered the three patients strapped into their beds somewhere in the basement of that vast facility, the dull yellow-tiled walls that never looked quite clean.

"Strap it down! Strap it down!" Was that high-pitched voice really Daniel's? Then, to Dorothy, "You should be watching Carter every minute! Wasn't that what you recommended? They should listen to you—you're the trauma expert there!"

"He's . . . he's . . ." She'd started to say *a grown boy*, but fortunately the line went dead. The walls of her bedroom were awash in waves of light.

Minutes later she was in her robe and racing down the stairs. She could see Randolph's door partway open below her, the light on. She wasn't surprised. He was always up late. It was Sunday. They'd had an early dinner together and she'd consented to keep him company while he listened to *The Shadow*. She cared little for the program but she did admire Orson Welles.

"Randolph? There was a call from the hospital. Your *early warning system*—apparently the three have detected something. Daniel is beside himself!"

The room was in shambles, but then Randolph's quarters were always in disarray: open books everywhere, papers spread across the floor, many full of the strange chirography he'd adapted for his alien appendages, food left out and darkening, gathering dust. But tonight was worse. Furniture had been shoved out of place, lamps and a bookcase upended, broken glass and tiny dark bits scattered across the floor, and there Carter was spread across his shabby burgundy brocade couch, half-dressed in shredded sleepwear. One arm was exposed and bleeding. A partially filled glass syringe lay on the rug. Also on the floor nearby was that comic book he'd bought recently, *Action Comics*, with the red-caped figure lifting a car over his head. And a large silver key she'd never seen before: tarnished and heavily inscribed.

"Randolph!" She ran up to the couch and started to bend over him, then stopped, holding her distance, reluctant to touch. He'd changed. But of course he was *changed* when she'd first met him, when General Craig had insisted that she examine him, interview him. It was supposedly her evaluation that would determine whether he would be given his new role, although she'd quickly decided that had been a bit of a ruse. J. Edgar Hoover wasn't about to lose Carter—he would use him however he could. He'd simply wanted some idea as to what he was actually letting himself in for.

When she'd first met her new charge she'd thought there'd been some kind of mistake. They'd told her he'd returned to the Dreamscape several times in order to undo the changes to his body. But they'd presented her with a child, a teenaged boy certainly no older than fifteen. He was short and slight, the initial dark hairs of puberty just beginning to pattern his oh-so-pale skin. When she'd asked him to stand he'd wavered as if he might faint. His nervousness had been palpable. He'd been quite modest, but as she'd slowly coaxed him out of his robe she discovered his deformities: The flesh on the right-side of the scalp burnt and melted, with similar warping and melting down that side of the face, around the neck and beneath both arms. A bronze metal eye patch had been fused to the skin over the right eye, and when she'd asked him what had happened there he'd said his first words to her: "It covers Zkauba's eye, and must not be removed." It had been the voice of a much older man, but articulated with some difficulty, as if the speech organs had been damaged, and the ability to speak relearned.

But none of that had prepared her for undoing the hefty canvas mittens that covered his forearms, and gazing at the long, clacking black claws that were his hands.

Those black claws were now more distinctly pronounced on Carter's right side—they were much larger than they had been before, sharper, and were currently partially embedded in the ripped cushion beneath him. But the left hand had been restored almost to a kind of normalcy: it at least resembled a human hand, with five fingers (although two of those appeared to possess an additional joint), which were curled into a painful-looking gesture. His mouth was frozen open in a silent scream. She thought he might be dead, or close to it.

She turned around and raced to the small liquor cabinet by the door, careful not to step on the glass, or these dark bits—were they dead insects?—in her slippers. She heard a faint scratching and saw movement on the wall above the cabinet and on the other walls and the ceiling. She glanced at this distraction: long lines of insects flowing across the wallpaper—flies, cockroaches, a variety of beetles—travelling in precise, needlepoint-like patterns. She jerked open the cabinet and retrieved the case with the syringe and the little red bottle, brought it back to Randolph, drained the bottle and plunged the contents into his shriveled belly. She had no idea what the bottle contained. Randolph had simply told her what to do if she ever found him this way.

There was a pause as the insect sounds seemed to multiply a hundred-fold and then Randolph jerked, limbs convulsing as he rolled off the couch and crashed to the floor. When she knelt beside him he grabbed her arm. "Was it him?" he said, his uncovered eye fixed and bloodshot. "Did he come through?"

"You're an idiot! We've all been counting on you!" Dorothy tried to calm herself down. She wasn't being professional. She sat down in a chair by the parlor window, watching for their car. She looked down at the hem of her uniform skirt, pulled on it, made adjustments to her stockings. Randolph, now in manic mode, paced the room, occasionally glancing at the small line of remaining insects as they marched across the wall, tracing drunken loops before disappearing into a crack in the baseboard.

"I deserve everything you might want to say, lieutenant." He was swallowed up in his outfit: oversized gray fedora and flopping topcoat. She could only see part of his scarred face and thin hand protruding. A hastily chosen yellow pillowcase covered his enlarged claw. When he turned, she noticed the rolled up comic book in his coat pocket. "But I thought a brief trip might . . . restore me to better functionality. And I'm much . . . much more intelligent when I am in the Dreamscape, I . . . swear. I thought perhaps I could do something from that side before slipping back through, and prevent future incursions. I thought it would make up for some of the damage I've caused with my previous trips."

"You should have asked, or at least told someone."

"But you would have said no, and then I would have had to do it anyway."

They were an adult man's words delivered through the somewhat whiny tones of an awkward and embarrassed teenager. Dorothy wasn't sure she would ever become accustomed to that. "We'll just have to assess the damage, and do whatever we must do."

"Perhaps there were no dangerous consequences this time. Perhaps I created but a small leak." He gestured toward the wall. "This insect activity may be a reflection of that." He looked pathetically eager for her to agree with him.

"Perhaps. But Doctor Andrews's patients—they were quite upset," she said. He turned away from her and gazed at the insects again. "Randolph, you said, 'did he come through.' What did you mean by that? Who is 'he'?"

He didn't answer at first. Then he turned around. "I don't know. I have no memory of saying those words. I may have been referring to some other version of myself. There are thousands of Randolph Carters, you see, all manifestations of some greater being."

She couldn't tell if he was being deceptive or not. He rambled on about his personal cosmology and the history of his "cosmic journeys" all the time. She'd grown a little weary of it—it didn't solve anything. Unexplained phenomena still occurred. Strange creatures still had to be tracked down. The push-bell rang. It was their driver.

"I have your car," the young soldier said. He stared at Carter for a moment, and then seemed grateful to turn his attention to her. He looked at her uniform. "Miss."

"She's a lieutenant, you know," Randolph said, sounding offended.

"Army Nurse Corps, Rand . . . Mr. Carter. The private here is correct. They call us Miss."

Randolph snorted. "But your degrees . . ."

"We should hurry," she replied, and ushered him through the door.

In the car on the way to the Washington Monument she scolded the driver for staring too much at Carter through his rearview mirror. It was a problem—no one wanted to take this disabled-looking teenage boy seriously. And Carter hesitated to deliver orders directly. He either communicated through her or by speaking generally to a group, looking somewhere over their heads, to make his wishes known.

There was still lightning, and an accompanying, hollow-sounding thunder. It lent a peculiar pastel glow to the smoky fog filling the D.C. streets. The fog seemed strangely active, fingers of it moving restlessly, finding new ways into alleys and onto porches, under bridges and into vacant buildings. And yet there was almost no breeze to account for such movement. Windows were dark and the streets were devoid of traffic, the sidewalks empty of people. Of course it wasn't even 4:00 a.m. yet, but this was Washington, the nation's capital. There were always people about.

Much of the sidewalks, the small lawns, were glossed over with a thin coat of frost, but it was summer, certainly the wrong time of year. She noticed glimmers of ice in some of the trees.

Carter appeared to have reverted a bit during their brief time in the car. A serious rash had developed over his exposed skin, perhaps a sign that he was much more distressed than he wanted to let on. Or was it contamination? Her hands worried at the clasp on her bag. It wasn't much larger than a purse, but it carried everything necessary. She started to open it and then closed it again.

He looked at her and she slid the bag behind her on the seat. He looked slightly desperate. "Lieutenant, how bad is it, do you suppose?"

"Randolph, we'll soon see. I'm sure they're monitoring things at headquarters."

"Has there been any further progress in the Hindenburg investigation?"

"They think almost surely it was a gas leak, and a spark—"

"But they can't be *sure*. And Miss Earhart, any word on her and Noonan?"

"None so far. But, Randolph, not every tragedy in the world has something to do with a breach into the Dreamscape. There is such a thing as a *coincidence*."

"You find that particular word reassuring, Lieutenant. I do not. Has Mr. Hughes answered any of my communications?"

"He has not."

"Perhaps President Roosevelt would care to smooth the way for us. A phone call from him might make Hughes more cooperative. Roosevelt is in his second term now—what has he done for us? Has he even been informed as to how bad things might become?"

"Mister Hoover decides what the president should know. The president is busy with things overseas. Germany annexed Austria only a few months ago—were you aware of that?"

"Vaguely," Carter replied, staring out the car window at the sky. "War is inevitable. Roosevelt must know that. I dream about it all the time. What if the Nazis have captured, or diverted, one of these, these . . . *visitors*?" He had straightened up, rolled down the window to look more intently at the sky.

"Randolph, what are you seeing?" She pressed her face against the glass. A vague but expansive curtain of ever-changing red and green and blue light filled the sky.

"In late January a brilliant aurora borealis described variously as 'a curtain of fire' and a 'blood-red beam of light' startled people across Europe, lieutenant. It was visible as far south as Gibraltar. If you check the records, I think you will discover we had a rather serious visitor from the Dreamscape around that time."

Once within the Monument, a private elevator took them down to the offices of the Human Protection League. Just inside the empty reception area they were met by FBI Agent Miles, Nathan Brady's direct representative. He stuck out his hand. Randolph failed to notice. Dorothy pretended not to. Agent Miles's broad face and flaky skin made him look vaguely ichthyoid. He also had a strangely off-putting odor. Dorothy didn't like touching him.

Miles put his hand away and stared at Randolph's face, then at the pillowcase, then at the somewhat restored hand. He looked questioningly at Dorothy. Randolph wouldn't look at him, but continued on into the interior offices while Dorothy stayed back. "Do we know if anything actually came through?" she asked. "I don't want to upset him."

"Upset *him*? *You people*. What did he do *this* time?"

Dorothy hesitated, but there was no point in hiding things. "He made a visit. A brief one, he says. He thought he was making the situation better."

"He's *your* charge, miss. You should be watching him better."

"I'm mainly his assistant, Agent. I'm not really his babysitter. I understand my job. Speaking of, has your team found Lovecraft's diary yet?"

"Every available agent is looking. We will find it eventually. We'd better catch up to him—I don't want your boy just wandering around the offices. He shouldn't be giving orders, you know. He's hardly qualified."

"Your people made him head of the Dream Division," she replied. "You'll just have to live with that. And remember, he's a veteran of the French Foreign Legion, and older than most of us."

"So you keep telling me—I suppose I'm just supposed to take your word for it. Some of the staff members *hate* him, did you know that?"

She'd already gone ahead, but threw back, "They have absolutely no reason to."

The inner offices were manned by a variety of agents, military personnel on loan, CID scientists, and a few private citizens recruited because they had been affected by the incursions. Randolph was attempting to ask some of them questions. For the most part they kept their physical distance and ignored him. One small woman did at least pretend to pay attention to him, nodding randomly at his comments.

"What did you want to know, Carter?" Agent Miles asked, scowling.

Randolph turned to Dorothy. "Ask him about Ettore Majorana. The Italian mathematician? A few months ago he disappeared."

Agent Miles was obviously annoyed, first trying to catch Randolph's eye, then giving up and addressing Dorothy. "I'm quite aware of that. He was travelling by ship from Palermo to Naples, but then he wasn't there when the ship docked in Naples. We've been working with the Italians. Still no sign of him, but I don't think—"

Carter interrupted. "He was actually a theoretical physicist working on neutrino masses."

"And what are those?" Miles asked Dorothy.

Dorothy shook her head. "I have no idea."

"I know, you're going to tell me it's just another coincidence." Randolph was agitated, waving his clawed arm around. The yellow pillowcase had begun to slip; a few inches of dark, chitinous surface were exposed. People around the office began to move away. "Just like the explosion at the New London school in Texas last year. More than 295 students and teachers killed, and they attributed all that to a natural gas explosion?"

"Because it was," Miles said.

"And just this February in Sydney. Three hundred swimmers on Bondi Beach dragged out to sea. They said it was because of 'freak' waves. Three freak waves in a row?"

"At least they managed to save all but five," replied Miles. "Carter, you're working yourself up. I appreciate that you feel responsible for, well, damn near everything it seems. But it doesn't help to make things worse than they are. These—*things*," Dorothy saw him glance at Randolph's claw, now almost fully-exposed, "—they're bad enough, but they're not *everywhere*!"

Randolph finally turned to look at him. "You haven't seen what I've seen, Agent. Yaddith and the sweetness, nameless aeons and the endless reaches of the galaxy, drowning in the voices of my multiple selves . . ."

Dorothy had been nudging Randolph toward the next door and away from Agent Miles. Finally she got him through. They descended a series of steps. "*Snow White and the Seven Dwarfs* is playing," she said. "An entirely animated movie—can you imagine? I'll take you, my treat."

"Thank you, Lieutenant." His voice was softer, slightly broken. "I quite enjoyed our excursion to New York to see *Our Town*."

"I wasn't sure. It seemed to upset you. I thought you might be uncomfortable, sitting in the back, wearing that hood and the oversized cloak."

"It was moving. In the final act the most prominent characters are the dead souls who already inhabit the cemetery, sitting in chairs at the front of the stage, and largely indifferent to earthly events. And earlier, the girl, Rebecca, talked of how Grover's Corners was contained within 'the Mind of God.' It's much as I have tried to explain—the 'real' world is nothing more than a set of mental images in the mind of some greater being that . . . that we cannot even begin to comprehend."

"It will take me awhile to get my mind around that." The truth was she didn't want to get her mind around that. She hoped that he was incorrect, that his experiences had unhinged him somehow. In fact she counted on it.

Finally at the end of a low-lit hallway they came to the door with DREAM DIVISION etched into the frosted glass. Randolph turned the knob and pushed the door in, then when it stopped after a few inches pushed it harder, and then had to really put his shoulder into it. Papers and a few books poured around the leading edge of the door with this final shove. They entered, stepping onto a layer of paper, books, and other reading materials. A large number of the papers were filled with his cramped and strange handwriting. Many of the others were Photostats of old documents and diagrams.

"Randolph, you promised me you would do better. It's hard to work in these conditions."

"This *is* better, isn't it?"

Dorothy stooped to pick some of it up.

"Stop!" he cried. "I know where everything is!"

"Really? What if Agent Miles were to come down here? Or Brady himself?"

"Hardly likely. They haven't . . ."

"But they *might*. You have to do something about this. They distrust you as it is."

But he had rushed ahead to a clean area. He got down on all fours, searching. "Did one of you do this?" he shouted. "Have you been in my things?"

Of course there was no reply. Their peculiar staff, Dorothy knew, would be indisposed.

There were half-empty bookcases on both sides of the room. She couldn't understand why they were so underutilized. A few of the drawings and Photostats had been nailed to blank sections of wall. The light was so dim in here she couldn't imagine how anyone could read what was on them, but then remembered that Randolph had a fancy aluminum flashlight for that very purpose.

A large cyanotype blueprint rolled off a pile of books leaning against the wall and onto her shoes. She scooped it up and unrolled it. It was an architectural drawing of a huge office building in the shape of a pentagon. Numerous notations had been made, some of them in Randolph's unmistakable hand. Some features had been circled. At the bottom it was labeled us war department.

"Randolph! You were supposed to submit your comments on Bergstrom's designs weeks ago!"

He sat down on the floor and looked at her. "Was I? Well, I had more important things to attend to. It will have to wait."

"They need to break ground on this! The Foggy Bottom building is too small."

He got up with a sigh and ambled over. "They should have known that and built a bigger building. They are a wasteful bunch, these government types." He glanced at it, made several more notations. "If they want maximum protection from future incursions they will need to move the electromagnetic generators *here* and *here*, and straighten those walls. And these . . ." He drew several arrows indicating points on the western side of the structure, the army section, ". . . between corridors four and five, are vulnerable to breach. They need to strengthen them." He tossed the blueprint back to her. “Call up upstairs. I need to know if there have been any sightings, and where.”

“Randolph, I’m not your servant.”

“I know. I once had a servant—Parks. He was much more respectful.”

She looked for a clean surface to put the rolled-up drawing on. There was an old wooden desk in a nearby room. She’d waded through the clutter and had laid the roll and her bag down when she heard the snoring. Peering around the desk, she found the low chaise lounge and one of Randolph’s selected “staff” asleep on top of it. Normally she would have pulled the man to his feet and scolded him, but then this was his actual *job*, wasn’t it?

He appeared to be a homeless man—they had thousands of them in D.C.—too poor to afford even a cobbled-together alley house, so they slept in the parks, or under things, like insects. His shoes were no more than tacked-together bits of leather, his shirt and pants long past saving. He had a fifth of whiskey clutched under his arm like a baby. He wore this contraption of wires and metal and ceramic plates around his head, pressed deeply into his greasy gray hair. It was of Randolph’s invention, and she wasn’t sure exactly how it functioned. Randolph’s simple explanation was “it keeps him focused on what he needs to focus on.”

She hadn’t been there for this man’s recruitment. Randolph had found him, supposedly questioned him extensively, and finagled one of the soldiers to bring him back to the Monument. Dorothy didn’t approve of Randolph going out like that, even with a soldier for protection, but she hadn’t been consulted. When she’d asked him why he chose this particular individual out of all the other homeless about, he’d told her, “We shared war stories.”

At least they could have cleaned the poor man up. He was caked in black dirt over his forehead and cheekbones. It was even crusted over his closed eyelids. She wondered if he could even open them.

His mouth was frozen in a grimace, lips pulled back to uncover his canines. He continued to snore, but his mouth was mostly closed. Still, the sound came from the direction of his head, somewhere.

There were several more of these men sleeping around the office, and one woman. She didn't always know where. There was a phone on the desk. She picked it up and dialed upstairs.

After the phone call she grabbed her bag and went to find Randolph. She preferred avoiding the extended parts of the suite. He'd promised he'd make them more comfortable for her—at least he appeared to want to please her—but of course he'd broken his promise. It simply wasn't in his nature to accept any ordering or organization other than his own.

There were a number of rooms. When Randolph first took charge of these quarters Dorothy couldn't imagine why they'd allocated him so much space. She'd initially been told that Dream Division would have minimal staff. But by the time she'd joined him a week later, the rooms were in more or less the same condition they were in now—bleak and overflowing with notes and research materials. When she'd asked him where it all came from he told her, "A room in Massachusetts."

Light in the deeper reaches of Dream Division was dim. Of course there were no windows, and lamps were few and appeared to operate inefficiently. Some fixtures were equipped with fluorescent tanning bulbs, for which Randolph had never offered an explanation. Once or twice she stumbled over a sleeping form. She mumbled her embarrassed apologies, but no one awakened, apparently too busy doing their job.

Now and then a phone would ring for a while in a distant room and stop. She heard no voices so assumed the calls hadn't been answered. Randolph hated phones and rarely used them, preferring that she answer the calls when she was there. She'd explained to him dozens of times that she wasn't his secretary, to no avail.

The short hall leading to his private office space (he called it his "cubby") was jammed with heavy steel filing cabinets, army-green and decorated with various dents and islands of corrosion. There had been no attempt to arrange them in a straight line—they appeared like wreckage from some terrible collision.

His space had no door but was marked by an intensification of clutter. She shuffled sideways between the tall stacks of reading materials.

Finally she found him bent over a small mattress containing his lone female sleeper. The poor old woman was weeping, her eyes rolling, her back spasms lifting her off the mattress. Randolph was stroking her hair away from her forehead, muttering, "Where, where?"

The phone began ringing again. She looked around. He'd stuffed it into a corner of the floor. "Randolph?"

"Answer it," he said, then added, "but only if you really want to."

She stepped over some books, bent, and pulled the receiver up to her ear. Apparently she'd joined an excited conversation midchatter. She could hardly distinguish the individual voices. Then Agent Miles was speaking to her directly. "Get up here!" he shouted. "There's been a sighting." Then she was disconnected.

"Randolph!"

"I know," he said softly. "Listen to her."

She stepped around and knelt beside him. She saw the pin fixed by the old woman's throat, that gold Red Cross pin. The wretched woman was babbling in a weak, cracked open voice. "Supernumerary . . . polymelia . . . supernumerary."

"She was a nurse. She's describing a birth defect," Dorothy said. "It's when the baby is born with too many limbs."

The woman's tone had changed. "Temple Court . . . skitter . . . skitter . . . southwest . . . the *Anarch* . . ."

"Close enough to see the Capitol's dome from there," Randolph said. "Whatever it is, it's moving through the slums."

They started out a couple of hours before sunrise, the streets still suspiciously deserted. In the deathly quiet the noise their vehicles made sounded like a circus parade. Dorothy kept scanning the horizon for signs of unusual activity. Her companions appeared to be paying no attention at all.

This time they had a bigger car and they'd squeezed two more soldiers in beside their driver. The older one carried a man-pack FM radio transmitter receiver. The other kept staring at Randolph surreptitiously. Finally Dorothy reached over and laid her hand on the young soldier's shoulder and shook her head.

Randolph probably hadn't noticed. He was deep in thought, unconsciously rocking back and forth. She'd seen this behavior from him before, so it didn't bother her. But usually he did this only in private.

They'd offered her a pistol but she'd declined. She'd lied that she didn't even know how to use one. She kept a tight grip on her bag.

Their vehicle was accompanied by several Marmon-Herrington converted trucks full of soldiers. Two M2 light tanks followed a block behind. Agent Miles's doing, she guessed. This amount of firepower worried her. They were in the middle of a large urban population, the nation's capital no less.

"I hear this is a big one," the younger soldier said as if reading her mind.

"Why would you say that?" she asked. "We have no idea what we're facing."

"Hmmm . . . scuttlebutt, miss," he replied.

She frowned at him. "You're not in the navy, soldier. I'd suggest you stow that talk."

Away from the government's Grand Plaza but still within sight of the Capitol Building, the convoy began to slow down. The brick houses here were progressively less grand, but still respectable middle-class homes. The alleys between the streets, behind these homes, were another story.

D.C. had been a city planned with spacious lots so, as the housing shortage for poor and migrant workers became increasingly acute, wealthy landowners discovered they could provide accommodations for these people in their backyards and along their alleys, giving birth to the alley slums, soon overcrowded with those who had nowhere else to live.

Old planks could be pieced together to make a short one-story dwelling with a makeshift roof, no windows or yard, the rickety construction thrown up right on the edge of the alley. A battered washtub could be set on top of each one to collect the rain.

Wooden additions could be tacked on to the sturdy brick backs of businesses even in otherwise wealthy neighborhoods, their wobbly balconies stacked three stories high. Or a number of one-room ramshackle boxes could be wedged into the backyard of a nicer house or hotel. No plumbing was necessary; all the toilets were outdoors. Water was provided by a shared hand-pump or hauled in half barrels. Clotheslines stretched above the crowded brick lanes. In the summer mattresses were set outside for the overheated kids. Trash could be sorted and sold. Everything was so dirty anyway, the working class residents often felt no urgency to pick up the accumulating rubbish.

The convoy turned suddenly into one of these narrow alleys and barreled forward at a frightening pace, splashing through huge puddles of drainage, clipping garbage cans and discarded furniture and even the occasional edge of a dwelling.

"Slow down!" she screamed. "Human beings live here!"

"Orders, miss!" the driver shouted back at her. "We were told this was where we were most likely to find the enemy! The tanks are too big—they'll meet us at the other end. Don't worry! I know what I'm doing!"

The enemy. She'd never conceptualized these manifestations that way, but in the final analysis she supposed that was what they were.

They rattled past rows of slight wooden structures made with ill-fitting weathered planks with countless broken and patched surfaces. The occasional gaps in these dwellings were crowded with cast-off furniture too imperfect even for these unfortunates, more drab shacks with broken-out windows and missing doors, and layer upon layer of flapping, hanging laundry, some of it dragged down and pulled under the wheels of their vehicle. Everyone in the car was silent except Randolph, who suddenly straightened up and asked, "Why are we doing this?"

At that same moment a dark emaciated figure leapt through the headlight beams, head rolling loosely and limbs all akimbo. The driver slammed on the brakes, the truck following so closely behind them screamed to a stop. Dorothy was tossed from her seat onto the legs of the men. As the soldiers scrambled to help her up she shouted, "Was that a child?"

The driver got out of the car and searched the area around the still-burning headlights. The other two soldiers joined the search with their flashlights, looking under the vehicle and among the garbage cans and assorted battered containers on the other side. The other military trucks coming up behind them turned their vehicles at staggered angles and used their lamps to illuminate a large portion of the slums on both sides of the alley. The soldiers piled out with their rifles. They stepped forward slowly. Dorothy expected the residents to come out, or at least some of them, to see what was going on. But no one came. There weren't even any curious faces in the windows as far as she could see. The entire complex of dilapidated housing appeared to be abandoned.

"Oh, I don't believe the soldiers should have gotten out of their vehicles," Randolph said beside her. "I don't think that was a good idea at all. Please call them back, Lieutenant."

"There may be an injured child out there. We have to do something."

"I do not believe these soldiers are here to provide aid. They have—what's the expression?—other fish to fry."

She stared at him briefly and then climbed out of the car. He came across as much less caring than he actually was. Many highly intelligent people presented themselves as unfeeling. She had to believe that.

It was so quiet. The soldiers were not speaking. The only sounds were the metallic ticking of the cooling engines and the heavy boots tramping on the gritty, refuse-littered paving bricks.

The sky had become a soft, glowing gray with the approach of morning. There were no more signs of lightning. The scattered clouds were pillowy silhouettes of drifting black. One of these silhouettes came down out of the sky and disintegrated into thousands of winged insects. They made a twisting, jagged dagger floating above the slow-moving soldiers. She heard Randolph getting out of the car behind her. A number of larger winged creatures, birds and bats, gathered into an immense moving cigar shape that darted rapidly from one side of the alley to the other before crashing into the pavement behind them, showering them with thousands of bits of feather, bone, and bloody flesh. The soldiers began to trot. Some were panicking, trying to scrape the organic slop off their heads, faces, and chests. Randolph grabbed her by the arm and pulled her, and then all of them started running toward the M2s parked at the other end of the alley. She heard a distressed-sounding buzzing noise. She was surprised to see that it was Randolph making the sound.

"Are you okay?" she shouted.

He was clutching his throat, massaging it. For a moment it appeared as if his neck had warped into something unrecognizable. Then everything looked normal again. "Run!" he shouted.

Several fast-moving shadows sprinted through their group, passing from one side of the alley slum into the other, brushing up against them, knocking them off their stride, slowing them down. The soldiers began turning around in confusion, raising their rifles. Dorothy thought of the terrible possibilities and shouted, "Don't fire!"

At the end of the alley a number of large, unidentifiable human figures stumbled out of the shadows, blocking their access to the tanks. They were too far away for Dorothy to see their faces, but they appeared to be adults, dressed in ripped-up clothing, and they were unnatural in their movements, jerking about, arms dangling. She thought of stringed puppets, or the veterans she had treated suffering from nervous system impairments.

Appallingly, they began climbing on each other. The soldiers around her stopped in their tracks. They were so surprised they lowered their weapons and stared. The frenzied activity at the darkened alley's end resembled the beginnings of some sort of acrobatic circus act. Except there was nothing athletic about the performance—certainly nothing graceful. The figures moved stiffly, and clambered over each other with no sense of muscle applied. They were stepping on heads and kicking into eyes, mouths, ears.

Many more of these people drifted out of the shadows and joined the others, climbed higher, or became additional support at the bottom for others to climb upon. The assemblage of various bodies soon reached a dizzying height. Dorothy even felt the urge to applaud. But then came this sudden, terrifying rush out of the darkness, out of the doors and windows and broken openings in the buildings, and bodies began filling the gaps, the spaces between the legs and around the arms of the others, wrapping their heads and curling around their feet, dozens and then hundreds of them, flying past her at inhuman speeds, children and teenagers and adults. Dark children, Negro men and women mostly, and then the occasional pale face, all of them in dirty attire: poor and ragged and disintegrating.

She tried to get a look at some of their faces as they flew past. Most of them were slack-jawed and expressionless, and many had their eyes shut or only the whites were showing. But now and again she could detect a presence: a pleading or an anguish in a chance glance or the turn of a head, a cry for help in an open mouth or a seemingly accidental gesture, the splaying of an offered hand or a lingering look, and it broke her heart.

This remarkable assemblage solidified before her, several stories high, studded with lolling heads like organic bolts, and it began to move. Its silhouette wasn't at all humanlike—there was nothing resembling a head, and if it had legs they were fused together. Now and then there were the beginnings of appendages which might have been arms, but these preliminary protuberances varied in shape and there were many more than two, as if the creature was undecided as to what its final form should be. It was slow and ponderous for a few steps, although they weren't exactly steps. The collection of bodies shifted and rolled on one edge and then the other, back and forth, progressing up the alley toward her and Randolph and the soldiers, not in a waddle as she might have expected, but in a shape-shifting wave as individual bodies drifted to the back in layers and others were brought rapidly forward.

And although its individual pieces remained silent—people, she reminded herself, these were human beings forced to participate in something no one could ever imagine—the composition itself groaned, and made snapping and cracking and splintering noises, and only after a few minutes of watching this shocking progression did she realize these were the sounds of bones breaking.

One of the soldiers started shooting, and then all of the soldiers were shooting, and screaming at the tops of their lungs as they fired in some kind of hysterical battle cry. She heard and saw the soldier wearing the man-pack radio shouting into his handset for reinforcements when one edge of the rotating bodies caught him and threw him aside.

"Stop shooting!" she screamed. "Those are human beings! There are *children* in there!"

Randolph grabbed her by the arm and dragged her with him back up the alley. "They're already dead, Lieutenant, or soon will be. Profoundly changed in any case, and undoubtedly better off killed quickly. Whatever is driving this doesn't need them alive. They are quite simply . . . *material*."

Some of that material extended itself—a gigantic arm consisting of entangled bodies—reaching down and swatting several soldiers with tremendous force, their frantic cries fading as they disappeared into distant shadows.

At that moment the Browning machine guns on the two tanks began firing, followed by the concussive boom of two 37mm shells, one after the other.

Randolph and Dorothy were suddenly showered in human debris. She turned and saw that the previously tightly-knit edifice of bodies had giant jagged holes through which she could see the sun just coming up behind the Capitol's dome. The left side of the colossal creature now had a ragged edge where bits of its various jigsaw humans had been blown apart, but it still managed to move.

There was another explosion from one of the tanks and the creature reeled as some of its supporting members vanished in a wash of red. More replacement bodies began pouring into it from the end of the slums as if they'd been sucked out of their homes. These figures were assimilated as soon as they arrived, each individual absorbed to make an invisible repair. The creature actually grew larger between each spray of machine gun fire and exploding shell. And still the bodies rushed in to feed its growth.

Then the entire sculpture of flesh and blood and bone turned and rolled onto the offending tanks. They bent and came apart beneath it. Dorothy could see the broken bodies of the soldiers sucked out of the tanks and fed into the creature, its center building out with each new addition.

It pivoted again and began its rapid movement back in their direction. Some of the soldiers had managed to get to the end of the alley when it went for the tanks and now fired back from the other direction, toward Dorothy, Randolph, and the others. The bullets passed right through the dead flesh of the thing and into the dirt and pavement at their feet.

"We must find shelter!" Randolph yelled into her ear.

They moved off to their right into the dark shacks. She could hear the pings on the metal washtubs. Lumber and brick were coming apart in small explosions around them. They crouched low behind some garbage cans as the butchered construction crunched past them. It appeared to be reconfiguring itself. Instead of a tall organism it was becoming a broad one as bodies flowed over each other and limbs altered their entanglement to become a series of grotesque appendages—dozens of them—spreading out into an insect-like arrangement scuttling over the abandoned cars and trucks.

Some of the soldiers made a stand just ahead, and they managed to stall it temporarily. A few of the massive legs swung back around in vaguely probing movements.

"Randolph! We need to get inside!" The words came out in a rasp. Could that awful thing hear her? She had no idea.

They went for the nearest opening, a raw frame missing its door, tattered bits of tile and rug just inside the entrance. A few feet in, Randolph stumbled and Dorothy went down on top of him, her bag swinging around and striking her painfully in the back of the head. She rolled off Randolph quickly and whispered into his ear, "Did I injure you?"

He stirred, groaned, and mumbled, "Just lost my wind for a moment." He rolled over onto his shoulder and gazed at her. "We are not alone in here."

She looked past him. The only light was whatever rays of sunrise had managed to filter their way inside. There was an antique stove against one wall, or pieces of one, the sections held together with wire and old metal plates. A low table with mismatched legs sat a few feet away. Much of the rest of the room appeared to be filled with large quantities of rags—rags a poor person might sell, or wear, or sleep in, or nest in. "Where?"

He motioned upward with his eye. She tilted her head ever so slightly and detected something large on the deeply shadowed ceiling. It began to move back and forth, rocking, and then it scurried across the ceiling into a corner. A black child, frightened, weeping. How did the poor thing ever get up there? Dorothy sat up.

"Lieutenant!" Randolph hissed.

"I think it's harmless. She. I believe that's a little girl up there."

Randolph sighed and sat up as well. "More than a little girl. She moved across the ceiling without falling."

Dorothy kept her eyes on the girl. "Poor child. She looks frightened."

"Of course," he stopped. Then he said, "Look around you. There are more."

Dorothy lowered her eyes. They'd adjusted to the lighting conditions inside the room. The walls were papered in mismatched patterns. Much had been stripped away to reveal the filthy plaster beneath. A thick portion of dust floated in the distinct rays coming through the empty doorframe. Two Negro children were curled together into one corner, their eyes fixed on her. Another lay half-concealed under rags beneath the low table. Two or three or four were mixed in with the rags in the darkest corner away from the door and nearest the stove. She supposed that normally that's where these children slept on colder days. And another one or two or three climbed the walls like giant flies and joined the original one who still looked so frightened. She thought of the patterns the insects made on the walls and ceiling back at the house when Randolph had returned from the Dreamscape.

"How can we help them?"

"We can't."

"Randolph . . ."

"Look at their heads, Lieutenant. Their necks are broken."

She studied each figure. Strange how it hadn't registered before—initially they had seemed almost normal, other than the fact that they could defy gravity and crawl up walls. Their heads were on backward, or tilted at impossible angles, or both. Or moved too freely, as if not connected to their bodies at all.

"My God. I would swear I could see signs of emotion glistening in their eyes, of intelligence."

"Perhaps you did," he said, "but that intelligence belonged to something else."

The other broken children had edged up the walls until they were all hanging there, impossibly, from the ceiling. And as she studied them she could see the abnormalities: the impossibly wide spread of legs and arms (because their limbs were broken), the complete articulation of the joints, the extra bends in their torsos, and just the insect-like jerkiness of their movements as they scrambled across the ceiling.

"Should we run?" She tried to contain her terror.

"I do not believe they intend to attack. I'm not even sure they are aware we are here. I believe they were forgotten, or perhaps they are spare body parts for that massive creature outside. But I suggest we might want to remain as still as possible for now."

So they waited for a very long time, and Dorothy contemplated their situation, and the circumstances of these children, living in the worst possible conditions within sight of America's very centers of power, Capitol Hill, the president, the Washington Monument of the Human Protection League itself, which was protecting, protecting . . . "Why was the breach here, in this poor neighborhood?" she asked.

He didn't respond immediately. "I have no idea. Even when I am in the Dreamscape I have no real insight into what they are thinking. They are like gods to us, completely alien. We cannot even begin to comprehend how their minds work, or even what their senses might apprehend."

"But why didn't it come through closer to you, to your . . . our quarters, since presumably you initiated this breach? Or even nearer the Monument, or the Capitol, where you spend most of your time? Or perhaps you no longer feel you have any connection, or responsibility, for these incursions?"

"Because . . . because . . ." He paused. She had heard the beginnings of a teenage whine in his voice. Perhaps he had heard them too. "You have to understand that the connections are unanchored. The passages float, they lack alignment. My silver key provides only a temporary anchor point, when used properly. We have nothing effective, as yet, against these breaches. No weapon. But a small electromagnetic pulse may sometimes *discourage* them from opening in a particular location. It diverts them some small distance. Central D.C. is protected in a small way via this method."

"A small distance?"

"A very slight diversion," he said.

"So certain other neighborhoods are threatened, Randolph. Certain, poorer neighborhoods?"

"That is up to the government," he replied, not looking at her. "They don't seek my input on those decisions."

She glanced up, thinking perhaps they deserved to have these poor children dropping on them, doing whatever they might. Perhaps she and Randolph could be some sort of food source for these malnourished children? It was a fantasy that smacked of justice.

The last of the children were leaving, crawling off the ceiling and into the empty door opening and disappearing outside. She helped Randolph up and they followed.

Outside it was early morning and overcast, the alley painted mainly in pewter tones with the occasional white or yellow reflection. As her eyes adjusted, brown and rust-colored stains became more evident, as did the torn and leaking anatomy. Her nose stung from the rank odor of slaughtered meat. They passed their automobile. It was useless—its hood and engine compartment smashed in. Two other trucks were seriously damaged; two others appeared intact and drivable. Farther ahead in the alley the giant conglomerated creature lay sprawled, its multiple limbs moving listlessly. Dorothy watched in amazement as the children—what had been children—she'd spent the last hour with climbed over bodies and locked themselves into place within the ragged edges of the form, making it more complete, bringing it closer to whole again.

"It uses the adults for the major muscles, the grosser movements," Randolph explained. "The smaller children give it refinement, more precision in its actions."

Several soldiers stood around, aiming their rifles at the creature. They appeared exhausted, barely awake. Dorothy saw no sign of their driver or the young soldier who had ridden here with them, but the older soldier with the man-pack sat by the side of the alley, looking stunned.

"Soldier, what's the status here?"

"Lots of casualties, miss, including Private Blake. I can't find the sergeant heading up this detail. He was in the truck behind us. Some of the men . . . this thing threw their bodies a long way. And it turned over the tanks, shook them like they were baby toys."

"Are you okay?"

"A little banged up is all. That damn thing broke my radio. I can't reach headquarters."

"We need to evacuate the remaining civilians."

"Ma'am, I don't believe there are any remaining civilians." He looked uneasily at the arrangement of bodies. "I think they're all part of that thing, the ones not blown up or shot to hell."

"Lieutenant."

Dorothy turned around to face Randolph. He gestured toward the creature. Several soldiers had dropped their rifles and were now calmly climbing over the previously acquired human beings and sliding into gaps, wrapping themselves around and between limbs, becoming additional parts of this creature from the Dreamscape.

She intercepted one such soldier as he was making ready to step up onto a leg, grabbed him by his arm and spun him around. "Stop!" she shouted into his face. He stared at her as if blind. His mouth moved loosely, as if chewing up food that wasn't there.

"There's no point," Randolph said behind her. "He's simply building material now."

The soldier started climbing again, fit himself into a hole. Once he was in place the creature shuddered into life again and began to rise. The stench was almost unbearable. Dorothy stepped back and rejoined Randolph and the soldier with the broken radio. They all watched as the colossal figure reached its full height and moved a few yards toward the street with thunderous cracking and popping. Some parts fell off, leaving a gruesome trail.

Dorothy asked, "Have you seen anything like this before in the Dreamscape?"

Randolph had to raise his voice as several bodies exploded when the great being began stretching, swinging its arms. "There is nothing like this in the Dreamscape."

"But *this* creature came through."

"No, no one saw this creature emerge. Because it did not emerge. Whatever Dreamscape god is involved, it did not come through the breach. I suspect the breach was very small, just as I originally believed, too small for one of those grand beings to pass. No, what came through were its intentions, its desires. And it is using the available organic material on our side of the breach to assemble a body for itself, a puppet which it can control from a vast distance."

The terrible collection of human bodies then began to pivot and shake. The soldiers still standing fired perfunctorily into the body of the thing, and when there was no visible effect they dropped their weapons and ran.

"But Randolph, how is it that it is still being controlled? The breach opens, something comes through, and then the breach closes again. That's the way it has always worked, or at least that is what you have told everyone."

Randolph looked perplexed. "I have no idea. It has always been a bodily voyage across those vast spaces between our worlds. The only uncertainty has been the exact nature of the physical form that arrives. I must have done something that has changed this. Somehow I am responsible for the deaths of all these people!"

"Randolph, you don't know that! You've done what you could. Without the early warning system you put in place . . ."

He stared at her. "We have to get back to the Monument!" He grabbed the radio operator's arm. "Can you drive one of those trucks?"

Once they were back at the Monument, Agent Miles was stunned by their appearance. He had dozens of urgent questions, but Carter waved him off and continued on to the office, insisting that Dorothy come along. They left their radio operator behind to explain everything, and by the time they exited the far door Miles was barking orders and calling the military.

"Randolph? Shouldn't we explain to him that their weapons aren't likely to do them any good, and the soldiers—"

"Our soldier will tell them what he can. They can draw their own conclusions, but of course they'll hardly listen. They're like children—they have to discover the truth in their own way. We have important things to do. May I have your bag?"

"Why, are you injured? Stop, let me look at it." But he'd already snagged the strap with his claw and taken the bag away from her. Things were so frantic, she hadn't even realized he'd lost, or removed the pillowcase. "Randolph? I need that. My medical supplies—"

"You'll get it back in a little while. I think I may have a need for it."

He struggled with the doorknob to Dream Division, and then forced the door open. It swung hard into the wall, cracking the pane. She could hear the weeping coming from several rooms inside, the small sounds of protests, and then toward the back of the offices, the screams.

"Exactly as I expected I'm afraid." They went into the closest office. The tramp she had last seen yesterday lay dead, apparently having choked on his own vomit. His eyes were still open, however, and glistening. She was convinced she could see something in the pupils, but Randolph was still moving and she had to struggle to keep up.

They found two more dead, but the others appeared to be alive, although in intense physical and mental pain. They finally reached his office. The old woman lay there on the low couch, arching her back and screaming. Randolph plopped Dorothy's bag down on his desk, and then opened it before she could stop him. He pulled out some of the medical supplies, finally a syringe and a bottle.

"This should calm her down a bit, give her a little peace. Please administer it, Lieutenant, if you would?"

"We have to be careful with any pain medication. I don't really know what's wrong with her."

"It's my responsibility, Lieutenant. And I sincerely believe she will survive that shot you're going to give her. Now."

She injected the poor woman and her screams gradually subsided into whimpers, and then nothing. But she was thankfully still breathing, although her pulse was wildly erratic.

Dorothy looked up at Randolph. He held the gun she kept in her bag. "I'm sorry, Randolph. I was told . . . I was ordered to carry it."

"Oh, no apologies necessary, Lieutenant. I told General Craig he needed to give you something, just in case. In fact I insisted on it. It's a Colt, isn't it? I don't really know that much about handguns."

"Colt M1911 semi-automatic service pistol," she replied.

"Why did he give you something so old? I told him you needed something reliable."

"Randolph, I'm told it's highly reliable. They were standard during the Great War, and the general swears by it."

"Well, if it's good enough for the general."

"Why did you want me to have a gun, Randolph?"

"Because you might need it, Lieutenant. Look at me. I had no idea what I might come back as or even, without any additional trips into the Dreamscape, if I would maintain this physical shape, or if my brain might undergo some unexpected mutation. I told you, those creatures, there's no fathoming their thinking. I was afraid there might come a time when I wouldn't recognize the difference between you and, well, *food*."

"Randolph, there are always other options."

"We've wasted too much time here, Lieutenant. I need you to call Doctor Andrews at Butler Hospital. My hand is full."

Randolph wasn't pointing the gun at her, but she understood that he intended to be obeyed. She dialed Daniel's direct number. He answered almost immediately. She could hear the screams of his three special patients in the background. He sounded breathless, panicked. "Daniel, this is Dorothy. Randolph Carter wants to speak to you."

"Hold the receiver up to my ear, Lieutenant." She did as she was told. "Doctor Andrews, I'm afraid my early warning system has proven to be a terrible idea. I can hear them—I can't imagine how you stand it. I need you to apply the remedy we agreed upon, the swift remedy. Yes . . . yes I know. Yes . . . I'm sorry too. But please, every moment we wait makes matters worse."

He handed it back to her. She heard three gunshots in succession, and after a pause, a fourth. Her hand shook and she dropped the handset.

Randolph turned and fired one shot into the old woman's head. "Randolph, no!" He marched out of his office and down the hall. She wanted to follow him, to stop him, but she was afraid. And although she didn't quite understand what was going on, she knew he was doing this for a reason, and no doubt for a very good reason.

The telephone handset made a steady *click-click-click* sound. She dropped it back into its cradle. There were five more shots, a minute or so between each one. She wanted to scream. She gripped the edge of the desk with both hands, squeezing her eyes shut.

Randolph walked back into the room, tears streaming down his cheeks. He looked very much like a sad little boy. The gun dangled from his hand. The clawed hand slowly opened and closed again and again with a steady, machinelike regularity. He gazed at her.

"I had not anticipated this. Perhaps I should have. My early warning system, those unfortunates I chose, they kept the passage open between us and the Dreamscape. Not very wide, but wide enough for directions, for orders to come through. They had no way of stopping it. They couldn't help themselves. The passage closed after my own trips, perhaps, at least I had a key—the full truth of that remains to be seen. But they had no such method available to them. Theirs was a one-way street."

"But was shooting them the only way? They were human beings; they had human families."

"Of course I know this, Lieutenant. The three at the asylum were my very own cousins—one was only in his teens. We Carters have always had certain inclinations; we have always been magicians of a sort. Butler has been the family asylum, just as it was for the Lovecraft family. Recruiting members of my own family seemed only natural. I understand their inherited abilities."

She walked around the desk and reached to take the gun from him, but he stepped away from her and held the gun up to his head. "Randolph, you should give that to me."

"I know very little about these pistols, Lieutenant, but I just shot six people in the head. Are there any more rounds in the magazine? You might as well tell me—I can always conduct a test."

"There is one round left," she said.

"Very good," he replied.

The phone rang. Her hand was shaking. She made a tight fist, opened it, and then picked up the receiver. She closed her eyes and listened, then cradled the phone again.

"That was Agent Miles. The creature has fallen apart into its component bits. There are no signs of movement, anywhere in the slums. It's over Randolph, and that weapon belongs to me, am I correct?"

He handed it over. Improperly, but he hadn't been trained. A line of insects made a series of loops on the wall behind him, then another pattern she did not recognize. Silently she begged him not to turn around.

SIX

The Stuff That Dreams Are Made Of

FIRST, I WAS TOTALLY minding my own business.

Second, if the pretty boy behind the bar had shown his hand sooner, maybe we wouldn't have had to wash what was left of two of his customers off the walls.

I'd been nursing a cocktail, the taste of which I like, but the name of which I prefer to keep private because it sounds like something Deanna Durbin might order if she was doing the town with the Pope, and I was waiting for Mike Bowman, my business partner. He was already spectacularly late, but that was hardly cause for alarm. With Mike, keeping people waiting is practically an art form.

I'm not going to lie to you. It's not like I hadn't noticed the blonde when she walked in—there was a lot to notice and hardly any of it was shy—but after that initial glance, I'd kept my eyes on the counter and my mind on whether the lead Mike had claimed to be following would turn into an actual case paying actual money. We could use it. It had been a slow month in a long winter.

The blonde wasn't alone anyway—a guy twice her age and certainly more than half her height joined her at the counter after wasting two minutes glad-handing a table of second-stringers from the *Chronicle*.

"Just making sure they're going to cover the opening of the new store," he said to her and to anyone within a hundred yards. "Prime location, Ruby," he added, though I suspect Ruby might have already had that fact mentioned to her once or twice. "Right there on Market."

"Are you going to make a lot of money?" she asked him. I know, I know. I wish I could tell you Ruby didn't actually say that out loud, but she did.

"Well, it's not like I'm hurting now," he said, and pulled something shiny from his coat pocket. It was a small green stone of some kind that hung from a thin gold chain, and he dangled it from his fingers to catch Ruby's eye.

"What is it?" she said.

He waved it in front of her eyes again, twitching his fingers so that it did a little shimmy for her. But he waited to speak until he slipped it back into his pocket, waited in fact until he patted the pocket to be sure his trinket was safely there, as if he feared some last-minute trick from an unseen magician. Seemed odd. Maybe he was crazy. But what the hell did I know? Maybe he *wasn't* crazy. Maybe Ruby's day job was Beautiful Assistant to some quick-with-his-hands vaudeville shyster, and they were setting this idiot up for a now-you-see-it, now-you-don't routine. Christ knows, wouldn't be the first time.

Done patting, he gave her a wink. "My ship came in," he said. Kind of smug, kind of teasing.

"That's nice, Albie," she said. "But what *is* it?" Flirting with petulant, heading for insistent.

Albie lent his voice as much drama and mystery as he could, which wasn't much, but you work with what you've got. "The stuff that dreams are made of . . . ," he said, and his eyes did their rheumy best to twinkle.

"On," said the barman quietly. He was wiping glasses down and not even looking at Ruby and her swain, but the latter believed he knew a challenge when he heard one.

"I beg your pardon?" Albie said. Little spin on it, like he was giving the guy the opportunity to plead insanity.

"On," said the barman again, looking up this time. "It's 'on,' not 'of.' It's Shakespeare, isn't it? *The Tempest*, if I remember correctly. 'We are such stuff as dreams are made on.'"

His voice was rich with that just-like-us-but-smarter thing that had once had women throwing themselves at John Barrymore. Ruby heard it too. Still worked, apparently. She smiled. "I love your accent," she said. "Are you British?"

"When the occasion calls for it, madam," the barman said. He gave her a small nod that managed to be both self-satisfied and self-deprecating, and the smile with which he backed it up was a clear signal that should she be looking for male company, he was more than willing to step into the breach once she came to her senses about the asshole she rode in on.

Before all interested parties could learn just what the hell Albie was going to do about that, the street door to the bar slammed open, loud enough to make everybody in the joint look over.

Revealed in the opening, framed against the rain that was just starting to fall outside, was an odd little fellow who was busy lowering the silver-topped cane with which he'd shoved the door open. Really quite splendid in his own bizarre fashion, he was a compact dandy in a formal dress suit, his hair slick with pomade, and only his eyes—slightly protruding, almost batrachian—spoiling his pocket-Adonis ambitions.

Those eyes fixed themselves on Albie, and a small and far from pleasant smile twitched across his tight little lips.

"Jerome Cadiz," I heard Albie mutter just before the barman stole my attention by tapping an unobtrusive finger on the counter in front of my stool. He'd laid down a small key—like something for a left-luggage locker at a train station or a bus depot—and slid it toward me.

"Got a little something for you, Steve," he said quietly.

I pocketed the key instinctively—what else are you going to do, someone hands you a key?—but it bothered me that he had my name, because as far as I knew, I hadn't been handing it out.

"Huh?" I said. And I'll have you know I said it pretty damn incisively. I didn't read those Perry Mason stories every month for nothing.

"I know how much you like your hats," the barman said, as if that explained anything.

"What?" I said. "Have we met before?"

"Depends what you mean by 'before,'" he said. And then the world went mad.

Albie suddenly pushed himself back from the counter, stool slamming to the floor behind him, and glared down the length of the bar at the little peacock he'd called Jerome Cadiz.

Whatever trouble Cadiz might have thought he was bringing to the party, it seemed that Albie was determined to head him off at the pass. "*P'hath bar nyleq'h hunq'a!*" he yelled at him. Or, you know, words to that effect.

"*Albie!*" Ruby said sharply, not like she feared for his sanity, but like he was embarrassing her, like he'd just told an off-color joke to a minister's wife or something.

But Albie wasn't done. And he certainly wasn't chastened by Ruby's disapproval. If anything, he looked like this might be the very opportunity he'd been waiting for to impress her.

"Behold the shard of the god!" he shouted, which was at least in English, even if it was still gibberish. He drew out that shimmering green stone from his pocket with his right hand, held it out threateningly at arm's length toward Cadiz, and waved his left hand over it in three consecutive, counterclockwise circles . . .

And then nothing happened.

You got to assume that was a bad moment for Albie, and I'm sure the contemptuous giggle that escaped Cadiz's mouth didn't help at all. Like the kind of jerk who sits down at the piano and plays a perfect "Moonlight Sonata" after you've just failed to play "Chopsticks," Cadiz also put his hand into his pocket and brought something out.

Not much of something, though. All he had in his hand was an unprepossessing mound of ashy gray dust. It looked like he might have scooped up a tablespoon's worth of somebody's dead relative from an unguarded urn, no more than that. It sat there cupped in his palm, doing precisely the same amount of nothing that Albie's shard of the green god had done. Until Cadiz blew on it. At which point it began to behave a little differently from your average pile of crematorium ash.

At first rising up in an arching line, swollen at the head like a king cobra woken by the charmer's pipe, it then swept upward and outward through the air in a curving arc, trailing more of itself behind it than should have been possible, and roiling at the head like a tidal wave about to break.

"Albie?" Ruby said, her voice small and unsure.

That voice, and Albie's devastated expression, were the last any of the rest of us knew, other than the deafening concussive roar of Cadiz's party favor as it reached critical mass and exploded.

I wasn't the last to wake up, but I wasn't the first either, and by the time I did, the uniform cops were already taking notes and sharing disbelieving glances.

There were a handful of us left in the bar, but there was no Jerome Cadiz. He'd gone, as had my curious friend, the key-dispensing barman. As for Albie and Ruby . . . well, they weren't *gone*, exactly, but they were unlikely to be giving statements to the lead detective. They were nowhere to be seen, unless you counted the two vaguely people-shaped bloodstains that were dripping their way down the back wall, already seeping and staining unpleasantly into the sawdust piles atop the bar's old-school tiled floor.

The detective though—in this case, a one-time beat cop bruiser named Dominic Coughlan whom nobody expected to ever make detective, let alone turn out to be good at it—certainly wanted to hear for himself what the rest of us had to say, no matter how ridiculous. He saved me til last, figuring with the license and all I might actually be of some use to him. On this occasion—and not, I'm sorry to say, for the first time—I was a great disappointment to Dominic, being as unconscious as every other idiot in the room when whatever finally happened finally happened.

The thing about senior investigative officers is this; like stallions or bulls, it's never a good idea to put two of them in the paddock at once, so when Tim Loory walked into the bar a few minutes later, I got an unfocused bad feeling. This jacket had clearly landed on Coughlan's desk, not

Tim's, so why was he here? I mean, it might've been a coincidence—cops have got to drink *somewhere*—but he was looking right at me like I was the guy he was looking for; and while the expression plastered on his big stupid Irish face was perhaps intended to be unreadable, I was pretty sure he hadn't shown up here to tell me he'd just heard from Bay Meadows that my horse had come in at twenty-to-one.

"Steve," he said.

"Tim," I said, and waited for him to tell me I was still the king of the snappy comeback. But he didn't. He didn't say anything, in fact, for a good three seconds, which is a hell of a long time for we who banter.

"You're waiting for Mike," he said eventually. Not a question.

I didn't answer. Just looked at him until his mouth twisted in what, for a cop, passes for sympathy.

Ah hell, I thought, and asked him if it was quick.

He spared me the bullshit. "It was not," he said and pretended to look at the painting behind the bar to prevent me reading just how not quick it had been.

"Out by the old railroad cross?" I said and then, off his nod, "Let's go."

"You don't want to see it," he said.

"The hell I don't," I said. I took a last belt from my drink and reached for my hat.

Tim didn't move, other than to point at my glass, a stunned expression on his face. "What in God's name is that?" he said.

"It's a drink, Tim," I said, planting my hat pointedly on my head. "We're in a bar."

"It's *pink*," he said.

"We should go."

"It looks like something they'd reward Little Lord Fauntleroy with for finishing in first place in his dance recital."

"We should go."

He came out of his trance and looked at me again, sympathy for the loss of my partner back in place. "You don't want to see it," he repeated, and this time there was something in his tone that actually slowed me down.

"On account of . . .?"

"On account of it makes what happened here look like a pat on the cheek in the kind of third degree we reserve for people with a long history of generous contributions to the Policeman's Benevolent Fund."

I waggled my hand like I was going to have to deduct a point or two. "A little elaborate," I said, not without gratitude for the distraction.

Tim's shrug was implicit. "My wife's cousin?" he said. "The head doctor? Last time he was around for Joan's veal Parmesan, he volunteered the opinion that I take refuge in colorful simile and metaphor because I'm uncomfortable with my emotions."

I gave it a moment while we headed for the door.

"This cousin of your wife's," I said.

"Yeah?"

"You let him have it once she wasn't looking, right?"

"She knows better than to leave him alone with me," he said, and I followed him out to the street.

As he drove us over to the old railroad station—the one that still did some storage business, but hadn't seen a train since they cut the big red ribbon at Downtown Union—Tim did his best to talk about other stuff and I appreciated the effort, even though he wasn't very good at it. He didn't have to try for too long—even though we were heading way across town, the trip took barely five minutes. Which might sound impressive to you, but then you're probably someone who doesn't have a siren sitting in your glove compartment for whenever you feel like cutting through traffic.

Mike, or what was left of him, was underneath the pedestrian bridge, mercifully hidden from the sight of casual passersby. Jesus Christ. It looked like something had clawed its way out of him, something powerful and frenzied. Like someone had force-fed him a mountain lion and then whistled it to come home.

Mike and I had never done well enough to afford an honest-to-God full-time receptionist, but Mike's sister's youngest came in two afternoons a week for pin money, and to let us look like a going concern for clients to whom that kind of thing mattered. It was she who'd told me yesterday that Mike was following up on a lead for a potential new client.

"What kind of client?" I'd asked.

"You know what kind," Valerie had replied, with a sparkle in her seventeen-year-old eye that would have been a great disappointment to the holy sisters back at her parochial school.

"Was it the kind that has a name?"

"It was," she'd said. "Kelly Woodman. *Miss* Kelly Woodman."

"That your stress or hers?"

"Oh, hers," Valerie'd said. "She was *very* emphatic about it."

All of which meant nothing more than that I had a name, which was something, but it wasn't likely to be enough.

Mike had never been great at the administrative side of the business. Stuff like filing receipts or keeping notes or making entries in a phone-log cramped what he liked to think of as his style. Fortunately, his aristocratic disdain for keeping house also meant he rarely cleared out the trashcan under his desk, and I found what I needed in there.

It was a napkin bearing the logo and address of a residential hotel, to which someone had added a handwritten room number. Someone—presumably the same someone—had also left a small and perfectly formed crimson lip-o-graph next to the number. Might've merely been happenstance—napkins were invented because people have to dab their mouths now and then, even people who wear bright red lipstick—but I couldn't help but wonder if it was also something to ensure that Mike was kept at full attention.

The Hotel Montana, which was apparently where Miss Kelly Woodman hung whatever hats she had, was the kind of residential hotel that didn't have lobby security—just a bellboy with his feet up on the front desk. And, if his employers had any of the usual disapproval of gentlemen callers, they certainly hadn't bothered to let him know about it. I made it all the way to the elevator without his eyes once raising from that month's *Terror Tales*.

Her apartment was on the fifth floor, and her door had its own little bell. I gave it a push.

When she opened the door, apparently fresh from the shower, she was still tying the satin belt of her satin bathrobe. I couldn't help but feel that that was all part of the floorshow, but that doesn't mean I didn't like it.

She gave me a brief appraising look and then cocked a loaded finger at me. "Mike's partner," she said, like I was not only the answer to the puzzle, but the lucky winner's grand prize.

"Steve Donnelly," I said.

"You found me, Steve Donnelly," she said. "Aren't you clever?"

"I don't know about that," I said. "You want to play hard to get, don't leave your address in a detective's office."

"Now don't be cruel, Steve," she said, then cast her eyes down demurely and gave a half smile. "At least, not yet."

Jesus Christ. Mike must've been putty in this one's hands.

"Come on in," she said, and stepped aside—but not too far aside—to let me pass.

"You'll take a drink?" she said, once we'd managed to reach her living room without anyone getting pregnant. Her question about the drink wasn't really a question. She may have been polite enough to make it sound like one, but the door to her cocktail cabinet was open long before I could actually answer.

"It's eleven-thirty in the morning," I said. "Not exactly sundown." It wasn't like I didn't feel that I could use a drink, just that I thought a mild protest was appropriate. After all, I didn't want Miss Kelly Woodman thinking I was easy.

"You know, Steve," she said, "one of the most pleasant revelations of my life was the moment when I found out that all that stuff you can do after sundown, you can do before sundown too."

"Really?" I said. "What was the occasion?"

"I was having my dress taken off by my best friend's husband," she said. "Bourbon or vodka?" She was holding up a bottle in each hand and wiggling them at me.

"Those are my choices?"

"What did you have in mind?" she said. "I like to be accommodating."

I gave a brief hopeful glance into the cabinet.

"Oh, that's right," she said, her voice full of teasing delight. "Mike told me. You like that cute little drink that sounds like—"

"Mike told you what I like to *drink*? How the hell long were you with him? I thought it was a half an hour?"

"Time is relative," she said. "Haven't you heard?" She made a show of looking into the cocktail cabinet. "Anyway, looks like I'm all out of cotton candy or sugar plums, so there goes *that* concoction." Her hands made the bottles of vodka and bourbon sway at me again, slow as a hula dancer's hips. "I'm afraid you're just going to have to go for the blonde or the brunette."

"That's fine," I said. "I'll take a vodka rocks."

"There's a big boy," she said and then, while pouring the vodka over the ice, "I heard about what happened to Mike, by the way. I'm so very sorry."

She didn't sound all that broken up about it, to be honest, but I tried not to hold it against her. She'd only known him half an hour, which works out pretty much as half an hour, however relative time might be.

"And all so unnecessary as it turned out," she said, handing me the drink. "If we'd known you were already on the case, we wouldn't have had to approach Mike in the first—"

"Hold on," I said, cutting her off. I put my drink down untasted on a side-table next to her white leather sofa. I saw how she threw it a quick glance, as if bothered that something wasn't quite going to plan, but I had other questions first. "What are you talking about, I was already on the case? And what makes you think—"

It was her turn to interrupt me. "You were in the *bar*," she said, and gave me a look like I was either screwing with her or had just had a small stroke. "Last night."

Well, that made things interesting. An old-timer from the Confidential Agency whom I'd got to know when he was just a few months shy of retiring had once said to me, "You'll find, kid, that when you're looking into something, there's no such thing as an unrelated incident." It was the kind of observation he liked to toss around when he figured he had a receptive audience, the sort of homily with which canny old operatives in love with their own legend like to dazzle the young and impressionable. The more kindly disposed among us like to call that sort of thing mythmaking, though I believe the actual scientific term is horseshit. But maybe the old Confidential Op had been smarter than I thought.

Before I could ask about the bar and what it might have had to do with whatever she'd been to see Mike about, the doorbell of her apartment rang. I felt the germ of a suspicion that it was not an unrelated incident.

Kelly made a tutting noise. "Look at me," she said. "Nearly noon and still half-naked." She turned and headed for what I presumed was her bedroom door. "Could you see who that is, Steve? I need to slip into something a little less comfortable."

I opened the apartment's front door to find that Miss Kelly Woodman of the Hotel Montana had another gentleman caller. That bellboy downstairs, I decided, was really not doing his job.

The new arrival was not much taller than me. He was, however, about three times as wide. And all that width was encased in a coruscating cashmere robe that seemed to billow and undulate around him despite the hotel corridor's surprising lack of gale-force winds. It was the kind of thing one would wear to an afternoon soirée at an opium parlor in a Cairo bazaar, I figured, though I should tell you right now that I've never been to Cairo, know nothing of its bazaars, and certainly have no idea whether or not they feature opium parlors. It was just what came to mind at the sight of the fat man and his vast and absurd caftan.

"Garland," he said, smiling at me. "Constantine Garland."

"Steve Donnelly," I said. "You here for Kelly?"

"Indeed," he said. "Aren't you?"

"Sure," I said. "But I didn't know it was a party."

He leaned a little to his right to cast a somewhat theatrical gaze over my shoulder and down into the length of the apartment. "Really?" he said, looking back at me. "Even though you were not the first guest to arrive?"

I half-turned and looked back behind me. Kelly had come out of her bedroom again and had brought a little surprise with her. Jerome Cadiz. The peacock from the bar who'd taught the unfortunate Albie a lesson in magic. Neither of them had a gun on the other, though both of them had guns. Both of them were smiling, too, and Kelly's smile was almost as unsettling as his.

I turned fast, ready to push my way past the fat guy and at least get his bulk between me and whatever bullets might soon start flying, but it turned out I was a tad optimistic. From somewhere within the labyrinthine folds of his ridiculous robe, Garland had already pulled out a nasty little hammer, raised it way above his head, and was swinging it heavily down toward the center of my brow.

I didn't even remember the moment of impact, let alone hitting the floor and being carried back into the living room.

By the time things swam back into focus, I was propped up in a perfectly comfortable chair sitting across from Constantine Garland, who was taking up most of Kelly's white leather sofa and who was beaming at me with the kind of benevolent indulgence he'd show to an old friend with whom he'd been enjoying a quiet hand or three of pinochle and who'd decided to take an unscheduled break to indulge in a little nap.

Kelly was sitting at a small letter bureau. She had the bureau's writing-lid down and was shuffling a pack of cards on it. Her eyes were on Garland and me and she was shuffling blind, but it was smooth and beautiful and expert enough to make it clear that should she ever find herself in Monte Carlo she'd have very little reason to starve. Cadiz was leaning against the doorjamb with a kind of louche elegance, as if waiting for a society photographer to immortalize his moment and passing the time until that happened by giving me the ambiguous benefit of his fishy stare.

Garland registered my return to the land of the conscious. *"T'reh faghul al aklo?"* he said to me. *"Thepha cantro? Cantro?"* Well, let me be a little clearer: I of course have no idea what the hell he *actually* said, but that's approximately what it sounded like. Once he was done, he looked at me with an optimistic inquisitiveness that was as meaningless to me as the nonsense that had been coming out of his mouth.

"How hard did you hit me with that hammer?" I asked him, tapping at my forehead with a couple of careful fingers. "My Pig Latin skills seem to have deserted me."

His eyes clouded briefly as if he suspected me of either lying or mockery, and his fat little fingers twitched instinctively, as if eager to reach for his hammer again. I could imagine how fully at ease he was using it as a tool of persuasion or punishment, so was relieved when I saw the moment pass, saw him choose to believe that I wasn't just playing dumb.

"So you are not of the elect, Mr. Donnelly," he said. "One always likes to be sure. I take it then that your interest in the spoils of the *Stella Noctis* is purely financial?"

"You got something against money?" I said. Other than the fact he was now speaking English, what he was talking about was still meaningless to me, but I've never found that admitting ignorance is a good way to get people to open up.

He gave a throaty little chuckle. "Against money?" he said "No indeed, sir. It is, after all, what makes the world go round." He gave a sidelong glance to Kelly. "At least for now," he said to her like a stage aside, like they had a little secret, and a glint of excitement came into her eyes, an excitement that didn't have a lot in common with the expert come-hither crap with which she dazzled saps like me or Mike.

"Let's say my interest *is* financial," I said. "How interested are you willing to make me?"

"You *have* it?" he said, suddenly eager. "You have the statue?"

"Never mind what I have or don't have," I said. "Let's just say my ship came in." I was taking a shot. I'd remembered that that's what the late lamented Albie had said to the late lamented Ruby, and figured that the *Stella Noctis* that Chubs here had referred to was very possibly the literal ship in question.

The anticipatory sigh that came out of Garland, and the way Kelly suddenly set her pack of cards down, told me that I was perhaps after all not as dumb as I look. Also, it wasn't as if I *didn't* have something. I just had no idea what it was for and why I had it. But, given that all this circling wasn't doing any of us any good and—as it surely wouldn't have taken them much longer to realize I had absolutely no idea what the hell any of us were talking about—I played the only card I had.

"Lookit, fats," I said, hoping he'd be offended enough to assume I must have a bargaining chip if I was willing to risk mouthing off like that, but not offended enough to take another swing with his hammer. "Let's get something straight. I don't give a shit about you or your little green god. I just want to know what you know about the key."

There was a moment of complete silence. Just long enough for me to wonder if I'd overreached. I'd been playing the same kind of association game that had scored me a significant point with the ship thing. *Shard of the God,* Albie'd called his small fragment of green stone. *You have the statue?* Garland had asked. So the Donnelly brains trust had put two and two together and risked making five by presuming that this week's trigger for the criminal lunatic population of the city to run around trying to kill each other was a green statue of a god of some kind. The silence can't have lasted more than two seconds, but I really felt I owed Kelly an apology for my earlier skepticism about time being relative.

Finally, Garland gave a slight chuckle. The amusement in it wasn't of the nicest kind, but I'd take it. "Oh, Mr. Donnelly," he said. "It's extremely unlikely we'd be having this conversation—delightful though it is—if I had the key or knew where it was."

"You wouldn't mind me wanting independent corroboration of that, would you?" I said, though I tried to make my tone suggest I really didn't give a damn whether he minded or not.

He blinked once as if to pardon my rudeness, but stayed polite, stayed amused. “Not at all,” he said. “Not at all.”

Cadiz was still lounging against the doorjamb, giving me the benefit of a lazy eye that was supposed to tell me something. He needed to work on his act a little—I couldn’t tell if he wanted to kill me or kiss me. At the sound of Garland’s snapped fingers, though, he looked over like he was about to be let off the leash.

“Jerome,” the fat man said. “Do I have the locker key in question?”

“You do not.”

“Do *you*, perhaps, have it?”

“I do not.”

Garland turned back to look at me, spreading his hands in a what-more-can-I-do? manner, but Cadiz had apparently been enjoying the game and wanted to throw in a new wrinkle.

“Perhaps *she* has it,” he said, and nodded in Kelly’s direction.

“Miss Woodman?” Garland asked him.

“Yeah,” Cadiz said. “Perhaps she has it.” He paused, letting his eyes take a good long look. “About her person.”

“And who’s going to search me?” Kelly said. “You?” The contempt was withering, but Cadiz just shrugged and gave a half smile. It was wry and boyish and, though I hate to admit it, almost goddamn charming.

“Nobody needs to search anybody,” I said. “*I’ve* got the key.”

That got their attention. In fact, it was kind of unsettling the way all three pairs of eyes swung as one to lock on my face.

“More importantly,” I said, “I know where the locker is. Which means I can get whatever’s in there. Which means, unless I miss my guess, that I’m the only son of a bitch who can get his hands on this statue you’re all in such a dither about.”

Thing is, I *did* know where the locker was. I hadn’t realized I did until remembering the key reminded me of the bartender and remembering the bartender reminded me of his crack about my hats. How he knew whatever he knew about me was still a mystery to me, but he'd used it to give me a clue. *I know how much you like your hats*, he'd said. Well, I do like my hats. And I don't like them from five-and-dime chain stores. I like them custom-made by an honest-to-God hat guy, and my particular hat guy was Stavros The Hat Guy—no kidding, that's actually what it says on his shingle—who runs his business out of one of those little storefront franchises on the west concourse at Downtown Union. He's sandwiched in between the shoeshine stand and the cigar store. And directly opposite the bank of left-luggage lockers.

Being polite about it—asking permission of my new friends before I stood up to cross the room and use the phone—I called Valerie, told her to get the key out of my desk drawer, head to Downtown Union, and bring whatever she found in the locker to the Hotel Montana.

"Really, Steve?" she said, like I'd brought Christmas to her early. "An assignment?"

She sounded thrilled. And then, when I told her to give the package to the pulp-reading bellboy in the lobby rather than bring it up to the room herself, she sounded devastated. If I got a chance, I'd make it up to her one day, but right now she'd have to stay devastated—I didn't want her within spitting distance of these people.

I paused at the cocktail cabinet on my way back from the phone, took out the bottle of vodka, and raised an eyebrow at Kelly.

"Help yourself," she said.

"Not drugged after all?" I said.

"Well, not the *bottle*," she said, like I was stupid. "You think I'm an amateur?"

"I do not," I said, pouring myself a shot. "It was you, wasn't it? You killed Mike."

She gave it a beat or two, wondered if the lie was worth it. "Not personally," she said.

I believed her—I'd seen the body—but that didn't stop her being guilty as sin. I swallowed the vodka and sat back down opposite Garland.

"What is it about this thing?" I asked him. "This statue. That makes people like you do things like that."

"Are you *fond* of anything, Mr. Donnelly?" he said, interlacing his pudgy little fingers across his great fat belly, as if settling in for Mommy to tell him a story.

"Kind of question is that?" I said.

"Oh, I mean no offense, I assure you," he said, though he seemed mildly amused at any offense he might actually have caused. "I have no interest in whatever worldly pleasures may delight you. I assume, for example, that like any vigorous man of your age, you find that wine, women, and song—or the equivalents thereof—have their inevitable attraction. I refer instead to the fascination that some of us feel for the artifacts of history, with their cargo of mystery and the ineluctable. There are some objects, some mysteries, for which—to those of us who are already on the journey—no price is too great. Objects which, once possessed, can bestow upon the bearer unimaginable power. The Scroll of Thoth, the Lament Configuration, the Ark of the Covenant, the Eye of Agomotto, the Spear of Destiny . . . these, and many other such artifacts, are being sought even now by our new friends over in Europe.

"Friends who, like us, worship a race that came out of the sky and existed upon this planet long before there were any men. They are gone now, inside the earth and under the sea, but they divulged their secrets in dreams to the first humans, who formed a cult which has never died. Hidden in distant wastes and dark places all over the world until the stars were ready again, we have always existed and always will exist until the Armies of the Night should rise and once more bring the Earth beneath their sway.

"This statue, Mr. Donnelly, was old before Atlantis drowned. It has been the stuff of legends and the destroyer of empires. Thrones have been traded for it, and thousands slaughtered. It is valued both for what it is—a thing of dreadful beauty carved from a stone not seen on this Earth for millennia—and for what it represents . . . the shining path to the Outer Reaches."

The bell to the apartment rang and Garland nodded to Cadiz who, moments later, was standing a newspaper-wrapped object about eight inches high on Kelly's kitchenette counter. Without waiting on Garland's permission, he whipped the wrappings away, letting them litter Kelly's floor, and revealing what was to my eyes a frankly not-very-impressive statuette of a squid-like but strangely regal monster. It was vaguely man-like in shape, but with the head of an octopus whose face was a mass of tentacles. Squatting on a rectangular pedestal covered with undecipherable characters, long, narrow wings folded back behind it, while curved claws gripped the front edge of the base. Carved from a greenish-black stone which glittered with golden, iridescent flecks, it was like nothing I'd ever seen before.

"Well, you tell a good story," I said to Garland, and nodded at the tarnished thing on the counter. "And this is it?"

"I rather fear that it is," Garland said, which seemed an odd response. He was on his feet faster than I'd have given him credit for, and the nasty little hammer was out of wherever it hid and in his hand before he reached the object.

"No!" Kelly shouted, but there was no time. The thing was in fragments before she or Cadiz could do anything.

"Calm yourselves!" Garland shouted at both of them. "Look!"

Nobody seemed to be too bothered about me anymore, so I stood up to take a look as well. Apparently, the statuette was important not for itself, but for what it contained. Within its shattered ruins, there was some kind of loamy earth. And within *that*, there were nine small objects. For one nauseating moment, I could have sworn they were wriggling in the stinking soil as if the decay-filled thing had bred worms within itself over the centuries. But, as Garland's eager hands swept the soil away from around them, I saw the objects were inanimate and stationary.

Figurines, I guess you'd call them. Small ornaments in a pearlescent green stone which put me in mind of Albie's sad little fake, although these things had a milky translucency that made them seem . . . I don't know . . . *denser*, somehow.

"Ni'ib shuggarath bah'im," Garland said, in an awed whisper.

"Ni'ib shuggarath bah'im," Kelly and Cadiz repeated, in unsettling synchronicity, like congregants echoing a priest's invocation.

Sharing a glance of mutual understanding, their eyes glittering with the fervency of religious lunacy, each of them reached down and picked up one of the figurines and then, stepping away from the ruins of their octopus god as if by unspoken assent, they moved back into the room, each of them pinning their figure to their clothes—to a shirt, a robe, a blouse.

Brooches? I thought. Jesus Christ. This was all for ornamental jewelry?

"Sit down, Mr. Donnelly," Garland said. "Please. This won't take long."

I sat—I didn't mistake that "please" for anything other than the order it was—and he sat too. He resumed talking, making no reference to the odd little ritual he'd just shared with his colleagues, instead moving on to a new theme—I'll spare you the circumlocutions and euphemisms—which was essentially the unfortunate necessity of removing the inconvenient Mr. Steve Donnelly from the picture.

The ornament in his lapel shimmered a little, catching the light and giving the strangest illusion of movement.

Garland continued to talk—was there ever a circumstance in which he didn't?—but I wasn't really hearing anything anymore. Because the movement I thought I'd seen revealed itself to be no illusion at all and I watched, appalled, as the small leg of the figure pinned to his lapel twitched spastically, as if in pain or shock. It wasn't shimmering. It was writhing.

Jesus Christ. This fat bastard had pinned to his chest, like some vile cross between a medal and a trophy, a living thing. Living at least until it could be released from its agony.

I'd had very little doubt that these were terrible people, but this seemed awful even for them.

Garland saw me staring at his wretched ornament, and must have read the horror on my face. His own face contorted in a small grimace, not apologetic, hardly even embarrassed, more a sort of facial shrug, like somebody caught doing something not discussed in polite society but entirely natural.

I looked quickly at Jerome and Kelly. Their figurines too. Pinned, dying, twitching, wriggling.

"You think it a cruel affectation, Mr. Donnelly?" the fat man asked.

I just looked at him.

"It's an optical illusion," Kelly said, her voice constrained and tight in a way that I didn't yet recognize as pain.

"Bullshit," I said. "Those things are—"

"That's not what she means," Cadiz said, and I heard something new in his voice too. Half-terror, half-wonder. I looked to Garland.

"While I never like to correct a lady," he said, "the illusion is not actually *optical*. Your eyes do not deceive you, Mr. Donnelly. The movement you see is real and the agony, I confess, is alarming. Your mistake is in assuming which is the pinner, and which the pinned."

His head twitched involuntarily as he finished speaking, and suddenly all three of them were jerking spasmodically, jaws loose and limbs twitching.

Something else was happening too. Their faces—no, not just their faces but everywhere their skin was exposed—were becoming suffused with a hideous soft green pallor. An involuntary shudder from Garland rolled his robe's sleeve back from his forearm, and I saw the veins pulsing against the skin, deep green veins.

I looked from face to face and while, for the first few seconds, there was an atavistic horror etched in each of them, it was slowly, horribly, replaced by what can only be described as delight. Unearthly delight.

It was a matter of moments before the possessions, the transmutations, were complete.

And then it got far too personal as, one by one, those inhuman faces turned to find mine and they each stood, still twitching, and moved in my direction, Garland's caftan now rippling and pulsing as if it concealed beneath it a writhing array of soft new limbs.

They advanced on me with a shuffling step as if whatever they now were had yet to fully learn the intricacies of human anatomy. But, however contorted, the expressions on their faces were alarmingly readable. Cruel. Eager. Hungry.

There was a sudden rising sound from somewhere around us all. It sounded vaguely familiar as it surged to a climax. I assumed it was their doing, until there was a brief second where what used to be Garland looked at what used to be Cadiz with a mutual incomprehension, before a concussive roar similar to what had put paid to Albie's ambitions the night before turned out my lights.

I don't know if there's an actual law about it, but being pummeled into unconsciousness by one means or another three times in two days seemed to me to be pushing the limits of reasonableness, if not legality.

But seeing the face of yesterday's barman looking down at me with benign concern was certainly preferable to the faces I'd been looking at before this last blackout.

He was holding a briefcase, which seemed a little incongruous, and was the only person in the room apart from me. There was no sign of the three impostors that used to be Garland, Cadiz, and Kelly, though I saw that the wreckage of the statuette was still on the counter, along with the remaining six figurines.

"Wha . . . ," I managed.

"The Olde Fellowes never see me coming," he said, just as if I'd asked an actual question, one that made sense. "Don't quite understand why. Perhaps because I'm a *very* old fellow." He paused, as if puzzled by something. "Though not as old as I used to be," he eventually said, more to himself than to me.

I'd have asked what the hell he was talking about, except that I'd already decided to give myself a break from shit that makes my brain hurt for a couple of days at least. So I stuck to more practical matters.

"They're gone?" I said.

"Unfortunately, yes," he said. "They managed to fold themselves into a gap in the continuum before I could complete the harrowing."

Well, who could argue with *that* explanation? I elected to focus on the fact that they were gone. It helped me breathe.

"This can't have been easy for you," he said, which showed what a very perceptive fellow he was. "Why don't we fix you a drink?"

He crossed to Kelly's cocktail cabinet and took out the vodka bottle, though I noticed he held it to the light and turned it a couple of times as if he wanted to be sure that it was, you know, actually of this Earth. It seemed to pass the test and he proceeded to fill, quite generously, a crystal tumbler.

"Sorry," he said as he handed it to me. "The former Miss Woodman doesn't appear to have had in stock the ingredients for a Pink Princess."

"You know, a barman is supposed to be a confidante," I said, as I threw the vodka down gratefully, "not someone who goes around giving away the name of someone's preferred poison."

"You don't like to name it?" he said. "Can't say I blame you. It sounds like—"

I raised a hand. "I've heard every possible riff on what it sounds like," I said and looked at him. "You *are* British, aren't you? You told our friend in the bar that you weren't."

"Come on," he said. "I work for the government. Can't trust a thing I say."

He moved to the kitchenette counter and opened the briefcase. I stood—I think the vodka had helped—and walked over to take a look at what he was doing. The briefcase had been customized, the inside fitted with a bank of specialized housings. Three rows of three. Nine in total. My friend—I really needed to remember to ask his name at some point—swept the remaining six figurines into their ready-made nests. I noticed that his movements were as quick as he could make them, and that he almost unconsciously dry-wiped his fingers against each other once he was done.

"Sticky?" I said.

"No."

"Wet?"

"No."

"Dusty?"

"No."

"I can do this all day."

"Fair enough," he said. "Malevolent. They're malevolent. And persuasive."

I'd have asked if he was kidding, but everything I'd seen in the last thirty-six hours made me fairly sure that he wasn't. "You came prepared, though," I said, nodding at the briefcase as he snapped it shut. "You knew what you were looking for."

He shrugged. "Playing a hunch," he said, which was obviously horseshit but, what the hell, I wasn't going to break his balls about the fine details. He'd saved my life.

"You saved my life," I said out loud, in case he'd failed to notice in all the excitement.

He wavered for a moment as if not sure exactly how to respond, and then smiled. "I know your granddaughter," he said.

What the hell? "Granddaughter?" I said. "I'm thirty-three years old."

"You won't always be," he said, and then looked to the window a second before a car horn sounded from outside. "Our friends from Washington," he said. "Impatient already."

"FBI?"

"No."

"OSS?"

"No."

"DAR?"

"No."

"We work on this a little harder and I can get us six nights and a Sunday matinee at the Orpheum."

He actually looked like he might have been interested in discussing that idea further. But the car horn sounded again. Twice.

He hoisted the briefcase from the table and gave me a wink, like it was all just a fun day at the office. I looked at the briefcase swinging from his insouciant hand, thought about the terrible things that were in it, and decided I needed to work a little harder on my brio.

"You're handing them over to them?" I asked.

"Somewhat reluctantly," he said. "They assure me they'll be safe." He didn't sound entirely convinced. "I'd like to take them back with me. Keep them out of the wrong hands. There's a war on, you know."

"Yeah," I said. "Last couple of days have given me that impression."

"No," he said. "I mean the other one. The one that makes the papers." He gave the case another shake. "And I hear Herr Hitler and his lapdog Himmler are rather fond of things like this. But you're right—there's a chill wind coming, Steve, such a wind as never blew on this world yet. It'll be cold and bitter, and a good many of us may wither before its blast."

I let him get to the apartment's front door and open it before I asked him.

"Jesus Christ," I said, nodding at the briefcase. "What *are* they?"

He gave me a look, like he couldn't believe how ready I was to be the Abbott to his Costello.

"Were you not paying attention?" he said. "The stuff that dreams are made of."

SEVEN

Junior G-Men vs. the Whisperers in Darkness

I

A WISE MAN ONCE wrote that from even the greatest of horrors irony was seldom absent. Mitford's irony was that its most pacific dreams were hatched through the cold incessant gnaw of paranoia. For these idyllic visions were only experienced on those nights spent in the tight, fear-stifled confines of bomb shelters, those buried safe spaces that the residents of Mitford had built in recent months as stirrings of a Red Scare thickened and encroached. The paradise each dreamer passed through was his or hers alone. The only unifying aspect to these hundreds of visions was beatitude, tranquility. No one dared speak of their dreams upon waking, so great was its empyrean peace. And after these dreams faded, much like the air-raid sirens that ushered them in, the people would crawl out from those tombs for the living and would go about their routines, if a bit less energetic after having paid the physical tariff for a night of deep reverie.

But Claude LeGoff always felt a bit melancholic after such nights. He had spent all of his sixteen years in the sluggish midwestern town, and its streets always seemed a bit paler after the golden roads he'd traipsed without his body.

As the one responsible for all reconnaissance and intelligence-gathering in the Junior G-Men, Claude felt that Mitford had transformed from a place rich in memories and associations to a timid creature cowering from the outside threats that seemed to be increasing daily.

This fear was no mere theory. Claude had witnessed it spreading through the town. Where there had once been block parties and town-wide picnics in Willowdown Park, there were now bomb shelters secreted beneath manicured lawns, and groceries were stockpiled rather than shared. Claude found the changes heartbreaking. In waking life his only real peace came from taking solitary walks along Mitford's pastoral outskirts. But it was not the peaceful atmosphere that drew him there, not the majestic trees or the skittering wildlife . . . it was the Witch House.

In a town as staid and utilitarian as Mitford, the Witch House was a monument to not only decadence but the unworldly. On the margin of the town, it stood out like a smug, gaudy peacock among the flock of drab pigeons that were Mitford's other dwellings.

The Witch House was properly called the Charles House, named after its designer and original owner, Anthony Charles, a nineteenth-century industrialist whose myriad business interests seemed uncannily immune to recessions. But it wasn't the man's fiscal prowess or his outré aesthetics that led to the rumors of his house being haunted, it was the fact that Anthony Charles had built his home in the thin valley between the ancient hills known as the Devil's Humps.

Ojibwe legend told of those hills being formed by the breath of a Mother Spirit and the bones of a primordial Father. It was the European settlers who first gave the hills their diabolical name and set down accounts of the barbarous religious practices that had supposedly occurred on those hilltops. Claude had always regarded the Puritan's records as colonialist hysteria.

Still, there were details about the area that seemed to betray something of a sinister aspect. Most markedly was the long and crooked trail that curved up from the valley and striped both hills. That this trail resembled a snake was plain to even the most unimaginative witness, for one end was meticulously tapered so as to resemble a tail and the other was capped with a rock whose size and chiseled features conveyed a serpent's head. Along the trail a total of twenty-two flat rocks were embedded. Each rock bore a carven pictograph or symbol. Together these rocks lent reticulation to the entire trail, a pattern of scales the likes of which one would find on a snakeskin.

The settlers, being strict and boastful adherents of the Gospel, interpreted the serpent mounds as some kind of Satanic shrine, a celebration of the Serpent that connived Adam and Eve out of Paradise and lured them into the hell of terrestrial life apart from God.

Folks around Mitford had never understood why anyone would have put down roots in a patch so markedly sour. But Charles had purchased the land at a time when the township was nearly destitute. He also, much to the bewilderment and suspicion of the locals, met with the elders of the local tribes and assured them that he had no intention of even slightly altering the hills, their shrines, or the serpent trail. It was rumored that during this meeting the elders of the Ojibwe ceremonially Recognized Charles to the sacred role of steward of the hills.

Anthony Charles died in the mid-1930s. The Witch House had stood vacant since his demise. Claude often wondered at how apparently no one in Mitford, except him, ever stopped to marvel at the structure, to lament its neglect.

It was a radiant example of Second Empire architecture. Its trio of storeys were inlaid with numerous windows that hosted the sheen and tint of volcanic glass. Each pane was surrounded with cornices and filigreed metalwork. A vast rectangular tower rose like the crowned head of some primordial god-form. The mansard roof was tiled in undulating bands of nickel. Weathervanes spiked the cupolas and arches like iron grave markers. The wooden exterior wore a coat of regal colors: scarlet, purple, royal blue. The double doors that served as the house's main entrance were difficult to espy through the baroque jungle that was the wraparound porch, but those that did cross the wide veranda were met with an entryway better suited to a vault than a homestead.

Thus, Claude's shock was profound when he wandered down the Devil's Humps and spotted moving vans parked before the Witch House.

For a moment Claude was too gobsmacked to do anything other than stare dumbly as men in coveralls lugged an array of expensive-looking furniture from the truck and into the main entrance. It was the first time

Claude had ever glimpsed the interior. Distance smudged many of its finer details, but the walls appeared to be papered in emerald.

His attention shifted once he heard the low rumble of a car engine. A dark sedan came creeping toward the house. The lane it followed had been unused for so long that Claude had forgotten it existed. An inexplicable surge of panic led him to crouch low among the brambles and thickets that bearded the footpath. Through thorn and tangled bough Claude studied the trio of figures that exited the car. The driver was a tall, whip-thin man dressed in a charcoal suit. His hair was brush-cut. His long face looked ill-suited for smiling. He moved to a passenger door and opened it, allowing the couple to exit the backseat. They were elderly but conveyed an air of regality. This was due not only to their expensive-looking attire, but also to the proud manner in which they carried themselves. There was an aristocracy to their presence. They were conversing with their driver. Claude strained to eavesdrop as best he could, his fear having given way to his sense of duty as a Junior G-Man. This was no longer a simple stroll, it was reconnaissance. The conversation was not in English. Although Claude was hardly an expert in the language, he heard the word *da* repeated often enough to recognize that the trio was speaking Russian.

His insides went cold. The couple followed their driver up the steps of the great wooden porch. Claude could scarcely wait until they were inside the Witch House before he fled. His head was swimming.

Mitford moved past him in a blur. Claude ran and ran. What began as a stitch in his side quickly escalated to a searing pain that forced him to stop and hunch over, pressing his palm against his belly.

The large clock before the town hall chimed twice, which allowed Claude a more informed guess as to where his comrades would likely be. Being Saturday afternoon, Leo and the other Junior G-Men would be taking advantage of Sheriff Bruckner's standing offer of a quick weekly debriefing at his office.

He rounded the corner onto Apple Road and immediately spotted the Chevy pickup that bore the Grassi Brickyard logo. His guess had been correct. Claude slowed to a walk and gulped greedily for air. His lungs felt scorched.

Scaling the steps, Claude entered the station.

"There are moving trucks over at the Witch House!" he gasped. The Junior G-Men, Mitford's most ambitious custodians of American liberty, were all huddled around the tombstone radio that Sheriff Bruckner kept in his office. The sheriff was seated behind his desk. He held a cup of coffee under his chin. His face was stony.

No music filled the wood-paneled office. Instead it was the sonorous voice of a newscaster. Claude was only able to catch the words *Korea* and *U.N.* He surveyed the faces of his friends, which hung in the gloom like masks of despair. When the news gave way to Nat King Cole crooning "Mona Lisa," Sheriff Bruckner leaned over and switched off the radio.

"What's going on?" Claude asked.

"Oh, nothing too grand," replied Leo, "just another world war!"

"*What*?" Claude felt the strength leaving his legs. He moved to a vacant chair and sat. "We only ended the last one five years ago!"

"Yessir," Leo said, scratching the side of his wide face. "We jus' heard it from Walter Klondike himself."

"It's *Cronkite*, genius," Luna interjected, "but yes, I'm afraid things are looking grim."

Claude swallowed. Hesitantly he asked, "Are we going to war with Russia?"

"Korea." This time it was Tim Wight who spoke. "The United Nations is sending troops there to fight back the communist invasion."

"Commies . . . ," Claude mumbled. "So what are we going to do about it?"

"You kids aren't going to do anything about it, understand?" Sheriff Bruckner's voice was firm. "There's nothing to be done. Not right now at least. Uncle Sam will handle that crisis. He always does. As far as the Junior G-Men are concerned, I need your eyes on Mitford, making sure everything here is status quo, understood?"

"But everything *isn't* status quo," Luna replied, "not anymore. My parents just finished having their bomb shelter installed. And Mayor Fenton has another air-raid drill scheduled for Friday. That's not exactly business as usual."

"Well, missy, we live in dangerous times, no denying that," said the sheriff. "But it's best to think of those kinds of things as precautions. Better safe than sorry and all of that. I think the trouble brewing in Korea and Russia is still a ways off from touching down in Mitford."

"I wouldn't be too sure . . . sir," Claude said.

Prompted by Sheriff Bruckner's expression of interest, Claude told what he'd seen.

"You're positive they were speaking Russian?" asked the sheriff.

"Well . . . pretty positive."

The sheriff nodded then reached for his desk phone.

The Junior G-Men stood awkwardly by while Sheriff Bruckner relayed Claude's story to Mayor Fenton.

"Yes, sir, Mr. Mayor." Returning the receiver to its cradle, Sheriff Bruckner said, "Well, Claude, looks like you've got yourself an appointment at town hall. You best skedaddle. Me, I've got an appointment with my wife's beef stew. The rest of you scamps keep out of trouble."

Once outside the sheriff's station, Leo suggested that the Junior G-Men meet at headquarters after supper in order to receive a debriefing on what the mayor had said to Claude. Tim and Luna piled into Leo's pickup truck while Claude walked toward Main Street. His approach had all the reluctance of one condemned to the scaffold. Reporting to Sheriff Bruckner was one thing; Claude had known him since the age of two and regarded the sheriff as a favorite uncle. Mayor Fenton was an entirely different story. He'd only been in office since the previous fall, but he always exuded an air of more genuine authority rather than neighborly warmth.

Claude made his way past the stone lions that guarded the town hall. Mayor Fenton's office was on the third floor. There was a security guard stationed at the head of the stairs. The man nodded stoically before parting the frosted glass doors that distinguished the mayor's office from the lobby.

It was a cold environment with marble floors and columns, and a monolithic desk where the mayor was seated. He did not rise to greet Claude. A forest of strange standing lamps shone over the mayor's shoulders like spotlights. Their position seemed strategic, as if to place any visitors under clinical scrutiny while Mayor Fenton sat in the dank embrace of shadows.

"Please have a seat." The mayor gestured to the pair of leather chairs that were stationed before the great desk. "Thank you for agreeing to see me on such short notice."

It was the first time Claude had ever heard the mayor speak unamplified. Without the aid of a microphone his voice was raspy, scarcely more than a whisper.

"Thank you for asking to see me, sir," replied Claude. He was too young to comprehend how obsequious he seemed.

"Sheriff Bruckner tells me that you and your chums have been a great help to our town. I want to personally thank you and the other Junior G-Men for the service you've been performing—maintaining the American way of life."

The mayor tapped his lapel, which was decorated with an enamel pin of Old Glory.

"Now, please tell me about what you observed at the Charles property today."

Claude obeyed. Mayor Fenton nodded periodically before ultimately asking, "This third man, the driver, could you describe him?"

The details he gave caused the mayor to lean forward. It was the first time Claude had gotten a clear look at him. He felt foolish that his first thought was that Luna had been right; the new mayor really *did* resemble the Hollywood actor Farley Granger. Luna had whispered this observation to Claude during a screening of *Rope*, when the Junior G-Men had all attended the Alfred Hitchcock film to celebrate their cracking a case where a college fraternity had been taking their hot rods for illicit drag races along Mitford's beach strip.

"Claude," he began, "I trust that as a Junior G-Man you know all about honor and discretion, yes?"

Claude nodded. The mayor rose from his desk and moved to the abstract oil painting on the wall. This he pulled back like a cupboard door. Claude heard the clicks and tumbles of a safe.

When the mayor returned, he placed a photograph on his immaculate desktop. "Does this resemble the man you saw this afternoon?"

"Yes! That's him, sir. Absolutely, that's him."

Mayor Fenton exhaled slowly before moving back to his silhouetted chair. "I'm going to need your word that what I'm about to tell you remains strictly between us. No one else can know of this—not your fellow Junior G-Men, not Sheriff Bruckner, not even your parents. Have I your word, young master Claude?"

He gave the scout's sign.

"Very good. What I'm about to disclose is not only of national importance. It is of global importance."

Claude tried to swallow, but found his throat dry. "Am I . . . I mean, are *we* in danger?"

"Yes," the mayor rasped, "and grave danger at that."

II

Leo had gone home just long enough to eat supper and then returned with the truck to the Grassi Brickyard. His father, who founded the business, had donated the unused storage shed at the lot's far end to be used as the Junior G-Men headquarters. The shed only had room for a desk, a filing cabinet, and four folding chairs, but it was enough.

While he waited for the others to arrive, Leo pondered the most useful way to spend his time, which he ultimately decided was to put his feet up on the desk and launch spitballs at the wooden ceiling.

He was on his fifth attempt to strike the ceiling lamp when there came a rapping on the headquarters door. He opened it.

"Since when do yous guys knock?" he asked the trio of shadows at his door. Luna was visible in the interior light. It was only after they entered that Leo realized the third figure that followed Luna and Tim into the headquarters was not Claude, but a tall, thin man in a suit and tie.

"You must be Leo Grassi," the man said, "leader of the Junior G-Men." His voice was sonorous and he wore his hair in a brush cut.

"Who might yous be there, Mack?"

The man flipped a wallet open, revealing a photograph of himself on a very official-looking identity card. Leo recognized nothing on the card beyond the US government seal. There were levels of clearance and sequences of numbers and letters, but nothing that really clarified who this man was.

"I'm Agent Telford McMillan. I work for a special security sector of the Federal Bureau of Investigation. And I'm hoping the Junior G-Men might be able to help me with a matter of urgent national defense."

"You want *our* help?" Leo's tone betrayed his shock. "Help with what?"

"Why don't we all take a seat?" agent McMillan suggested. "This may take a while."

Luna dragged the last pair of empty chairs from the corner and sat. "We're listening," she said.

"During the war, I was part of the secret service under President Roosevelt," agent McMillan began. "I respected that man more than I can say. You're all too young to remember his inaugural speech of course, but I'm sure you're familiar with his statement that America has nothing to fear but fear itself?"

The Junior G-Men uniformly nodded.

"Unfortunately, Roosevelt was wrong. This country, this *world*, has a great deal to fear."

"You mean the Reds?" asked Leo.

"Not entirely, no. Now, don't misunderstand," the agent said, raising his hand, "a lot of those dangers are very real indeed. But there's far more to the story than what we see in the newspapers or hear over the radio. In my current job I've seen a great many things, things that have convinced me that there is one irrefutable truth about this world."

"What truth is that?" asked Tim.

"Nothing, and I do mean *nothing*, is ever what it seems."

"So there really is communist danger here in Mitford?" Tim asked.

The agent cleared his throat. "My division has had eyes on Mitford, the Charles House specifically, for a very long time. We received word that the house was about to become occupied again."

"Occupied by *Russians*!" interjected Leo.

Agent McMillan nodded. "Yegor and Dominika Volos. Better known in their native Moscow as *Drakon ubezhishcha*, the Seekers of the Dragon."

"Seekers of the Dragon?" said Leo. "What are they? Some kinda zoo-keepers?"

"They're stage illusionists," Agent McMillan replied. "Or rather, they *were*. They retired years ago, but around the time of the Russian Revolution they were a famous duo. They performed all over Europe. They went into hiding just before the outbreak of the Second World War. My division had been doing our best to keep tabs on them, but the Voloses were basically ghosts until this year, when we received information that they had resurfaced."

"But why Mitford?" Luna asked.

"The Witch House . . . ," muttered Tim.

Agent McMillan touched the side of his nose.

"But what would two Russky magicians want with a haunted house?" Leo asked.

"Their routine was based not on entertainment but on sorcery, on real magic."

"Are yous telling us that their prestidindigestion is real?" Leo interjected.

"*Prestidigitation*," Luna corrected.

"Yes," said Agent McMillan.

"But every magician tries to convince their audience that their tricks are real," said Tim.

"True enough. But the Seekers of the Dragon weren't just pulling rabbits out of top hats or linking rings together. Their stages were designed using very precise geometry and symbols. Instead of locking cabinets and silk handkerchiefs, they used double-cube altars, Circles of Evocation, black mirrors, things like that. Their act, if you can describe it as that, was calling up spirits and demons that they believed lurked in certain corners of the Earth. That's what was most peculiar about them; they didn't tour per se, instead they selected specific sites that they believed had occult power."

"You don't buy that anarchy do you?" asked Leo.

"I believe you mean *malarkey*, Leo, but yes, I do. I've seen enough strange things in my time to leave me open to the possibility of spirits and demons."

"So what you're telling us is that we should steer clear of the Witch House," Luna said.

"Quite the opposite; if anything I need you all to stick close to the place. We could really use the Junior G-Men's help on this one."

"You sure you don't have us mixed up with some other club?" asked Leo.

"I'm positive. You all know this town much better than I do. And you're known faces around here. We consider that an advantage."

"Who is the 'we' you're referring to?" Luna asked. "I mean, it might not be any of our business, but the initials on your identification aren't FBI, they are HPL. What does that stand for?"

"I'll explain everything at the proper time. Right now I'm asking all of you to trust me when I say that the closer you stick to the Charles House, the more you'll be helping us. I'm going to leave you this card. It has the telephone number where I can be reached day or night during my stay in Mitford. Anything you can find out about the comings and goings of the Dragon Seekers would be greatly appreciated. Stick close to them, but not so close that you might be seen. I'm trying to stay inconspicuous, so instead of staying at the inn I've rented a room at Elsie's Boarding House over on Eleventh Street. You can reach me there."

"Pardon me," Tim began, "but this all . . . well, sounds kind of dangerous."

"That's because it is." Agent McMillan's voice was level and firm. He thanked the Junior G-Men for their time and exited the headquarters.

The group sat and listened to the agent's car engine rumbling and then the sound of tires passing over the gravel lot.

"Boy," Leo said, breaking the cloying silence, "it feels like the whole town is being turned upside down."

Suddenly a shadowy figure emerged from behind a pallet of bricks.

"Claude!" Luna cried. "You startled us."

"I'm sorry," he said. "I had to wait until that spy was gone."

III

"Claude, I'm telling yous, that agent was as American as you or me," Leo said.

"Says him," Claude returned. "But like I just said, he was with those Russians today."

"But Agent McMillan just told us that he was keeping an eye on the Russians," Luna explained.

"There's a difference between 'keeping an eye on' and chauffeuring the enemy around and chatting with them in Russian. I promised the mayor that I wouldn't tell you any of this, but that was before I saw that spy trying to infiltrate the Junior G-Men. I say we listen to Mayor Felton and give those three a wide berth."

"Let's not get batty, Claude," Leo interjected, "nobody's giving birth to anybody here!"

Luna rolled her eyes. "Your English teachers really did a number on you, didn't they, Leo?"

"I went to the same school as yous guys. Anyways, I'm still the head of the Junior G-Men, this is still my pop's property, and what I say goes; and I say we do our civic duty and help out this government man. I'm at my uncle's tomorrow, but why don't at least one of you go and meet him at Elsie's Boarding House after church tomorrow?"

All the Junior G-Men nodded, save for Claude, who raised his hands in resignation. "You do what you like. But I can't follow you."

"But we're a team!" Luna said.

Two years earlier, when the friends decided to put their patriotism and sense of justice to productive use as the Junior G-Men, Tim had produced a quartet of handmade identity cards that outlined each member's title alongside the Junior G-Men logo. It was this card that Claude removed from his wallet and placed upon Leo's desk; a gesture that robbed the other members of speech.

"I'm out," Claude said before moving to the exit. He crossed the brickyard with a deliberate slowness, secretly hoping that his chums would come rushing out to stop him, to beg him to reconsider. But they never did. Shock and unease about the future of not only their club but the world at large kept them pinioned.

The following morning Claude's heart was filled with a mighty desire to attend Sunday Service. It was not grace or faith that inspired him, but a wish to speak to the mayor. Shaking hands and chatting with their mayor had become woven into the fabric of Mitford's Sunday routine ever since the election in November. It was now a common sight for the procession of churchgoers to shake the minister's hand and then a few paces down stop and gab with Mayor Fenton if they so desired. Unlike previous mayors, Elder Fenton did not even attempt to pass himself off as a family man. On Sundays his only companion would be his stone-faced secretary, whom Claude had never heard utter a sound. When asked about his confirmed bachelor status, Mayor Fenton quipped that he was wedded only to his duties as mayor.

The sermon was a tedious thing. Claude felt awkward when he caught a peripheral glimpse of Tim seated with his family, so he kept his eyes locked on the nave. Unsurprisingly, there was no sign of the double agent or the Russians from the Witch House. Claude did spy Luna's parents but not Luna. Leo, he presumed, was in the next town attending Catholic mass with his father and brothers.

Mayor Fenton sat in the back pew. Claude counted the seconds until the congregation at last rose and began to file out. Fate delivered him an opportunity when his parents slipped into a convivial chat with a couple they'd not seen in weeks. Claude was fascinated by how, despite the fact that the mounting crises in Korea and the Soviet Union were clearly on the fore of everyone's mind, not one word was spoken of it. Instead, recipes were exchanged, queries were made about the wellbeing of such and such, innocuous jokes were told.

There was a painful moment when Tim called Claude's name and began to advance toward him, but Claude dodged him, instead making a beeline for the great willow tree beneath whose somber boughs Mayor Fenton stood.

"You have something for me, son?" the mayor whispered before Claude could even speak.

"Yes, sir. That man you told me about, that double agent . . . I know where he's staying."

A cold gleam brightened Mayor Fenton's eyes. After a pause he said, "Go with your family now, Claude. You've been a great help. Leave everything to me. Go home and stay put. I'll call on you again when the time is right."

Claude slipped back with his parents just as they were saying their goodbyes to their friends.

Within minutes the streets were vacant and tranquil.

They remained that way until the afternoon idyll was unexpectedly pierced by the awful scream of the air-raid siren. As there were no drills scheduled for that day, everyone in Mitford was overwhelmed by the realization that this was for real.

IV

As to the exact reason behind her determination to visit the Witch House on Sunday morning, Luna couldn't say. Perhaps it was a desire to curry favor with Agent McMillan, or simply to prove Claude wrong. Either way, Luna departed solitarily for the outskirts of town once her family had left for Sunday Service. She felt guilty for lying to her parents about feeling unwell, but desperate times . . .

It was an unseasonably cool, overcast day in late June, and Luna wished she'd had the forethought to wear a jacket. When she reached the valley of the Devil's Humps the atmosphere was fittingly gloomy.

The glow in the Witch House's main-floor windows would have likely gone unnoticed had the day not been so dim. Set against this leaden atmosphere, the amber light appeared as dramatic as the jack-o'-lanterns that lined Mitford's leaf-padded streets on Halloween. Luna squinted in order to sharpen her distance vision, but her eyes took in merely shapes, impressions. The glowing orange light was unquestionably moving, for Luna was able to see it pass from one parlor window to the next. There also appeared to be figures bearing that light, but these figures were obscured to the point of being shapeless silhouettes. Or were they dressed in hooded robes?

Then figures and light and movement all became subsumed by the Witch House's deeper recesses. Luna felt herself in a push-pull as to whether she would be of more service to the Junior G-Men if she were to phone for Agent McMillan or to follow the authentic, but admittedly more perilous, route of pursuing the lead she'd just witnessed.

She chose the latter. Luna approached the house in a roundabout way in order to take advantage of the great obscuring oaks and apple trees that loomed large over the rear of the property. Crouching behind the final apple tree, checking for any signs of the Russians, she saw none.

The backdoor was stained the purple of spilt wine. Its handle was carven in the form of a gargoyle squatting amidst ugly castle stones. Unsurprisingly, a turn of this grotesque proved the door locked. But Luna had learned a number of skills since associating with Leo and the Junior G-Men. In his youth, Leo's father had been, by his own admission, a hood, but some of the knowledge he'd gleaned from the streets of Brooklyn still came in handy. When Luna had lost the key to her bicycle lock two years ago, Leo's father had schooled her in the art of lock-picking. Ever since then she always kept a hairpin clipped to her keychain.

The lock on the Witch House was somewhat more sophisticated than the padlocks she had practiced on, but after a few minutes of fiddling and poking Luna heard the thrilling *click*. She pressed down on the gargoyle and slipped inside the forbidding building. She felt more than a little like a child in a Grimm's fairy tale.

The Witch House interior was singular, a place thoroughly domesticated and yet so very rich in strangeness. The walls were high and regally adorned with wallpaper whose emerald background practically glowed against the intertwining arabesques of black velvet. Sconces were mounted just below the cherry-wood molding, each of which bore a single burning taper. These wan flames allowed Luna an impression of the long and latticed carpet that seemed to lure her toward the double doors.

These she approached and silently opened. She was then able to fully appreciate the care these old Russian magicians had invested in order to transform this ordinary chamber into a shrine dedicated to their career. Based on the sheer scope of this collection, their obsessions had been long and dearly held, for there was no speck of the room that did not bear some relic of the magical career of Yegor and Dominika Volos. Posters and news-clippings, all in Russian, spoke of *Drakon ubezhishcha*. One of the framed clippings offered her a full view of the couple. Dominika was not what Luna would call beautiful, but as a young woman she had been undeniably striking. Her countenance was haughty, as though she viewed the world from an elevated plane and thus was able to view the smallness of most things. Her eyes and hair were silver. Yegor Volos appeared much younger than his paramour and partner, for there was vitality in his piercing stare, and both the shock of hair on his head and the sculpted Van Dyke beard that framed his thin mouth were free of gray. He wore many necklaces, each of which were weighted with what looked like carven stones. On his brow was a black spot, which Luna thought could be either a mole or simply a flaw in the photograph.

Along with the printed ephemera the Voloses' had displayed, there were a variety of handcuffs in nickel and iron, a gilded cage that held a stuffed dove the color of porcelain, and a pair of mannequins dressed in the stage costumes of a glittering scarlet woman and a top-hatted prestidigitator. But mixed in among these props of industry were items less of magic and more of mystery: bundles of stinking weeds impaled on long, imposing nails, devils carved from corn cobs drowning inside jars of vinegar, a staff of crooked wood. As she neared the great stone fireplace, Luna noticed that it was immaculate, without so much as a trace of ashes.

Perhaps the Russians had kept this fireplace unused in order to preserve the massive firebrand that decorated the back wall of the hearth? Hammered into the iron slab was a work of art akin to what Luna had seen in history books dealing with ancient Mayan or Aztec religion. There was a vast serpent-like creature coiled inside what looked to be an egg. Perched on the outer shell of the egg were a cluster of human figures armed with fire and rods of lightning. A second egg sat adjacent to the other, but there the human figures were inside the egg, walking through what seemed to be winding entrails.

No, not entrails, she realized.

Tunnels.

This insight, which Luna had gained from who-knows-where, then led to a second realization: these were not eggs, they were hills—hills so very much like the Devil's Humps that flanked the Witch House.

Agent McMillan had warned that the Voloses were not mere illusionists and that their knowledge reached far deeper than sleight-of-hand. Was this what had brought them to Mitford, this site? Not the hills themselves, but something *within* them.

Luna backed away from the fireplace, unsure how to feel. She stood numb and useless, staring at the firebrand while her mind reeled with no stable thoughts at all.

Something then drew her gaze to the edge of the hearth, where an iron pull-ring hung as if in waiting. Luna couldn't help but sense that something had just extended to her a forbidden invitation.

She accepted this invitation not out of curiosity or reverence, but simply because she couldn't stand this vertigo of helplessness any longer. She gripped the ring and pulled it. The firebrand parted from the wall with neither resistance nor sound.

What it revealed was an abyss. Dumbstruck, Luna leaned her ear toward the round aperture. There she heard a silence beyond silence; the muteness of a place that felt less abandoned and more sworn to some oath of secrecy.

Inspired, she darted to the corridor and retrieved one of the burning candles from its mount. This she carefully ushered back to the secret doorway.

The introduction of a lone taper to this sprawl was akin to attempting to light the heavens with a single star. The flame gave Luna no perspective on how large or deep this next world was, but what it *did* reveal was another sign that she couldn't help but perceive as welcoming. Set into the blackish clay beyond the hearth was a series of flat stones. They descended down and down with a crafted symmetry—an ancient rung ladder that was built to admit men to a place not made for them.

Looking into an environment so startling and so unspeakably foreboding froze her.

She had a grip on the pull-ring and was about to set the firebrand back in place when a hand lunged out from the shadows and grasped Luna's blouse. Shock and unthinkable horror turned her muscles to jelly and allowed her captor to pull her through the hole with ease. Her attempt to cry out was stifled, and she was dragged rapidly down the hideous steps.

V

Tim and his family had just settled around the dining room table for their customary early Sunday supper when the siren started wailing from the town hall. It pressed through the streets and into the less-populated stretch of town where the Wight family farm stood. The sound caused the dinnerware to rattle on the walnut table. The chicken fidgeted on its platter as though reanimated.

"Everybody outside!" Tim's father cried.

The Wights did their best to follow their well-rehearsed protocol, but the authenticity of this siren made their routine jerky and sloppy. They reached the rear of the unused barn where Tim's father had installed a pair of incongruous orange flagstones in the soil.

"Help me lift them, Tim," his father instructed. Tim heeded and the stones rolled back on the metal hinges that transformed them into a trapdoor.

The world below those doors always struck Tim as being like something out of a dream. Perhaps this was because he always dreamt so richly during the drills, which although they were designed to last only moments seemed always to stretch until after sunrise, with everyone in Tim's family sleeping soundly underground. Perhaps this boded well: it meant that in case of the real event—like today—they knew they could survive down there.

A set of well-sanded wooden steps led down from the hole in the earth to a smooth concrete floor.

"Go on down and grab that pull-chain at the bottom of the stairs, son."

The light's pull-chain felt cold in Tim's fist. The illumination it spawned was clinical, raw.

Down there, two sets of bunk beds stood against one wall, their spotless linens folded military-crisp. The wall opposite hosted a larder whose shelves were weighted with canned vegetables, fruits, and meats, all of which bore the same labeling: text that identified the can's contents and the Home & Hearth Inc. logo.

H&H had also provided the shelter with distilled water, toilet paper, toothpaste, soap, linens, even a selection of magazines, crossword-puzzle digests, and a wall calendar and pencil on a string, presumably so the shelter's occupants could mark the days of their internment like prisoners awaiting parole.

Home & Hearth had installed everything and had done so on a payment plan that fit the Wights' budget. The same deal had been struck with dozens of households throughout Mitford. Home & Hearth had been brought into town at the behest of Mayor Fenton at the dawn of the communist threat. The mayor had assured everyone in town that Mitford would remain safe provided they heeded his instructions.

Heed they did. Shelters were installed and stocked. And the drills began, growing more and more frequent as the news poured in from around the world about spies and government secrets and a vast chaotic threat to American liberty.

Tim hadn't noticed the faint, mechanized wheezing sound at first. But now that his ears had grown more accustomed to the tomb-like setting the noise was sharp and clear, almost percussive. Such tight confines made sourcing it a quick process. It was coming from the large fan that was spinning behind an iron grill in the wall, which Tim's mother had switched on.

"It's cold enough down here already!" Tim's brother cried.

"That's for air circulation, champ," Tim's father said, his voice uncharacteristically shaky. "Let's just relax now, everyone. This will all be over soon."

Tim wondered if his father had intended that phrase to sound so fatalistic.

The family sat on their bunks and listened to the muted scream of the siren, which soil and distance had mangled into the plea of a maimed animal. They listened also to the lulling whir of the ventilation fan, which was a balm to the Wights. Tim stared at the rotating blades and a sudden exhaustion blanketed him. His eyelids felt weighted and a tingling sensation numbed the inside of his skull.

He tried to speak, but what escaped his slackening mouth was a murmur. He was attempting to tell his parents that the fan had started to turn the wrong way, but the dream paradise had begun to beckon, and its wordless call was somehow more powerful than even the dire sirens that now felt a million miles distant.

VI

Across town, Claude hunkered down with his widowed mother and his sisters. Their shelter was less than half the scale of the one he'd seen being built on Tim's family's land, but it was secure and well-ventilated, stocked with foodstuffs and distilled water. That was enough.

Being the eldest child and the only son, Claude had found himself being cast in the paternal role, which he accepted simply because he could sense the immense and sorrowful burden that had been placed upon his mother. Here, in this ugly predicament, Claude found himself consoling his siblings, whose fear was raw and deep and palpable. He wished he could somehow draw it from them.

By the wan light of a lone lantern, his mother sat mute and stared at the ceiling as though it was adorned with Sistine-style murals rather than being the drab concrete it truly was. Was she contemplating the catastrophe that was brewing above the ground, Claude wondered? He gathered his sisters on the bunk and began regaling them with the French folktales his father had passed on to him in childhood: stories of the Castle of the Sun and the peasant who sang down a star for his beloved. The girls went from panicked to soothed to sleepy. As the blades in the wall spun and hummed, Claude watched over his sisters as they slept on their cot.

"Why don't you sleep, too, *maman*?" he asked.

His mother nodded lazily, as though halfway to slumber already. He helped her onto the shelter's second and final cot and slid the blanket over her.

"*. . . you . . . yousleeptoo . . .*" she urged him in a slurred voice.

"I will," Claude told her. Fatigue was pressing into his muscles and his mind as he settled into the corner of the room. He used his jacket as a rudimentary blanket and shut his eyes. Yet despite his mounting exhaustion, sleep would not claim him. Claude's mind was submerged in a chaotic storm of images, his conscience weighted with guilt. He dwelled on the memory of his departure from the Junior G-Men. The shocked expressions of his friends haunted him. He thought, too, of Agent McMillan. For some vague, inexplicable reason, Claude felt that he had somehow made a grave error in judgment. He now viewed himself as being resonant with the characters of those old French folktales—the fool who'd struck a bargain with the Devil.

A violent tremor shook the shelter. It snapped Claude out of his reverie. It shook canned goods from the shelving unit. It caused the cots to shift like boats on rough waters.

What it did not do was awaken Claude's mother or his sisters. Claude rose and donned his jacket against the deepening chill. Had it been this cold when they'd first sealed themselves in?

A second tremor rocked the room. Claude gripped the anchored shelving unit to keep himself upright. This one lasted several seconds longer than the first. Claude shouted for his family to wake up.

It was then that he noted the fog. The whitish mist blanketed the shelter and rendered its details hazy. Claude's mind frantically connected the mist with the violent pulsations in the earth and realized that these were not tremors but surely the effects of powerful bombs.

The invasion was real, and what Claude was now witnessing was the poisonous smoke from the fallout insinuating itself into their supposed safe room. His hands made clumsy by panic, he grabbed towels from one of the footlockers and doused them in distilled water. Though it was likely futile, Claude pressed one to his face and then rushed to do the same to his sisters.

But the mist was not invading their sleeping forms. Instead it was gushing *out* of them.

Claude refused to trust his eyes. How could this colorless fog be flowing from his sisters? What manner of horrid communist weapon could cause pale mist to come leaking out from slack mouths and gently breathing nostrils? What was this ghostly substance that also came gusting out from beneath closed eyelids?

A backward glance at his mother confirmed that she was also suffering the same ugly fate. He gripped his mother's shoulders and shook her.

A tremor then seized the shelter and shook it. The lantern flew from its hitch and shattered. Claude immediately beat out the tiny kerosene fire using one of the wet towels. The shelter was now in darkness.

Despite his panic, Claude had to resist the urge to simply curl up and go to sleep. Perhaps it was because he was plainly overwhelmed by the awfulness of his predicament. At the same time, he was only able to marvel at the way his family could appear so content despite the danger and the mania that swarmed about their sleeping forms. He wondered if they were dreaming the same glorious dreams that he had enjoyed during previous drills.

Those dreams . . .

But only ever during air-raid drills, and only when Claude and his family had cloistered themselves down here . . .

Again, a vague intuition began to heat him. These were all clues, he knew, but clues to what mystery?

There came the sound of shifting in the distance. Claude braced himself while also trying to shield his sleeping loved ones.

The tremor never came. Instead, it was light. At first Claude thought it was his eyes playing tricks in this stifling blackness, but the orange glow was plain. The faint illumination was visible through the twirling blades of the ventilation fan. The shifting he'd heard, he now realized, was footsteps. Someone was moving on the other side of that fan. Who it was and how such a thing was even possible were questions Claude set aside in his mind. For now he crouched low and watched and listened.

Whispers.

They came slithering through the slats of the fan's frame like eels of sound. Their tone and their indecipherable content caused the blood to surge cold through Claude's veins.

"E'yayayayaaaa . . . ngh'aaaaa . . . Nasht . . . Kaman-Tha . . . Nyarlathotep . . ."

The entire grill of the fan was now illuminated by the amber gleam of lantern light. Through the slats Claude was able to discern vaguely human shapes. As the susurrus of their chanting filled the shelter, Claude watched in amazement as the fog began to slip back through the vent. Was the fan somehow drawing this alien substance out rather than pulling in fresh air? Surely this was a trick of lantern-glow and shadows.

The whisperers then moved along, taking the light with them, leaving Claude in the bewildering blackness. Seized with fear, the boy felt his way to his mother and listened for her heartbeat. It sounded sluggish, as did the heartbeats of his sisters. It was as if whatever essence had been leeched from their sleeping forms had left them diminished.

Another tremor rocked the shelter, knocking Claude clean off his feet. His head collided with something firm. He did not lose consciousness, but when he touched the smarting area on his scalp he felt blood. Frustration tangled his insides. Claude knew that something had to be done, but what? If bombs were the cause of these shocks, he could not risk irradiating himself or his family, but he could not simply sit by and watch them slip into a potentially permanent slumber.

The fan. Claude reasoned that if those figures, whoever they were, were able to move along the opposite side of the shelter's vent, there must be some kind of access.

Through touch alone Claude found the iron bar from which the kerosene lamp had hung. This he pried from the stone wall. Steeling himself against the risk he was about to take, Claude held his breath and began to push the bar through the slats in the vent. The fan blades clanged horribly against the foreign object. Mercifully, the fan did not spin with great velocity. This made Claude's task of feeding the bar through to the far side of the grill somewhat easier.

The blades now locked in place, Claude began to pull back on the grill. The fan's engine was beginning to wheeze. He wondered how much time he would have before it completely overheated. Putting all his weight into the task, Claude finally managed to yank the grill free. He fell to the ground. The grill made a horrible clang once it struck the stone floor. Panicked, Claude huddled against the wall, his ears straining to hear beyond the struggling fan motor for any sounds of people. The whisperers were apparently too far gone to have noted the noises. Their lanterns were out of sight.

Propping himself at the foot of his mother's cot, Claude lifted his legs and began to kick at the fan. He prayed that he wouldn't knock the bar loose and set the fan slicing into his ankles. Each kick seemed deafeningly loud. He winced every time, terrified of discovery.

The seventh attempt sent the unit out of the hole that had been carved into the wall to mount it. The back grill and the fan crashed down on the opposite side of Claude's shelter. Sticking his head through the now-vacant aperture, he could sense a tunnel. The blackness beyond that shelter was so complete, Claude knew that attempting to feel his way through would be disastrous. His brain cobbled together a quick solution.

The footlocker held two large cans of kerosene for the lamp, along with a large box of long matches. Claude took these and the last two hand-towels. With care, he climbed through the hole in the wall, landing on the other side with as soft a thud as possible. He felt around for several minutes but at last found the iron bar, which, thanks to the towels, some kerosene, and a match, he transformed into a torch.

He was in another world, one older and stranger than he could even fathom. The tunnel in which Claude now stood was a ragged chute. The walls were braced with a zigzag of wooden beams, all of which seemed to conjoin at weird angles, forging a kind of textured cuneiform whose message was too alien to decipher. Cautiously, Claude began to creep through the tunnel. In the gloom beyond his meager torch there was the sound of foul drippings and a soft but incessant whirring.

He rounded a bend in the tunnel and immediately spotted the pools of faint light that stippled the blackness. Like a moth, Claude moved to them and found their source. Peering into those small shafts of light, he found himself staring into another underground shelter. Though slightly larger than the one that Home & Hearth Inc. had installed in Claude's own backyard, the shelter was of an identical design. He did not recognize the occupants, both of whom were lying on cots, dreaming deeply. He could just make out the vague remnants of a heavy mist lingering inside the chamber.

Each dimly-lit vent connected this vast labyrinth of seemingly-ancient tunnels to the newly-built shelters. Claude saw the good people of Mitford lying oblivious to whatever hideous plan was unfurling here in these dank, chthonic halls. He moved slowly, fearful that he would at any moment encounter the whisperers. The tunnels all seemed emptied, just as the various bomb shelters had been drained of the strange fog.

His ears suddenly detected a sound in the distance: whispers again, only this time they were in chorus. The voices, though soft and keen, ricocheted through the passages. Claude did his best to follow the sound. Eventually it began to grow louder.

Louder, and brighter, for whatever chamber these tunnels fed into was large and lit by flickering fire. Claude could now see shadows and dancing light. He was close. His torch had burned down to the iron. He set down the useless tool and advanced.

He had almost reached the mouth of that great open chamber when something grabbed his arm and yanked him backward. Claude nearly cried out, but a rough hand was pressed across his mouth, muzzling him.

A face emerged from the darkness. It was the face of a mad-looking old woman. And it was a vaguely familiar face. Claude suddenly remembered where he had seen it before: at the Witch House. The Russian woman. His captor, he could only assume, was the woman's husband.

Claude's struggle to break free ended the instant he saw a third figure step out from behind Mrs. Volos's robed form. It was Luna. Claude felt his eyes widen with disbelief as the girl pressed her finger to her lips.

VII

"I knock!" Leo cried. Setting his cards on the kitchen table he added, "Straight flush. Read 'em and weep, ladies!"

"Bah!" spat Leo's Uncle Vincent. "See? What did I tell you? Mitford boys don't know how to play rummy without cheating!"

"Cheat nothing! I'm what yous call a card shark!"

"It's card *sharp*, Leo," his father replied. "And I think it's time we shut down this casino and got headed back to Mitford. I've got an early-morning delivery tomorrow."

The Grassi family piled into the pickup truck and made their way out of Cedar Falls and back toward Mitford. The sun was well into its western descent. Leo and his siblings laughed themselves hoarse singing along to the radio's broadcast of "I Wanna Be Loved" by the Andrews Sisters.

"Okay, you mooks," their father advised them eventually, "pipe down. We're home now."

Passing the sign that welcomed them to Mitford, the Grassis found themselves facing a veritable ghost town. It was deathly still. At first Leo wondered if there might be another air-raid drill, but the sirens at the town hall were silent. There was no sign of anyone on the streets and every house they passed was unlit. The darkness of the town was near-complete, save for one patch.

"Holy frijole, will yous look at *that*!" Leo exclaimed, jutting a finger out of the open truck window.

The hills on the outskirts of town appeared black, for they were back-lit by a weird colored luminescence that shimmered and pulsed in the sky.

"Could be a fire, Pop," Leo said.

"Not like any fire I've ever seen," replied his father.

"This isn't right, I'm telling yous. Let's go infestigate around up there."

"Uh-uh," replied Leo's brothers, one shaking his head.

"Leo's right," his father replied, "somebody could need our help out there. We'll drive past and then double-back to the fire station to get help if need be."

They drove on toward the Devil's Humps. The Witch House came into view. The sight of it caused Leo's father to slam on the brakes.

Multicolored light came beaming through the building's every window and door. The entire house seemed to be shaking like some carnival attraction.

And the hills . . . the hills . . .

The Devil's Humps were pulsating, flexing, and shrinking to an impossible, horrifically drastic degree. None of the Grassi men could speak. They simply stared at the lights and the motion.

And then they felt the rumble. It was a savage tremor that seemed to intensify endlessly until at last it reached its zenith.

The Witch House began to fracture. Like a house of cards, its moldings and its sturdy walls and its framing began to collapse in upon themselves.

And from this buckling structure fled a stream of figures. Leo leapt from the truck and watched in disbelief as these people, all of whom were dressed in monkish black robes, scattered like bugs. Seconds later there was a rush of headlights and screeching tires as a manic motorcade came racing toward the truck. Leo leapt onto the hood to avoid one of the careening sedans.

When the frenzy was over, the Devil's Humps were still once more and the lights in the sky had faded.

And in the moonlit valley, just a few yards from the ruins of the Witch House, a trio of figures stood. One of them lifted their hand as if to wave. Leo squinted. "*Claude*?" he gasped. Beside him, dressed in a black robe, was Agent McMillan. Luna leaned against the agent. Leo could see that she was crying.

VIII

Earlier, while lost in the grim, stifling tunnels, Claude stared at Luna in disbelief. A storm of questions surged through his mind but, instead of asking, he decided to heed Luna's gesture for silence. Slowly, the hand that had been clamped over his mouth was lifted away.

The man who'd been standing behind him now stepped into view. It was the Russian he'd spied at the Witch House, only now he was not dressed in finery. Instead, his form was draped in a dramatic robe of crimson satin. A great sash crossed his breast. Strange symbols had been embroidered upon the sash in glinting gold thread. Amulets of stone hung from his spindly neck.

His wife was dressed similarly. She held what looked to be a bolt of silk against her breast. This she unwrapped, revealing what appeared to Claude to be a great pendulum resembling a paddle. It was a rectangle, approximately three feet in length, fashioned in some form of polished wood. The rope it was attached to resembled a withered vine.

Around the bend in the tunnel, flames danced and chants echoed. The tremors had begun to increase in both frequency and power. Claude could not help but believe that the end was nigh.

Yegor Volos gently guided both Luna and Claude to one side. From the folds of his robe he removed a golden flask. He muttered something in Russian. Mrs. Volos traced invisible words in the air with her finger. Sparkling water poured from the flask. Yegor used this to baptize the polished board. He rose and nodded. The couple embraced quickly. Dominika Volos then unexpectedly placed a kiss on the brows of both Luna and Claude.

The hierophant moved toward the entrance to the chamber. He gripped the vine firmly. The wooden pendulum swung to and fro as if ticking off these last few seconds. Dominika pressed her hands together in prayer. Luna found herself mimicking this pose.

Yegor rounded the corner. His wife immediately followed. Whatever fear of discovery the couple might have had was now vanquished, for the old man was bellowing words that the two Junior G-Men could not understand, yet they sensed were not in Russian. It was a tongue far older—a long-dead language resurrected, perhaps to meet a threat as ancient as this spell.

A deep pulsating sound now filled the air. Claude scurried to the entrance and peered into the brighter chamber.

What he witnessed was a drama of the abyss, a nightmare made flesh.

The room was a vast oval cavern. Torches blazed from mounts in the earthen walls, their fire illuminating the procession of black-robed figures that paced a slow widdershins ring around what looked to be a bottomless pit in the floor. This vast opening was framed by large blocks of shimmering black stones, four in total. Each stone formed a trapezoidal wall. The hooded figures were each carrying what looked to be incense censers, the kind used to perfume cathedrals during Mass. But what billowed and swirled about these chained bowls of copper seemed less like smoke and more like . . . fog.

Claude felt his jaw drop. It was the selfsame mist he'd seen filling his family's shelter, the fog that had come spilling out from his loved ones.

The hooded shapes were in turn pouring this mist into the pit. Each new offering was met with a fresh and fiercer tremor.

The chorus of whispers chanted in cycles: "*E'yayayayaaaa . . . ngh'aaaaa . . . Nasht . . . Kaman-Tha . . . Nyarlathotep . . .*"

Standing upon a dais, elevated above this moving snake of devotees, was the celebrant. His robe was a vivid yellow. He held a gleaming kris sword, its wavy blade suggestive of a surging serpent.

"Oh my God," Luna whispered in Claude's ear.

"Mayor Fenton," Claude added.

Mayor Fenton did not seem interested in the feeding of the pit, for his gaze was fixated on a higher object. Claude looked upward and was horrified by what he saw.

Hanging upside down above the pit was Agent McMillan. Naked as the day he was born, his limbs bound by ropes, and his mouth gagged, he dangled above the pit, wriggling in a vain attempt to free himself.

But when Yegor and Dominika Volos charged into the chamber, the mood of the ritual was instantly shattered. Mayor Felton snapped his head around to face the couple as they moved swiftly toward the pit.

The rhythmic pulse that Claude and Luna had heard was coming from the wooden pendulum, which Yegor was now swinging above his head. As the pendulum hummed and circled around, it created a great wind that began to draw the mist out of the copper censers being held by the robed figures. The fog of Mitford's dreaming started to lift away from the pit, and soon began to dissipate in the higher climes of the great chamber.

There was an immense howl of rage. It came from Mayor Fenton, who charged down from his dais. He stopped just a few paces from Yegor Volos, who cursed at him in a sonorous shout. Gripping the kris sword with both hands, Mayor Fentor swung.

With one cold and accurate stroke, Yegor's head was sliced free from his body.

Like a malfunctioning automaton, the old man's decapitated trunk somehow managed to continue swinging the purifying board. But then his arms twitched and groped sightlessly. Yegor's heart pumped his life's blood out where it stained the ancient stones of the cavern. His body crumpled. The pendulum clattered to the ground.

Dominika Volos unleashed a cry that was the single most awful thing Claude or Luna had ever heard—a mewling howl that was equal parts anguish and horror.

Mayor Fenton lifted the blade again, taking a step toward the woman.

Her demeanor instantly transformed. She released a spiel of phrases and gestures.

The sword shot out of Mayor Fenton's hands. It clanged as it struck the far wall of the cavern. Unfazed, Mayor Fenton advanced and began to strangle Dominika. His face was a feral, evil mask.

By now the procession had broken. The chamber was in chaos. Robed figures were hurriedly pouring what little fog they had left into the pit, others were beginning to saw at the ropes that held Agent McMillan in place. Their aim was plain: to feed him to whatever was inside the pit.

Before Claude had even registered what was happening, he caught sight of Luna bolting past him. She ran fearlessly into the chamber. With unbelieving eyes, Claude watched her rescue the pendulum from the gore that had once been Yegor Volos. She immediately resumed the old magician's task, spinning the wooden board around above her head.

When Claude spotted two of the robed men charging toward Luna, he raced into the chamber and picked up the kris sword. On instinct, he swung. The blade sliced both men, one of whom cried out while the other dropped without a sound.

The other men drew daggers from their rope belts. Claude tried to grip the sword as best he could with trembling hands.

Above the pit, Agent McMillan's one arm had been cut free. He knew that within seconds he would fall headlong into that hungry abyss. As a last ditch effort, he yanked the gag from his mouth and pronounced:

"*Ateh Malkuth ve-Gevurah ve-Gudalah le-Olahm Amen!*"

At this, the entire world seemed to shift, and shift violently. The once-whispering congregation now scattered like insects, darting for various tunnels that led out of the chamber. A few were actually flung off their feet, their heads striking stone. The entire cavern rumbled and shook. And the dark pit was suddenly rinsed with light.

Claude raced and helped Agent McMillan free himself. Once safely on the ground again, the agent stepped over the lifeless bodies of Dominika and Yegor and hurriedly peeled a robe off one of the unconscious devotees and donned it.

"Let's go," he told them. "And bring *that*." He pointed to the pendulum tool that Luna still held.

Together they rushed through the dark caverns, holding hands in order to stay together in the impenetrable dark. Agent McMillan clearly knew these tunnels well, for their travels were swift, and in a moment they were climbing up a set of rugged steps. Luna recognized them.

Claude was disoriented when he climbed out of the hearth and found himself inside the Witch House.

"It's not safe in here," the agent advised them. "Come on, this whole place might cave in at any moment."

They ran outside, into a night that was strangely tranquil. Claude had never been happier to see Leo's face.

IX

When they had gathered at the pickup truck, Leo finally asked the burning question, "What was all that about?"

The group then listened raptly as Agent McMillan divulged the history and aims of the Human Protection League, as well as the details he could reveal concerning their archrivals, the Olde Fellowes.

"So the Voloses have been working with HPL all this time?" Claude asked.

"Yes," the agent replied. "Their skills in magic were all that stood between humanity and a god they call Nyarlathotep, the Crawling Chaos. Nyarlathotep lurks in the endless void between the Dreamscape and this world. When the Olde Fellowes learned of the Red Scare, Elder Fenton developed a plan that I grant was nothing short of genius. He came to a zone of occult power, here at the Devil's Humps, and created a network of tunnels where he could collect the dream-essence of Mitford's sleepers. Being in those shelters put you and your neighbors too close to Nyarlathotep. That rite we just witnessed was the final feeding of the Crawling Chaos. If I'd been served as the main course, like the Olde Fellowes had planned, Nyarlathotep would have broken through into our universe.

"Had it not been for the Voloses' help and their abilities, the Crawling Chaos would have emerged right through those serpent mounds. The spells that the Ojibwe tribe used to keep It bound to the depths were growing weaker and weaker over time, and Elder Fenton was using all the powers of the Armies of the Night to awaken It. The Voloses were our best defense. That's why I urged the Junior G-Men to stay close to them."

"I feel just awful . . . ," Claude muttered.

"Don't," Agent McMillan replied, placing a hand on Claude's shoulder. "Fenton's very persuasive. I don't blame you for letting him know where I was. Besides, the way I see it, you're a bona fide hero."

"What I don't understand," Luna began, "is why the Human Protection League had only one agent here in Mitford. I mean, the threat was huge, so why not send reinforcements?"

"Believe me, they tried," Agent McMillan replied, "but unfortunately the League is stretched very thin. Most people aren't aware of the preternatural dangers we keep at bay, day in and day out. The threat to Mitford was just one of many. We do what we can, where we can."

"I can't believe this is the world I live in," Leo said.

"You remember what I told you? Nothing is ever what it seems. Well, it will be dawn soon. The good people of Mitford will soon be waking up safe and well rested. They'll have no idea how close they came to an apocalypse. And we must never tell them."

"Why not?" asked Luna.

"They'd never believe you, for one. And secondly, the job of the Human Protection League, of which the Junior G-Men can now consider themselves honorary members, is to fight secret threats by secret means. Keep the shadowy things in the shadows. It's better that way."

"Just one last question, sir," said Claude. "How did the HPL even know about the Witch House in the first place?"

"We own it," Agent McMillan replied, "or *owned* it I should say. We've been at this for more than a decade now, and our resources have grown markedly thanks to the support of some generous benefactors. Where we can, we make it our business to know the zones of occult power all over the world, and we do what we can to keep them sealed. Shortly after the League came into being, the building you call the Witch House was bought up by us."

"Well, that's maleficent," exclaimed Leo.

"I think you mean *magnificent*," laughed Luna, "although in this case you could be right . . ."

EIGHT

At the Hills of Hollywood

"WAIT FOR IT, BABY."

I pumped my fist up and down Little Arty, getting ready.

"I could do that for ya, ya know. I mean, ain't that why we're here?"

"Be cool, honey."

Slow, then fast. Slow, then fast.

"Or I could do it with my mouth. I don't mind. Boys usually like that."

From the set, through the not-quite-closed door, I could hear the *whirr* of the crane. The click as they locked it down.

"Hush now, baby. It's almost time."

A hoarse voice from the set called, "*Ready*?"

"Oh, yeah," I whispered.

The naked blonde was invitingly splayed over a purple-and-green divan left over from some Tony Curtis sword-and-sandal pic. She frowned over her shoulder, narrowing her baby blues at me.

"Whatcha doin' over there, anyway?" she said.

"*Roll sound*," came the call from the studio.

"*Speed!*"

"*I'm* gonna roll *you*, baby."

She licked her lips.

"*Roll cameras*."

"*Marker*."

"Say it, say it, say it," I begged. I stepped up, grabbing hold of her with a couple of slaps.

"*Set!*" came the call.

"Set," I said.

"I never done it like this," said the girl. "It's a little unusual."

"*Action!*" called the director.

"*Yes*," I said, rocking my hips.

That's when it went off.

"Shit!"

I let go of the girl and looked for my pants.

"*He-e-ey!*"

"Hold your giblets."

I found my clothes dangling from the tip of a balsa scimitar. Some wit had etched BERNIE'S A BENDER into the wood with a penknife. I reached into my keys-pocket for the little black orb which buzzed and vibrated in my palm.

"Fuck a duck," I said. I couldn't ignore this.

"What's *that*?"

"Nothing, darling." I slipped the device back into the pocket and pulled my trousers on. "Just a gadget to tell me somebody needs me. I've got to go."

"But what about . . . ?" She indicated her exposed loins with a bob of her chin and cupped her breasts.

I sighed. "Duty calls."

"What about my audition?" she said.

"You're a star, babycakes, I can tell. I'll pass a good word on to Mr. Dmytryk. Hand to God."

I could see my lie in her eyes.

"What kinda crap is this, anyways?" she said, folding her arms across her chest.

"Hollywood, baby. It's Hollywood."

"Burns! Arty Burns!"

Fat little Lemkovitz charged at me as soon as the director called, "*Cut.*"

"Hey! What's the scene, Jimmy Dean?"

“Hah?”

“What d’ya want, Larry? I’m on the move.”

“You don’t talk to me like that, *shmendrick*. I’m the producer here . . .”

“Associate.”

His tiny, bald head went puce. “Yeah, well you’re associate nothing. Goddamn studio security, so-called. What the hell do you secure, anyway? I’m missing a gold pen. A keepsake, even. Gone, *poof*, like the Lindbergh baby.”

“Just like,” I said.

“RKO used to be a nice place to work, you know.”

“Someone took your little pen?”

“Gold.”

“Solid or plate?”

“It was pl—what the hell? I’m reporting a theft here.”

“You know I won’t sleep until the culprit’s in the hoosegow and you’re back in the ink. But right now, I’ve got to see the big man.”

“Listen to me, you little c—” My words caught up with his mouth. “The big man?”

I nodded just enough to crush him.

“Mr. Hughes?” he mouthed.

“There a bigger man here?”

“No,” he croaked, then cleared his throat. “No, no, of course not. But, but . . .”

I held back the big smile I felt.

“Would you pass on my kind regards?” he said, gently stroking my elbow. I bet I could have scored a hand job off the bastard, if I’d wanted.

“I’ll mention the pen,” I said.

“No,” he yelled. “No, please, don’t do that . . .”

But he was already in my dust and I wasn’t feeling so bad about missing out on the blonde.

"Hey, Sweet Knees!"

I stood up a little straighter before turning around.

"What's cookin', good lookin'?"

"Hi, Faith," I said.

She stopped in her tracks, cocked a hand on her narrow hip and pouted those thick lips at me as if I'd just taken her teddy bear away. She wore an orange and pink sarong-y thing that begged to be unwrapped before Christmas. I don't normally dig brunettes, but Faith Domergue was an exception to prove any rule. A string of tiny, pink flowers had been woven into her velvety brown hair.

"Is that the best you can do for me, Arthur?" She added a dirty look.

"Sorry, gorgeous, I'm distracted. I'm on my way to . . ." I stopped, pointed at her clothes. "We lensing a South Seas pic? I don't remember hearing about it."

"What? This old thing?" she asked. She gave a twirl, just as a breeze kicked up, raising the hem high enough to see the lighthouse at Bora Bora. "You like?"

"Jeez, Faith, you sure could drive a fellow places."

"I've got the car if you've got the key." And she let out a laugh like clinking highball glasses.

"Maybe I could fill her up a little later?"

She gave a furtive look around, an impish grin on her puss. She reached up and plucked one of the little pink flowers from her hair and pressed it into my palm.

"You just got *lei*ed," she teased.

"You wonderful, dirty girl!"

"*Vroom-vroom*," she said. Then she got all serious. She looked around again, then beckoned me closer. Little Arty throbbed with anticipation.

"Did you hear?"

"What?" I asked. I licked my lips and placed a hand on the small of her back.

"Bob Shayne got named," she whispered.

"Huh?"

"You know Bob, don't you? I did that awful mad scientist thing with him. He's a sweetie."

"A cherry sweetie, you mean."

She looked confused.

"He's Red."

"I don't believe that."

"You got to watch yourself, darling. They're everywhere. Even if they're not."

"What do you mean?" She seemed genuinely puzzled. God bless her.

"Just stick with me and you'll be fine," I said.

She looked scared for a moment, then leaned in and bit me on the neck. She scampered off in the direction of the commissary.

I was still holding her pink flower in my hand. I gave it a sniff, smiled, and tucked it in my pocket.

What a town!

I stopped in the men's room and straightened myself out. Hair combed, tie and fly double-checked—Faith had Little Arty straining at the leash again—and most importantly hands washed. I got a surgeon to show me how to do it right. A while back, Mr. Hughes had me chuck a PR out a window when he spotted a curlicue of mustard under the nail of the guy's pinky finger. Only the second floor, but still . . .

His secretary—*another* Jane Russell lookalike; Christ in a D-cup!—nodded at me and brusquely pointed to his door. Once, she'd caught me perving on Lizabeth Scott during a wardrobe change and she's lemon-faced me ever since. Christ, as if it would make any difference to Lizzy the Lezzy.

I opened the door and walked down the narrow corridor to a second door. This time I knocked.

The door opened automatically and I entered the darkened office.

Along with clean hands, there were two things Mr. Hughes liked more than anything else in this world: airplanes and boobs.

The office was full of both.

"It took you over fourteen minutes to arrive here from my signal, Mr. Burns."

"Sorry, Mr. Hughes, I got hung up on the way."

He sat behind his great mahogany desk, glowering. He had a wad of chewing gum tucked in his cheek and fiddled with that great gold signet ring he wore. He nervously twisted it round and round on his left pinky finger. The ring bore the image of some mythological creature I didn't know: one of those weird combinations of animals the old Greeks had such a hard-on for. Part-eagle, part-barracuda, part I-don't-know-what-the-hell. It was a lot of gold in any event, and the eyes were flawless rubies.

You never shook hands with Mr. Hughes. I think he only ever directly touched pendulous bits of female anatomy.

"You stopped to flirt with Miss Domergue," he told me.

"You saw that, huh?"

"I see everything. She should know better than to twirl in that dress."

"She's a lovely gal. And I think it was a sarong."

"I've had priapic encounters with her on a number of occasions."

"Uhhhh. Yes, of course. I mean . . . of course."

"Her performance was entirely satisfactory, with some minor reservations and notes." He fondled the nose of the model plane on his desk. "Her second act is weak—at vital moments, she is prone to issuing a distracting rasp. She is also somewhat under . . . *sophisticated* in areas that are of significance to me."

"You mean her, ummm . . ."

Boobs. In the office. I think I mentioned that the place was full of them. And airplanes. That maybe sounded a little confusing.

Pictures is all I meant: glossies. Just about every busty actress in town. Nothing crude or obscene—nothing you couldn't find in a gossip rag or a legit agent's file drawer. But a lot of them, blown up big and plastered all over the walls. Enough cleavage to secrete a regiment in. Cavalry, even. And on the wall behind his desk, a big oil portrait of Jane Russell—the

Madonna—herself. If you stared at it long enough, you'd swear you could see that bosom heave.

Or maybe it's just me.

And then there were the planes, natch. Models hanging everywhere, resting on every shelf and surface. Beautiful things, finely crafted, dangling from almost invisible wires, lit up by tiny, hidden spots. The HF-11 he'd crashed that caused him all his pain and made him pop those little pills. And, on the desk, a precisely machined H-4 Hercules in solid platinum. Ironic given that the real one was wood, but probably worth more than I'd earn in ten lifetimes.

He liked to stroke it.

A small cough from the darkest corner of the room just then. I hadn't even noticed her sitting there. Very sloppy of me.

She leaned slightly forward in her chair and one of the invisible spotlights caught her fine, blonde hair.

Like a splay of harp strings. I could even hear the music.

She raised her head and looked at me. Long, hubba-hubba face, with a sharp chin and nose, and thin lips that might just cut your tongue if you were lucky. Lots of angles there.

I love to play the angles, me.

"Do I know you?" I tried. Something about her . . .

"Mr. Burns," Hughes said, "this is Miss—"

"V," she rasped. Oh, what a voice. Lauren Bacall with a chest cold. "Call me . . . V."

"How do you do, Miss V," I said, starting to get up.

She sat me back down with a flick of her brown eyes.

"No 'Miss.' Just V."

"V," I repeated. Little Arty cleared his throat too.

"Arthur," Hughes said. And I knew I was in trouble. Mr. Hughes never called me Arthur unless it was business of the worst sort.

"Yes, sir?"

"We have a problem."

Obviously. I wouldn't be here otherwise.

I nodded.

"It requires . . . fixing."

"Of course, Mr. Hughes. Whatever you need."

A snort came from the skirt. Hughes ignored it.

"Do you like"—he glanced over at V—"what are they called again?"

She proffered the flimsiest of smiles, which seemed all the prompt Hughes required.

"Monster movies!" he said. "What do you think about monster movies?"

V moved so silently, it was like walking with Theda Bara.

"You seem to know your way around the lot pretty good," I said.

"It's my business."

"I'm still not too clear on exactly what that business is."

"I work for a man. A private investigator."

"Really? I don't . . ."

Then I remembered.

"It's that big, dumb lummox isn't it? The one who shot the psychiatrist. It was all over the papers a while back. Your picture too. What's his name? I know . . ."

"Let's leave names out of this, shall we?"

"You know who *I* am."

"I'm sure I'll forget that soon enough."

"That's not very nice, honey."

She spun on a stiletto heel, dropped down, and somehow flipped me over hard onto my back before I knew I was down. She was on top of me, her right hand bunched into an odd fist that pressured my chest in a way that made breathing very unpleasant.

"This is business, Mr. Burns, and I take my business very seriously. Are we as one about that?"

She eased the pressure off my chest and I gulped some smog.

"We are one," I agreed.

"Excellent! And it's not 'honey,' it's V."

With a smile that could cut a diamond, she reached down and pulled me up to my feet.

I might just have been in love.

"So why the hell are we going to the Valley? And why the slow road?"

"Shall I pick up the pace, then?"

She didn't wait for an answer, but dropped a lead foot on the gas and whipped us around the bends of Coldwater Canyon.

Bad enough riding shotgun to a frail, but V drove the big Caddy with one loose hand, the other twirling that fairy-blonde hair.

"Easy, sister . . ."

She shot me a long glance even as another sharp curve was coming.

"V. I mean, V. Jesus, would you keep your eyes front!"

Another tinkle of a laugh, a jerk of the wheel, and we shot around the bend.

"Don't you like the scenery?"

"I want pretty pictures, I'll buy a copy of *Life*."

"Oh, an intellectual."

As we shot gravel off the edge of another hairpin turn, I decided enough was enough. Knockout blonde or otherwise.

"Listen, lady . . ."

"Where do your loyalties lie, Mr. Burns?" she said.

"Hah?"

"Your loyalties. Your allegiances. In what and whom do you put your faith?"

"That's a funny question to ask in this town."

"It's the question being asked everywhere at the moment, isn't it?" she said.

"I'm no Red, if that's what you mean."

"And what do think about these . . . Reds?"

I watched her expression: just that sly trace of a smile. She threw me a glance, raising a pencilled eyebrow.

"I think like Mr. Hughes: they're a menace to our way of life and they have to be dealt with. They're monsters. I've had to do some things."

"So I understand. You're faithful to Mr. Hughes. That is commendable. It also keeps food on your plate and blondes in your bed. But there are loyalties and there are *loyalties*."

I narrowed my eyes at her and she seemed to sense it. She turned her full, gorgeous face to me and showed her teeth. I couldn't work out if she was smiling or hungry.

"What's your game, lady?"

"Monsters, you said. What a wonderful choice of words."

She looked back at the road in front of us and I did too. We'd reached the top of the Hills; the Valley sprawled below us.

V eased her foot off the brake, and I sensed it was going to be a fast plunge down.

"Let's go kill some monsters," she roared.

The Encino Ranch lot was plumb in the middle of nowhere. I've never liked the Valley or anything in it. The north side of the Hills is like a desert to me, with the promised land of Hollywood on the other side. It's brown and parched and dull and feels as flat and empty as Kansas, even as you're coming down an actual hill. The land's cheap, though—or used to be—so the studio bought it up for the big backlot. But it's always hotter than hell in the Valley and the air itself tastes dry and stale.

And twice now, I've caught a dose of the clap in the Valley.

V didn't have to flash more than a smile at Pete at the studio gate and in we drove.

"You seem to have a way with people," I said.

"I'm a woman of many talents."

"Do tell."

We drove around a set of trailers and a big construction site. Some peculiar façades were going up and I couldn't work out what pic they might be for. RKO mostly shot oaters out here, though as I recall Capra took it over for that sappy Christmas picture, and Hawks used it for his outer space carrot-creature thing. I always heard tell that Hawks only insisted on shooting up here because of a favorite whorehouse in Tarzana that imported the roughest trim from Mex and the smoothest single malt from the Highlands.

As we came around an equipment warehouse, we were confronted by a huge set in mid-construction. The scale of it was genuinely impressive and a little dizzying. Oddly shaped, futuristic structures rose up from what looked like burnt-out ground in front of us. But there was something off about the geometries of the buildings. The longer I looked at them, the dizzier it made me. Of course they were only fronts—no way could such monstrosities exist as real structures; physics wouldn't allow it—but the longer I looked at them the more I felt like I wanted to barf. When I was a kid, I used to walk around the house staring down into my mom's little, round makeup mirror so it felt like I was walking upside down. This set gave me the same feeling, only I was looking at it right side up.

I think.

"What the hell?"

V shook her head ever so slightly and said a word that sounded like a sneeze.

Before I could ask her to repeat it, she zipped into a parking spot on the far side of the set and jumped out of the car. I moved fast, caught up with her, and put a restraining hand on her arm.

She raised one of those thinly pencilled eyebrows.

I abjectly held both hands up as if she'd drawn down on me.

"You want to tell me what this is all about?" I said.

"Let's go see the man."

I shook my head, but followed her into the offices.

Once again, V nodded and smiled her way past phalanxes of guards and secretaries without so much as a word or a halt in her gait. Walking with her was like wearing an invisibility cloak.

She finally stopped outside a door marked head of production in shiny, gold block letters. I could see my distorted, puzzled face reflected in the "P." She knocked this time, but opened the door while a phlegmy "Come in" was still being sputtered.

"Oh," the man behind the desk said.

"It's V, actually," she said. I think she was making a joke.

I recognized the guy as Bill Alland, though we'd never really met. He'd produced a bunch of B pictures at RKO—always making money, though not a lot—but for some reason he was one of Mr. Hughes's fair-haired boys. Not that there was a lot of it on that balding head. He had the standard producer look: lips a little too flaccid, eyes a little too dead, suit a little too good for the *schlepper* wearing it.

"Rosebud," I said.

V tittered.

"Gee, that never gets old," Alland said.

Alland had started as an actor, an old pal of Orson Welles—in fact he was once Welles's Boy Friday. His only memorable performance so far as I knew came in *Citizen Kane*: he played the reporter chasing Kane's story whose face you never see.

Good casting.

Kane was from before my time—and Mr. Hughes's—at RKO, but people still talked about it. Supposedly the main character was originally based on Mr. Hughes. I can still remember seeing the movie when it came out. A fucking sled!

"I should have guessed he'd send you," Alland said to V. He didn't look happy. He glanced my way, narrowed his eyes, drummed his fingers on the desk.

"Waters?" he tried, pointing at me and squinting.

"Burns," I corrected. "Call me Arty."

But he'd already dismissed me.

"What's with the crazy set out there?" I asked. It made him look my way. I tried on a smile that was last year's cut. "What are we shooting?"

"*We*?" Alland snorted.

"Jeez, Louise. What are *you* shooting."

"Big new picture. Monsters. Outer space. Lots of screaming dolls in tight spacesuits."

"What's it called?"

Alland came to a dramatic stop. He slowly spread his hand across the air in front of him as if engraving the Ten Commandments in stone: "*Cthulhu! Creature of Destruction!*"

I laughed. "You are shitting me. All of that for a rubber-suit pic? What was that name? Cashew nuts?"

I glanced over at V, expecting her to share my mirth.

She looked very serious.

"*Cthulhu*," Alland said. "And I have personally convinced Mr. Hughes of its potential. You can see from that set the budget I have. This is no B picture, no stuntman in a gorilla suit and diving helmet jumping around to scare the kiddies. This is big-time."

"Cast?" I asked.

"Stewart Granger. Bev Garland. Great comer name of Connie Clare." He cupped his hands in front of his chest. Clearly a Howard Hughes production.

"Pinch me," I said. "Directing?"

"Menzies," Allard said. I nodded my approval.

"Who wrote it?" V asked. She looked hard at the producer.

"What kind of question is that?" Alland said with a sneer. "Who gives a rat's smelly ass about writers?"

V nodded.

"So what's your problem?" I said. "If you have the world by the"—I could still see that peculiar set in my mind's eye and had to suppress a shudder—"square balls?"

"What are your politics, Mr. Burns?" Alland asked.

I glanced at V, but she studied the producer.

"I'm a citizen," I said.

"No . . . subversive leanings?"

"I put ketchup on my burgers and mustard on my hot dogs," I said. "Like every good American should."

"And if someone here—a paid employee of Mr. Hughes—was found to . . . squirt the ketchup where it didn't belong?"

"He might find a different kind of red sauce dripping down his chin."

"And if this *he* was a *she*?"

I flicked another glance at V. She was watching me now.

"I do what is needed to secure the best interests of Mr. Hughes and this studio," I said.

"And the country, of course," Alland said.

"What's good for Howard Hughes is good for America," I declared.

"Good answer," Alland said.

"Now about this woman . . ."

"Television!" I said.

V was driving again. I saw one of those strange little smiles curl her lip, but she didn't glance over at my exclamation. She just went faster.

"You are aware that your Mr. Hughes is investing heavily in television. Building a new broadcast studio atop Cahuenga. Do you own a television, Mr. Burns?"

In fact, I had two: kickbacks from an RKO contractor for not ratting him out over a skim he'd been running on the props department. I barely watched either one—maybe the occasional Saturday night at the fights.

"You don't have to call me Mr. Burns. Arty is fine. And yes, I do own a set."

"What do you think of the medium?"

"The medium?"

"The thing itself."

"The picture sucks. I can only get two channels where I live. Three if the wind's blowing the right way."

"Yes, yes. But what do you think about television's potential. As a means for reaching the masses, rendering unto them that which is their fondest desire?"

Recalling the way she flipped me, I hesitated, then said what I wanted to say.

"Guys want cooze and a snooze, dolls want a hug and a ring on their finger. That's your fondest desires. TV gonna give them that?"

She actually laughed. I exhaled.

"Is that really how you see the world?"

"That's the way it is, hon . . . V."

"What about the cinema, Mr. Burns? What does that give people?"

"Arty, please. I don't know. Couple of hours in the dark to escape their lives. Maybe a moist squeeze and a quick ball at the end of the night if they're lucky. Jujubes."

"And that's all you think of the movies?"

I let out a sigh that accidentally turned into a Bronx cheer.

"I don't know, lady. I've met a lot of people in this burg who buy into that 'Dream Factory' hokum. I mean, I like a good picture as much as the next guy. Give me a nice Western or a pirate pic—Errol Flynn pig-sticking Basil Rathbone—and I'm a happy little hog in shit. But you know, they're just stories, right, and they don't usually make any sense if you think about them for five minutes after. And in the end you still got to go home and walk the dog."

"Do you own a dog?"

"I'm talking—what do you call it?—metaphorically."

"Ah, but it is precisely in their metaphors that the movies are so rich."

"What? Like that overblown cashew nuts thing? Monster movies?"

"*Cthulhu*. But you know that, don't you? I don't think you're half as dumb as you play."

"Yeah, yeah, *Cthulhu*. What's your metaphor there? Monster chases screaming babe. Monster gets killed. Hero gets babe. You gotta love that three-act structure."

She slowed down slightly—thankfully—thinking. She actually pulled over before she spoke.

"You underestimate the monsters."

"Howzat?"

"Don't you understand the appeal of such movies? The deep truths they reveal?"

"Go on, then."

"The stories are a veneer, a scrim behind which shines a meaning that would be too blinding to look upon uncloaked. We laugh and shriek at the monsters on the screen in order not to think upon the monsters we most deeply fear in our lives. There is no place so deep to hide as out in plain sight. Mr. Poe taught us that long ago."

"Poe. Producer at Metro, right?" I said.

"You know what I'm talking about."

"Nevermore," I said.

She smiled. "I think maybe I'm starting to like you, Arty."

"Welcome to my dark den," she said.

The KTTV studios were up on Sunset, on the site of the old Nassour complex. I did a brief hitch as security for Ed Nassour on an Abbott & Costello pic. Christ, you've got to go back to Cain and Abel to find two guys who hated each other more than that pair. I spent most of the job chasing hobos back onto Van Ness and hitting on Hillary Brooke, though I never got so much as a handful of thigh off her.

The confined set was totally wild. Barely even room for cameras. And it had an actual ceiling—what the hell?—mosaiced with a complicated pattern of stars. They were kind of weird, too: not constellations, exactly—no crabs or archers—but after I looked away from them, I thought I could see pictures lingering in my head. Shapes that didn't quite make sense and made my stomach roll. I tried not to look at them, but I could feel them hanging over me, threatening me or something.

The floor was covered with grass—fake, I thought, until I saw a couple of caterpillars doing the dirty bop in a weedy patch and reached down to touch it. Creeping vines, thick and gnarled as an old sailor's arm, snaked up the walls, reaching for those nasty stars. A huge black divan sat in the middle of it, with a glass coffee table in front and a big, illuminated crystal ball resting on the top. Smoke swirled around the crystal, and I had to admire the skills of the effects team on a super-low budget, late night TV show. Skulls—I don't know from what kinds of critters—had been propped up in a circle around the globe. Fish-heads? Frogs?

"It is good of you to see us, Enchantra," V said. I'd not heard her sound so solicitous to anyone.

"Always for you," the woman sang.

"Enchantra?" I asked.

"My colleague, Mr. Burns," V said.

"Call me Arty," I said automatically and put out my hand.

She didn't so much reach out as float her arm in the air until it bobbed my way. Her hand felt cool and soft and kind of melted at the touch. Her skin was as white as Grace Kelly's teeth.

Her face had an odd shape: oblong with a thin, witchy nose. Pretty, though, in an Yvonne De Carlo kind of way. Her neck was too long and her head a half-size too small. Her hair had been razored into a widow's peak in front, but flowed long at the back, nearly to her (very pert) ass. Her midnight-black dress was cut as low as you can go without begging a visit from the Vice Squad, and Mr. Hughes himself would surely have admired the . . . *sophistication* of her chest. The dress streamed all the way to the grass, hugging her lower half, and her legs seemed as long as the Nile.

Little Arty sent me a telegram about launching an expedition to discover their source.

"Enchanted, darling," she said.

Enchantra enchanted. Ha-cha-cha!

She had an accent, an intonation—something European, I don't know, from overseas—but it sounded so B-movie Lugosi that it could have been a put-on. On the other hand, there was something generally . . . other-*ish* about her.

"Quite the digs you have here . . . Enchantra."

"I do try."

"Not bad for TV," I said.

Her eyes and cleavage narrowed.

"You don't like the television?"

You think my baby's ugly? she might as well have hissed. I hate to be rude—well, circumstances permitting—so I tried to make nice.

"I like it fine. Hell, I've got two TVs," I said.

"Television. Is. The future."

"Yeah, sure," I offered. "Great for sports, huh?"

Enchantra looked over at V. "What is this you have brought to me here?"

"Hey!" I said.

"I believe there's more to him than meets the eye," V said.

"There would have to be."

That was enough.

"Listen, lady," I said. "I dig your groovy ghoulie get-up, and those love puppies of yours could make a dead man jump up and jive, but I think you're on the wrong side of who's leading the band here. I . . ."

She spat a word.

I don't know how to describe its sound: mice with hangnails sliding down a mile-high blackboard; a freeway pile-up played back at 78 r.p.m.; the stumps of broken teeth chewing the glass from a bottle of battery acid.

Not nice. Uh-uh.

I felt something wet on my lip, touched the back of my hand to my mouth and saw the blood that dripped down from my nose. I wobbled slightly, had to lock my knees to keep from tumbling over. Reaching out to steady myself, I grabbed onto one of those weird vines: it was prickly and slick and pulsed like a heart. I quickly let go.

I looked over at the crystal ball on the table, which now blazed with light. Where the hell was it coming from? The light flared through the fish/frog skulls, lending them an even more alien quality. For a second I thought I could see the flesh that once encased them.

"What . . . is going on here?" I said.

"There is a war coming," V said. "In fact, it has already begun."

"The Reds, I know. I already told you . . ."

"No," Enchantra said. "That is a mere proxy. A feint. A . . ." She looked at V.

"It is a deception," V said. "A disguise for the true battle that is at hand."

I shook my head.

"Great forces gather. Ancient enemies. Powers beyond your perception," V said. "And sides must be chosen."

"Uh-huh," I said. "Like Warners versus Fox?"

"You are not believing, Mr. Burns?" Enchantra asked.

"You're not the most credible source I've ever met," I said, gesturing at the surroundings.

"She's full of shit," a voice called from behind.

I spun around and saw two big guys standing in the doorway. They both had guns in their hands.

Or . . . something.

As they walked into the room, lit by the glowing crystal ball, I saw that what I took to be guns were actually—I don't know—animal horns? Curved, ivory things anyway, wrapped around their fists. They pointed them at us as if they were gats. The pair wore identical gray suits with black ties and gray Homburgs.

Feds? Feds with . . . bones?

No.

I started to reach for the spring-loaded sap in my jacket pocket.

"Ah, ah," one of them warned, raising a femur.

"What are you going to do? Scrimshaw me?"

"Careful, Mr. Burns," Enchantra warned.

"Careful of what? Who are these guys? What the hell is going on here?" I turned to V, who stood still as a cigar store Cheyenne, watching. "I've played tag along long enough. I'm . . ."

"Dick-deep in shit, so shut your yap," a nasally voice informed me.

The two bone-men stepped aside to let a little guy into the studio. He hitched up his pinstriped trousers as he walked, then stuck a thumb in each pocket and spread his stubby fingers over his thighs. He smiled, kind of, but it didn't hang right on him—like a bargain-store suit. I saw the yellow of his crooked, horsey teeth. And the dead blackness of his eyes.

"I know you," I said, a memory from an old wrap party rising slowly out of its box. "Yeah, it was that Fritz Lang picture."

A spread of the ill-fitting smile in reply.

"I had to toss you, I remember now. You got fresh with Miss Stanwyck."

"Skank!" he spat.

"You're a . . ." I remembered his name now: Berkeley. "A fucking writer! You've been singing to the committee about Reds in town."

That took a bit of the glint out of his smile. "It's Burns, isn't it?" he said.

"Call me Arty."

"You belong to Hughes. We're on the same team, friend. So what are you doing with"—he nodded in Enchantra's direction—"*that*?"

"Still haven't learned how to talk to a lady, huh?"

"Lady!" He laughed a little man's girly laugh. "Don't you know what *that* is?"

The gunsels—bonesels?—had each taken a couple of steps back and to the side. The three of them formed the points of a triangle between us and the door. Remembering that crazy karate move she pulled on me, I shot a glance at V. Her eyes never left the little guy, Berkeley, and I sensed the tension in her body.

I could suddenly feel something else, too: a vibration. It rang in my fillings first, then penetrated right down to my ankles. Little Arty thought a party had started without him.

A light so bright it staggered me shot out of the crystal ball. Like someone had flicked on a thousand-watt Kleig under the table. All of us threw our hands over our eyes and I went down to my knees on the grass. I heard a little explosion and knew it had to be the crystal. The light dimmed and I could open my eyes.

Squinting, I saw one of the gunsels on the floor, blood pouring down his face. He was riddled with tiny shards of glass and moaning in pain. V was already on the move for the weird bone-gun he'd dropped. The other was still shaking off the blast.

In the middle of the set, Enchantra and Berkeley stood like a pair of gunfighters staring each other down in an Anthony Mann western. Their eyes were locked on one another and their lips moved. Berkeley had one hand up over his head, fingers curled, palms toward the sky. He chanted something in that high-pitched voice. It sounded like a rabbit in a lawnmower and it hurt my ears something fierce.

Enchantra stood with her hands in front of her, splayed fingertips pressed against each other. In the gap between them, an ultraviolet light hovered and glowed as if she had some purple sprite trapped in the cage of her hands. She chanted, too, but deeper and more resonant, like a hippo breathing through a snorkel.

Off to one side V and the remaining gunsel were engaged in some bizarre duel with their bones. Sparks flared every time the objects touched, the air around them sizzling.

I got to my feet when Enchantra's eyes widened and she thrust her arms out, separating her hands to send the purple sprite spiraling toward the little writer. His high-pitched chant reached a peak and he started spinning madly. He spun so quickly that his weasley features became a blur. The space around him appeared to bend. I could swear that the very fabric of the air had been torn and a chilling *nothingness*—something far beyond the most starless night—began to emerge from the crack.

My very flesh objected to what transpired around me. It felt like fire and ice battling inside my skin to decide which would have the pleasure of consuming me first. My throat constricted, and wetness—tears or blood, I couldn't tell—ran down my cheeks from the corners of my eyes.

Enchantra's purple sprite exploded against the ebon rent emanating from Berkeley's still-spinning form. The whole room shook, and the grass below burst into green and yellow flames. Those weird vines started exploding around me, releasing a warm sienna ichor that burned where it touched. The flames were consuming the vines as well, racing toward V and her attacker who rolled on the grass, bone-guns glowing. I fell back to my knees.

This was no good.

I don't know what made me do it.

An impulse, a whim. Nothing better to do.

(I thought I heard a voice.)

Though the crystal ball had shattered, the fish-frog heads on the table still stood, glowing white from a source unseen. One of the heads had particularly sharp teeth—dozens of tiny, bone flechettes.

I grabbed it. (It felt so cool.)

I raised it up and for a moment I saw not the skull, but the creature whose flesh it once bore.

It was hideous, sickening, indescribable.

Beautiful.

Utterly inhuman.

And it laughed.

I hurled the skull at the void that had started to envelop Enchantra's purple spell. It screamed like a giddy fish-girl as it flew.

It met the black tear in space and everything stopped.

For an instant, I was someplace else, with no ups or downs, and where the very idea of life was a punch line.

Someplace . . . impossible.

There was black. Then there was purple. Then there was white.

Then all was well and truly dark.

I woke to the smell of Camels.

The cigarettes, I mean.

Without so much as the aid of a forklift, I raised my head. It was pretty dark. And it smelled.

Like camels.

Not the cigarettes.

"Bleughh," I said. Or something very similar. It fully expressed my feelings.

"Do you smoke, Mr. Burns?"

"Call me . . ."

"Do you smoke, Arty?" V asked.

I started to shake my head, but that wasn't fun. "Uh-uh," I managed.

She sat on a three-legged stool. It looked like a milking stool. No cows, though. Or maybe that was the smell. V's expensive skirt was soiled and torn, and her exposed skin dirty and covered in bruises. Other than one lonely strand, which strayed down over her right eye à la Veronica Lake, her hair was still perfect. Damn!

I had a look around, but there wasn't much to see. A cabin, furnished in a very cabin-like manner. I lay on an old sofa, more springs than cushion. It creaked like a newlywed's bed with every movement. So did I.

"Who looks worse?" I asked. "You or me?"

V took a long drag and breathed the smoke out through her nose as she sized me up.

"You," she said, then nodded.

"That's a shame," I said.

"Meh," she said.

I roused myself to a proper sitting position, shifted to get a spring out of my asshole, then settled down again. Unbidden, V scooped up a bottle of Old Grand-Dad and tossed it to me in a delivery worthy of Bob Feller. She moved like a big cat, and even in my pained condition I couldn't help but wonder how it would feel to have her moving beneath me.

She narrowed her eyes as if she could read minds. Hell, given all the weird shit of the past day, who's to say she couldn't.

I took a swig of hooch.

"Good stuff," I said.

"Mr. Hughes pays the bills."

"What happened to Berkeley?" I asked.

"He's gone . . . for now."

"You maybe want to tell me what's going on?" I said.

"What do you think?"

"I don't get paid to think," I said. "That's why *I* work for Mr. Hughes."

"Tell me about him."

I sighed. Bourbon surely wasn't the right medicine for my condition or this conversation. I took another swig. Then I tossed the bottle back to V with about a tenth the grace she had demonstrated.

"What's to tell?" I said. "You obviously know him better than I do. He doesn't let *me* sit on his office furniture."

"All you need are D-cups."

"Amen, sister, amen."

That brought a slight upturn of her lip on one side.

"What if I told you," she began, "that your Mr. Hughes is not at all the man you think him to be."

"Let me guess: he's secretly a monk sworn to celibacy. Chasing every juicy flap of cooze between Sunset and Pico is just a cover."

"Maybe that's not so far from the truth," she said.

I sat up.

"Not the celibacy bit," she added.

"Thank God. A man's got to be able to believe in something in this world."

"Yes. Belief."

She picked up the bourbon and stared at the label so hard I thought maybe she was planning on slipping Old Grand-Dad the tongue. She delicately put the bottle down having arrived at some decision in her head.

"May I show you something, Arty?"

I was about to mouth smart about whether it involved taking off her panties, but I decided the moment wasn't quite right.

I nodded instead.

"It will change your . . . beliefs."

She stood up and walked toward me, undoing the buttons of her no-longer-white blouse. I realized that I had only ever seen her with her top buttoned to the neck. I swallowed hard, the panties quip still lingering at the back of my tongue. I don't know what I expected. Nah, I do: flawless fun bags of creamy fleshiness. With cherries on top. I certainly didn't expect what I saw.

It wasn't milky white under there. It was dark. A tattoo, I thought at first. But it was so dark. Dark as crow's feathers at the bottom of a hole in a cave. Dark as the depths of a studio chief's heart. Dark as . . .

As my deepest fears.

She continued toward me, shirttails flapping behind her as that darkness grew in my sight. I tried to look away from it, but I couldn't see V, couldn't turn away to the light. There was no light.

Except in the middle of the darkness.

A pinpoint. Then a pattern. Swirls and matrices and spirals that surrounded and ate each other as they spun through the blackness. The shapes took on dimension and grew impossibly large.

Or I shrank improbably small.

The patterns enveloped me, wrapped me up like a bean burrito and took my breath away. I closed my eyes, but still the patterns burned my brain. Once seen, they could not be unseen. They filled my head, my throat, my stomach.

And then a voice. It was V's voice, but amplified across a stage, a field, a world.

"This is what lies behind and beyond," she sang to me, though the voice came without words. "This is the truth that you cannot allow yourself to see."

I wanted to talk—no wising-off this time—but I had no lips, no tongue or throat; I was nothing in this vastness. Just a hole in an emptiness.

I would have wet myself, but Little Arty was on holiday too.

"There are worlds and more beyond this one. Dimensions so ancient and vast that your universe is but an inkblot on a page of crumpled paper in a small room of a forgotten shack."

"*My* universe?" I managed. I don't know where my voice came from.

"Battles rage across these dimensions among beings ancient when your world was rock-dust spinning about a newly-birthed star."

"My world."

"These intelligences are enormous and cruel. And petty."

"Like movie producers. Well, not the intelligence part."

The darkness in which I was immersed exploded into light. I had no eyes in this place, but could still see in my mind. I couldn't shut those mental eyes, however desperately I wanted to. And what was illuminated was too awful to behold. Shapes of . . . things, alive and dead, twisted and deformed and inside out—though how the outside could ever be in was not comprehensible. Through eyes that were not eyes, I saw . . . other eyes. Millions of them, billions. Watching me, wanting me, desperate to feed. Blinking randomly to mercifully hide—however briefly—the monstrous souls to which they were the windows.

"Unnnhhh," my voiceless voice said.

"Yes," V hissed. "Unnnhhh, indeed."

For a moment—and thank God it was but the slightest of moments—I thought I saw something else. An impossible thing too inhuman to even recognize. Once, when I was in the service, we came across a Panzer that had taken a direct hit not far from El Alamein. You always had to check these things out and I was on point. Three Nazi bastards had been cooked inside. And they'd been in there for a while. The smell was indescribable. Sometimes, at night, I still wake up with a trace of it in my nose.

The thing I saw used that scent for aftershave.

Then a flash and it was all gone. And V and I were back in the cabin. She tossed the bourbon back to me.

"Are we dead?" I asked her.

"You should be so lucky, Arty."

I gave Old Grand-Dad a very long kiss.

"Why me?"

V scowled. "Why not you?"

"Can't you ever just answer a simple question?"

"Maybe I would if you asked one."

"Cripes!" I said. "If all else fails you can write for Sid Caesar."

Before, I would have described the moonless night we drove through as dark, but after the things I'd seen, well . . . the unlit road into the Hills felt like Pismo Beach at noon.

"Look, V, I'm just a regular guy . . ."

She guffawed. "You're factotum prime for one of the most powerful men in the world!"

"Deep down, I mean."

"Few of us know what we are deep down," she said. All serious now.

"I suppose you're one of the lucky ones."

"No luck involved," she said. "No such thing as luck exists. There's only knowledge, design, and hard work."

"So what are you? Deep down, I mean."

She dropped down a gear, never taking her eyes from the winding canyon road. She didn't flinch as something furry squished beneath our wheels.

"I'd like to say I'm a warrior," she said softly. "I like to think of myself that way. But I'm just another pawn, dreaming of being a castle or a bishop. All a dream within a dream."

"Is that what this is? A game of chess? Why not dream of being a queen or king?"

"You've caught a glimpse of the sovereigns of this game," she said. And now she did turn her head and looked me square in the eye. "Would you aspire to so terrible a condition?

"No," I whispered.

I was still trying to make sense of all that V had told me. The Arty of two days ago wouldn't have believed a word of it—wouldn't even have bought it as the script for *Cthulhu*—but now . . .

A war. A vast and ancient war. Beings—gods?—beyond anything we little humans could even conceive, battling for . . . what? That bit I still didn't really understand.

Just for the hell of it, it seemed to me.

But some of them—I hesitate to say the bad guys, 'cause I couldn't really see any white hats in this picture—want what we have. "Our dimension," V had explained back in the cabin. Our space, our world, our stuff.

Us.

They poke and probe and seek ways in. Those vast and unspeakable eye-things that V allowed me to see. They want to take us.

I hadn't been able to stop thinking about it.

"What's so great about this place, anyway?" I asked.

"What?" V asked, but kept her eyes on the now tortuously winding road.

"These . . . beings. What did you call them?"

"The Great Old Ones."

"Yeah, those guys. What the hell do they see in this place? Earth. Why the razzamatazz? Why here?"

For some reason, she shook her head. Then said: "Our world is a kind of conjunction. A point in space and time where the dimensions meet. Kind of a revolving door in the cosmos. That's why there's life here, how it arrived in the first place."

"You mean like cavemen?"

"No. Not like cavemen. Is your entire knowledge-base gleaned from low-budget movies?"

"Not entirely. I used to read dime novels too. Doc Savage was great."

"I think the Man of Bronze would have known better."

"We could sure do with him now. We need someone on our side."

"We are a force to be reckoned with, Arty. We are part of a tradition that has stood against the Old Ones for many years. We are still here."

"And they're still trying to get in."

"Yes."

"And we have to stop them."

"Yes."

"Us."

"We're not alone."

"You, me, and Enchantra then. Watch those giant space monsters run."

"We have Mr. Hughes."

I still couldn't believe it. But V had told me that Hughes's persona as an obsessive, fast-living, vulgar, womanizing, breast-obsessed, billionaire arms mogul was a front.

"You're kidding?" I'd said.

"Well, mostly a front," she'd replied.

In fact, Hughes was one of the de facto leaders in the war against the Old Ones. His whole life was an illusion to make him look like anything other than what he was: an invisible hand guiding—and helping finance—those who were trying to hold the line against the return of these elder . . . gods?

"Everything he has done has been in the service of our cause. His aviation business, munitions interests. All his investment and riches have allowed us to build up a war chest. The real weapons he forges are to be raised against a far more profound enemy than the Russians."

"And the film studio?"

"This, too, is part of the fight. Hearts and minds are important in war as well. And there are messages in the films. Of course, people go for the thrills, the romance . . ."

"The popcorn?"

"Yes. They go for the emotional pleasure, the visceral kick, the kinetic charge. But they get a message too. Sometimes when they are least aware, the message penetrates the deepest. When their guard is down while they are watching silly little comedies or—"

"Monster movies," I'd said, as a cog fell into place. "*Cthulhu! Creature of Destruction!*"

"Exactly. It is a warning, a way of putting out to the many what could never be said, what would never be believed if stated directly. Surely the preponderance of monster movies these last few years has not escaped your notice?"

"But who goes to see them? A bunch of B movies at the drive-in. Horny teenagers looking to get to second base in the dark?"

"'Give me the child until he is seven and he is mine for life.'"

"Isn't that the church?" I'd asked.

"Are we not speaking of gods?" V had replied.

Touché.

"And Mr. Hughes's crusade against the commies?"

"A front against another front." She'd practically spat.

V explained that the Red Scare served as a cover too. A classic diversion.

"Leave the masses in terror of a false threat, to keep them from seeing the real one," she'd said. "Turn all your guns to one flank, leave your rear unguarded."

"But the government, the Feds . . ."

"Some know of the threat and are doing their best to oppose it. Some are blind. And some—very high up—are quislings, serving the Ancient Ones. All's fair, as they say."

I thought of some of the Reds I'd put the boot to. I didn't cotton to playing the pawn for anyone.

"What about Enchantra?" I'd asked.

"Television will be the most powerful force at our disposal. A signal into every home, every room."

"You mean who can afford it."

"That will change. Television will be everywhere before you know it. Imagine a world littered with screens, all sending out the same hidden message: *Watch the skies! Beware!*"

"Crazy," I'd said.

And crazy it still felt. Even as we hurtled through the dark to meet the enemy face to face. Eyeball to . . . eyeballs?

"You have got to be kidding me," I said.

"Have you no sense of irony, Arty?"

"Irony I can do. But this is pushing the boat out."

We'd arrived at our destination. Or was it our destiny? V pulled off the dirt track we'd been rumbling up and announced we'd have to hike the rest of the way. I didn't have the shoes for it, but I didn't have much choice either.

She'd managed to get the car about two-thirds of the way up Cahuenga Peak before that dirt road petered out entirely. Mr. Hughes owned most of the mountain—he'd bought it after he proposed to Ginger Rogers. (Apparently he thought its shape was a dead ringer for her right breast. Romantic or what?) When Ginger decided he was too nutty for her, he abandoned it. I only knew because I once saw the tear-stained plans on his desk for the mountaintop castle he'd planned to build for her. He'd rambled to me about her betrayal as he scrawled dirty words and obscene caricatures of Fred Astaire all over the blueprints.

Just to the east, atop the slightly smaller Mount Lee, stood the mighty Hollywood sign. The altitude at which we stood left us about level with it.

"You can take the Elder Gods out of show business . . . ," I started.

That actually elicited a laugh. Short-lived, though.

"Come on," V said. "It's a rough walk."

Los Angeles always looks better at night, and from atop Cahuenga the basin sparkled like an upturned bowl of stars—a mirror below of the vastness above. Did the same monsters lurk in both? A warm breeze rattled the thin rows of pines and rasped the back of my throat. I reckoned we'd be in the teeth of a proper Santa Ana by morning.

We'd been walking a good hour before V stopped. My feet had swollen in my Stacy Adams and my shirt was soaked through. Don't ask where my boxers had ridden. I'd long since taken off my jacket and thought about just tossing it into the brush now.

Even in the dim glow thrown up by the city lights I could see that V looked as fresh as a sailor in a shore-leave cathouse.

V pulled something out of the small leather bag she carried over her shoulder: it looked like a glass pyramid. She murmured a word I couldn't make out and tapped the top of it. It let out a bright white light.

"Ancient artifact?" I asked.

"Hammacher Schlemmer catalog," she told me.

She placed the pyramid on the ground, pulled another item out of the bag and held it up. "*This* is the artifact."

Between her thumb and index finger she held a green, star-shaped object. I thought it was a sheriff's badge, but as I looked at it, the thing changed shape, grew in her hand. The sharp edges I had taken for points on the star seemed to extend and retract. It looked like it was made of sandstone or perhaps jade, but it also seemed . . . alive. Like some weird sea urchin or ocean-bed creature pulsing in her fingers. Kind of disgusting, but also hypnotic.

"What is that?" I asked, leaning over to get a better look.

"It is you, Arty," she said.

And she thrust it between my lips.

An anise bomb exploded in my mouth. It tasted like Good & Plenty, only without the Plenty (or is it the Good?—I've never known which bit the licorice is supposed to be . . .). I started to gag as I felt the pulsating blob dance around my mouth. Then it scurried—I swear I could feel the toes of its nasty little feet *galumphing* down my gullet. I felt sure I would puke it up, along with my stomach lining, when . . .

Everything changed.

Once, long ago, I found myself at the bottom of an old well (don't ask). I screamed for help and the sound echoed back and forth, around and through me, such that I felt like I could hear with every fiber of my bones and organs.

This was that times a million.

The light had changed around me too. Every tree, every rock, every skittering bug and blade of grass had grown sharper in focus and buzzed with a deep purple luminescence. There was no darkness now, no night—the world was a shimmering violet wonderland. I looked up at V: she had become an angel, her blistering white aura extending ten feet high, her smile an argent slash that set off chimes in my skin—then I raised my gaze to the skies.

Where I saw them all.

"My gods," I issued.

"Yes," V sang.

Others emerged from the brush. Where they came from I couldn't say, but they were inhumanly beautiful. Soldiers, I knew, though their faces and forms were strange to me. And at the last—her true essence a roiling silhouette of orange and blue, veined with madder rose—I recognized Enchantra.

"Are we ready?" V asked her.

I knew the answer before I felt Enchantra's reply.

We were one. We were ready.

We advanced.

The doorway into the hillside of Mount Lee could not have been seen with human eyes, but in my new state it was as obvious as King Kong at a cookout. With a gesture, Enchantra blew it open and our little platoon of the otherworldly poured inside.

In my heightened state, all senses merged into one. I could hear the tightly packed dirt of the path that had been torn out of the side of the mountain and down which our cadre moved. I could smell the determination and pride that passed between the warriors both in front of and behind me. I could taste the bitter sweetness of the ancient un-human extremities that had forged this trail.

I could see, hear, taste, smell, feel—in colors, along wavelengths previously unimagined—everything.

I saw everything.

They came at us all at once through the rock. Shapeless, yet deformed. Empty, but bearing the weight of worlds. Throatless, yet screaming with a fury beyond time, beyond dimension. These things were not of this world. No human could have dreamed them. I didn't know how they could even be alive.

Maybe they were not—it was way out of my league.

The warriors—I still don't know who or what they were—met them. The mountain rocked. The great sign on the hilltop above us teetered on its supports, Hollywood on the brink of falling.

To the millions below it must have felt like an earthquake; to our ethereal company, it was a rocking of the stars themselves.

Light of hitherto unseen chromaticism exploded as the forces met.

Flanked by V and Enchantra, I pressed on as the battle burned around us. Glimpses of . . . things—tentacles, eyes, organs blacker than the pit—penetrated my expanded consciousness, staggered me. Always, though, the women on either side held me up, edged me forward.

Then, in a fraction of a blink, Enchantra was gone. A mouth—inside of it a thousand mouths, and within their maws an infinity of onyx teeth flailing with foul life—opened and took her. I tasted the rending of her soul in my heart.

It tasted a little like chicken.

V and I pressed on as the trail inside the mountain widened, finally opening out into a vast chamber of stone. Every inch of the walls was poisoned with a graffito—the symbols and figures carved into the rock a mad god's vandalism. To even glimpse these obscenities was to feel elemental pain.

At a very center was not a darkness, but an absence. A hole in everything, the enemy of light and reason. The nothing—this impossibility in reality—nonetheless glowed somehow. It glowed with a blackness that burned like a sun.

"What in the Sam Hill?" some piece of me said.

As we neared the heart of the cavern, stupidly approaching this radiant blackness, V reached inside—I want to say her pocket, but if so, that pocket was sewn somewhere inside herself. Her hand went wrist-deep inside her torso. Just a day ago that alone would have made me kack my skivvies. Now I just thought: *copasetic*!

When she drew her hand out again, the light of her aura slightly dimmed, but on her finger I saw a ring.

It was Mr. Hughes's pinky ring—the one he was always fiddling with. I recognized the crazy hybrid-creature etched in the thick gold.

Now that gold was glowing, and the ruby eyes blazed with fury.

And the creature was somehow emerging from the metal.

It is not possible to explain what this . . . being was. I had no eyes to see it, nor ears to hear, but I knew it deep in my soul (as I knew in that moment, for the first time in my life, that I actually had a soul).

It was light. It was power.

It was . . . majesty.

The creature leapt into the glowing orb of black.

There are no words to capture the struggle that ensued between the light and the dark, only feelings—terror, grief, pain, tendresse, anger, ecstasy, hunger, despair, orgasm.

Yes, it was like ejaculating excrement.

For a moment, the light deepened and took over the chamber.

Then the dark grew again and that soul I'd only just shaken hands with shriveled.

"We are lost," V cried.

I wanted to, had to, do something. I didn't know what. I was nothing against the cosmic vastness. I am no warrior: I had no skills, no abilities, no weapons.

Like a fool, I patted myself down, reached into pockets. I had some coins and keys, a monogrammed hankie, and a pigskin wallet.

And one other thing.

(*Yes*, something said.)

Letting loose a scream that bloodied the inside of my throat—but which was less than a pin dropping on mile-thick carpet to the roaring chaos in front of me—I plunged my hand, and the tiny item it held, into the pulsating blackness.

I heard a real scream then—it was the dying scream of universes.

It burned me to a cinder.

There is nothing in this life duller than having to listen to someone talk about their dreams. So I won't detail what I experienced. Except to say . . . they weren't nice.

Then: a voice.

"What's cookin' good lookin'?"

Faith Domergue, naked as that wonderful, proverbial jaybird, approached and straddled me. She gave Little Arty the bestest birthday present any boy ever had and then she got really dirty. Holy, Lady of the Angels!

Okay, *that* was a dream. But at least it wasn't dull.

I opened my eyes.

I looked around.

I saw airplanes. And breasts.

"Mr. Hughes's office," I croaked.

I managed to raise my head enough to see that I was lying on his great leather sofa. I had to suppress a shudder thinking about the fluids that must have befouled it over the years.

"Hello, Arty."

V. I quite literally knew that voice inside and out now.

"Mr. Hughes won't like this," I said. "He'll have the sofa burned. And me with it."

"He isn't here," she said. She came over and sat beside me. She reached down and stroked my hair. "He's . . . gone away."

"That's nice," I said. I meant the stroking.

"He's fought a long, hard battle."

"*He's* fought a battle?"

"He's been at it for years. It has cost him dearly."

I raised a finger and gestured at the luxurious surroundings. "Not exactly a shotgun shack," I said.

"I don't mean money. He's paid a price with his mind. The war has left him damaged. Beyond repair, I fear. He's been taken someplace to try to help him recover. But giving up Winfield's ring . . . that was all that held him together. Without its binding force, I see little hope for his future. He will probably sell the studio now. Sad. But he has been valiant."

"V . . . ," I began.

She pressed a finger to my lips.

"Best not to ask too many questions, lest you walk the path of your Mr. Hughes. The battle was won. The dark things, the Old Ones, have been . . . deterred."

"But not defeated."

"No," she said. "Defeat is not a possibility, and there will be greater battles to come. But this is a victory even so."

I pondered that a while.

"Can I ask you a question, Arty?"

"I'm spoken for," I said. "But if you really want to . . ."

She rapped my forehead with a steel knuckle. It hurt.

"What was in your hand?"

"Howzat?"

"In the chamber in the mountain. When all seemed lost, you thrust your hand into the nothing. It held something that saved us, but I couldn't make it out. What was it?"

I thought about it for a moment, not sure what to say about the little pink flower that Faith had given me on the studio lot.

"It was . . . a token."

"*What*?"

"More than that, I suppose. Call it . . . an obscure object of desire. Though quite a pretty one. It was just a flower, V."

She tilted her head back and laughed the loudest, most heartfelt laugh I'd ever heard.

"Beautiful," she said when she stopped laughing. "Perfect."

"Perfect?"

"Life, beauty, desire—humanity. All wrapped up in the smallest of organic packages. There could have been no better weapon against the dark. How did you think of it?"

"The only other thing I had on me was a cherry Lifesaver," I confessed.

"You, Arthur Burns, are a great warrior." She started laughing again.

"Not just a pawn, then?"

She stopped laughing. "I knew there was more to you than first appeared," she said. "Something in the blood, perhaps in your genes. Your line has been touched, I think. I was wrong about you."

"Everyone is. How do *you* mean?"

"You're not a pawn at all, but are transformed—you have become a knight."

"Really?"

"You know how they move on chessboards? All aslant? That is definitely you."

"And knights have big lances, right?"

She shook her head at me. She leaned over and gave me a kiss on the lips, so soft it might have been the tap of a butterfly's wing.

"I think our paths may cross again," she said and made for the door. She paused and turned to study at me again. "Or if not you, perhaps your heirs."

"Heirs? Say what?" I tried to get up to stop her, but I just couldn't move.

Then I was alone in the room. I stared at the model airplanes for a while and thought again about Howard Hughes. Who could have imagined? I let my gaze drift to the photos on the walls: the starlets all at their peak-a-boo bests. Backs arched, lips moistened, eyebrows plucked, skin shimmering like the sea's surface under a full moon.

One of the smaller glossies hung in a slightly darker corner of the room. After a while I managed to get up, limp over to it and take it down. I laid it flat on Mr. Hughes's desk and stared at it for a while. Little Arty came to look too.

Trying my luck, I punched the button on the intercom. Hughes's haughty secretary asked if she could help.

"Faith Domergue," I said. "Could you see if she's on the lot? Ask her to come up to the office if she is?"

The secretary said she would see what she could do.

Me too.

NINE

Arkham House on Haunted Hill

IVERSON HOUSE WAS A hideous sight, even from a distance. It squatted on the misshapen hill like a huge malevolent toad, looming over the town of Arkham below, gray against an even grayer sky.

Once Frank was past the clutching arms of the skeletal trees and onto the crumbling path leading up to the house, he could finally see it properly. The compact, boxy structure looked as though it was drowning in the shadows that cloaked its walls. Even the air above it was host to a murky miasma that made it look diseased.

From where he stood, the place just looked like solid brick, dull and rust-colored, cold and comfortless, without a window in sight. He couldn't imagine what the architect must have been thinking, designing something so unapologetically ugly—and then actually building it.

There were several hills dotting the rural Massachusetts landscape—larger, higher, and more picturesque. Why choose the smallest, most malformed one on which to build this horror?

He was so distracted he stepped off the path. His foot squelched into mud the color of dying flesh. With a muttered curse, he jumped back onto the cracked paving stones and stared in dismay at his ruined shoe. It felt like an omen, a sign of bad things to come. Not that he believed in such things.

For a moment he considered turning back, but then abandoned the idea. He'd been hired to do a job and he wasn't the kind of man to let someone down. Especially not a man like Arthur Leland. And especially not for the kind of money he was being paid: $5,000 up front and another

$5,000 on completion of a week's stay in the house. That was no small amount.

Still, he found the assignment curious. He'd told Mr. Leland quite emphatically that he didn't believe in ghosts or anything to do with the supernatural. In fact, he'd confessed, he wasn't even a Christian. But Leland had insisted. He wanted an architect in the group, and he had chosen Frank's firm. Frank had known why, of course.

Twenty years ago, at the beginning of his apprenticeship, he'd been witness to a strange event. He had only helped draw up the blueprints for the little shop, so it was sheer coincidence that he was at the building site at all that day. That was to say, he had no special connection to the place—or the events.

The sky had suddenly darkened, plunging the framework of studs, beams, and girders into shadow. The plastic sheeting over the unfinished walls had begun to crackle and billow even though there wasn't a breath of wind. Suddenly there came a thunderous boom, like an explosion. And then the upright posts had collapsed like dominoes and the entire structure, scaffolding and all, had come tumbling down. Several men had been standing in the middle of the building site, including Frank, and it was a miracle no one was killed. At the time, the local paper had marveled at the occurrence and called it "inexplicable," but never went so far as to suggest that ghosts were responsible.

Leland had questioned him about the event, of course. And Frank had given the old man the same answers he'd given everyone else all those years ago. Sometimes these things just happened. As far as he was concerned, there was always a rational explanation; it was just that people often didn't look hard enough for it.

But Leland didn't care whether Frank believed or not. "I have to know what's in that old house," he'd said. "Grant a dying man his final wish."

Well, who was Frank to argue with that? More to the point, who was he to turn down $10,000? For that kind of money he was happy to play along. Hell, he might even be tempted to embellish his report with something just as "inexplicable" as what he'd witnessed all those years ago.

“Would you hurry up?” Gregory urged.

Val looked up to see that he had already started up the path with the suitcases, leaving her behind to struggle with the smaller bags. They’d parked halfway up the hill on the crooked little outcrop that served as a forecourt, but the path leading up to the house was at least another hundred yards long. Even with just a bag of groceries it would feel like a mile.

“I’m hurrying,” she shot back. “You’re always rushing me!” She yanked at the bag but it wouldn’t come free of whatever it was snagged on in the car’s trunk.

“Because you’re always so sloooow.”

“Well, I could move a lot faster if you’d help me!”

With a sigh, Gregory turned back and made a big show of setting down the cases and unlooping the shoulder strap of her bag from where it had caught on the tire iron. He deposited it at her feet with a thud. “There. Are you happy now?”

Val rolled her eyes and picked it up, hauling it over her shoulder with the two other satchels she was already loaded down with. “No thanks to you.”

“Hey, don’t throw a double duck fit. Those are heavy.” He jerked his chin at the cases. She could see sweat stains blooming under the arms of his white T-shirt. “If you didn’t have to pack everything you own . . .”

She crossed her arms and waited for him to finish.

But he trailed off as he met her exasperated expression. “Are we going to argue all week?”

After a moment she relented. “No,” she said. It had been a long drive from New Jersey and they were both tired and cranky. “I’m sorry.”

He slammed shut the trunk of the Buick and gave his beloved car an affectionate pat before heading along the winding path with Val.

When the monstrous house became visible through the trees, Val felt a flutter of unease in the pit of her stomach.

“Ugh,” she said, “it doesn’t look very nice.”

Gregory smiled. "A spook house *shouldn't* look nice. Come on, it's what we've always wanted. Don't chicken out on me now!"

Val relaxed and allowed herself to smile. Yes, it *was* what they'd always wanted—to see an actual haunted house. And Iverson House was rumored to be the most haunted house in New England. Maybe in all of America.

They'd never actually seen it before, not even a photograph, but they'd read newspaper articles about the unexplained phenomena recorded in the house over the years. Strange noises, screams, flickering lights. And Arthur Leland had told them even more. Three people had apparently vanished without a trace after exploring it five years ago.

When he'd interviewed them for the assignment, Mr. Leland had said he was very impressed by their enthusiasm. They didn't have the experience of older, more seasoned investigators, but he said their youth would work in their favor. They had fewer preconceived notions and ingrained ideas, he'd told them. They were more open, more receptive.

Val had asked whether that might make it more dangerous for them, to which Gregory had responded with a withering look.

But Mr. Leland had merely offered her an avuncular smile and patted her hand. "Of course not," he'd said reassuringly.

"Gee, it sure is ugly," Gregory said, sounding excited. "*Real* ugly."

And it was. A great hulking mass of crumbling—was it brick? Stone? It looked like something the ground had tried to swallow and brought back up.

Val wrinkled her nose. "I sure hope it's not full of bugs. Rats and bats I can handle, but if I see a spider like the one in New York that time . . ."

Gregory laughed. "Don't worry, I'll stomp it." And he demonstrated by bringing his boot down hard on a dry leaf, pulverizing it into dust.

For some reason the sight made her shudder, and she suddenly realized how chilly it was. She'd only worn a light cardigan over her blouse, and her pedal pushers left her calves and ankles exposed. Once the stony path came to an end, the ground was unpleasantly soft and squishy. Thank heavens she'd worn her old saddle shoes.

"Almost there," Gregory said, reading her mind.

It took them several minutes to find the door. Where a normal building would have the entrance in front, the way into Iverson House was around a corner. Val shook off the unpleasant notion that the door was hiding from them. It was tucked into an alcove that didn't look like it belonged with the rest of the structure, as though someone had blasted a hole in the wall and covered it up with a crude porch and a slab of oak with a hinge.

They stood staring. It did not look inviting.

"Do we just go in?" she asked.

"I suppose so. We are guests at this party after all."

The door was horrible. Warped and twisted. Like something that had been dredged up from a swamp and battered into place by cavemen. It made her skin crawl. What if the rooms inside were just as primitive?

Gregory reached for the handle, but Val grabbed his hand. "No, wait! Let's knock."

He frowned at her for a moment, then laughed. "You think we might have the wrong house? Val, for Pete's sake!"

But he hesitated anyway, standing there with his upraised knuckles inches from the wood. There was something in his expression he couldn't hide from her. He looked just as scared as she felt.

Frank was standing in the main room of the house when he heard the faint knocking on the door. He turned toward the sound. It hadn't even occurred to him to knock when he'd arrived. The place was supposed to be deserted after all. Well, unless of course there really *was* a ghost.

It had been a chore to pry the front door open so he could get in, and the wood squealed and juddered against the floor as he dragged it open once more. He stared in surprise at the clean-cut young couple standing on the porch, loaded down with bags. The boy had a blond crew cut and the girl wore her hair in a ponytail with a red-checked scarf tied around it. They looked like teenagers.

“Hi,” Frank said, adopting a welcoming smile for them. “You must be Mr. and Mrs. Robinson.”

Their smiles dissolved and they turned to each other with an expression of mutual horror.

“Um, no,” the girl said after a moment.

The boy shook his head. “We’re not married.”

“Oh,” Frank said. Honestly, he didn’t see what was so shocking about that, and he was about to say so, but then they both spoke in unison, each pointing to the other.

“He’s my brother.”

“She’s my sister.”

Frank covered his mouth, then allowed himself to laugh. “I’m so sorry,” he said. “I thought—the shared last name. Just—” he shook his head “—come on inside, will you?”

The boy regained his composure first. “Hey, don’t sweat it,” he said with a friendly laugh. “Honest mistake.”

The girl gazed wide-eyed around the room as they entered. “Wow,” she breathed.

Frank didn’t see much to inspire awe. It was a profoundly dull, empty chamber. The lopsided walls were the same muddy red as the house’s exterior, devoid of paint or wallpaper or any kind of decoration. The only furniture was a battered wooden table and four rickety chairs, sitting at odd angles on the uneven floor. It all had the air of a monastic cell, something functional but never intended for comfort.

He had been surprised to find that the house had running water and electricity, although neither the pipes nor the wiring were concealed within the walls. It was hard to imagine that anyone had ever actually *lived* here. Even painted, carpeted, and furnished, Frank couldn’t see it being at all livable.

After a quick glance around, the boy stuck out his hand. “I’m Gregory,” he said, “and this is Val.”

The girl smiled as she peeled herself free of all the bags she was carrying and dumped them on the floor.

"Pleased to meet you," Frank said, shaking both their hands. "I'm Frank Edwards. Are you twins?"

They both laughed.

"People always ask us that," Gregory said.

"But I'm actually a year older," Val finished.

Frank looked down at all the luggage they had brought. "I take it you're the ghost hunters."

Val winced. "Paranormal investigators, *please*," she implored.

"Yeah," Gregory said. "No one takes you seriously if you call yourself a ghost hunter!"

Frank didn't have the heart to tell them that no one took "paranormal investigators" any more seriously, but he didn't want to spoil it for them. Leland really must be off his rocker, sending a skeptic and two kids to explore his haunted house.

Gregory ran his hand over the nearest wall. Red flakes came off on his palm. "Yuck!" He laughed as he dusted it off on his jeans. "It's like being inside a brick."

"Or something collapsing on a pottery wheel," Val added, a description Frank thought was apt. "Have you had a look around yet, Mr. Edwards?"

Frank bristled a little at the name. Well, he supposed he *was* old enough to be their father. He chuckled. "Please just call me Frank. And no, I just got here too. I've seen the kitchen, which is fully stocked, just as our host promised. But that's it."

Gregory was still trying to wipe away the red dust from the wall. Now he was scrubbing his hands on a towel. "Who's missing?"

"Missing? Oh, you mean our fourth?"

"The psychic. Mina . . . something." He looked over at his sister.

"I think Mr. Leland said her last name was Cloudminder."

Oh brother, Frank thought. He tried not to look too disdainful at the mention of a psychic. Would she turn up in a riot of colorful, swirling skirts, a headscarf, and huge golden hoops in her ears? Would she have a crystal ball? More to the point, how was he supposed to interact with these people? Him, the sole nonbeliever?

Val had already begun unpacking the first of many bags, pulling out odd-looking devices and electrical equipment, scattering them haphazardly across the table. Some were patched with duct tape. Others just looked homemade. There was something that looked like a hybrid of an old box brownie camera and a circular saw. It all gave the impression of a school science project gone wrong, and Frank decided not to ask what any of it was.

"Come on, Sis," Gregory said, pulling Val away from the table, "we can set up later. Let's explore the house first!"

"Good plan," Frank said. He was eager to see for himself how the interior looked, given the appalling appearance of the exterior.

Gregory grabbed the two suitcases that looked as if they might actually contain clothes and headed for the stairs. Val followed, taking one of the smaller bags with her.

"When was this place built?" Gregory asked.

"No one knows for sure. The locals claim it's always been here."

The stairs were of the same material as the walls and floor. Frank could almost imagine giant fingers hand-sculpting the house and everything in it out of the same wet red clay. The image made him feel a little queasy, and he steadied himself against the wall as they reached a bowl-shaped landing.

"Hey, you okay?" Val asked.

He shook off the feeling. "Yeah. Just lost my footing for a second."

The upper floor was even uglier than the lower one, and Val's pottery image came back to him. The walls looked like they were in the process of disintegrating. Perhaps they had been ever since the place was built. And the floor was even more concave than the landing, as though worn by the passage of many feet, over many years.

The girl clutched her arms and gave an elaborate shudder. Frank was grateful for the display, as it disguised his own similar reaction.

"It's so cold," she said, pulling her sweater tightly around herself.

"Aww, don't be a wet rag," Gregory said, giving her a shove down the hallway. He turned to Frank, affecting a world-weary expression. "If it's not too cold, it's too hot. Or too dark. Or too bright."

Val glared at him. "Or too full of brothers," she grumbled.

Frank closed his eyes as he realized he was probably going to end up playing peacekeeper all week. He ignored their squabbling and opened the first door that looked like it might lead to a bedroom. To his surprise, it actually contained a bed, along with a dresser and a chair. A pile of folded linen rested on the bare springs beside the rolled-up mattress.

"Well, that's a relief," he said. "At least we won't be sleeping on the floor."

"It looks like a prison cell," Gregory said. He sounded excited at the prospect.

Frank went to the window and pushed aside the tattered brown curtains, releasing a shower of red dust that made him cough. The light was fading, turning the trees into clutching shadows. He followed the line of the path all the way to the forecourt and smiled at the one spot of color in the bleak landscape.

"Say," he said. "Now *that* is a thing of beauty."

Gregory hurried to see. "What is?"

Frank pointed at the jazzy blue and white convertible.

"Oh," Gregory said, a huge grin spreading across his features. "Yeah, isn't she sweet?"

"I'll say! Buick Skylark, right? What is she—'53, '54?"

"'53," Gregory said, beaming with pride. "I spent all summer restoring her."

"I helped."

Frank saw Gregory spare his sister a grudging glance to acknowledge her contribution. "Yeah, a bit," he allowed, and she slugged him in the arm.

The kids clearly had money. Cars like that didn't come cheap, not even fixer-uppers. Frank felt a wave of envy as his eyes drank in every detail. "Just look at those lines. Does she have the new Nailhead V8 under that hood?"

"Sure does! Lowered beltline and the new Sweepspear too."

Val shoved in between them. "Her name's Smiley," she said.

Gregory rolled his eyes. "*You* call her Smiley," he grumbled. "*I* call her Bettie."

The girl gave a snort and looked to Frank for support. "Don't you think she looks like she's smiling?"

Frank took another look. The polished chrome grille did resemble teeth, with the headlights either side giving the appearance of wide, inquisitive eyes. Such a young, beautiful car. And sitting next to his battered old Chrysler. Suddenly he felt very old and obsolete.

"She sure does, kid," he said wistfully. "She sure does."

Val left them discussing every minute detail about Smiley and went to find the best bedroom for herself. There were five in all, and she laid claim by dumping her stuff on the bed that looked the least rickety. It was also the smallest room, which she hoped meant it would be the warmest. For once she was glad she'd listened to her mother and packed an extra blanket.

The bathroom was primitive, but at least it had hot water. She supposed they were lucky the house had electricity too. She didn't like the idea of watching for ghosts by candlelight.

She was setting up the first of three cameras downstairs when a noise made her jump. She froze, listening intently, but all she could hear were the muffled voices of Frank and her brother upstairs. Jeez, were they still going on about cars?

"Hello!"

The unexpected female voice made her cry out and she dropped the tripod she'd been assembling. It clattered noisily to the floor. Val whirled around, half-expecting—and half-hoping—to see a spectral figure floating behind her. But it was only a woman. A flesh-and-blood one.

The stranger laughed softly. "I'm sorry, I didn't mean to startle you."

Val blushed, pressing a hand to her chest to calm her galloping heart. "Oh," she panted, "you didn't scare me." Then she blushed even deeper at the ridiculous lie. She'd only jumped straight out of her skin.

But the woman was kind enough to ignore it. "I believe you were expecting me," she said. "I'm Mina Cloudminder."

Val drank in her appearance: her stylish dress and black gloves, her upswept auburn hair and elegant dove-gray coat. She didn't look like a psychic. But then, Val really had no idea what a psychic should look like. Maybe they all looked like they'd stepped off the cover of *Vogue*.

The noise had brought Gregory and Frank running, and they drew up short when they saw their guest.

Val took special pride in introducing the glamorous newcomer to the others, as though they were old friends.

Mina clasped her gloved hands as she gazed around the room. She looked as out of place as Marilyn Monroe would at a truck stop.

"Well," Mina said after a while, "this really is quite an unusual house."

"Are you picking up any psychic vibrations or anything?" Gregory asked eagerly.

Oh boy, Val thought, suppressing a giggle, *he's in love*.

Mina only offered him an enigmatic little smile in response as she made a circuit of the room, peering into the crooked corners and gazing up at the sagging ceiling. "Extraordinary," she said after a while. "It's like melting wax."

Frank nodded in agreement with her description. "I don't know what keeps it from collapsing," he said. "I had a look upstairs and there's no evidence of any internal support or reinforcement. No studs or beams. I think the whole thing was molded out of clay from the hill."

"Like an adobe house?" Val asked. They'd learned about it in school and she was keen to show off her knowledge.

"Not quite. Adobe houses are essentially mudbricks stacked together and then covered with more mud. They're extremely durable. This place behaves almost like a liquid. A very slow-moving one."

"Melting," Gregory mused. He grabbed Val by the arms and shook her excitedly. "What do you think about that, Sis? A melting house!"

She could barely contain her own excitement. "A *haunted* melting house," she added.

Frank looked faintly embarrassed, while Mina smiled indulgently at them.

"You two seem eager to meet a ghost," she said, her eyes sparkling. She slipped off her gloves one by one to reveal immaculately manicured hands, with scarlet nails to match her lipstick. "I do hope the house won't disappoint you."

"I've always wanted to see a ghost," Val gushed.

Gregory nodded, sharing her enthusiasm. "Can you sense them? How many are there?"

"Are they trapped here? Are they sad? Can we help them?"

Mina laughed softly and held up her hands to ward off their barrage of questions. "One thing at a time. As you must know from your previous paranormal investigations—" she gestured at the equipment arranged around the room "—the spirits will only make contact when—and if—they're ready."

Val felt herself positively glowing at the fact that Mina had used their preferred term and not the dismissive "ghost hunters." But she could see Frank scowling and shaking his head behind Mina's back. Before Val could say anything, Mina beat her to it.

"I gather we have a skeptic among us as well?"

Frank looked startled for a moment before regaining his composure.

Mina turned to him, still smiling. "It's all right. You're part of a grand tradition of people who don't follow blindly, and who don't just take the word of others for things that can't be explained by conventional means."

He seemed surprised by her praise. "That's true," he said. "And I'm a big believer in those conventional means. So unless one of these alleged ghosts appears right in front of me . . ."

"You trust the evidence of your own senses," she said. "That's perfectly reasonable. So do I. It's just that *my* senses . . . show me more."

She closed her eyes and tilted her head back, as though scenting the air in the room. "When you heard the sound, you thought it was an explosion. Paul jumped out of the way first, but one of the beams hit Jerry. No, Jimmy. But he wasn't seriously hurt. All you could hear was the rattle of the plastic sheeting as it tore away from the collapsing posts. The rhythm made you think of a song, which you found funny, but only for a moment."

The room was silent. Val and Gregory exchanged a wide-eyed glance before turning back to Frank, whose mouth had fallen open.

"What song?" he whispered.

She met his eyes. "'Sing, Sing, Sing.'"

Val had never heard of it, but Frank clearly had. For long moments he just stood there, gaping at Mina. His face was like a movie screen, all his emotions playing out across it in plain sight.

Mina went to him and touched him lightly on the shoulder, as though to wake him up. "Sometimes our eyes aren't enough," she said softly.

Gregory had chosen the bedroom next to Val's, but he was too excited to sleep. After a brief argument over whether or not they should sleep in shifts (Val said no way), he'd decided to move his stuff downstairs and stay with the equipment. Honestly, she was such a lightweight. She got all excited over the idea of staying up all night watching for ghosts, only to start nodding off after half an hour.

He'd actually been hoping that Mina would stay up with him. Her performance earlier had knocked his socks off. Whatever she'd been talking about with Frank, she'd obviously been right on the money. He was dying to ask her all about it, to ask what she could pick up from the house. But she'd cried off, saying it had been a long journey and she was tired. She'd let him carry her bags upstairs for her, and it was only once he was back in the main room that it occurred to him that she could probably read his mind as easily as she had Frank's. The thought made his ears burn.

He fiddled with the cameras and microphone to make sure they were ready to go. This was nothing at all like their previous adventures, when they were just kids creeping around derelict buildings with their dad's old camera. The first time they'd encountered something supernatural, they'd been acting out spy stories in an old factory. Gregory was a G-Man and Val was a Russian agent who'd hidden a Soviet decoding device somewhere on the premises.

At first he'd thought the strange knocking sounds were Val, trying to lure him into a trap. But then he ran into her on the factory floor and she looked as surprised as he did. When they realized that neither of them was responsible for the knocking, they'd run home to get their father's recording equipment. It had sounded like Morse code, but when Gregory transcribed it, it proved to be only gibberish. It didn't deter them, however. They *knew* it was a ghost. And while the ghost didn't seem to know Morse code, it was nonetheless clearly trying to communicate with them.

Ever since, they'd been wild about the paranormal. They believed they were sensitive to the presence of spirits, if for no other reason than that they were both desperate to experience something not of this world. They had felt cold spots in rooms and a host of minor incidents had convinced them that they shared a psychic link. People told them that was normal for siblings as close as they were, but they were positive that it was more. Fortunately, Mr. Leland had agreed. And Iverson House was probably the best opportunity they would ever have to put their skills to the test. Their first professional gig.

It was pretty boring sitting here by himself, though, waiting for footprints to appear in the flour they'd sprinkled by the windows and doors. Or for the motion sensor to trigger one of the cameras. Gregory could hear the trees outside rustling in the wind, but inside all was silence.

Deep and deathly silence.

He found himself getting sleepy in spite of himself. He could pretend he was a sentry on guard duty, like he had when he was a little boy. But pretending was no fun without his partner in crime. He missed the old days of acting out stories with Val, and he found himself thinking of the time they built a rocket ship and went to Mars. The planet's surface was covered with hot red lava and they had to jump from rock to rock—well, from the couch to a chair to a rug—to avoid stepping in the shifting pool of liquid death. When the Martians attacked, they fought back with ray guns and escaped into a forest where dinosaurs lived.

He stood up, intending to patrol the room like a soldier to keep himself awake. But as soon as he moved, he felt the floor shift beneath his feet.

He froze, staring straight ahead, afraid to look down. In their Martian adventure, the floor had never actually moved. But if it had, he was sure it would have felt just like this.

Like melting wax.

The house was warping underneath him. The movement was subtle, and for a few moments he almost managed to convince himself that he'd imagined it. But then it lurched hard enough to make him stumble. He fell to his knees, grimacing as he landed, but there was no pain. The floor was all wrong. It was soft and yielding. He pressed a hand against it and found it was as malleable as clay. When he drew back, a perfect imprint of his hand remained. Then it faded as the substance slowly reformed itself, erasing the evidence of his touch.

The walls were wavering, too, shifting and oozing, as though the whole place was about to slump into an enormous pile of goo. What had Frank said about it behaving like a liquid? The table and chairs were sinking, the level of the floor inching slowly up their legs.

Gregory scrambled to his feet, backing away. But there was nowhere he could go to escape the spongy floor. It moved like thick red waves, tripping him. He fell more than once as he made for the stairs, and he would have welcomed the pain of bony knees against unyielding stone rather than the doughy give of the awful substance he was mired in. He seemed to sink deeper each time he moved. He thought of a fly trapped in syrup, burying itself farther with its frantic struggles. The image horrified him and he finally cried out.

"Help!"

The liquefying floor oozed over his legs, pulling him down until he could hardly even crawl.

"Val! Help! Frank! Anyone!"

He was barely aware of the clatter of hurried footsteps and the shouting voices that followed. The clay was up to his chin and he couldn't hold his head up any longer. He closed his eyes, struggling helplessly even as he felt himself drowning.

"Gregory, it's okay! It's me!"

He screamed, thrashing against the awful muck.

"Wake up!"

At last he opened his eyes, expecting to see everyone sinking into the mire as the house dissolved. But there was nothing there. He looked down at himself, bewildered to find that he was sitting on the floor. The hard, solid floor. Val was crouched beside him in her pajamas, staring wide-eyed into his face. He had a death grip on her arm. Frank and Mina stood a few feet away.

"It was just a dream." Val cupped her hands around his face.

He shook his head and pushed her away as he got to his feet. "Uh-uh," he said. "No way. That was no dream."

He looked at the others. It was obvious that they hadn't seen anything out of the ordinary. Frank shuffled his feet, but Mina's expression was rapt and serious.

"What happened?" she asked him.

"The house," he said. "It was melting. The whole floor, it just—it turned to liquid, like mud, and it was . . . trying to swallow me."

Frank picked up one of the chairs and rapped its legs against the floor.

"It wasn't like that before," Gregory insisted. "I was sinking!" He looked down at himself, brushing at his arms and legs, but there was no evidence of the oozing substance that had almost devoured him. He looked pleadingly at Val. "I'm not making it up."

"I believe you," she said, putting her arm around him.

"I know you do."

He didn't dare look at Frank, couldn't face seeing the doubt in the other man's face. Instead he cast a helpless glance at Mina. She still looked impossibly glamorous, even in her dressing gown, and he had the sudden thought that if *she* didn't believe him, he would die of shame.

But Mina nodded. "I believe you too."

Relieved, he sagged into a chair.

"I don't think anyone should stay down here alone," Mina said. "There is something very bad in this house. I think it wants to separate us."

Mina Cloudminder wasn't the first person to have approached the Human Protection League for help. Nor was she the first person Agent Dehner had ever impersonated.

The real Mina had been terrified by the invitation to be part of a formal investigation into the notorious Iverson House. She knew its reputation. At least two people had died exploring it, and several others had gone missing over the years. It was an evil house, on an evil patch of ground. Once tribal land, the area had been claimed by white settlers after a bloody battle in the eighteenth century. No one knew the origin of the odd little house, but the ground it stood on had come to be known as Headless Hill.

Mina had wanted nothing to do with any of it, and she had been on the verge of saying no. But then a friend put her in touch with the "Lovecraft Squad," as he called them, and Director Nathan Brady had assigned Liz Dehner to the case. Fortunately for both women, Arthur Leland had never met the psychic whose services he'd requested, and Liz had easily stepped in to replace her. She even thought of herself as Mina now.

Iverson House was well known to the HPL, having been the site of so many unexplained events over the years. But they had never had a chance to investigate it. Until now.

Mina/Liz believed Gregory's account of what he had experienced. She knew better than to dismiss such things as "just a dream" or "overactive imagination." She was sure the two would-be investigators had had their share of such patronizing reactions before. They were passionate and committed to the cause, but also terribly naïve. As such, they were easy targets for malevolent forces. And this house was most certainly malevolent.

She had sensed it from the moment she'd laid eyes on it. The whole design of the place was wrong. The air was heavy with menace and the uneven floors and walls seethed with hidden power. Whispers lurked at the edge of perception. Gregory had already heard them, and Mina felt certain that Val would hear them too. There was something monstrous here, and they were all in grave danger.

"What do you mean, it wants to separate us?"

Mina was disappointed that Frank was still so skeptical after her demonstration of her abilities. But then, he had probably spent the past few sleepless hours finding ways to rationalize what had happened.

"We're easier to attack on our own," she said. "More vulnerable."

He frowned and shook his head. "I'm sorry. I just can't believe any of that stuff. It's three in the morning. Everything is scarier at night. It's a primal instinct. It's also when we have nightmares. It's perfectly normal."

"There was nothing normal about it," Gregory snarled.

But Frank wouldn't be deterred. "It's all just a lot of spooky nonsense."

"But she read your mind," Val said. She turned to Mina. "Didn't you?"

"She made some good guesses," Frank said. "But honestly, it was so long ago I couldn't tell you who was standing where when it happened or who moved first and who got hurt or didn't. It was in the papers at the time and all our names were in it."

"But the song!" Val protested. "You were white as a ghost when she said that."

He pursed his lips, still shaking his head.

Mina could see the struggle in his mind between cold hard facts and the possibility he didn't want to accept. She knew he would be trying to remember if he'd ever mentioned that detail to anyone else, if there'd been someone she could have got the information from. She didn't blame him for it. Most people wanted to believe that there was a rational explanation. It was far less frightening than the alternative—that there were forces at work beyond human understanding, forces that might wish us harm. The most stubborn of skeptics could never see that often their supposed "rational" explanation was actually more far-fetched than the idea of the supernatural.

"Well, I'm going to listen to Mina," Gregory said. "You weren't here. You didn't see what I saw."

"I'm not calling you a liar, son. I'm sure it felt real to you. I just—"

"It *was* real!"

Val put her arm around Gregory's shoulder in a show of solidarity. "If my brother says it happened, then it happened."

Mina decided not to intervene. Nothing was going to convince Frank.

The architect sighed and looked up at the ceiling in frustration.

"You said yourself the house was weird," Val reminded him.

"Yes. It's weird." He gestured around the room. "It's probably the worst design I've ever seen for a house. Definitely the ugliest. But that doesn't mean it's haunted. There's no evidence that . . ." He broke off as his eyes fell on the recording equipment.

Val followed his gaze and her eyes widened. "The cameras!"

Gregory's expression mirrored her own and he leapt up from his chair. "They must have caught something. Why didn't we think of it before?"

Mina knew why they hadn't. The house hadn't *wanted* them to. "Can you develop the film?" she asked.

Gregory glanced up from the camera he was inspecting.

"Yeah. But, um . . ." He exchanged a look with Val. They both looked nervous.

"We left all the darkroom stuff in the car," Val said softly.

Frank gave a harsh bark of laughter. "Oh, and now the ghost hunters are afraid of the dark," he said. "Marvelous!"

Mina rounded on him. "The boy has just had a traumatic experience in this house. It's hardly surprising that he doesn't want to go out there, and I certainly don't think there's anything funny about it."

He blinked in surprise and then nodded sheepishly. "You're right. That was uncalled for. I'm sorry, kid."

Gregory just looked embarrassed.

"If it will make you feel any better," Frank said, "*I'll* go get it."

"Really?" Val asked.

"Really. Just give me the keys." He smiled. "That is, *if* you trust me not to drive off in that little beauty."

That lightened the mood, and Gregory visibly relaxed. "Sure. No problem." He gave Frank the keys and Mina handed him a flashlight.

"Be careful on the path." It was all the warning she dared offer, knowing he would spurn any suggestion of anything more dangerous than broken paving stones.

The kids set about turning the adjoining room into a darkroom. Mina was curious to see what the pictures would show. She didn't doubt Gregory's story at all, but whatever power was at work had likely made sure there would be no evidence after the fact.

Frank muttered to himself as he headed off. Things were going just as he could have predicted, with the three fruitcakes siding together against the voice of reason. He shouldn't have made fun of the poor kid, but really—if he and his sister wanted to poke around scary old buildings looking for ghosts, they needed at least one backbone between them.

The flashlight beam bounced along the winding path. The moon was almost bright enough not to need it, but he didn't care for the idea of stepping off the stones into that awful mud.

The path looked even more treacherous than he'd remembered. Jagged edges of pale paving stone stuck up from the ground like claws, and he edged carefully around the worst areas. How the hell had Mina done this walk in high heels?

He was so intent on watching his feet that he didn't notice the hulking shape directly in front of him until he was almost upon it. He drew up short with a gasp, thinking it was a bear. Instinct kicked in and he threw his hands up to cover his face. The flashlight flickered out as he stood there trembling, stranding him in the eerie glow of the moon. Slowly he lowered his arms, and as his eyes began to adjust, he saw the smile. It was wide and bright and filled with gleaming teeth.

For several seconds he could only stare at it, frozen with shock. Then he relaxed as he realized what he was looking at. It was only the car. Smiley. Or Bettie. Or whatever. He laughed as his galloping heartbeat began to slow down. And then the laughter died in his throat as he understood what was wrong with the scene.

He hadn't reached the forecourt yet. He hadn't even gone halfway down. The car was parked on the steep path, as though it had been making its own way up to the house.

Frank shook his head to clear it. Maybe *he* was the one dreaming. If so, he was ready to wake up now. No, it was more likely that Gregory had come down in the night and moved the car here. But why? And how? Surely the incline was too sharp for it to manage.

Before he had time to wonder further, the headlights flashed on, blinding him. At the same time the radio exploded into life at such a deafening volume that it made him jump. He stumbled and landed hard on the broken paving stones. The song started with a lively, bouncy piano riff that led into the harmonizing arpeggios of four male voices. Frank knew it. Such a harmless, playful song, but "At the Hop" sounded like a living threat here in the dead of night, blaring from a radio that no one had turned on.

And then the car began to move.

The engine wasn't running, but the car was definitely moving. Inching closer. *Creeping*. Slowly it shifted its tires, alternating them like legs, pulling itself along at a slow, deliberate pace. Every forward lurch was filled with menace.

Frank was already backing away, crab-walking over the sharp stones to get out of the way. He couldn't seem to get his footing. He kicked his legs out, scrabbling for purchase, but the jutting stones seemed to slip away from him, vanishing into the quagmire. When his feet also began to sink into the mud and clay he fought back a surge of panic. Gregory had been telling the truth.

He was helpless against the cloying ooze. And just like Gregory, he began to scream. It was no use. Inch by inch, the car moved closer, wriggling toward him, still blaring that infernal song. The others would never hear him over the noise. For a moment he dared to hope that they might at least hear the radio, might look outside and see what was happening. But then the right front tire came down on his stranded legs and pushed him deeper into the wet ground. By the time the tires reached his head, he was already gone.

Mina left Val and Gregory working on the darkroom while she went upstairs to get dressed. No one would be getting any more sleep tonight, and she felt vulnerable in just her dressing gown. She didn't like feeling vulnerable.

The tight black slacks and black turtleneck made her look like a cat burglar, but it also gave her more freedom of movement. It had helped her once before, in a case the League had called "The Breathing Shadows Affair." She'd been able to blend into the darkness and defeat the strange phantasmal swarm attacking the graveyard in Providence. She'd kept the outfit on hand ever since as a kind of good-luck charm. Tonight they needed all the luck they could get.

She was hurrying back along the hallway when she felt a sharp pain in her head. For a moment she was blinded and she cried out. A quick succession of images flashed before her. The moon. Stones. A bear. She smelled something wet, like turned earth. Then a ghastly Cheshire cat grin swam out of the darkness, dancing in front of her.

"Mina? Are you okay?"

The voice seemed to come from far away, but when she opened her eyes, she saw Gregory standing right in front of her. She was on her knees in the hallway. She had no idea how long she'd been there.

"Here, give me your hand," he said.

After a moment of disorientation, she put her clammy hand in his and he helped pull her to her feet. She was shaking all over. That awful grin was still there in her head, wild eyes blazing on either side of it. It was all she could see.

Gregory shook her slightly. She opened her mouth to reassure him that she was fine. And then she heard the song. At first she thought it was just her, but she could tell from Gregory's reaction that he was hearing it too.

It was so loud it might be coming from the next room. Frank's room. They both hurried inside and ran to the window, yanking the thin curtains aside.

"Oh my God," Gregory breathed.

A car was halfway up the path, its radio blaring and its lights blinking on and off. It was rocking crazily from side to side, like an excited child. The carefree nature of the song only heightened the savagery of the car's motion. There was something trapped beneath the wheels, something gradually sinking into the wet red clay of the hillside. *No*, Mina thought, suddenly feeling sick. *Not sinking. Being* buried.

"Don't look," she said sharply, trying to pull Gregory away. But it was too late. He'd already seen it. Frank's hand, rising from the mud beneath the tires, jerking with the vicious rhythm of the car. Then it was gone.

Mina closed her eyes, pushing the image out of her mind. She had heard Frank's screams inside her head, tasted the vile clay as it filled his mouth. She had felt his dying moments. And now she needed to clear her head of all of it if they were going to get out of this alive.

"Where's your sister?"

The music had stopped. Gregory was still staring out the window. He looked shell-shocked.

She asked him again, and his eyes went wide with fear. "Val! I left her downstairs!"

He ran and she followed, stumbling in the open doorway and falling headlong into the hallway, where she landed in a heap. A lump of clay had emerged from the floor and tripped her. She was sure it hadn't been there before. As she watched, it contorted, lengthening into a curling tentacle that reached for her exposed ankle.

Gregory was shouting his sister's name as he pounded down the stairs, and Mina thought she heard the girl calling back. She scrambled to her feet, but it was hard to balance. The floor was moving, warping. Just like Gregory had said. It was happening downstairs too. She could sense it, *feel* it.

Mina took a deep breath and focused intently on the house, trying to exert her influence and halt the spread of its power. The evil here wanted to drag them all down into the hideous mud.

Hand over hand, using the wall for balance, she made her way down the hallway. The floor moved like a billowing sheet beneath her. Each time she touched the wall, her palm sank partly in and it took real effort to pull it back, as though she was battling glue.

At last she reached the stairs . . . and gave a cry of dismay at what she saw. The treads had been absorbed into the shifting clay. There was no banister to hold on to, no rail for support. Just an undulating ramp leading down. The last thing she wanted to do was sit down and slide to the bottom, but she had no choice.

Downstairs she could hear Val and Gregory calling her name. Before she could change her mind, she dropped to the floor and shoved herself forward. The writhing substance tried to stop her, clutching at her with coiling fingers of clay. Her training kicked in and she curled into a ball, letting herself tumble the rest of the way down, landing on the rippling floor. It gave under her weight as it tried to draw her down into it. In her mind she forced herself away, sending out a powerful psychic pulse to repel it, to make the floor solid where she placed her feet.

The kids were struggling as well, as though sinking in quicksand. They'd made it as far as the front door, which was wedged shut by an oozing wall of mud.

"Mina," Gregory panted, "the door's stuck!"

"Try the window!"

Even as she said it, she knew what a long shot it would be. Suddenly it seemed miles away, and there was nothing to stop the melting house from sealing it off before they could make their way there.

Val was crying and starting to panic, batting frantically at the moving walls and dripping ceiling.

"Try to stay calm," Mina urged, knowing it was a lost cause. They were scared to death.

"What is it?" Val sobbed, yanking at the gobbets of clay that fell into her hair from above. "Is it ghosts? What did we do wrong?"

Gregory grabbed her arm and hauled her toward the window, dragging her. Her heels gouged lines in the glistening floor.

"It isn't ghosts," Mina said, trying to remain calm herself. She could feel the presence pushing at her mind, probing for weakness, looking for a way in. She gritted her teeth as she focused on her training, forcing it away again. She pictured the house as it was before, solid and unyielding. She tried to mold it in her mind.

"What do you mean it's not ghosts?" Gregory said, his voice rising. He was catching his sister's panic. "What the hell is it then?"

There was no point in lying to them. "The house isn't haunted," Mina said. "It's *alive.*"

They froze, staring at her in wide-eyed horror.

"The house, the hill, the clay. It's all one living creature. And now that we're here, it's trying to pull us down inside it."

"It can control things," Gregory said darkly. "Like my car."

She nodded. "Like the trees, the stones, anything it touches. Now come on. I'm holding it back now, but it's taking all my strength. It's very powerful."

The floor had settled, but only a little. They were able to pull their feet free and make their way to the window at last. But there was no way to open it. It was a solid pane. Gregory grabbed a chair and made to smash the glass. The chair bounced away, as though the window were made of rubber.

Mina's scalp prickled with unease. "It's not glass," she said, peering closely at it. "It's an eye." She shuddered at the malevolence she felt directed at her from the sightless yet staring pane.

They were sealed in. Beneath them the floor was quivering. Mina sensed the same kind of savage glee she'd seen emanating from the car outside. A hunger combined with a lust for killing. It was readying itself for another attack, and Mina was growing weak. She wouldn't be able to hold it back much longer.

In desperation she closed her eyes and let it in, let it touch her mind, let it show itself to her.

It was ancient, this creature. Ancient and evil. She saw unfamiliar galaxies, mind-boggling distances. She saw its true form, gelatinous and vile, a pulsing amorphous being, like a jellyfish. Wherever it had come from, it had settled here in Arkham, attaching itself like a parasite to the land. No wonder the Native Americans had always believed the area to be cursed.

At first it had been alone, weakened by the unfamiliar world. But over time it had begun to absorb images and memories from the people it took, to learn from them. It learned how to mimic, how to appear harmless. It learned how to control objects. And people. Mina's stomach churned as the sickening truth became clear. Someone had tended the house, made it appear normal. Someone who knew what it needed to survive. Someone willing to *feed* it.

"Arthur Leland," she hissed.

"What about him?"

Gregory's voice came from beside her and she realized that they were holding her by the arms, keeping her up off the floor. She must have collapsed.

"He did *this*," she said, panting. "Brought us here. To die."

Val stared at Mina in disbelief. "That sweet old man? Why would he do that?"

"I think it's keeping him alive," Mina said, "to *serve* it." Her psychic link with the creature was fading, as was her hold on it. "I think he's far, far older than he looks."

She peered around the room. It was like seeing under water. Everything wavered and flickered, moving out of focus. Her whole body felt out of focus along with it.

The kids were huddled together by the table, clutching each other for support.

"How do we get out?" Val whimpered.

Mina put her hands down on the table, bracing herself as well. The floor rocked and shuddered beneath her. The house was returning to its natural state. Soon it would melt entirely, and take them all with it, devouring them. How many people had it consumed in this way over the years? She couldn't banish the appalling image of a carnivorous plant, trapping its prey inside to be slowly crushed. Dissolved.

Her eyes widened suddenly as an idea came to her. They might have one weapon. There was something that all living things feared. There was no reason an alien should be any different.

"Gregory," she said. "Go to the kitchen and find some matches. Val, gather up all the paper you can find in here."

They both nodded, understanding at once, and raced off.

Mina grabbed one of the chairs and smashed it against the floor. At first the wood only dented the soft surface, but Mina sent a volley of images at it—stone, iron, steel—and it solidified long enough for the chair to shatter. She dropped to her knees, momentarily blinded and dizzy by the effort, but then she gathered her wits and collected the broken chair legs.

Gregory came running back with a box of matches and Val was piling the table with newspapers.

"Here," Mina cried, thrusting a stick at each of them. "Wrap some paper around them and set them on fire. We're going to burn our way out of here."

Her assertiveness seemed to give them confidence. They did as they were directed, and soon they had three blazing torches.

"Good, good. Now I want you both to concentrate. Focus on burning a hole through that wall. I don't know how much time we'll have, but as soon as you can fit through, do it. Ready?"

Val swallowed and looked at her brother. He looked terrified, but he gave a single nod. Val copied him.

"Okay. Go!"

They rushed the wall like a trio of soldiers, brandishing their torches. When they pressed the flames against the trembling flesh of the house, there came a high-pitched shriek that almost made Mina drop her torch. She also felt the creature's pain—a surge of scorching agony that set her nerves alight.

She turned her howl of pain into a battle cry as she forced the licking flames farther into the weeping red wall. A hole opened up as the clay retreated from the source of pain. It rippled as she ran the torch around the edges of the opening, widening it.

To either side of her she saw Val and Gregory doing the same. In moments Gregory was already clambering through. Mina aimed one last jab at the area closest to the floor and then launched herself through, ducking and rolling as she hit the soggy ground outside and came to a stop. Gregory had landed a few feet away and he was pulling himself up when they heard Val scream.

She was trapped. The hole had closed around her like a vise, leaving only her head and one arm—the one not holding the torch—outside.

"Gregory, Mina, help me!"

They both ran to her. Mina's torch had gone out when it hit the ground, but Gregory's was still just about alight.

"Cover your face," he cried as he wielded the flame, thrusting it like a sword at the wall that held his sister. Val screamed as the torch brushed her and she wriggled helplessly, trying to squirm free of the wall.

Mina sent black thoughts to the creature, trying to force it to let go, but the fight had drained her. She felt the monster's fury as it tightened like a boa constrictor around Val.

Gregory was shouting, his words drowning out Val's cries of pain. "Let go! Let go of her!" He jabbed at the house again and again, but the flames were no longer having an effect. The creature had adapted to the pain. It was holding tightly to its prey, refusing to let go.

It had also adapted to the psychic intrusion, driving Mina out with a mental jolt that threatened to shatter her skull. There was nothing she could do. Nothing at all.

Seconds passed like hours as Gregory fought against the monster. But it was hopeless. Gradually Val's voice weakened and her cries grew fainter. After a little while they stopped altogether. Mina moved to Gregory's side and tried to drag him away from the limp and silent body of his sister. The girl hung there, trapped in the closed iris of the wall. Then they both watched in horror as it slowly pulled her back inside.

Gregory shook Mina off, beating helplessly at the house with his fists, calling Val's name over and over.

"She's gone," Mina said. "You have to let her go. We have to get out of here."

The hill was beginning to rumble with renewed fury. Red tentacles burst from the ground, clutching at the air like vicious talons.

"Run!" Mina cried. She grabbed Gregory's arm and yanked him, dragging him with her. He followed, dodging the living sea of mud as it surged and swelled beneath them, trying to trip them.

They ran past the car, half-submerged in the hillside, and continued down to the forecourt without a second glance. They stopped for a moment to catch their breath, and Mina debated whether her own car would be safe. But if the creature had managed to drag one car up there and then bury it along with its victim, it could just as easily do it again. They couldn't trust anything on the hill.

She didn't want Gregory to stop running anyway. He was still in shock and the grief would cripple him if she gave him time to surrender to it. She grabbed his hand and they ran again, heading for the lights of Arkham below.

Mina risked one final glance behind her. Iverson House was gone. It had melted entirely, and the awful hill was smooth once again.

Arthur Leland smiled as he reached the top of the hill. A few days ago he couldn't have made the climb, would have had to lean on his cane and stop to catch his breath several times. But he felt better now. Refreshed. Revitalized.

The house looked brighter too. Stronger and sturdier. He stroked the red clay surface, then licked the coppery dust from his fingertips. It tasted rich and meaty.

It was a pity about the psychic. She would have been a much more nourishing meal for it. Especially as she wasn't even who she'd claimed to be. What a prize that would have been—a member of the Lovecraft Squad! He knew it was only a matter of time before they sent other agents to investigate Iverson House. And him with it. Well, let them, he thought. The house had not only absorbed the false Mina Cloudminder's thoughts and memories—it had also absorbed some of her power. And with it, the collective knowledge of the Human Protection League itself.

"We'll be ready," he said, smiling. "Oh yes, the Armies of the Night will be waiting."

Liz Dehner stood proudly as she watched the ceremony. It was bittersweet, but at least something good had come out of that failed mission a year ago. She dabbed at her eyes as Director Brady held up the certificate.

"And it is with great pride that we welcome our newest recruit to the HPL, Gregory Robinson."

The room deep beneath the Washington Monument was filled with the sound of applause as the young man strode to the front of the circular chamber and shook Brady's hand. He posed for a photograph, and although his face was smiling, Liz knew the bittersweet emotions behind it. She had sponsored him and helped train him. Her job was done. Soon he would be sent out on his own missions.

No one blamed her for what had happened, not even Gregory, but Liz still felt she had failed them. Especially Val. She watched as everyone congratulated the new agent, and she decided it was time to go.

Just as she was about to slip out the door, a hand fell softly on her shoulder. "Liz."

She smiled. "Agent Robinson."

He blushed and looked down. "Hard to get used to."

"You've earned it. And I know you'll be a great asset to the League. I'm so proud of you."

"Thanks," he said sheepishly. He didn't need to say what else was on his mind. Liz could see the thought as clearly as if he'd spoken aloud. *If only Val could be here too.*

"Your sister would also be proud," she said, reaching out to straighten his tie.

He nodded. "I know. Of course she'd also be driving me crazy, and we'd probably end up yelling at each other and scaring all the ghosts away."

"Probably."

"But then maybe, I think . . ." He stopped himself, lost in thought for a moment. His eyes met Liz's. "Hey, I don't have to tell *you* what I'm thinking, do I?"

She shook her head. "No you don't. And I hope you *can* find her. Not all our agents are corporeal, you know. Ask Agent Carter."

He looked up at the high ceiling. "Hear that, Sis? You don't get away from me that easily."

"Good luck," Liz said, and kissed him on the cheek. "To both of you."

She closed the door behind her and stepped out into the crisp autumn evening. Leaves skittered across the grass and a bold red moon was just beginning to rise. She opened the envelope Director Brady had given her earlier and read the contents. A man had been digging in his basement and opened a portal into another dimension. Now its inhabitants were creeping through into this one. It was another job for the Lovecraft Squad, and for her talents in particular.

"On my way," she said, smiling.

TEN

The Color Out in Space

Prologue

IN SEARCH OF THE woman who asked me to save Yuri Gagarin, I have come to Arkham.

Arkham, England, that is. Not the place you probably heard of, in Massachusetts. Although I never heard of that, either, before Peabody approached me. This is Old Arkham, in the valley of the Kielder Burn, in Northumberland.

I bet you never thought about it, but it's logical that such a place should exist. Many North American place names were imported from Britain, or Europe—York, Boston. So there must have been a British Arkham, right? And here I am.

Not that there is much to see. This is wild, open country, scoured by vanished glaciers and cropped to the rocky ground by wandering sheep. Old Arkham itself is just a tracery of worn stones that here and there make a rough line that might once have been a wall, a vague angle that was a corner. I'm an American, and I'm forever astounded by the depth of time you encounter here in little old England. Even now, the only way in is by a marching track laid down by the Romans. You'll find Arkham in the Domesday Book from the eleventh century: a few families, a few fields, a few animals. But it's been abandoned since the 14th century, supposedly because of the Black Death. Nobody has ever proved that, so far as I know.

I ought to look up total solar eclipses in the 14th century.

Not that the place is hard to find. I took a solo flight over the valley, and from the air these ruins are the heart of a circle of gray. You walk in, along that old track, past clumps of wood that are kind of odd, the trees growing too thick together, too fat and tall. And, yes, at the center of it, gray: desolation, like ash, a circle of blight, of blasted heath. Even the heather in the fall comes up spindly and colorless, the locals told me. And on the ground the grass blades crumble under your boots, gray and dead almost to the root, and oddly odorless.

You wonder why nobody ever came back here, to rebuild. The place has some bottomland, some water. Not a good place for the imagination, I guess. My eyes keep being drawn to that Roman road, the only straight line anywhere in sight. The only bit of rationality in an irrational landscape. I'm a pilot; I like to find order, control. The secret harmonies of situations. I have to force myself not to bolt.

Who the hell would take the name of a place like this across the Atlantic? Maybe the founders of Arkham, Massachusetts, knew something about their site even before the turf was cut. Black humor.

Squadron Officer Mabel Peabody, of the Women's Royal Air Force and the Human Protection League, didn't come from this place. She never told me where she did come from. Military family, I guess. But, in the few hours we spent together in orbit, she told me about this, about Arkham. She was brought here as a kid for hiking vacations. Can you believe that? To a medieval plague village. Some kids get Coney Island. And then she came back during her training—there are big military ranges in the area. Childhood nostalgia amid the live firing exercises. Or maybe it was all some subtle grooming to prepare her for recruitment into the HPL.

Three months ago, Peabody needed an experienced Gemini pilot, and I was the best available. No, scratch that. I was the best there was, at that time.

I flew with her to rescue Yuri Gagarin. Not for the Lovecraft crap.

But everything changed.

I

My name is Magnolia Jones. I was born on a cotton farm in Atlanta, Georgia. On Saturday, July 20, 1963, I really did fly a Gemini spacecraft into orbit to save Yuri Gagarin. I guess it was the most extraordinary thing I ever did. So far, anyhow.

Now, as you'll remember, that was the date of a total solar eclipse over North America. That was no coincidence. And you'll know that no Gemini craft has publicly flown yet. Our flight happened anyway. And Yuri Gagarin is still alive, officially; after his alleged first-ever manned spaceflight, he is still working behind the scenes on the USSR's space program. If you have the appropriate clearances you'll know how much of this is true, or not. Otherwise, just accept it. Very little of what you've been told, all your life, is true.

We were to launch from Tarooma, which is a British-American space center in the dead, red heart of Australia. Dead for hundreds of miles downrange, anyhow, where for years spent rocket-boosters have been raining down on Aboriginal holy grounds. It's a hell of a sight from the air: desert and scrub, and craters from launch failures, and nothing much to see at the center itself but tin huts and rockets.

Everything was a rush, from my recruitment to launch day. Unlike the two Blue Gemini flights I had already made for the USAF to that date, there had been no real mission preparation, no simulations—there was barely a checklist, as it turned out. I would learn that official permission for our flight had been slow in coming, and it was only the imminence of that July eclipse that forced the issue, although it was a while before I understood why.

I didn't even meet my co-pilot, Squadron Officer Peabody, until we were actually on the transfer bus to the launch pad.

By then I'd already gone through a major part of the pre-flight ritual, which was the same in Tarooma as it ever was at Cape Canaveral or Vandenberg. You start stripped naked, and the techs (all women for us Gemini 21 girls) stick med sensors all over your bare skin. Then it's on with the cotton underwear and the urine bag, and if there's one barrier to women in space it's that damn catheter. Into the pressure suit, which is a kind of limbo dance until you force your head through the neck ring, and a zip up at the back, and the helmet forced on, and you start to breathe that sweet oxygen.

And then a short walk, carrying your portable air unit to the van, which will drive you to the pad itself.

That was when I met Peabody. She was already in the van, suited up as I was, with her own air unit on the bench beside her. She was around forty; through the glass of her visor I glimpsed a strong face, a handsome Roman nose, blue eyes. The drivers were in a sealed cabin up front.

There was one other in there with us. A man, shorter than either of us, in a loose environment suit of his own—sealed up, but not vacuum-ready. That's protocol; you're supposed to protect your astronauts from infection before a flight. My sharp pilot's eyes read the tag on his chest: GARDNER, DR. MAXWELL EDISON, alongside a British flag. I figured the guy was around forty also; he had a weasely look, and he was hunched over, like he was underfed.

And he had a kind of valise at his side, leather and metal, of which I was immediately suspicious. In fact I thought I recognized it.

The van rolled off.

"Officer Peabody," I said, to break the ice. "We talked on the phone. Good to meet you." I went to bump her gloved fist with mine; she went to shake hands, and we had an awkward laugh at transatlantic misunderstandings.

"Likewise," she said. "On such a momentous day." She waved a hand at our companion. "Dr. Gardner is a friend and colleague. "

"Ain't too much room in that old Gemini for a passenger."

"Indeed not. Maxwell is here to transfer the package he's carrying. Specialist medical supplies, for treating Gagarin and his colleagues in the *Zarya* station, if they survive. Security protocols. Those Soviets, you know."

Specialist medical supplies my ass.

That name sounded familiar, though. *Gardner*. I dug in a pouch on my leg and pulled out a battered, lurid pulp magazine. *Amazing Stories*, September 1927. "This was the only bit of briefing material you sent me, about the HPL side of the mission."

"Lovecraft's account of the 1882 event." She smiled. "What did you make of it?"

"Weird. Insane."

"But the truth," she said quietly.

"Gardner, though. That's the name in the story."

"You're correct, Captain Jones," Gardner said. "My great-grandfather was Nahum Gardner, whose farm was the center of the event. The 1882 'Color Incursion,' as it's called by the League.

"My grandfather was Nahum's fourth son. Sickly, even before the Color Incursion. Got sent away as an infant, to an aunt in Boston, and raised there. And was kind of forgotten. Never mentioned in H. P. Lovecraft's account, although he always claimed he dreamed it, like so many of his so-called 'stories.' After the deaths, what was left of the family came back to England; they were only a couple of generations out of the old country. But we remembered Nahum's story. After majoring in medicine, well, I got drawn back to the strange family history. I even did a placement at Miskatonic U."

If I was looking for sanity and reassurance from Peabody I wasn't going to get it.

She said now, "I did a placement at Miskatonic also. And as you know, while I am a serving officer in the WRAF, I also hold a senior position in the League, or what we like to call 'The Lovecraft Squad' around here, an international affiliation. This flight is a joint RAF-USAF-HPL mission, in fact. Judging from the fragmentary data we have, the ongoing situation in *Zarya* is thought to share some similarities with the 1882 incident. You'll learn more in the next few hours. Need to know, however."

"Oh, of course."

Gardner's accent was, to my ears, a neutral British. But now he surprised me by breaking into what sounded like a convincing New England twang. "*Jest a color . . . an' it burns an' sucks . . . it come from some place whar things ain't as they is here . . . one o' them professors said so . . . he was right . . .*" He grinned at me, as if anticipating my reaction.

Peabody glared at him. "He's quoting the Lovecraft piece. Stop showing off, man. You know, your handlers are well aware how you use your connections. Dribbling classified information for a bit of notoriety, is that the game?"

Gardner, unperturbed, kept grinning at me. "I do know some famous people. Spooky stuff is fashionable. Dirk McQuickly says he'll write a song about me some day."

Peabody shook her head impatiently. "We're there. Thank Him."

The van drew up at a launch gantry.

We climbed out into dim but dazzling sunshine. Above us loomed the familiar slim profile of a Titan, an ICBM crudely adapted to carry humans to orbit, and with the complex cone-shape of a Gemini capsule on the top.

As we took our short walk to the elevator that would take us up to the spacecraft itself, we passed a Perspex cordon plastered with logos from previous flights. I found myself staring at mementos of launches by something called the British Experimental Rocket Group: the Q-I, 1953; the M-76, 1956; the Q-II, 1958. . . . Beyond the barrier, techs and other workers desultorily clapped for us astronauts. Farther out I saw a few Aborigines, dressed in T-shirts and shorts and leaning on brooms. They weren't clapping.

At the foot of the rocket, waiting for us behind the barrier, stood a senior RAF officer with a couple of nervous-looking aides. He must have been midseventies, with a crimson face obscured by a huge white handlebar moustache. In his ornate uniform, he looked like he'd been inflated.

"The ceremonial bit." I could almost hear Peabody gritting her teeth as she led us forward. "Marshal. How good of you to come see us off in person."

He stepped forward to greet us, and would have caromed off the

Perspex if an aide hadn't stopped him. "Ah, quite right, quite right, no touchy feely, eh? Privilege to know you'll be flying the flag in the great beyond, Officer Body."

"Peabody, sir—"

"And here's your copilot."

"Strictly speaking, sir—"

"Ah, how I envy you. Once it was my privilege to fly to Heaven and back, eh? . . ."

An aide hurried him away.

We made it to the comparative haven of peace that was the gantry elevator—just me, Peabody, and Gardner with his package. The open cage began to rise with a whir, and the Red Center opened up around us.

"Sorry about that," Peabody murmured. "He was a First World War flying ace, and he still is a First World War flying ace, if you see what I mean. Old bugger won't retire, but he's been shuffled off into this wilderness where, they think, he can do little damage."

"His day is done," Gardner said brutally. "Old warriors like that, with their nice clear wars to fight. Well-defined enemies. Hasn't got a clue about the modern day. Only here as a PR front, a distraction."

"He's harmless," Peabody said. "'To Heaven and back.'" She laughed. "Good old Flasheart. Drives Prof Q. crazy."

"Speaking of PR," Gardner said, "what a shame for you that the Soviets sent up Tereshkova just last month. First public announcement of a space flight by a female."

That, at least, was one public untruth I was aware of. I shrugged. "I'd rather have the flying than the fame."

At the top of the gantry a couple of techs in coveralls waited to load us into the capsule. A Gemini is kind of like a very small boat, a conical body with a big circular heatshield at the rear and a cylindrical docking unit for a nose, all stood on its end. The two crew climb in through hatches and squeeze in side by side, into couches you won't be leaving, aside from walks in space, until you return to Earth, and there's barely room for the two of you in your pressure suits.

The techs gave us thumbs-ups when they were done. But at the last second Maxwell Gardner muscled in and passed over that "medical pack," which Peabody stuck in her foot-well. Then he handed her a slip of paper, which I guessed was some kind of authorization code. I was increasingly certain what that package was.

And then they put their heads together, faceplate to faceplate. They seemed to murmur something like a prayer, of which I caught only a couple of words: *Great Azathoth*. If I'd had a glimmer about what that meant, I'd have got off that bus there and then.

Gardner withdrew. I never saw him again, from that day to this. Read about his trial for serial homicide, though.

In a Gemini, you actually have to duck down to avoid your head being cracked when they close the hatches.

The Tarooma controllers walked us through a checklist, every detail familiar to me from my two previous Blue Gemini flights. But the damn list was mostly handwritten. That's how loose this whole thing was.

We settled into our home away from home. We were tight in there, in our little boat. We had to connect oxygen hoses and comms lines to our chest panels, and parachute harnesses to our suits in case the launch failed. The oxygen from a Gemini feed doesn't taste the same as from the support packs; it has an antiseptic tang.

"So," Peabody said to me. "Here we are heading for *Zarya*."

"*Zarya*. You mentioned that name."

"The space station—that's *spring* in Russian." Stiff in her suit, she looked over at me. "Everything is on a need to know basis, as I said. Our orders are to rendezvous with the station, assess the situation, save Gagarin and any surviving colleagues, and take any further appropriate action."

I shrugged. "Sounds straightforward. However . . ." I tapped a button that shut off our downlink comms. "Just us, Officer Peabody. Before we launch. Tell me why you brought a backpack nuke on board my spacecraft."

She just glared at me.

"Come on, Peabody. I'm USAF, remember. I recognize the model. RAF issue, is it?"

She gave in, icily. "Royal Marines, actually."

"So the 'appropriate action' of your orders includes taking out the space station with an atomic bomb? You see, my problem is this: when you approached me, I looked up the Human Protection League, as best I could. Asked around. And one thing I know for sure is they're opposed to the use of nukes in orbit. For fear of—what? For stirring up trouble from outer space?"

"Actually, more likely from inner space, the oceans . . . Oh, hell, Jones. Look—I'm both WRAF and HPL, remember. And believe me, there was a high level debate between those two services about the necessity to carry this nuke on such a mission. In the end, the armed forces won the argument. Global security against the outside threat, you see."

"But you accepted the mission even so. Despite your HPL conscience."

"Even so. Look, I was in the League long before I thought of joining the armed forces. Recruited by a tutor who picked me out when I was a student at Lonsdale, actually. My Oxford college. Jones, think of me as like a pacifist who nevertheless sees the logic of fighting a particular war—against the Nazis, say, or other, more dangerous groups—a war that had to be waged. That's me, do you see? I have clear orders from my command chain in the WRAF as to when and why I should trigger the nuke. And if the situation arises, I will do so. Can you not see that the logic of its use will be all the more compelling if *I* choose to make such a call—I, a member of the Lovecraft Squad?"

I studied her. On the surface, it was as if she'd opened up to me. But I still didn't trust her. I just knew there was more to come. More layers. "Anyhow, our prime objective is to save Gagarin."

"Gagarin, yes. And you need to be prepared for him." She dug a small tape recorder from a suit pouch. "This is a downlink taped at an American communications station on the Canaries—part of their global network. We're not sure if he was even intending to broadcast it . . ." She pressed a button.

I heard a hollowness, an echoing. That was my first impression, before I separated out any specific sounds. Then there was a kind of scratching.

"Like tree branches against the window," I blurted. "When I was a kid—"

"I know. Keep listening."

Now a human voice, evidently a man's, but a husky whisper, heavily distorted by the lousy radio link. A lot of panting, as if he were in pain, or exhausted.

"I can't tell the language. Russian? But I can hear it's broken up."

"Russian indeed, and difficult even for native speakers to translate. There are few complete sentences, and what there are seem to be oddly constructed. Many in a passive mode. About how things are done, rather than something doing those things, you see?" She consulted notes on a pad attached to her sleeve. "Things are moved and changed, and *fluttered.* Ears hear sounds which are not wholly sounds. Eyes see colors which are not true colors. Something was taken away from him. He was being drained. Nothing was ever still in the night. The walls, the station partitions, shifted and changed. The very shape of the station was *restless.*" She glanced at me. "As you may have guessed, based on our fragmentary information to date, the phenomena we're dealing with here do seem to show some correlation with the 1882 incident Lovecraft reported."

"You mean the *Amazing Stories* yarn?"

"Nothing Lovecraft wrote was fictional," she said bluntly.

Listening to Gagarin, I thought I picked out a word, or phrase, repeated over and over. "What's that he's saying? Sounds like *Tiger Lily*?"

She frowned. "Some of the analysts think that's *Poyekhali.* What Gagarin famously said as he was launched in Vostok One: 'Let's go!'"

I looked at her. "Whereas you think it is—"

"*Tekeli-li! Tekeli-li!*" When she said this her tone of voice changed, became an odd, caw-like cry. She coughed. "Which has other significance. Anyhow, you can tell that the man is in serious trouble. Or was."

"Was?"

"These recordings are weeks old. Since then, we've had no communications of any sort. Even the automated telemetry is failing, apparently."

"Any reason why the Russians aren't up there saving their own?"

"Pad explosion at Baikonur. They can't fly, not before the eclipse deadline."

"And so they asked for help from their mortal enemies? They sanctioned this mission?"

"Let's say they're aware of it," she said, British-dry.

Meanwhile the countdown had continued, all but unnoticed, without a hold. That Titan is a reliable beast.

We got to *twelve, eleven, ten*. The whole bird shuddered. Peabody looked faintly alarmed.

I was the veteran here, in the left-hand pilot's seat; I considered ribbing her about "need to know," but I'm too good-hearted. "Gimbal tests," I said. "Rocket nozzles swiveling this way and that. Shakes the whole stack."

Eight. Seven.

"Grab that D-ring."

"What D-ring?"

"Between your legs. Operates the ejection seat."

"Ejection seat? Him in the Gulf!"

Five. Four.

And she said softly, "*Tri. Dva. Odin.* We're coming, Yuri."

I hear the fuel pumps throb into life.

The pushback is gentle at first. Then there are more jolts as the thrust nozzles gimbal, twisting this way and that in an ongoing effort to keep the whole damn tower balancing on a pencil of flame. The noise begins now, a rattle, a deeper thrum you feel in your chest. Then the *pogoing*, vibrations along the length of the stack that throw you back and forth. I laugh, cruelly. "*Poyekhali*, Officer Peabody!"

But she just mutters, over and over, "*Tekeli-li! Tekeli-li!* . . ."

We go supersonic and smooth out. The Gs reach a peak of four or five.

Then the first stage cuts. An instant of surreal peace: no weight, and the air is filled with debris, with loose or lost bolts and shreds of sealing putty and scraps of paper. Which all rains down around you as the second stage cuts in.

At last, it's over: flame-out.

I glance out the window, at the spent booster stage tumbling past, and I look at the mission clock. "Five minutes fifty-four seconds from the pad. Five hundred thirty miles downrange. Speed seventeen thousand, five hundred miles per hour. We are in orbit, Officer Peabody."

She's peering out at a sunlit Earth. "The place where there is no darkness."

II

My passenger was anxious about time.

That eclipse was setting us a deadline, for reasons I had yet to understand. Lovecraftian logic, no doubt. Anyhow, we needed to rendezvous with a Russian space station, deal with whatever the hell mess we found in there, and get out again, all within the next five hours, because five hours from the moment of our orbit injection was going to be totality of the eclipse.

For a good while, all I could tell Peabody was that everything was going as planned. Happily she was an experienced flyer, if not an astronaut, and she'd been briefed well. She knew that spaceflight imposes its own constraints, and that chasing another craft in orbit was going to take its own sweet time.

We checked out the systems of our sturdy spacecraft, following the checklist: the oxygen tank, the fuel cells. I blipped the attitude thrusters, beefy little rockets that sounded like a punch on the hull when they fired. We had patient, expert support from mission control at Tarooma, as relayed by comms stations on islands and ships around the world. For me the Tarooma voices were an unaccustomed mixture of American and British accents with the odd Australian nasal twang.

Our call sign was *Angel.* We were on a mission of mercy, officially.

I stole a few glances out the window. This was my third mission in a Gemini, and you never tired of the view: the jet black above, the rind of atmosphere on the horizon, and the dazzling view down below, bright as a tropical sky. I always liked the ocean, myself—the shallows at the fringes of the continents and around the islands, where you get complex waves and reflections, easily visible from space. There's my sense of pattern again. Remember the Roman road?

Peabody, though, I noticed, kept looking up at the black sky, with a complex expression. Fear and longing at the same time, so I thought.

Two hours thirty into the mission, I began our hunt for *Zarya* in earnest, with my first approach burn. The maneuver was on the money, as showed by the ground's estimate and my own navigation sightings of stars and Earth's horizon.

I broke out chicken sandwiches, and a water gun that delivered half-ounce squirts into the mouth. "Over an hour until we begin the final approach phase. I take it Lovecraft Squad officers are allowed a lunch break?"

She took the stuff without commenting.

"You know," I said, "the one thing I regret about having to make my secret flights is that I can't tell anybody about *this*. The experience. Earth from space. I was raised on a cotton farm in Georgia. Big family. Lots of nieces I could tell it to."

She glanced at me. "I saw your file."

What file? Kept by who? I didn't trouble to ask such questions.

"I admit I only take in the relevant technical material. I remember you're unmarried. Farm been in the family awhile?"

"The first generation of Joneses who owned it were bought-out slaves. But I was never a farmer. Always distracted by flying, whenever I could get near it, the barnstormers at the shows. My family encouraged me. After a few years of crop-dusting and stunt flying, I took courses on commercial and military engines. I couldn't get close to the military back then, not as a woman pilot, but I got some training on the Lears and de Havillands—civilian ships, but jets. And then I got signed up by Boeing as a test pilot. A lot less discrimination in the civilian sector."

She looked at me. "Over gender, or color?"

"Both. Anyhow, with all that behind me, when there was talk of hiring women to train up as astronaut candidates—it was never official NASA policy, of course—I was in the box seat. Missed out on the Mercury 13, but I made the Blue Gemini 21. Joined the Air Force, officially. Blue Gemini is their covert program for the spacecraft, while NASA uses it to prepare for the Moon landings."

"And you got to fly in space."

"It turns out we're useful," I said dryly. "I've ambitions to fly on the MOL. You heard of that?"

"Of course. The Manned Orbiting Laboratory. Space station for surveillance, supported by Gemini technology. Actually the League helps sponsor it."

"Why aren't I surprised? The point is, you see, that male astronauts are would-be heroes; as soon as NASA picks them they get *Time* magazine deals and whatnot. Whereas the women are invisible, at best a token. A joke. And so if you want to hide away a couple of astronauts for forty days on a spy station, photographing Eastern Bloc sites with big old Dorian cameras—"

"Make them women, because, unlike the men, nobody notices if they go missing."

"That's the idea." I decided to try a little fishing. "I guess the one benefit of all this covert spaceflight we seem to be running is that it's giving more opportunities to pilots like me."

She shrugged. "I doubt if you know the half of it. Well, you've glimpsed some of it at Tarooma.... Look, the British alone have an extensive space program going back a couple of decades. All kick-started by the Germans' wartime work, of course. We had our first artificial-satellite lunar orbiter back in 1950, the experimental Q-ships from 1953, and even a venture to Mars in 1956."

"Mars? Seriously?"

"Didn't go well. Meant to be a flyby—crashed—one man survived. Still up there. The type who's always annoyingly useful on camping holidays. Now he's doing archaeology! Needless to say the Russians and Americans have been beavering away just as busily, and with just as much mixed success."

"But the triumphs: Sputnik 1, supposedly the first satellite in orbit, Gagarin himself—"

"Everybody is pretty miffed at the Soviets going public with all that. There isn't really a space race as such, you see, because so much of it is hidden from the public. It's more a race for prestige, for publicity. And the Soviets are cheating."

"Hmm. But right now they need our help to salvage this *Zarya*."

She seemed distracted. "I won't bore you with details of my own career. Suffice it to say that I reached the top, at Oxford, in the WRAF and in the Human Protection League, because I was far better than the best of the men. Simple as that. There was no choice but to take me. Some day, you know, women will be elected purely on merit, for space missions as in everything else. I have a niece too. Bright as a button ..."

That was when she told me about Old Arkham. How she'd tried to take her niece up there, to that desolate place, as her parents had once shipped her.

"Here we are—it's 1963. I hope that by 1999 my niece is chief science officer on the first U.N. expedition to Venus. Or leading the investigation of the magnetic anomaly in Tycho."

I frowned. "Tycho, on the Moon?"

"I said too much. How's our rendezvous coming on?"

Back to business.

The mission milestones unfolded.

Three hours after launch, the solar eclipse began. The Moon's great shadow was already sweeping across the Earth.

We paid attention only to the timing. The total duration of the eclipse would be five hours, with a couple of minutes of totality in the middle. We expected to be at the station in a couple of hours, leaving us thirty minutes before totality.

At three hours fifty minutes after launch, we were in a circular orbit under *Zarya*'s track. Being lower, our orbital speed was faster, and we gradually overtook the target. After four and a half hours, I made another burn to raise our orbit, with intercept to follow thirty minutes later.

When we were twenty-five miles below it, *Zarya* was a speck of light in the sky. My main job was to keep the ship's nose pointing at the target. I measured the rate at which the nose rose up, relative to the horizon of the Earth; that kind of number gave me another way to estimate the closing distance and speed.

"We won't be able to dock with this thing. I suppose you have a key to the porch?"

"So to speak," Peabody murmured.

I glanced at her. "Come on. Nobody here but us chickens. How? Soviet space secrets are notoriously hard to crack."

"We turned Doktor Merkwürdigliebe."

"Who?"

"One of the Nazi rocket scientists who built the V-2. We got von Braun; the Soviets got Merkwürdigliebe. Nutty as a fruitcake. Anyhow the *Zarya* was pretty much his baby."

"So how did you get hold of him?"

"The Americans promised him he could work on their nuclear weapons program." She grinned. "What could possibly go wrong?"

We closed on the station. In the final phase, Peabody helped me by reading out the numbers. "Eighty-three feet per second, two miles . . . forty-four fps, one and a half miles . . . eleven fps, three tenths of a mile . . ." Rendezvous is a precise art—basically you have to arrange it so that both range and relative velocity go to zero at the same time. An orderly process, and pleasing to me because of that.

But I didn't get it quite right, this time. In the final close we went into a whifferdill, a complicated spiral around the target. I had to fix it with blasts of my attitude thrusters. I am a professional; I was annoyed I wasted a little fuel, and irritated at my lack of precision.

Peabody couldn't care less. "As long as we still have enough for re-entry." She pulled on her helmet and began to close up her suit, and she glanced up nervously at the sun.

I looked through the smoked glass we'd brought for the purpose. I could see a substantial chunk of the sun had gone dark already. A clear geometry, a brilliant remnant crescent of sun—an eerie sight as we drifted beside that darkened station.

"Let's get on with it," Peabody said.

"*Poyekhali!*" I replied.

She didn't smile.

III

We were going to have to spacewalk over to the *Zarya*.

Like everything else about this mission, the procedure was half-assed and not rehearsed at all. But at least, as the experienced astronaut, I was in charge. I'd even done an EVA before—an extravehicular activity—even if it was only to stick my helmeted head out of the hatch of a Blue Gemini, while my male colleague drifted around in space working an experimental atomic-radiation sensor.

Anyhow, we put on our helmets and closed up our suits, and I pressed the button to open the valve that vented our cabin air. There was a soft sense of pressure as my suit inflated. I opened the hatches over our heads, and from the enclosure of the cabin my visual field unfolded, to reveal infinite space, pitch-black, a slice of blue Earth, and the dark mass of the *Zarya* only yards away.

I opened my couch harness and turned to Peabody. "So you wait for me to come back and get you before you even take your seat belt off. Okay?"

An impatient thumbs-up. Too polite to give me the finger, probably. God bless the British.

I straightened up, stood on my couch, and pushed out into space.

I trailed an umbilical line that attached me physically to the Gemini, and which contained an oxygen feed for my suit. But I also had an oxygen bottle dangling from my waist. We didn't know what we were going to find in the *Zarya*, and couldn't depend on there being breathable air.

And, to help me move around, I had a reaction pistol, like a little portable maneuvering rocket. I hung onto the Gemini and squirted this a couple of times to test it.

Then I turned my back on the *Zarya*, made sure my lines weren't tangled up, and pulsed the gun a couple of times. It gave me a firm shove, and when I turned around again I was drifting across space toward the Soviet station.

Compared to the tidy, somewhat tinselly and baroque NASA tech, *Zarya* looked heavy, crude. "Looks like it was made in a tractor factory."

"Just tell me what you see, Jones."

"It looks dead. No lights . . . I see three cylinders, attached lengthwise. They get fatter as you go down the body. The whole is, what, fifty feet long? The smallest cylinder must be about six feet across. Right where I'm heading."

"That's where the EVA hatch is, and the airlock. Where we'll enter."

"Copy that. There are antennae everywhere, and big solar panels folded out like an insect's wings . . ."

Insectile. That was one word for it. Antennae and wings. The hull was dark metal, like chitin, like the carapace of some great beetle. On the hull I could see bits of engineering, such as handrails for cosmonauts doing their own EVAs, I guessed. And . . .

"I see runes, Peabody. Carved into the hull. Must have taken some effort to do that in zero-G. The reaction when you apply a torque—"

"Skip the John Glenn patter. What kind of runes?"

"Like stars. Five-pointed. Like pentagrams."

"Five-pointed. You're sure?"

"I can count. Coming up on that EVA hatch now. Oh, there's one more element, a big old ugly sphere attached to the end of the stack."

"That's the crew return capsule. The Soviets are developing a three-crew ship, the *Voskhod*. Haven't flown the thing yet. Not officially anyhow. They flew up their crew one by one in Vostoks, but this is for the return."

"Three crew, then. Including Gagarin."

"Yes. If they're still alive, we have food packs and med supplies to treat them. And we're to stuff them inside that recovery capsule and send them home. But to achieve that we're going to have to go in and find out what's what. Jones, those three chambers. Probably sealed-off from each other. We'll have to clear them one by one."

"Understood."

I reached *Zarya*.

I sailed close enough to the hull now to grab a handrail, on that narrowest cylinder. A part of me flinched as I made physical contact with the station, but it was just metal, in the shadows, cold through my gloves.

I worked my way around the cylinder until I got to the EVA hatch. It had labeled instructions in Cyrillic that meant nothing to me, but there was a big red wheel whose function was obvious. I turned it, it stuck a little before it gave, and soon I had that hatch swinging open sweet as a nut. Inside, the airlock was a dark little cave. I wasn't about to go in there alone, nor was I about to say so out loud.

I swung back out into the light. "Okay, Peabody, all is copacetic here. I'll tie-off the umbilical and come back to get you."

And as I guided her along the cord across that stretch of space, mostly trying to avoid tying ourselves in knots with our various umbilicals, it did not surprise me at all that she insisted on carrying over her case of "specialist medical supplies."

At the station we disconnected our umbilicals from the Gemini, tested the sweet juice from our suits' oxygen bottles, pulled ourselves inside that airlock, and closed the hatch.

I was in the mouth of the whale.

We flooded the lock with air and I tried to open the inner hatch. The next red wheel was stiff, heavy, an over-engineered chunk of Soviet tech. When it cracked at last, around its edge I could see light—green-filtered sunlight—and what looked like branches. Tree branches, like pines, bristling with needles.

I could hear the branches rustle.

I glanced at Peabody. "Sounds as if there's air in there, at least."

"Let me check it out." She had a simple sensor attached to her chest unit that she inspected.

Meanwhile, still fully suited-up, with my reaction gun dangling at my waist, I drifted through the hatch and into . . . green.

Look, I'm from Georgia. I'm no expert on the northern forests. But I recognized pine, larch, spruce, cedar, all growing out of pots of earth fixed to the metal walls. There were even fruit bushes; I thought I recognized cranberries, blueberries, big and swollen. An incongruous place to be in a spacesuit.

Wan sunlight filtered through lichen-smeared portholes into this crowded vivarium. I wondered uneasily how close we were to the totality of the eclipse.

"It's safe to crack your helmet," Peabody called.

I did so. I lifted the helmet off my head, let it dangle at my waist on a cord, and took a cautious sniff. I smelled rot, like bad compost maybe. "I'm still alive."

Peabody nodded. I noticed she kept her own helmet on.

I pushed deeper into the green. "Wow. Looks like a bonsai laboratory. What's the tree stock, Canadian?"

"Not Canadian. Siberian. Specifically, flora from the Tunguska region."

I fumbled to pick a blueberry with my gloved hands, tried again. The fruit was huge, soft and mushy. Some zero gravity effect, I thought at the time. "Tunguska?" I had to search my memory for the reference. "Where the comet fell? Flattened all those trees. In . . ."

"1908. The Soviets have always done experiments on life in space. Plants, animals."

I remembered. "Like that poor dog they put in orbit. Laika? More famous than Lassie, for a while. Funny how they never admitted they had no way to bring her back to Earth."

"That was the cover story, yes."

"Why bring Tunguska trees?"

"There was a reason. Are you going to eat that blueberry?"

I looked at the fruit doubtfully. It was huge, but looked swollen, almost to the point of being rotten. "What, am I a lab rat now?"

She just waited.

I bit into the fruit. It was bitter, sickly bitter, and the texture was like mold. Disgusting, literally. I spat out the mouthful of flesh and dumped the berry.

And as I was telling Peabody about this, I thought I saw a figure, deeper inside that small, forest-choked chamber. A tall shadow.

Peabody was making a note on a pad attached to her suit sleeve. "Abnormal fruiting is typical of Color Incursions. In Lovecraft's account of the 1882 incident—"

"Peabody. I think I see somebody. At the rear of the compartment."

"Moving?"

"No." And the more I looked at it, the less human it seemed—a tall shape in the green, a suggestion of a head, of limbs . . .

The hell with it. I pulled my way zero-gravity style through that Siberian foliage, toward the figure.

You think I'm exaggerating, for dramatic tension maybe. Maybe you're looking at a plan of the station as you read this. It was an expedition of only a few feet.

But believe me it felt a lot farther than that. Partly, it was the way I had to push through that toy forest, I guess. But there was something subtler at work, inside that station. Distances were deceptive, deeper, or sometimes shallower, than they ought to have been. One of the League's C.I.D. double-domes who debriefed me later said the interior volume might have been "non-Euclidean." Look it up—I had to. Space in there was distorted, the way Einstein describes the whole universe. It was "characteristic of incursion architecture," the scientist told me.

Well, I got through my miniature odyssey, and boldly faced that figure.

Which was, when I got close to it, not human at all. It was kind of like a scarecrow, built around a coverall—blue, tagged with Russian lettering—that looked to have been roughly packed with clothing and other garbage to make a barrel torso. But the top of it, the "head," was made from a cut-open, splayed-out packing case, like a plastic flower, as was the base, the "feet." Bits of cable were draped about, suggestive of arms, or tentacles maybe. And plastic sheeting was draped behind this thing, like half-folded angel wings.

This was, I saw now, only one of a row of several of such figures, all roughly human-sized or larger, all evidently improvised from the ship's stores. I'd never seen anything like them. And yet they looked vaguely familiar. I couldn't explain that feeling then, and I'm not sure if I can now.

Peabody came to join me. I was floating in the air at the far-left end of this row, with Peabody more central, to my right. She still wore her helmet. These dispositions turned out to be crucial to what followed.

"Somebody's been busy," I said.

"The cosmonauts," she said. "Clearly. Obsessed by visions, dreams they could not understand. Trying to realize them in the waking world. Again, this is typical of such incursions." She touched the topknot of one of the crude sculptures, the splayed casing. "See? Five-fold symmetry. Like a starfish. And the base too."

"Like I saw scratched on the hull."

"Quite."

"Dreams of what?"

She began to detach her helmet, lifting it off the neck ring and over her head. I was aware then, I think, of movement farther down that grotesque row. Just a subtle shifting of the light. That was almost subconscious; I was distracted by what she was saying.

Which was: "Magnolia Jones, meet the Great Old Ones."

That was the first time I heard the name. But not the last. No, not the last.

I responded as you would have. "Who?"

"The ancients of days. Those who filtered down from the stars when the Earth was young. And who concocted life on Earth as a joke. Or a mistake, perhaps—"

I saw the lash, an instant before it hit her face.

Or would have. She had her helmet half-off, lifted in her gloved hands. I just balled my fist and punched down on the top of her helmet so it slammed back into place.

And the lash—curling in that cramped space, it must have been eight, nine feet long—slapped against the helmet, and I saw some kind of venom squirt against the glass. Some of it caught my gloved hand, and it stung like hell, even through the tough vacuum-proof fabric.

I dragged Peabody out of the way. Shocked, maybe a bit dazed from my punch, she was like a statue herself.

And now I faced the thing that had emerged from the foliage. It was kind of a big mobile plant, coming out from that line of rough statues. *Where it had been hiding*, I realized with a kind of deep horror. Bent over under that low roof, it might have been ten feet tall. Up top there was a kind of funnel, like an immense, drab flower, from which that venomous sting dangled. A straight stem twisted and writhed as the thing tried to get closer to me. I saw that it was actually chained up. A plant that hid, waiting for prey. Waiting, maybe, for Peabody to take off her helmet so it could get at her face.

I took in all this in about two breaths. That sting was winding back for another lash.

I shot it with my reaction gun. My personal rocket pistol: call me Buck Rogers. I shot it in the funnel, which splashed and scattered, I shot it in the stem in two, three, four places. A kind of oil filled the air, droplets of it, leaking from the broken flesh.

Peabody had recovered. "Thanks," she said laconically. "If that had got me in the face—"

"What the hell was it?"

"A triumph of Soviet biological engineering. I imagine the cosmonauts were instructed to do experiments on how it adapted to weightlessness."

"Too damn well, I'd say. Why the hell would anybody engineer such a thing?"

"Biofuels," she said simply.

"And do you think this is what killed off Gagarin and the rest?"

"Oh, I doubt it very much."

That polite British understatement scared me more than all I had seen so far.

"I can see the hatch to the next compartment. We go on."

She nodded. "We go on."

Without letting myself think about it, I shoved aside the crude statues, yanked aside the foliage to expose the hatch, and turned the next red wheel.

And I saw, from the corner of my eye, that as Peabody passed the Great Old Ones statues, she gave them a kind of salute—a bow, like a zero-gravity genuflection, and a splayed-hand salute. A five-pointed star.

I trusted her less and less.

IV

More forest. That was my first impression, as I pushed my way through the hatch.

More of those damn trees, pine and fir. Another chamber, like a great green mouth, swallowing me up. How could there be so much vegetation? What was feeding it? Maybe this was a living version of the sense of space distortion I'd had since we'd swum into this pit in the sky. Just as this station was too big on the inside, so it contained too much *life*. If you could call it life.

There was an odd glow too. Sometimes I thought there was a kind of sparkle about the needles on those pine trees—like the St. Elmo's fire I've seen a few times on the rigging of splashdown recovery ships. And something more elusive. The air in there was wet, almost misty, and there was a glow about that mist, a color I couldn't put my finger on.

Peabody had pressed ahead. Now she called me. She'd come to a kind of clearing in the choked-up forest.

Here, I could see more details of the workplace that this station was evidently intended to be. There was cosmonaut stuff on racks on the walls—spare pressure suits, bottles of water and air, instrument panels, electronics racks. Big TV screens which, no doubt, had once relayed images of US ICBM sites and naval bases. More mundane features. An exercise bike, a treadmill. Seats around a table, bolted in place so they didn't drift off. Photos of wives and girlfriends and little kids, pinned to a notice board. Sunshine and pigtails. It was like an explorers' shack, in the wilderness of space. It was kind of heartbreaking, when you thought about how these guys had ended up, obsessively cutting up their stuff to make those statues of the "Old Ones" that had, evidently, plagued their dreams.

Peabody told me to take a look for anything like a lab bench. There must have been some kind of samples of extraterrestrial materials in here, she said. Maybe like meteorite samples. I took a look, at the little work tables, the instruments, microscopes and spectroscopes, the sample dishes held down by little clips. Everything was murky, covered in mold and slime and dirt. But I couldn't see anything like meteorite rock. When I reported that back to Peabody, she wasn't surprised.

I thought I heard something, then, deeper inside the choking green. A kind of whimper. A child, an animal?

But Peabody hadn't heard, and now she was beckoning me farther in. "Come see."

"See what?"

"I found our cosmonauts."

If not for the coveralls and soft boots they still wore, I don't think I'd have recognized the remains as human at all.

Lodged in the foliage, they were two gray figures, spilling out of those uniforms. The bodies were bloated and swollen in some parts, shriveled in others. One had his head turned aside, and something of his face had survived. His mouth was stretched grotesquely wide, like a cartoon scream of agony. Bits of gray, like ash, drifted out of that mouth—the remains of his tongue, perhaps. His eyes were holes.

They had bled out, these cosmonauts, and some of that blood had dried on the hull plate. I was distracted by little hard knots of white, stuck by the blood to the plate. They were human teeth.

Peabody placed a cautious gloved hand on the head of one of the cosmonauts. At the touch it imploded, like a puffball fungus. We both flinched back. I had an immediate, visceral dread of breathing in any of this gray, ashy stuff.

"I ought to take a sample," Peabody said. "But I can see it's the same symptoms as the 1882 infestation in Massachusetts."

"Only two of them."

"Yes. And neither is Gagarin; these two have nametags on their coveralls. We need to get to that third chamber."

But again that whimper. I glanced at Peabody; this time she had heard it too.

"Something's alive in here," I said. I turned away, and pushed deeper into the foliage-choked chamber.

And I found a dog.

She was strapped into a kind of frame, what looked like the remains of a gutted electronics rack. She had tubes inserted into her body through crude, seeping wounds, tubes that led to flasks of what looked like water and some kind of gelatinous food, and to tanks of urine and feces. The food and water were nearly drained, and the waste tanks nearly full.

And her head . . .

The skin and flesh had been removed from one side of the skull. The brain was exposed under clear plastic. Electrodes dug into the soft gray matter. A thick cord of wiring led from the back of her head to a kind of distribution point on a control panel nearby. What looked like a power lead was plugged into one eye socket.

And she seemed to be attached to the infestation of vegetation in the station too. Her frame rested on a kind of cradle of wood, shoots and lianas curled up through the metal, and green tendrils snaked into the gray stuff inside her head, alongside the electric leads.

None of this technology looked *human*, even though it had evidently been fixed up with scraps and materials from this human installation, this station. It was too advanced. As if a modern engineer had improvised a space rocket from the ruin of a James Watt steam pump, and placed her inside . . .

Her. I knew who this dog was. I remembered the pictures the Soviets had put in the papers when she had had her few days of extraordinary fame. I recognized the long snout, the big perky ears, the one bright eye. This was Laika.

She looked at me, and whimpered again.

I cupped her face, the unharmed side, and stroked her neck. We always had dogs in Georgia. Whole happy packs of them. "So they got you back, did they, babe? But look what they did to you. Look what they did. Does it hurt? Well, it won't hurt any more."

I raised my rocket gun.

I felt cold metal in the back of my neck. "Lower it, Jones."

Cautiously, I obeyed. And when I turned around, just as cautiously, I saw Peabody, sitting there beside her backpack nuke, pointing a revolver at me.

So. I knew she'd been lying to me, on some level, since before we launched. Now the game was on. It was almost a relief.

"You won't shoot," was my opening gambit. "Because if you do you'll blow a hole in the side of this station and kill yourself."

She smiled. "Funnily enough we thought of that."

Supercilious Brit.

"Soft-nosed bullets, low velocity. Designed to kill people, not blow up space stations. The choice of whether to test the design is up to you."

I looked down at poor Laika. "Why don't you want me to kill the dog?"

"Because, obviously, she's become an integral part of the system. Oh, I imagine she was retrieved here as an extension of the experiment that sent her into orbit in the first place. A study of the effect on the body of years in space. But of course the *Zarya* has . . . evolved. And so, it seems, has she.

"Look at her, Jones—you're enough of an engineer to see it. The ship itself is alive now, in a sense. Infested, transformed, a blend of the human, the technological, the biological—an amalgamation of the terrestrial with the alien. Inextricable. And Laika has clearly become a part of the systems that keep this place running. Her brain is being used as a natural processor to—"

"What do you want, Peabody?"

She said nothing to that. Even then, I suspected there were many more layers to this than I was guessing. That maybe she was betraying everybody, the military as well as the Lovecraft people. Not to mention me.

Time to go fishin' again, Mags, as my pappy used to say.

"Look—you can't kill me, Peabody. Not without killing yourself. Good luck with getting back to the Gemini alone, let alone piloting it downstairs."

She frowned. "My personal safety isn't the only consideration."

"How did I know you'd say something like that? Come on, Peabody. You're no strip-cartoon fanatic. Your life is a consideration, at least.

Think how valuable you are to the cause." Whatever the hell that cause was. "Maybe you'll achieve a win-win, maybe you'll reach your goals *and* survive. But to do that you're going to have to start telling me the truth. And time's running out, remember. You still want to be out of here before totality—right?"

She thought that over. At my side, Laika whimpered again, and I stroked her again.

"Very well," Peabody said, at last. She sighed. "You're going to have to see the bigger picture, Jones. Keep your small mind open."

I shrugged. "Shucks, I'll try."

She looked at me, intent. The gun not wavering.

"Here we are out in space, Jones. I know you have an orderly mind. And I bet you like to think that the universe is just as orderly, don't you?

"Well, it's not. We suspected the existence of—anomalies—in the solar system even before we ventured into space ourselves. Look at the 1882 incursion. How could all that stuff *get* here? And since we sent out probes it's all been confirmed. The solar system is riddled, like Swiss cheese, with . . . holes, Jones. Tunnels that connect *here* to *there*, out beyond distant Yuggoth."

"Yuggoth?"

"The Ninth Planet . . . Oh, it's not just a question of short cuts—of all those four hundred billion stars in the galaxy suddenly bumping up against the gardens of the sun. It's a question of categories of existence clashing. Places where different kinds of reality mesh, like the components of a machine. The flaws, the gateways, are called time-convergent funnels. Or more strictly, chronosynclastic—"

"Gardner."

"What?"

"In the transfer van. He said the same thing, or quoted it: 'It come from some place whar things ain't as they is here . . .'"

She nodded. "You get the idea. Well, for a long time—longer than you will guess, Jones—these flaws have allowed various entities to, um, *influence* the story of our Earth, and ourselves. Zellaby, who died in the Midwich changelings incident, wrote of an 'Inventor' who repeatedly meddles with life on Earth. Like dropping cultures into an already crowded petri dish. I think it's more random than that, and multiple agencies are involved, but that's the essence. Invasions from space.

"As for the Great Old Ones, they may have been the first of all. First discovered, scientifically anyhow, by the Dyer expedition to the Antarctic in the 1930s, in a layer of Precambrian rocks, a billion years old."

That didn't mean much to me. "Seems kind of early."

She raised a cultured eyebrow. "Kind of early, Jones, yes. Life on Earth was only just beginning to experiment with body plans more complicated than the amoebas. The fossils Dyer's people found—" She jerked a thumb over her shoulder, at the chamber we'd left, the statues.

"The Old Ones?"

"They came here from somewhere else. They may have—I would say *probably*—kick-started the evolution of complex life on Earth, and exploited it, but didn't meddle with its evolution beyond that. This is the secret of life, Jones. Our life.

"And they stayed here, ever since. They built cities. And they suffered extraterrestrial invasions of their own. The spawn of Cthulhu. The Mi-Go—you know them as the Yeti—"

"But humans evolved regardless."

"Yes. But we're aware of incursions by other kinds of beings, which surely did affect our evolution. There's an abnormal humanlike skull, twelve million years old, found in Kenya—much older than the conventional chronology. Fendelman Industries, linked to the HPL—we use them for missile-guidance systems—is putting a lot of money into studying that one. Five million years ago, a ship apparently from Mars crashed to Earth under modern London—it's thought that Piltdown Man may have come out of that."

"Piltdown? I thought that was a hoax."

"Of course you did. And, just recently, the space probes have detected slightly younger magnetic anomalies, a pair of them—one in the Olduvai Gorge, in Africa, with, remarkably, a match on the Moon."

"Tycho."

"I mentioned that, didn't I? Olduvai, you see—right on the spot where the Leakeys have shown that modern hominid evolution was kick-started, and the right timing, too, three million years ago."

I thought that over. "Magnetic anomalies. Pilots know about those. We call them dragons, popcorn, echo haze."

"Sure. And the records kept by the airlines and air forces have been analyzed by the League and other agencies, in our search for such anomalies. We found one just last week in Maine, a town called Haven . . .

"And we're not alone, in suffering these incursions. Even on Mars, Jones! Even there the Inventor has been tinkering! Since 1956, our resourceful Robinson Crusoe has been sending back reports of some tantalizing archaeology. A worldwide catastrophe that Ivor Dare of Cardiff dates back two hundred thousand years, caused by some kind of hive mind from space, perhaps."

"Ancient history, Peabody. And time's running out." Again Laika whimpered, and again I stroked her. "Not long now, girl."

"All right, all right. Look—of more immediate concern are the incursions that are happening right now. I mentioned the Midwich event in middle England: that one began with something like a meteor fall. And five years ago we had an unusual pattern of meteor strikes *in the oceans.* All in the deeps. There has been some . . . interaction since."

"Interaction?"

"Well, to be blunt, a US Navy carrier called the *Keewenaw* has been lost, near the Marianas. Harriman Nelson is still urging attempts at contact. Ideally we could form an alliance with these particular visitors—even use them as a picket around R'lyeh."

"Woah. What's R'lyeh? . . . Never mind."

"Anyhow, you can see what we're having to deal with here—"

"How come nobody knows about any of this? We've got the radio, television."

She snorted. "Do you ever *watch* television? Sports and soap operas. Consumed by a population already sedated by cheap alcohol and fast food. Television was designed to distract, not inform."

I shook my head. "Yet some do get to report this stuff, in a way. Lovecraft for one. That copy of *Amazing Stories*—"

"Oh, certainly. There has always been a dribble of truth escaping in quasi-fictional accounts. Lovecraft himself saw it all clearly, with the mind's eye, at least. It's probably safest if you believe that all the fiction you read is true, and all the factual content is a lie. *Fiction is truth: truth is fiction.* Hmm . . . That could be pithier. *Ignorance is strength*, perhaps." She actually made a note of the phrase in her notebook.

I thought the light was diminishing. I didn't know if we ourselves would pass into the zone of totality ourselves.

I said: "Tell me about the Color."

"Once again we have to thank Howard Phillips Lovecraft for the clues. It was eclipses that proved the key.

"He saw at least one total eclipse himself—in North America, in August 1932. He left an account of it in his letters . . ." She thumbed through the pages of her notepad. Evidently she had brought, on a space mission, pithy quotes from long-dead nutjobs. "Here we are. 'When the crescent waned to extreme thinness, the scene grew strange and spectral—an almost deathlike quality inhering in the sickly yellowish light.' Typical Lovecraft!"

"And the Color?"

"Now, look, on May 17, 1882, there was an eclipse over Egypt. And at the moment of totality, with the sun's glare gone, observers saw an object close to the sun itself. They thought it was a comet—called a Kreutz comet, a sungrazer. All right? And then, just a few weeks later, in June 1882, the Color incursion, on the Gardner farm. Where something landed." She stared at me. "Come on, Jones. You're the space pilot. Work it out! Suppose that wasn't a comet that was seen in May, close to the sun? If it was some kind of craft—"

"It was decelerating," I said, figuring it out as I spoke. "If you come in from interstellar space, and you want to dump velocity with the greatest efficiency, your closest approach to the sun is the place to do it." I looked at her. "So this thing flies in from the stars—"

"More likely at high speed through some time-convergent funnel."

"It slows up at the sun, and two weeks later lands on Earth."

"That's it. Look, we're not sure what the link is with eclipses. Maybe they use them as cover for their operations—hiding in the shadow of the Moon . . .

"The Color is some kind of parasite, we think. Characterized chiefly by a draining of the local life-force. Apparently it somehow uses that life energy to escape. The witnesses at the Gardner place saw bolts of light shoot up from a well, back to space. We know of further incursions that were probably made by the same class of entity. In 1896, the 'Saliva Tree Incursion' at a place called Cottersall in Norfolk, England.

"And then, 1908. On June 20, an annular eclipse. Two days later, Tunguska. Acres of forest flattened. The Tsarist authorities didn't know what to make of it. But after the Revolution, the Soviet scientists were fascinated. Look, Jones, the Soviets see themselves as having waged a war of existential struggle since the moment their regime took power. Anything they can use to get an edge—"

"Are you saying they tried to capture this alien horror, this Color?"

She shrugged. "In fact they followed a British example. You saw the plaque at Tarooma, the Q-I mission? 1953. Experimental deep space flight. In that case an alien infestation penetrated the ship itself, and was brought back down to Earth. Anyhow, the Russians figured, maybe they could similarly lure the Color into some kind of technological trap.

"There was a total eclipse due in February, 1961. The Soviets anticipated a fresh Color Incursion. So they launched this station, manned by a military crew—this was before Gagarin publicly flew, remember. And they loaded it up with flora from Tunguska, as much as they could cram in. The idea being, hopefully, to attract the newcomer to the relics of a previous visitant."

"And trap it up here. Why? To harness it, as yet another Cold War weapon?"

She shrugged. "Maybe not. The two sides have been known to cooperate over the incursions. Remember Zellaby and Midwich? The West cooperated in the nuclear destruction of a Russian changeling nest at Gizhinsk, near Okhotsk. This was last year, just before the Cuba missile crisis. That operational-level contact did a lot to help defuse—"

"So they trapped this Color in here, in *Zarya*."

"That was the plan. It worked. And when it came here—you know, the 1882 landfall attracted lightning. Electricity. The Color trapped in *Zarya* seems to have set off a global electromagnetic disturbance called the 'Ring of Fire.' You must remember that . . . ?"

"If some kind of meteorite hit this station . . . Quite a trick to survive that in the first place." I glanced around—if there was any evidence of damage repair it was hidden by the foliage. "Where the hell is it?"

She sighed, impatient. "You should have read the briefing more carefully, Jones. There's always a kind of rocky shell which contains the Color itself, which is . . . intangible. And the rock disappears. Sublimates maybe. In some cases physical traces remain."

I shrugged. That was the least strange thing I'd heard in the last half hour.

"Well, the Color was trapped in here, but it broke out of control, inside the station. The crew was killed. But there doesn't seem to have been enough living matter on the station for the Color to consume and escape altogether."

"So the Soviets have this unholy menace bottled up in here, stuck in orbit. Then what?"

"Then, as best we understand it, Yuri Gagarin, already a national hero, volunteered to lead a fresh crew up here, scientifically qualified, to attempt to save the first crew, if any survived, and deal with the Color. An expedition that failed in its turn. And so I was ordered to find out what became of Gagarin and his crew, and to deal with the Color once and for all. The nuclear sanction was very much a last resort. But I was clearly instructed to take that resort, if all else failed."

I watched her carefully, trying to read her. "Aha. Whereas that's the last thing you intend to do."

"I couldn't let that happen, Jones. I infiltrated the mission, made sure it was *me* who brought up the nuke, so I—we—could be sure it would *not* be used . . ."

"Who's 'we'? Not the British authorities, not the Human Protection League or the US government. You're somehow on the side of this Color."

"It's not that simple. I asked you to keep an open mind, Jones. Given all I've told you, can you not see how everything is changed? How everything you ever believed is wrong? The life forces from beyond the Earth haven't just come into our homes, our petty planet, like movie monsters. They are into everywhere. Every *when*. Inside *us*. And we have to embrace that—"

"Who's Azathoth? I heard you, with Gardner, before the launch, like you were praying. *Who's Azathoth*?"

But she seemed beyond speech now. Her eyes were bright—and seemed to me then to shine with that strange, elusive non-color I'd already glimpsed in this station, in the moisture in the air—but she did not speak further.

Still she held the gun on me.

What happened next has become controversial.

Look at it from my point of view.

I was bewildered by all the talk of multiple alien invasions, and the distortion of humanity's evolution, its entanglement with life on Earth itself, and yakety yak. If any of it was true, what did it mean for me? What was good, what was evil, in such a context?

Well, I had a moment of clarity. Right here, right now, in this standoff, there was only one unimpeachably good action for me to take. So I took it.

I shot the dog.

V

I found out later that the instant I pulled that rocket-gun trigger was the moment the sun passed into totality. I didn't, couldn't, know that at the time.

Sometimes I think there's something in all the spooky stuff.

Anyhow, all hell broke loose.

The main lighting failed, to be replaced by a sick emergency-red wash, and wan eclipse sunlight leaking through murky, slime-coated windows. Alarms howled, including some kind of recorded voice of which I couldn't understand a word. I guessed Peabody was right that poor Laika had somehow been used as a sort of canine computer to run the station—or whatever gestalt thing this station had become. Now I'd shut her down.

And the trees, the damn foliage that crowded out the place—I'll swear they stirred and moved, the branches stretching like short skinny limbs, the needles raking, like they were trying to reach me.

Peabody, hanging in the air, had her hands pressed to her face. Even now she had that backpack nuke, floating with her.

And something was hammering on the other side of the hatch to the third compartment. Something massive and heavy, like a dumb animal ramming its head against the bars of its cage. But I heard a human voice call: "*. . . eez-vee . . . eez-vee-neetee . . .*"

Something was coming through.

I was plunged into nightmare.

I muttered to myself, "What now, Jones? Well, you came here to rescue Yuri Gagarin. Not for this Lovecraft crap."

I pushed my way to that damn hatch, to the third chamber. It bulged with each blow, as whatever was beyond was slammed against it.

Another red wheel. I turned it and hastily shoved myself out of the way.

The hatch slammed open.

The thing tumbled through.

It was like the others, the corpses. A human body, still jammed inside a ragged, filthy blue coverall, but swollen, distorted—the spine bent, the joints looking dislocated, parts of the torso alternately shriveled or swollen. Like it was stuffed with outsize copies of its internal organs, the liver, the bowels. The head was a grotesque balloon, as if the skull had been inflated. And all of this rendered, not in the texture of human flesh, but in a crumbling gray, like the ash-ghost of a log you sometimes see on a hot fire, holding its shape, just before it collapses to cinders.

But this one, unlike the other cosmonauts, was alive.

Still he moved, scattering flakes of ash-gray in the air as he did so. One shoulder was smashed, flattened, and I surmised this was what he had used to beat against that hatch. I wondered if the other two crew had forced him in there, or if he had tried to save himself from them.

Alive. When he moved, pulling himself across the deck, he made a sucking, sticky sound. That pumpkin head twisted now, and a face looked up at me—stretched, distorted, flaking ash. I recognized him. Of course I did. That broad peasant face was one of the most famous in the world. I felt like saluting.

And he looked at me, with eyes that had somehow survived, like glass beads in a hearth. "*Eezveeneete* . . . *Eezveeneete* . . ."

Peabody seemed to have calmed, even as the shriek of the alarms continued. She looked down at this figure. "*Polkovnik Gagarin.*"

Those eyes turned to her. "*Eezveeneete* . . ."

"What's he saying?"

"Sorry," she said. Her expression was complex—pity, I thought, warring with exultation. "He's saying sorry."

"What's he sorry for?"

And now she had her gun again, pointing at my head. I cursed myself for not getting it off her while I had the chance.

She said, "He's sorry because he lured us up here. Look, Jones, the Color is a parasite on life-forces. In Massachusetts it consumed animals, vegetation, people—the Gardners. And why? So it could build up the energy to get back into space, and move on, to find some other place to settle, and feed again. Grow, maybe. Spore.

"Now, think about it. The Soviets lured the Color here. It broke out, but it was trapped. A few pot-plants and three skinny cosmonauts weren't enough to fuel its escape, right? Colonel Gagarin here led up a second crew. Again the Color overwhelmed them, consumed the new crew. Still not enough to escape."

"But it spared Gagarin—"

"Yes. Spared him deliberately. *It kept him alive.* Maybe it understood how it had been lured here, and trapped. And now, you see, it used Gagarin to lure us."

I looked down at the Gagarin monster, those clear human eyes in the distorted mask of gray. I knew his story, as much as anybody in the West did back then. The boy raised on the collective farm, who survived the German occupation. The technical school student who studied tractor-building. The volunteer air cadet. The first in space, as far as the whole world knew. After all he'd achieved, he wasn't yet thirty years old. And now, this.

"*Eezveeneete . . . Eezveeneete . . .*"

"He knows who he is," I said. "The Color left him that much."

"It seems so," Peabody said. "The lure wouldn't have worked otherwise, would it?" She raised the pistol. "And it has worked, you see. It lured *you* here. His name alone. And now—"

"Now you're going to feed me to the Color."

"Us, Jones. *Us.* Me too. Do you see, Jones? Do you see? They gave me this bomb to bring here. Oh, I was never going to use it. All I ever intended was to bring *you*. You and myself. Two of us, you see, perhaps with this Gagarin morsel. It will be enough. The Color will destroy this toy, and return to that center of ultimate Chaos, and speak to Him in the Gulf of our petty world, and its readiness for consumption . . . Do you see, Jones? You with your petty ambitions, your infantile clinging to illusory order. Embrace the Chaos! The Crawling Chaos . . . !"

I just stared.

Now, if I'd been her, I'd have pulled the trigger there and then, disabled me, and fed me to the Color, whatever. Instead she started to chant, in a kind of frenzy—to Lord Azathoth, Him in the Gulf, Lord of All Things, Father of the Nameless Mist and Darkness, the ancestor of Yog-Sothoth and Shub-Niggurath and Cthulhu in the Deep . . . And she started shrieking, "*Tekeli-li! Tekeli-li!*"

Meanwhile, you see, I still had my Buck Rogers rocket pistol. Which she had forgotten about, in her turn. I pressed the nuzzle up against the back of Gagarin's swollen head, and figured trajectories.

I'll swear to this day that Gagarin knew what I was planning. He looked at me. "*Spaseeba . . . Bal'shoye spaseeba . . .*" I didn't understand what he whispered to me. But I memorized it syllable by syllable and found out later. *Thank you. Thank you very much.*

In turn I used the only Russian word I knew. "*Poyekhali*, Yuri."

I fired.

Yuri Gagarin's head was blown to smithereens of ash.

And the pulse passed through that fragile shambles of a head, and, just as I planned, hit Peabody on her right shoulder. The shoulder holding the pistol. The gun went flying.

After that, I had to move fast.

I dumped Gagarin, a corpse at last, and pushed through the air. I landed on top of Peabody and slugged her to make sure she was out.

And I got hold of that backpack nuke, fumbled with it until I found the panel that opened to reveal the command keys. Then I searched Peabody's suit pockets and pouches until I found the piece of paper Maxwell Gardner had slipped her before the launch. It was, of course, the bomb's enabling code. I punched this in.

And then we had five minutes to get away. Think a classic countdown, red-digit counters clicking over. James Bond, you should have been there.

I closed up my suit and Peabody's, and hauled ass out of there, through the second chamber, through the first. I had to get her out, you see, and I couldn't afford to kill her, because I wanted to destroy that damn Color, not risk feeding it, not even with the energy of Peabody's miserable life. I was flying on instinct, on reaction, and that was my deepest, most profound reaction. This thing had to be killed. So I plotted how I'd do it.

If that sounds like clinical, rational, professional decision-making, believe me, it wasn't. It was a kind of sublimated panic. Because when I shot Yuri Gagarin, the whole crazy place got even crazier.

You have to imagine those tree branches scratching at me as I passed, furious, spouting electric sparks from their tips. I think if those damn Siberian pine trees could have uprooted themselves like that Russian biofuel plant and come after me, they would have done.

At the hatch, I looked back. The emergency lights were a sullen red glow, and it was an infernal scene in there, with the trees lashing now, lashing and straining to get at us, their branches shedding sparks and flashes.

And then there was the water. The air was already misty, and now there were detonations like grenades, and I saw that stainless steel Soviet-engineered water tanks were cracking and spewing their contents in the air. Back in 1882 the Color had, in the end, infested the Gardner farm's water supply, a well. So it was here. The air in that place was quickly full of it—not a formless mist, but something alive in itself, an animated miasma that rippled and pulsed and smashed in great spouts against the station windows, seeking release. Like a fire-hose let go, perhaps, gushes of it spraying and splashing.

Water that glowed, with the Color itself—that was the first time I'd really seen it, not a color from the spectrum you learn about at school, something different, stranger. Literally indescribable. A Color out of space.

I got us out of that insanity. I even remembered to fix our helmets before swimming out into vacuum.

I scrambled over the umbilicals back to the Gemini, stuffed Peabody into her couch, closed the hatches, piloted that sweet, responsive bird out of there. Wary of radiation, I positioned us with the heatshield between us and the nuke, and maybe a mile of space.

I jammed my eyes shut.

Peabody was out cold, through the whole of it. In fact, I made sure she stayed out until we'd been picked up in the ocean, after re-entry, by the boys of the helicopter carrier *Guadalcanal* just off Puerto Rico, a few hours later.

And the sea air had blown away the last shreds of the Color from my lungs.

Epilogue

So here I am in Arkham, England. A plague village centuries dead. Trying to find out a little more about Squadron Officer Mabel Peabody, who played here as a child. Trying to understand.

Not that the Human Protection League understands, or the RAF. The Lovecraft Squad are mortified somebody managed to infiltrate to such senior levels. It's sent them and their government masters into a kind of existential crisis, I think.

Peabody was taken away after we splashed down, and is probably being interrogated in Washington right now, under maximum security. As for me, I think I see the character logic a little more clearly. You could say she was a traitor to her race, for trying to lure down Azathoth—which seems to be some kind of horror behind the horrors that have been pressing down on us from space since the time of the Great Old Ones. She was certainly dazzled by all that.

But it wasn't so simple. Peabody was operating in the human world too. She, and others like her, believe they see a better way for the world to be ordered. I've done my research on these characters. As you've no doubt figured out by now, I'm methodical. They call themselves names like the "Olde Fellowes." Or, the "Armies of the Night." Very hard to pin them down, or to establish any connection between them. Yet they exist, they are already scarily powerful, and they ain't going away. Why, Peabody herself managed to infiltrate both the RAF and the HPL.

There is no real social progress. That's the basic thesis. Inequality is embedded in our species. There will always be struggling masses, propping up an elite. So maybe, the argument goes, in this scientific age, we should formalize all that. There is talk, at a level higher than governments, of perpetuating the Cold War as a means of social control. . . . And better yet, what about drawing down a menace from space itself—a source of unending, undefinable peril, to cement that control for good?

That's the theory. A quiet war, but an unending one, with *them* in charge, forever.

And given all that, should I have set off that damn nuke?

Opinion is split. On the one hand, me. On the other hand, all the experts.

The Lovecraft people were up in arms. We were somewhere over the Pacific when the atomic bomb went off. The detonation was visible as a brilliant flash in that strange, eclipse-shadowed sky. Most people thought it was some kind of solar effect. And the crew of the SSRN *Seaview* saw it, from their station at 48° S, 127° W. Captain Crane's log reported "massive disturbances" in that part of the deep ocean in the Pacific, after our bomb exploded. Meanwhile, back on land, asylums went crazy as patients all over the world appeared to suffer from simultaneous psychoses, and thousands of sleepers awakened suddenly from the worst nightmares they had ever experienced . . .

But that, I guess, is a story yet to be told.

In the aftermath of the mission I met Peabody's niece, who she mentioned once. Just a kid, bright as a button, as she said. Jocelyn, she's called. I think she'll go far. When you see kids like that, you think there's hope for humanity yet.

But there's another eclipse coming. I can't help but look up at the stars and wonder what is going to happen between now and then.

Next for me, however, is Mars.

Next year I'll be part of a British-American crew going in search of the crazy Brit who's been stranded alone up there since 1956. This time I'll be part of a properly equipped crew. A real expedition. But nobody will know about it. That's another thing I learned from Peabody—there are more secrets and lies in the world than there is truth. Far more.

Well, soon Old Arkham is going to be a secret too. They're building a reservoir here, to feed the growing towns, industry. Old Arkham and its blasted heath will be lost beneath the waters, taking its mysteries with it.

An invisible country. Or a mask over the horror. Maybe I'll come back to see it one day.

But I sure as hell won't be drinking the water.

EPILOGUE

The Shadow Across 110th Street

AFTER THIRTEEN HOURS, THE power came back on.

One moment, the large hall of Mordecai Vault's Undertaking Parlor on West 116th Street was lit only by the weak, wavering beams of cop flashlights . . . the next, overheads flickered and buzzed and harsh light filled the room.

She saw bodies—twisted, broken, rent apart, bled-out—strewn around. Men and women. All black. It looked like the whole congregation had been hit. The Harlem Hounfor was the voodoo cathedral of New York City. Damage was done to the sacred space. Bullet holes in the walls, of course. Trestle tables and pews smashed to splinters, with blood and other stuff mixed in. A live goat nuzzled the open chest of a dead man whose face was chalked to look like a skull.

The obeah man. So this was Mordecai Vault.

She knew an autopsy would confirm Brother Vault's heart was missing. Powerful juju—the heart of a sorcerer. There'd be buyers if it came to auction.

She didn't believe this was just about that, though.

Along with light came music—drumming, a wind instrument, wave sounds, organ tones. That only lasted a few seconds, until someone found the switches that turned off the bank of tape machines. She was surprised Vault used prerecorded music in rituals. Sign of the times.

"Special Agent Gauge," said a florid-faced cop.

"Lieutenant Brake," she acknowledged.

"So, where were you when the lights went out?" he asked.

"At the opera. *Macbeth*. They say it's unlucky."

"I thought you were overdressed for a crime scene."

Agent Whitney Gauge was still in evening wear—black silk jumpsuit by Valentino, with a deep V cut-out back, sleeveless fitted bodice with bias front draped at the neckline, and cuffed, straight-legged pants pleated and darted into a V-shaped waistline.

The matching jacket that completed the ensemble had got shredded when she wrapped it around her right forearm to take the opportunist's knife away from him. Walking alone from the abandoned performance to Central Park West, she'd run into a dude who'd most likely been waiting for the power to go out city-wide so he could jump the first woman who passed his alley. Unlucky for him, Mr. Would-Be Rapo drew Whitney—first in her Unarmed Combat Class, and used to far more terrifying infractors than this random mook. She was six foot tall, even without the heels . . . her assailant was five-eight at most.

She took away the knife but let the creep have the jacket, which she told him to keep pressed against his bleeding neck while not moving. She guessed the paramedics would get around to him after approximately fifteen thousand more deserving patients got seen to. It was one of those busy nights. She had taken his driver's license—what kind of amateur sex offender carries ID while prowling?—and would see about getting Peter Gerard Stallman busted if he was alive at the end of the week. Indeed, if anyone was.

There was an off-chance the Hounfor massacre was the first sign of the coming apocalypse they were always being briefed to expect. Some older agents had been contemplating the end so long she thought they'd welcome it. Otherwise, they'd wasted their careers when they could have been earning citations busting regular heads rather than probing the sort of arcane mysteries no one thanked you for solving. With Nixon still in the White House, Whitney wasn't especially warmed by the prospect of a presidential medal of anything—so she was happy to stick at the job in comfortable obscurity.

"Our first thought was shoot-out in the dark," said Brake.

Whitney shook her head. "Uh-uh . . . our vics, the congregation, were the ones with guns. This man here was shot . . . but by mistake, by that woman there . . ."

A concealed .38 pistol with a red chicken design picked out on the grip lay near a dead, middle-aged woman who wore only a thousand-bead necklace and a feathered headdress—she wondered for a moment where the woman had packed her piece. Whitney wasn't that up on voodoo, but supposed she was a priestess.

The skull-painted corpse was the *houngan*, the high priest.

From what she knew, the goat had had a lucky escape.

All being normal, this morning should have seen the goat sacrificed and the voodoo worshippers happily exhausted from a night of abandoned dance and licentiousness sacred to Damballah and Erzulie Freda.

Instead, something had come in here and killed the whole church.

She and Brake were the only white people in the room, living or dead. The three uniforms on the scene—two men and a woman—were all Negro officers. They were quiet—shocked rather than angry.

The big doors of the hall that served as voodoo temple and undertakers' chapel were caved in, as if a mammoth had charged through. Part of the front wall was collapsed. Black teak coffins were crushed flat, red plush linings in strips. Maybe fifty or sixty dead.

Only three cops.

Any other time, the scene would be crowded. The 32nd Precinct would have every available uniform here, and call in reinforcements from the 28th. This would be the red ball case to end all red ball cases. But after last night, when city blocks went up in flames and whole streets were looted, the NYPD was spread thin over the whole island.

"They made a movie about the last big blackout," said Brake. "The one in '65. With Jerry Lewis. If they make a movie about this one, it won't be a comedy. It'll star Boris Karloff."

"Karloff's dead," said Whitney.

"He's always been dead," said Brake. "But he comes back. You and me, we know that stuff ain't just the movies. That stuff happens."

She looked around the room.

"These folks aren't coming back. Not even as zombies. The murder was spiritual as well as physical. Brother Vault's gone. His followers obliterated. No second chances. No return from the grave."

Brake headed the NYPD's Cults Unit. Whitney had worked with him before. When the yippies tried to levitate Cleopatra's Needle by joining hands and chanting Beatles songs around it, they'd broken the circle before anyone had a chance to see whether the trick might work.

"Was this a crime of opportunity?" she asked. "I ran into one of those last night—more than one. Some sickos just mull it over and wait for the darkness before acting out their greasy fantasies."

Brake shrugged.

"That's what the local cops thought. Lots of scores got settled last night. But it didn't only happen here. So far as we can put it together, two minutes after the lights went out—and ConEd still haven't told the Mayor why that happened, and why the phones went down, too—something came in here and laid the big hurt on Brother Vault and his followers. At the same exact time, all over the city, others got it the same way. The Temple of the Seven Golden Fists in Chinatown—none of their chopsocky helped keep out whatever it was. In the Village, the Children of Aquarius were torn to pieces. Montresor Mountmain's Chapel of Satan in Hell's Kitchen is up in flames. The penthouse of the Pyramid Building on Wall Street was sheared off, taking the Financial Wizards with it. The golem sweatshop in the Garment District is a mess of writhing clay—the *dybbuk* who ran the place *drowned* in it. We could wind up the Cults Unit tomorrow. Our whole damn Watch List is out of business."

"But you won't . . ."

"Nature abhors a vacuum. Especially a *spiritual* vacuum. What was done last night just made a hole in water—more water will rush in. This was a power play. A night of long knives. Someone was behind it—not just the mindless things let loose here and at the other places—but someone with a brain and an idea and a game-plan."

The cop was right.

Something was slouching toward Manhattan to be born.

"What about the Esoteric Order of Dagon?" she asked.

Brake looked like he had a sour taste in his mouth. "That's an old name. We've got files on them, but they've been off the scene since before there was a Cults Unit. Your Bureau pretty much shut them down in the '40s, I heard. Here in Harlem, a wealthy colored man called John Bronze went to war with the Esoteric Order. He was one of those vigilantes we're not supposed to approve of. Son of a genius inventor and a seven-foot-tall Waziri warrior princess. Had a bunch of misfit pals. A jazzman who could call-up spirits with his horn. A heavyweight champ raised from the dead. A snake dancer, Nubia Dusk. Bronze wound up marrying her. All shudder-pulp stuff."

Whitney knew all about Mr. Bronze. The Bureau had a fat file on him. And she knew who was running his family business these days. She was hardly ever off magazine covers . . .

"You should check all the old places the Esoteric Order of Dagon hung its shingle. They were big once. They may still be big, but in new packaging. I'll have a list of affiliates teletyped over. They tie in with the Olde Fellowes, Starry Wisdom, GEIST, and one or two of those white supremacist science fiction fan groups. All bastards under their pointy hoods. We hear whispers that the Esoteric Order is back. My guess is they'll have active premises in the city. Uptown and down. And if none of them got this treatment, then . . . well, then we'll have something interesting to chew over."

"Is all this your case, Special Agent?"

"Do you request help, Lieutenant? We're like vampires, you know. You have to invite us in . . ."

". . . and put up with you never leaving?"

Whitney shrugged. Her shoulders ached. Her feet hurt too.

She'd walked practically the length of Manhattan in heels.

What was the collective noun for mass murders? She didn't really want to know.

"Lieutenant, ma'am . . ."

It was the woman officer. Her badge gave her name as Terrell.

She was hesitant about speaking up. Whitney could guess why. Not many women on the NYPD. Not many black women among them. Even in Harlem, Terrell would be stuck with the sort of things male cops thought female officers were for—holding hands, fetching coffee, smiling at fumbled passes, typing detectives' reports for them. Only on a day when everyone with a badge—including the station janitor—was out on the streets would Terrell be padding around a room full of bloody dead folk.

"What is it, Officer?" Whitney asked.

"That's not Brother Vault," said the woman.

Brake looked again at the dead man with the skull-paint. A crushed top hat lay under his shaved head. Brake peered closer, but didn't touch the corpse.

"It *looks* like him," he said.

"Uh huh," said Terrell. "It's his cousin. Brother Vault is over there, with his head caved in. He wasn't *houngan* no more. There's been a succession . . ."

"And you know this because . . .?"

"Because I live in Harlem, Lieutenant. Everybody knows there's been a changing."

Whitney looked at Brake, who showed empty hands.

"The Cults Unit's stretched at the best of times," he said. "We don't get federal funding. Or opera tickets, unlucky or no. Last we took a census, Mordecai Vault was Heap Big Voodoo Chief. The 32nd know it's their job to pass on intelligence like this."

Whitney noticed Terrell's lips tightening.

"Did you have a special reason for pointing out our mistake, officer?" she asked. "Do you know who that is?"

Terrell nodded, solemnly.

"Sebastian Cutter. Brother Cutter."

Whitney looked again at the dead man.

"A short reign as voodoo king, then?"

"Sure enough," said Terrell. "But that ain't what you need to know about Brother Cutter. You need to know who he's married to . . . separated from, but still married to. Then you need to hide, because she's going to take this bad . . . and this place, this terrible place, won't be the worst we see this week. Before it's over, we'll look back at this and think it was . . . *nothing*."

The cop spoke evenly, as if giving evidence—but she was scared, and also a little excited. Some folks waited with an eagerness they could never admit to themselves for city-wide power cuts . . . for a woman walking by an alley alone . . . for a time-locked bank strongroom to pop open when the clocks shut down . . . for rain of fire on Central Park . . . for tentacled star-beasts of the Apocalypse in Times Square.

Brake was perplexed.

"Okay, Terrell, I'll bite," he said. "Who is—who *was*—this dead guy married to?"

Terrell smiled, like a cultist naming the angel who was coming to smite the wicked and drown the world in blood.

"Her," Terrell said, looking past Whitney and Brake at the smashed-in door.

A woman—tall enough to look down on Whitney, heels or no—stood there, framed as if for a magazine cover. As an Olympic decathlete, fashion model, political activist, and Top 40 recording star, she'd been on more newsstands than Watergate and the Moon landings put together. Her leopard-skin wrap didn't quite conceal the red leather shoulder holsters that held her father's famous eleven-shot bronzed automatics. Her crimson dress was slashed to the navel and thigh, belted with gold links, which matched her necklace and nose-stud. Her spherical Afro was a giant black dandelion clock around the face of an African goddess. Her emerald eyes were coldly furious.

"*. . . Nefertiti Bronze*."

DON'T MISS

NEFERTITI BRONZE VOODOO VS. CTHULHU!

Another Thrilling Chapter of

THE LOVECRAFT SQUAD

IN THE NEXT VOLUME

DREAMING

ACKNOWLEDGMENTS

Special thanks to Claiborne Hancock, Iris Blasi, Katie McGuire, Michael Fusco-Straub, Sabrina Plomitallo-González, Douglas Klauba, Lisa Morton, and Michael Marshall Smith.

STEPHEN JONES was born in London, England, just across the River Thames from where his hapless namesake met a grisly fate in Hazel Heald's story "The Horror in the Museum." A Hugo Award nominee, he is the winner of four World Fantasy Awards, three International Horror Guild Awards, four Bram Stoker Awards, twenty-one British Fantasy Awards, and a Lifetime Achievement Award from the World Horror Association. One of Britain's most acclaimed horror and dark fantasy writers and editors, he has more than 145 books to his credit, including *Shadows Over Innsmouth*, *Weird Shadows Over Innsmouth*, and *Weirder Shadows Over Innsmouth*; *H.P. Lovecraft's Book of Horror* (with Dave Carson), *H.P. Lovecraft's Book of the Supernatural*, *Hallowe'en in a Suburb & Others: The Complete Poems from* Weird Tales, *Necronomicon: The Best Weird Tales of H.P. Lovecraft*, and *Eldritch Tales: A Miscellany of the Macabre*, along with the *Zombie Apocalypse!* series, and twenty-eight volumes of *Best New Horror*. You can visit his web site at *www.stephenjoneseditor.com* or follow him on Facebook at *Stephen Jones-Editor*.